PRAI

THE MEMORY OF
LAVENDER AND SAGE

"Some books are simply a joy to read. Aimie K. Runyan's *The Memory of Lavender and Sage* is one of them. Sensuous . . . dreamy . . . romantic . . . *The Memory of Lavender and Sage* is a mélange of tastes and smells, magic and romance. Aimie K. Runyan weaves a sumptuous tale of mystery and magic, family and friendships, reminding us that it's never too late to find the home of our heart. If you long to be transported to a charming village in Provence, surrounded by loveable characters and secret spells, grab a cup of tea and immerse yourself in this magical novel!"

 —LORI NELSON SPIELMAN, *NEW YORK TIMES*
 BESTSELLING AUTHOR OF *THE LIFE LIST*

"In Aimie K. Runyan's signature heartfelt voice, *The Memory of Lavender and Sage* is a warm, generous, and utterly satisfying novel about the power of kindness, character and finding purpose and love where you least expect it."

 —ANN GARVIN, *USA TODAY* BESTSELLING AUTHOR
 OF *THERE'S NO COMING BACK FROM THIS*

"Aimie K. Runyan wows in her latest atmospheric novel about the power of family, the beauty of change, and the transportive magic of finding where you truly belong. Set against the backdrop of an idyllic village in Provence, *The Memory of Lavender and Sage* reminds readers that every moment should be savored and that, sometimes, the simplest pleasures are the greatest gifts. Runyan has proven herself as a standout voice in women's fiction. I was captivated from the very first line."

— KRISTY WOODSON HARVEY, *NEW YORK TIMES* BESTSELLING AUTHOR OF *THE SUMMER OF SONGBIRDS*

"*The Memory of Lavender and Sage* is an enchanting novel that sweeps you away to France on a journey of self-discovery, uncovering family secrets, and learning how love lives on. With a home renovation and a charmed greenhouse filled with herbs and plants that lovingly grow for their keeper, this family saga bridges the generations together with understanding, compassion, and forgiveness but not without a lot of misunderstandings in the middle! Friendships are forged, romance is cultivated, and magical moments abound in the captivating small French town. For readers who love *Under the Tuscan Sun* and *Chocolat*, this is your next heartfelt, delightful read."

—JENNIFER MOORMAN, BESTSELLING AUTHOR OF *THE MAGIC ALL AROUND*

The
MEMORY *of*
LAVENDER
and **SAGE**

ALSO BY AIMIE K. RUNYAN

WITH J'NELL CIESIELSKI AND RACHEL MCMILLAN

The Castle Keepers
The Liberty Scarf (Coming November 2024)

HISTORICAL FICTION

Mademoiselle Eiffel (Coming Fall 2024)
A Bakery in Paris
The School for German Brides
Across the Winding River
Girls on the Line
Daughters of the Night Sky

DAUGHTERS OF NEW FRANCE

Promised to the Crown
Duty to the Crown

The

MEMORY *of* LAVENDER *and* SAGE

A NOVEL

AIMIE K. RUNYAN

HARPER MUSE

The Memory of Lavender and Sage

Copyright © 2024 Aimie K. Runyan

Published by Harper Muse, an imprint of HarperCollins Focus LLC.

This book is a work of fiction. The characters, incidents, and dialogue are drawn from the author's imagination and are not to be construed as real. Any resemblance to actual events or persons, living or dead, is entirely coincidental.

Any internet addresses (websites, blogs, etc.) in this book are offered as a resource. They are not intended in any way to be or imply an endorsement by HarperCollins Focus LLC, nor does HarperCollins Focus LLC vouch for the content of these sites for the life of this book.

Library of Congress Cataloging-in-Publication Data

Names: Runyan, Aimie K., author.
Title: The memory of lavender and sage / Aimie K. Runyan.
Description: Nashville, TN : Harper Muse, 2024. | Summary: "Bestselling author Aimie Runyan makes her contemporary women's fiction debut with this charming escape into the lavender fields of Southern France and a young woman who discovers her family's secrets and the hope for her own future"-- Provided by publisher.
Identifiers: LCCN 2023041887 (print) | LCCN 2023041888 (ebook) | ISBN 9781400237258 (paperback) | ISBN 9781400237265 (epub) | ISBN 9781400237272
Subjects: LCSH: Women--Fiction. | Family secrets--Fiction. | Self-realization in women--Fiction. | LCGFT: Novels.
Classification: LCC PS3618.U5667 M46 2024 (print) | LCC PS3618.U5667 (ebook) | DDC 813/.6--dc23/eng/20231003
LC record available at https://lccn.loc.gov/2023041887
LC ebook record available at https://lccn.loc.gov/2023041888

Printed in the United States of America

24 25 26 27 28 LBC 6 5 4 3 2

To J'nell Ciesielski, international treasure

Chapter 1

WINTER

GREENWICH, CONNECTICUT

The odd thing about a forbidden space was that when its owner died, it still felt . . . forbidden.

I crossed the threshold of my father's bedroom and, though he was powerless to stop me, presumably far beyond caring that I trespassed into his private lair, felt like an errant teenager once again risking a lecture on boundaries and respect. I was instinctually prepared to double back at any moment and retreat to the safety of what had once been my bedroom.

But it was foolish. Dad wasn't around the corner and the room wasn't his any longer. Even though his essence still permeated every inch of the dreary space, nothing belonged to him, and he belonged to nothing and no one anymore. I wished the tears would have welled up and blurred my vision. Dad deserved that much, I supposed. But try as I might, they didn't come.

My eyes stayed dry until I saw the faded yellow tome of Mamà's on his nightstand. I opened it to the first page and read the lines, as ingrained in my childhood memory as Mother Goose was to every other child in Connecticut:

> *I sing the love of a Provençal maid;*
> *How through the wheat-fields of La Crau she strayed,*
> *Following the fate that drew her to the sea.*
> *Unknown beyond remote La Crau was she;*
> *And I, who tell the rustic tale of her,*
> *Would fain be Homer's humble follower.*

Mamà would read the old epic poem in Occitan aloud to me in bits and pieces each night and explain their meaning. Like spoon-feeding psalms to a child, Mamà taught me to know this poem like it was Scripture. It was the story of forbidden romance and tragic loss. It was Romeo and Juliet, though rife with class struggles in place of family feud. She loved the story that was written more than a hundred years ago by Frédéri Mistral as a tribute to the dying language—and culture—he loved.

I was surprised to find the battered book Mamà had read from on Dad's bedside table. I'd scoured the house for it a million times in the years since she died and never been successful. I'd assumed Grandmother had found it and tossed it out, as she had so many things over the years. The cover was yellow with black script. No image to lure in the reader, a charming trait of many French books. They felt the words should be enticement enough to the reader without the draw of a descriptive, artful cover. I had loved the rough, deckle-edged pages and the neat stanzas printed on thick cream paper, Occitan on the left with the French translation on the right. It felt like the secret code shared between mother and daughter.

I would snuggle next to Mamà and listen to her read from the book in her lilting accent, somewhere between standard French and Italian. I would learn about Mirèio, the daughter of a wealthy farmer, and Vincen, the lowly son of a basket maker, whose match was forbidden by her father. They loved each other and tried so valiantly to make a life together, but their love was ultimately denied. Each time, as we reached the story's conclusion, I'd hope that somehow it might end better for them. But sadly, it never did.

I'd have given the world to have Mamà read it to me now, though when I was young, I would sometimes grow bored with the endless stanzas in a language I understood only vaguely from her recitation. I'd plead with her to take a break and tell me the story of the night I was born instead. She always obliged me.

"You were born as the wind howled and the rain thrashed against the roof. There could be no name for you but Tempèsta. You summoned the mistral winds all the way from Provence to celebrate your birth. You were born with a headful of curls the color of burnt sienna and blue-green eyes like the Lac Sainte-Croix near my old village. You charmed the nurses and stole our hearts, even as the thunder threatened to shake the hospital windows from their panes."

Mamà had told me the story of my birth a million times, but I loved it each time. Though I was probably far too old at the age of twelve, I curled up in her lap in the oversize rocker in the corner of her bedroom and drank in the scent of lavender, sage, basil, and lemon, with the barest hint of olive oil, that seemed to seep from her pores. I snuggled in closer and twirled one of her long corkscrew curls with my index finger.

The bedroom she shared with Dad was full of love drenched in sunlight. My favorite part was the embroidered quilt, with all the rich colors of Mamà's native Sainte-Colombe. Bright yellows, vibrant reds, lively greens, and blues so deep you could get lost in them. The very sight of it made me feel safe.

"And what about Wal, Mamà?"

"He was born two years later, on a calm day in May, the very image of your father. He was all dimples and smiles and never caused a bit of fuss."

"How boring," I proclaimed. And Mamà, as she always did, dissolved into giggles. Dear Wal. Walter Francis Luddington IV, the next in the proud line of succession of Luddington men. There had been the original Walter, then Grandpa Wally, our dad Walt, and now Wal. I sometimes wondered what we'd call Wal's son as the name was getting progressively shorter . . . just a guttural *Wuh* sound to call the poor kid from the playground? It had to be hard, being given a name that carried the weight of so many generations of expectations.

With a name like Tempèsta, all anyone expected from me was a bit of chaos. It was easier that way.

When Mamà was alive, she'd made sure that Dad remembered that Wal wasn't just a torchbearer for the family name; that he had to be allowed to have hopes and dreams of his own. But then, far too young and far too suddenly, Mamà was gone in a senseless car accident, and everything changed.

And now I stood in that same room, the one she'd shared with Dad for their almost-fourteen years of marriage. After Mamà died, Dad forbade our entry into the space, claiming he needed one refuge from us.

Never mind that he had his study, the office, the gym, and his country club. It seemed unnecessary to shut us out of here too. But we never questioned him about it. Never dared to incite the wrath that would have ensued if we contravened his orders.

I hadn't stepped foot in this room in the fifteen years since Mamà had died, and nothing was left of the joyful space I remembered. The chair we'd rocked miles in, a huge oaken affair with an overstuffed green cushion, had been replaced by a muted, dove-gray velour bench. The mismatched wooden furniture Mamà had collected from yard sales and flea markets had been replaced with uniform, glossy, piano-black pieces, all selected from the same collection on a high-end furniture showroom floor.

The vibrant hues of the beloved quilt Mamà had embroidered herself, with designs recalled from memory from her native Provence, had been replaced by a duvet with alternating stripes of matte and shiny dark charcoal gray. Perhaps worst of all, the airy gossamer curtains that had framed the windows had given way to the thick blackout variety from the nearby home-improvement store. He claimed they helped him sleep. But the truth was that when Mamà died, he chose to block out all the light in his life . . .

And that included Wal and me. We were just kids, thirteen and eleven when she died, and we had to bear our grief alone.

Dad had systematically removed every trace of Mamà and locked it all away in the basement. There was a small shelf of plastic tubs with meticulously printed labels that read *Nadaleta's Clothes*, *Nadaleta's Books*, *Nadaleta's Papers*, impeccably organized and, like so much in the house, not to be touched. It seemed tragic to see her life reduced to one small corner of a basement.

Within two weeks of Mamà's funeral, Grandmother Luddington came to live with us to manage Dad's modest but stately house. With her arrival we got a string of tutors, music lessons, extracurricular activities, and a nightly lecture over dinner from Dad about some topic he thought would help mold our young brains and turn us into productive citizens. Punctuality. Financial management. Real estate. Living life "the Luddington Way," he called it. It was the closest he could come to nurturing us.

I had chided that he ought to write a self-help book called *The Luddington Way* to help all the poor, driftless souls in the world find some direction. He didn't appreciate my humor.

Wal ate it up. He began to bring a leather-bound notepad and fountain pen to the table every night to take down Dad's words like he was in law school and prepping for the bar exam. Dad lived for Wal's obsequious journaling of his life philosophies. I listened attentively too, though I refused to mimic Wal's note-taking. I was able to parrot back every word Dad said on the frequent occasions when I was accused of not paying attention. But the difference between Wal and me was that I didn't want to accept these lectures as a replacement for affection the way Wal seemed willing to.

"Are you ready?" Wal's baritone sounded behind me from the doorway of his bedroom, snapping me back to the present day.

I turned and stepped back into the hallway, clutching the book of poetry to my chest like a shield. He was, as a twenty-six-year-old man, even more the spitting image of Dad than he had been as a boy. Tall, sandy-blond hair, blue eyes, patrician features. His classic black suit and red power tie were indistinguishable from those in Dad's closet. It was a morbid thought, but with Dad's passing, Wal's wardrobe would effectively double if he could bear to wear his things. Wal's only concession to Mamà's genes was the glow to his skin that allowed him to tan, while poor New Englander Dad, true to his Yankee roots, was lobster-red within a half hour.

The room behind Wal had shelves stuffed with medals and trophies. The walls were covered in plaques and college pennants. A shrine to Wal and his successes. My old bedroom became Grand-

mother's "sitting room" when I left for college, which I always felt
was more appropriate for an Austen novel and not modern-day Connecticut. Even now, she had rooms here but spent most of her time in
the city, living in the penthouse she had shared with Grandpa Wally.

This sitting room of hers doubled as a guest room when it was
needed to serve the function, so my bag was tucked away in a corner
next to the impossibly uncomfortable foldout sofa, doing its best
not to impose. I dashed in and hid the book of poetry in my bag,
even taking care to nestle it between layers of clothes so it wouldn't
tempt Grandmother's grasping fingers that loved nothing more
than to toss anything connected to my mother. Or me.

My half-finished art projects, my tattered notebooks full of
horrible poetry, my collection of (admittedly dreadful) music Dad
and Grandmother despised were long since gone. I had an apartment the size of a shoebox in Queens stuffed to brimming with all
the detritus from my youth that wasn't welcome here.

Dad had insisted I major in finance, which I did. What I never
disclosed to him was that I actually triple-majored, adding journalism to the mix for me and French for Mamà. Occitan studies weren't
an option, so French was the best I could do to stay connected with
her. I'd tried working in finance to please Dad, but after the fourth
horrid job in a windowless cubicle, I put the journalism degree to
use and found a position with a paper. It was as a restaurant critic,
which never would have been my first choice, but it was by far the
best job I'd had.

I'd always hoped to have a job as a travel writer, visiting far-
flung places and bringing the exotic sights, sounds, and, yes, tastes
of the world to those trapped in the rat race in New York. So in a
sense, being a food critic was just a geographically limited version
of what I'd hoped to do.

Wal and I walked together down the wide marble staircase to the main level of Dad's house, not bothering with words. He caught a glimpse of me from the corner of his eye. For a moment I thought Wal might speak, but he seemed to change his mind with an audible click of his teeth clenching shut.

Grandmother Luddington was waiting in the foyer wearing an impeccable black suit. Her makeup was understated, and her gray hair was coiffed into a sleek bob. She refused the close-cropped-with-a-perm 'dos of her contemporaries, though she did feel long hair was practically vulgar on a woman of advanced years. The bob was her concession to aging gracefully.

She eyed me, appraising with the jaded eye of a jewel collector who expected to be cheated. She seemed satisfied with my conservative black dress and low black heels. Most of my wardrobe—like that of virtually all my colleagues at the *New York Tribune*—comprised black or other dark hues, but after I'd sifted through my second-hand wardrobe three times, there really wasn't anything funeral appropriate. The dress—which wasn't designer but was reasonably well-made—was the best I could find at my favorite thrift shop on short notice.

Her eyes lingered at the bronze necklace with charms of rosemary, sage, thyme, and parsley at my throat. It had been a five-dollar impulse buy at the thrift shop jewelry bin. The necklace seemed the sort of thing Mamà would have loved, and that was a lure I struggled to resist.

"You couldn't wear a simple strand of pearls?" she said by way of greeting. We hadn't exchanged more than a few words in three years, but I would have been foolish to expect anything warmer.

My hand reflexively went to my throat, ready to remove the offending bauble, but the sensation passed as quickly as it came. I didn't have to protect her feelings anymore. "*What* pearls? Where would I have gotten pearls?"

It wasn't as though she'd handed down any of her heirlooms to me prematurely, and Dad had never been one to lavish gifts unnecessarily. Certainly nothing so frivolous as jewelry. A briefcase embossed with my initials and a laptop, very much appreciated but not exactly sentimental, had been the last gift Dad had given me after my graduation seven years before. Since then, I was lucky to get a rushed phone call on my birthday.

But then, Grandmother's circumstances had always been such that it probably didn't occur to her that buying a strand of pearls would have meant going without other little luxuries—like food—for months.

She set her jaw. I knew she longed to roll her eyes but would never stoop to something so crass. "We haven't time to find you something suitable now, so just put the necklace in your clutch. It looks ridiculous."

"No." The word reverberated through the foyer like a muttered curse in a silent church.

When I'd lived under this roof, I would have complied. I suffered the muted colors and drab designs Grandmother had insisted were classic and suitable for a young girl bearing the Luddington name. But I wouldn't allow her to cow me into submission any longer.

"Tempy," Wal said, his tone warning me. He folded his arms over his chest, just as Dad used to do when he expected me to back down.

"No," I repeated. Both stared at me, stunned at my defiance. But I'd disappointed them often enough before that once more would make no difference.

"We cannot be late," Grandmother said as though I were blocking the exit.

"Then let's go." I gestured to the door where the car would be waiting for us.

She exhaled, her nostrils flaring. She turned on the ball of her stiletto-clad foot and crossed to the door, her heels clacking on the polished marble.

"You couldn't just ditch the necklace?" Wal still stood with his arms crossed, like the statue of a Roman sentinel. "Her son has just died, and it didn't occur to you to make that little gesture today of all days?"

"In case you forgot, my *father* died too," I hissed. "I'm here, aren't I? Wearing a dowdy black dress and heels to boot? I'd rather be anywhere else, and she damn well knows it. I showed up for the two of you. And it didn't occur to *her* not to nitpick today of all days?"

"We'll discuss this later."

"Doubtful." I would stay for Dad's funeral and the gathering afterward but planned to be on the first train back to the city in the morning. I walked past Wal and took my place next to Grandmother in the town car.

According to Grandmother, the service simply *had* to be held at Christ Church, the Episcopal church in Greenwich that dated back to the late 1700s. Every major family event, from baptisms to funerals, had been held there since the place opened its doors. The notable exception had been Dad's hasty wedding to Mamà when they were only twenty-two years old. It had been held in a tiny garden upstate with only a handful of friends present.

An offense that Grandmother never let Dad forget. No doubt she'd been mentally planning the wedding of her only child for years, and she'd been robbed of that opportunity.

The church was packed with his colleagues and business acquaintances, all clad in black suits or dresses with designer labels and sunglasses to hide the tears they weren't shedding. Why would they? He was someone they all knew but never well. He simply hadn't let anyone into his life to that degree in years. I never caught wind of him dating or even going on social outings that weren't at least tangentially related to work. Dad was friendly and charismatic, to be sure, but no one knew what he'd been like outside of work.

Sadder still, the memory of the once-carefree father from my earliest days, the one who carted me around on his shoulders, who told the very best ghost stories around the campfire, who loved calling me "Tempest-in-a-teapot" because it made me giggle, and who always made sure I had my own popcorn at the movies, was so faded around the edges, I barely remembered it.

After the priest gave his sermon and a few colleagues waxed on about Dad's work ethic, sense of humor, and brilliant golf swing, we lined up to walk to the front of the church to see him one last time. He wore a navy suit and red tie, cut just like Wal's, and looked as though he were sleeping. And he should have been. Asleep in the sun on a beach, relaxing with a Hendrick's gin and tonic and counting the minutes until his retirement. He was only fifty-one when the heart attack claimed him.

I wished I could wake him up, even if it meant I'd be subjected to another lecture on my shortcomings. Because as much as we'd driven each other mad, he'd deserved better than literally dying at his desk before he had the chance to retire and get to know himself outside of the office. But hopes, as I had learned over the years, counted for precious little.

Chapter 2

By the time the last guest left, my feet throbbed in my thrift store shoes, and I was so tired that not even the medieval torture device Grandmother called a foldout sofa would impede my sleep. As the door clicked shut behind the last of the mourners, I kicked off my shoes and shook my head at the table laden with half-eaten food and empty drink cups. The mess would have to wait. I expected Grandmother would have help coming in the morning, but I could help clear some of it away before my train if she had, uncharacteristically, overlooked that detail.

She'd begged off almost an hour ago, and I was envious that at her advanced age of seventy-eight, though spry as the rest of us, she was able to break away from the crowd who assembled to pay their respects.

Wal worked in fundraising, just like Dad, so he knew everyone in attendance. Most of the guests seemed only vaguely aware, or even mildly shocked, that Dad even had a daughter.

Wal crossed the now-empty living room to the bar, pulled out one of the etched crystal tumblers from the cupboard, and poured himself a measure of Dad's good scotch. Not the top-shelf bottle he'd saved for the best of good news, like a major donation to one of his causes or national recognition for some of his work, but good scotch nonetheless.

"Want some?" Wal asked before replacing the stopper.

"Thanks, but I'm going to bed." I mustered a weak smile. "I'm catching the early train. I have to work Monday."

"Really? Is work not giving you the time off? The foundation gave me a week."

I pinched the bridge of my nose and exhaled. "Because your last name is Luddington, and you work for a foundation that just so happens to bear the same name. And the person who died happened to have worked there for three decades. Never mind that you're not living on a newspaper columnist's salary. You can afford to take time off."

"You didn't have to leave finance, even if you didn't want to work for Dad. You had some good entry-level jobs. You'd be better off at one of those firms than trying to scrape together a living in a dying medium."

I bit my tongue. Working for Dad had never been on the table. Grandmother had personally seen to that. Not that I'd have wanted it. Wal went to Yale, like the rest of the Luddington men, and followed Dad's plan to a T. He never explained why, but he thought Sarah Lawrence would be a better fit for me, though Yale had been within reach. But I didn't fight him on it and graduated summa cum laude. Instead of earning me praise, those achievements were cast in my face when, time after time, I failed to clear the ever-rising bar of their expectations.

"I hated each and every last one of those jobs," I said. "But I don't want to rehash this now. I had this fight with Dad far too many times. I like my job now. Money isn't everything."

"Temp, that's—" He cut himself off. "Listen, if you insist on rushing out of here at first light, we need to discuss the will now."

I blinked. It wasn't something I'd even considered. I had somehow expected Dad to outlive us all and hadn't given a second thought to what would happen to his estate after he died. "Pour the scotch, then."

"And one for me," Grandmother said, entering the room. The arrangements of flowers from the funeral seemed to shrivel when they felt her glacial presence. She was still clad in her pristine suit that had nary a wrinkle. Whatever she'd been doing, she hadn't been napping. Likely, she was bored of accepting condolences from people she didn't care about and was perfectly content to let Wal and me handle the crowd once she'd been seen by the people who mattered.

Wal pulled down two more crystal tumblers from the cupboard, poured a generous measure of the amber liquid into both, and slid them to each of us as we took our seats at the bar.

"Dad named me as executor," he began.

"Naturally, that duty would fall to you as the oldest son." Grandmother shot me a glare that dared me to contradict her. "You don't have your brother's head for finance."

I stifled a scoff and was sorely tempted to challenge Wal to compare transcripts. I didn't remember hearing about any special accolades at his graduation, and there was no way I wouldn't have been told a dozen times if there had been.

"Primogeniture in full effect in the twenty-first century. I'd expect nothing less," I said, though I felt no real animosity about

Dad's decision. Wal had a brilliant mind for planning and details. He was the natural choice.

"I won't bore you with the details of the minutiae, but he has bequeathed a fair amount to his causes." He took a sip from his glass.

"That's good," I said. Though the Metropolitan Opera and the Museum of Modern Art likely had plenty of money, Dad *had* cared passionately about them, and it made sense that he should leave a bit of a legacy there. His name on plaques and in programs, *In Fond Memory of Walter Luddington III*, all over town was the sort of thing he would have loved.

"He, of course, made some provisions for Grandmother," Wal continued. "He assumed you'd still have money from your portion of Granddad's estate but wanted to make sure your future was secure."

"He was always so thoughtful," she said. For the first time since I came home, I saw a few tears welling up in her eyes. I reached over to rub her back, but she stiffened at the contact so I removed my hand at once.

"He left the rest of his personal estate to me," Wal said quickly, not meeting my eye.

I exhaled. I hadn't known what to expect, but maybe not *nothing*. "Um, well, it was his money to do with as he wished. It's fine."

Grandmother snorted into her tumbler.

I turned to her. "What does that mean?"

"Why, nothing, dear." She took a long drink from the heavy tumbler. *Dear* rolled off her tongue like an insult, but she never referred to me by my name, calling the moniker "ridiculous." She'd even tried to persuade my father to have it changed—to Millicent, of all the horrid names—after Mamà died, but for once, he ignored her.

Nonetheless, Grandmother spent years trying to mold me into the prefect "Millie" she'd dreamed of. The biddable granddaughter who attended prestigious schools, went into a respectable career for a short time, then married into the right family and gave up the career for children and high-profile charity work. That I refused to melt myself into a puddle of wax for her to shape was the bitterest disappointment of her life.

"That wasn't nothing," I said. "Spill it."

"Your mother was a gold digger." She turned to me. "I don't have to pretend otherwise for your father's sake any longer. Why would you be any different?"

"Grandmother, that's hardly fair."

I felt my eyes widen, surprised that Wal had come to my defense at all.

"She's just like her mother," Grandmother insisted. "Not like you. You're your father's son through and through. She doesn't *deserve* the same consideration."

"I hardly think—" Wal said.

"Your father made his wishes clear," Grandmother pressed. "And I insist you follow them precisely."

"I won't contradict Dad's will," Wal said. "But you aren't right about Mom either. It seems she had money of her own that Dad saved for Tempy."

"I don't believe it." Grandmother pursed her lips into their natural state. "That bit of bohemian trash couldn't have had two dimes to rub together."

"You're wrong. It wasn't a Vanderbilt fortune, but it's a tidy sum," Wal said. "And it's all to go to Temp. Dad saved it for her so the estate would stay intact but she'd have a little something of her own."

He pulled a folded document from the breast pocket of his suit jacket and slid it over to me. I scanned the legalese to the section concerning me. Mamà certainly had a comfortable nest egg, and Dad intended it for me. I swallowed back the tears.

He hadn't forgotten me entirely.

I wouldn't let Grandmother see me cry, but it was a reminder that I had once been loved. It was a reminder of how much I missed that sensation.

"I can set it up in an index fund for you when it clears probate," Wal said. "It shouldn't take long."

"That won't be necessary," I said. "I can manage things on my own."

Like Dad, Wal had the ability to remain composed while he was inwardly fuming. He crossed his arms over his chest and shot me a glare because I wasn't falling in line and obeying his commands. I was, to use Grandmother's favorite expression, "being difficult."

"I think it's best if you invest the money in something prudent, and soon. Your retirement can't be in great shape." Another barb. My work had few fringe benefits, and I was currently on track to retire at the spry young age of 117. And to Wal, without a hefty 401(k), a job could have no value.

"You may be right. But I'll make the decision without your help."

"Why do you choose to be so hardheaded, Tempy?" Wal countered. "You're always so impetuous. It would be easier for everyone if you just listened to reason."

I set the crystal tumbler down on the granite counter with a decisive clunk. "I'm sure it would be easier. For you. Maybe it would be easier for me, *little brother*, if you'd stop treating me like a child. I never asked either of you, or Dad, for a single thing once I graduated college. Despite what you think, I'm not wholly incompetent. I don't need your advice on how to live my life."

The tendon in his jaw twitched as he gritted his teeth. He'd been given precedence in the family for so long, he loathed being reminded that he came behind me in any respect—even birth order.

"Listen, Wal. I don't give a damn about Dad's will. Keep this godforsaken house and everything in it. Keep his filthy money and may you enjoy every penny, though I don't expect you will. I just want what Mamà left for me. And her things in the basement, if you don't mind."

"And here I'd hoped to have a New Year's bonfire," Grandmother said, the scotch already eating away at her already-flimsy filter. "The sooner you get that garbage out of here the better, if you ask me."

"You can have her things," Wal said, more diplomatically. "It probably wasn't right to leave it all boxed up for so long, but I don't think Dad could bear the sight of it."

I softened slightly. Wal's alliances might have fallen with Father, and with Grandmother by default, but he *had* loved Mamà. "Is there anything of hers you want? If there's something precious to you, you should have it."

"He doesn't need any of that tramp's refuse," Grandmother insisted. "Why would he?"

I kept my eyes on my brother, hoping he'd have some sort of an answer. Perhaps a bracelet of hers he remembered fondly that he could pass down to an eventual wife or daughter. Maybe some of her needlework or a piece of the local art she'd loved that Dad had taken down and stored after she died.

He opened his mouth but paused a moment to regroup. "I'm fine. If Dad's legacy is going to be mine, her legacy should be yours."

* * *

The death trap of a sleeper sofa, paired with the contents of my discussion with Wal and Grandmother, rendered me unable to sleep despite my exhaustion. Insomnia was nothing new for me. It plagued me for years after Mamà died. Dad, always helpful, had told me to count sheep. Wal told me to listen to soft music, which did help, but Grandmother claimed to be able to hear it from her room, so that was forbidden. Funny that she claimed she couldn't hear the same music from Wal's room, which was perfectly equidistant to Grandmother's room as mine. Grandmother told me to stop complaining about my troubles and, for heaven's sake, go off to school.

I tried reading from the novel I'd brought along for the train ride. I meditated. I even counted Dad's stupid sheep. I imagined them in suits with power ties leaping over golden fences, but it didn't help. Finally, as the old clock radio, one of the few things I'd left behind that hadn't been discarded, read 2:00 a.m., I gave up on the attempt to sleep.

I tossed off the blanket and padded down to the basement to the perfectly labeled rows of identical plastic tubs that held Mamà's things. It was a miracle that Grandmother hadn't convinced Dad to get rid of the lot of it, but at least Dad's loyalty to Mamà extended as far as her personal effects, which had been neatly categorized and tucked away on a shelf.

I immediately decided against taking the train later that morning. I'd borrow suitcases and pack all this away and take a rideshare back home, despite the cost. I wouldn't risk Grandmother disposing of anything. It sounded spiteful, but she was more than capable of it.

In the earliest days after Mamà passed, I'd asked Dad if I might have her perfume bottle to keep in my room. It was etched crystal with a long, elegant stopper. It was always a special occasion when Mamà permitted me a bit of scent. She would gently tip the bottle and remove the stopper, letting the excess perfume drip back into the bottle. I would shiver in anticipation as Mamà brushed the cool crystal gently against my warm skin.

Mamà's preferred scent was somehow both floral and earthy. Clean, bright, not overpowering. A lot like her. I would lift my wrist to my nose and breathe in deeply when I thought no one would notice. It felt impossibly grown up. But when I'd asked Dad if I might have the keepsake for my own room, he'd grown sullen and banished me from the living room with a barked order to go do my homework.

I could see it now, wrapped in bubble wrap in one of the bins containing the most fragile of her possessions. I unwrapped it, knowing I'd have to rewrap it carefully for transport back to Queens. But after fifteen years of separation, I longed to hold that memory of her in my hands.

Two inches of scent still remained in the bottle. When I removed the decorative crystal top and tipped my nose to the rim, it was as though Mamà were back among the living and right in this cold basement alongside me. After bathing in a cloud of the floral notes in her perfume, I could almost feel her arms around me. And it was painful when the embrace did not materialize.

I understood then why Dad hadn't allowed me to keep the bottle. The smell of her in the house would have felt like her ghost trailing us all. But it made no sense to leave all her memories down here to gather dust when we might have enjoyed having the remembrances of her around us.

I dabbed a bit of the perfume at the hollow of my neck and in the crooks of my elbows. Warm places that would release the scent. I knew it had to be a higher quality than the drugstore sprays I used, for the smallest amount seemed to last all day. While my own seemed to fade before I'd left my apartment.

My hands shook, feeling my mother so close, as I rewrapped the crystal bottle and placed it back in the tub. I ran my fingers along the rest of the tubs. Her clothes, her beloved books, the precious things she'd deemed worthy to cart across an ocean. The things she'd accumulated in the years after she met Dad. But then I saw what I was searching for, taking up one entire tub all by itself: Mamà's quilt.

She'd made it herself when I was small, using threads in the deepest of jewel tones and delicate pastels. It had graced her bed every night of my life before she died. It was one of the first things to disappear after she passed. I removed it from the tub and pulled it around my shoulders. The yellow was sunny and warm. My mood always lifted when I saw it. The blues, reds, and greens, rather than being discordant, played off one another, making a happy medley of color I imagined mimicked the vibrant landscapes of Sainte-Colombe where Mamà had spent her youth. She'd lovingly embroidered every stitch as a gift for Dad, and it was a crime that it had been left untouched and unloved in a plastic bin for over a decade.

Sainte-Colombe was a small village in Provence, nestled into jagged rock formations. It seemed as though the first settlers of the town had crammed the village into the side of the rocks by sheer force of will, and I always pictured the residents as being hardy folk who refused to yield to the whims of nature. Below the town were lush hills, fertile and verdant, tended by farmers who lived in pristine stone cottages. Mamà had promised to take me, but as with so many promises, she'd not been granted the years necessary to realize them all.

I'd always been fascinated by the place but never had the means to travel there, nor had Dad been willing to take us. So I wrote reports about the village in school. I'd taken French classes when Dad had urged Spanish or Chinese. I read everything about the village and the region I could find at the school and city libraries, which wasn't much.

When I closed my eyes at night, my vision was filled with the image of the warm, sand-colored buildings with terra-cotta tiled roofs and brightly painted shutters and doors all built along a winding road that led up to the top of the hill and the village square.

Thanks to Mamà's nest egg, I could easily afford the ticket and some time off. If I couldn't see my mother, it would at least be a chance to see where she was from and all the places she'd loved. It would be a way to learn more about her since she wasn't here to tell me more herself.

Chapter 3

NEW YORK CITY

Hell, I can't tell if this is salmon or pork," my editor, Carol, whisper-shouted from across the table, angling her plate to get a better view of the food. She practically had to scream to be heard over the blaring techno music that emitted from so many speakers, the din was impossible to escape. We'd come directly to the restaurant after a long day in the office, and while she seemed keen to try the new hot spot, I'd have much preferred to grab some takeout and curl up in my apartment with a movie or a book before falling into bed. But sadly, there was no takeout in my future, and that bed was several hours away.

Though she was just five years older than me, Carol was light-years ahead of me career-wise. I was convinced it was in no small part due to how much she loved New York. She was short and curvy, with a sassy brown bob and a sleek wardrobe to match.

Everything about her screamed "urban sophisticate" in the best possible way.

"I didn't see any pork on the app menu, so if it isn't salmon, they've gone off book because they figured out that we're with the paper." I shook my head. If they knew I was a critic and showed off, I couldn't do a write-up. Any observant restauranteur would know if a critic was in-house; they often came in groups and ordered a huge sampling of dishes to pass around and discuss at length. I preferred to go in a little more low-key, with a friend or two at most, and more often alone. If a place couldn't make a solo diner feel welcome, I thought it spoke to a poorly run front-of-house that had been made to feel like any open seat was a waste of revenue. To be fair, it was true, and the restaurant business in the city was brutal, but that was not a burden to place on the shoulders of a guest.

But no matter how incognito I tried to be, about half the time, I was recognized as a critic. A rookie chef might try to pull out the stops to impress me, but a truly savvy restauranteur would pretend they were none the wiser and then quietly cook their tush off so as not to risk losing the free publicity from a good review.

The lights inside Nava, the new "concept restaurant" in Chelsea I'd been assigned to critique, were so impossibly dim, it was hard to see the food on my plate, let alone the fork to eat it with. I'd have to ding them for that. Mood lighting was one thing, but lights this low could be designed to hide a multitude of culinary sins.

Renowned chef Edward Fairbanks was at the helm and had, in his words, sought to create a "dining experience that immersed the guest in the harsh realities of late-stage capitalism." The restaurant was made to resemble an industrial warehouse that boasted the wildly ineffective light fixtures we struggled under. Servers in coveralls seated patrons at stainless-steel workbenches and served food on hammered chrome dinnerware. The flatware was so large and heavy it was almost unwieldy, especially given the appetizers' comically small portions. Another ding.

According to the menus, printed on cheap, quad-ruled drafting paper and presented on metal clipboards that displayed a disturbing number of fingerprint smudges (yet another ding), the name *Nava* meant "lovely," though they never specified in which language. But in any of them, it was a horrendously obvious attempt at juxtaposition. I hoped at least the food would live up to the moniker, but I wasn't optimistic.

"Salmon!" she shouted triumphantly over the incessant beat of the music. I shot her a thumbs-up, not wanting to raise my voice unless I had to. Ding, ding, ding. It was never a great article when I was ready to pan a place before the main course showed up.

My appetizer was tangerine-glazed chicken wontons with blue cheese. There were four of them, each about as large as a Wheat Thin, served on a plate the size of a hubcap. I cut one open with the massive knife and fork provided, though both were so outsized it made a mess of the tiny wonton. I gave up on the cutlery and popped one in my mouth with my fingers, too exasperated to worry about the table manners that had been drilled into my head. At first it was done lovingly but insistently by my mother, who believed food deserved respect. Later, the lessons were hammered in relentlessly by Grandmother Luddington, who I think simply delighted in chastising me.

The chicken, cloyingly sweet, tasted like something from a cheap, fake-Asian drive-through and didn't marry at all with the tang of the blue cheese. The wonton itself tasted unremarkable, and I guessed they were simple store-bought sheets cut into quarters. To the kitchen's credit, it was fried perfectly, but the flavors were a mess.

Carol looked at me expectantly. I shook my head and passed her one of the two remaining wontons that hadn't been eviscerated by the flatware designed for some twenty-foot giant.

"Oh God." She turned her head to both sides to see whether anyone was watching and spit the noxious mess into her napkin before taking a deep draught of her overpriced red wine. *Foul*, she mouthed. She passed me one of her bite-size almond-crusted salmon tarts, and though the coating of teriyaki overpowered the whole thing, it was far better than mine. I took subtle notes on my phone, trying to think of the kindest way possible to pan the place.

The server arrived with my Kobe beef slider, which I generally thought was a waste of prime-quality meat, but they boasted it as one of their signature dishes, so I felt compelled to order it. Carol's choice was lobster served with a truffle beurre fondue. I turned on the light on my phone to be able to see the burger better, only to be rewarded with a peevish sigh from the server.

"Chef believes the lack of light serves to heighten the other senses. He doesn't want you to eat with your eyes but to experience the tastes, textures, and scents on a higher plane."

"How very interesting." I forced the corners of my mouth upward and switched off the phone light. I could have offered the poor woman an entire TED Talk about why the chef was full of it but spared her. "I find it a captivating choice that he decided to deprive us the visual experience only to overload the aural." I gestured to the speaker above my head.

"It isn't meant to be a *comfortable* experience but rather an *intense* one."

Clearly it was a line of nonsense the server had been forced to memorize, but it was clear she believed it as though it were foodie scripture. The Word according to Edward Fairbanks.

Carol's shoulders shook with laughter when the server finally departed. Her lobster was fine, though the truffle masked any of the gentler notes in the tender flesh of the shellfish. It was a shame, really, as the lobster itself was excellent. The slider was utterly underwhelming, tasting no different from an eight-dollar chain restaurant offering. The garlic-Parmesan fries they served with it were the most solid offering of the night, but that was hardly glowing praise, given that this was a world-class kitchen.

"Can we please skip dessert?" I yelled to Carol when I finished my slider. I had no desire to sample whatever ethically sourced chocolate-saffron-foam-topped nightmare they had on offer. She nodded and settled the staggering bill with the paper's credit card.

We stepped into the frigid night, bundled in our heavy black peacoats. While most journalists were famous for not paying attention to their appearance, the Culture section of the *New York Tribune* felt compelled to dress well. Designer labels—mine thrifted—and usually in shades of black, charcoal, or navy that would help us to blend in while we were on assignment. It reminded me a bit too much of the bland beiges and pastels Grandmother had shoved me into, but I could at least see a purpose in trying to blend into the wallpaper in my line of work.

"I have an embarrassing question." Carol pulled on her cashmere-lined leather gloves.

"Yes, we can get a real dinner. I'm famished. Antonio's?"

"Obviously."

Antonio's was our standby. Good pizza with house-made mozzarella, drinkable wine, and a pleasant ambience that allowed people to speak. It was just a couple of blocks away, and we were settled in our favorite booth with Chianti at the ready within minutes.

"That place was a nightmare." I rubbed the life back into my fingers after our walk in the glacial night air. "I don't know what the hell Fairbanks was thinking."

"It's high-concept." She waved her hand dismissively, as though it were a legitimate explanation for the culinary assault we'd just endured.

"The food ranged from bad to mediocre. I don't care about the 'statement' the chef was trying to make." I leaned my head back against the familiar red vinyl of the booth. "I'll have to let him have it. If he were a rookie, I might be compelled to be generous, but he's been in the game long enough to know better."

"Tempy, you can't pan the place," Carol said. "Fairbanks's chief investor is also a major advertiser for the paper. We'd lose a major account if you do."

"Carol, I can't in good conscience encourage people to spend a week's pay eating in that dreadful place."

"It's an experience. Some people will love it."

"Dining out should be a *pleasant* experience. Otherwise, what's the point? At the end of a long week, who wants to go out and be made to suffer? Do you know anyone who has it so easy they'd find that sort of thing enjoyable?"

She paused, contemplating. "I know plenty of people who would love to brag about paying through the nose for 'the Fairbanks Experience,' at least."

"They're welcome to it, but I can't praise the food."

"I'm sorry, Temp. I can't run the article if you trash it. We'd both lose our jobs."

I sighed. I mentally concocted an article that talked around the food and focused on the uniqueness of the venue, but it made me vaguely nauseated to do it, even in my head.

Our server, Gina, was part of the fourth generation of her family to run Antonio's. I'd met Antonio himself when I first moved to the city and had even attended his funeral when he died a few years back. She placed a simple cheese pizza in front of me and one in front of Carol.

"Look at this," I said to Carol. "I can actually see what I'm eating. Crust made from a hundred-year-old recipe. Homemade marinara and mozzarella. Fresh basil probably grown on the back patio. Baked to perfection in a wood-fire oven. And it's fifteen bucks. Not three hundred a plate for food that left us hungry. And not to mention Gina here, who is a New York City treasure."

"Damn straight." She patted my shoulder as she headed back to the kitchen. "I'm giving you the family discount for that one."

Carol sighed. "I know, but it's business. Is it worth losing our jobs over giving Fairbanks an honest review?"

I sat there staring at her. Willing my mouth to open and say, "Of course not, you're absolutely right."

But I couldn't. I couldn't live with myself if people wasted their hard-earned money and precious time outside their offices at such a massive disaster of a restaurant. If some superrich elites wanted to waste their money on an "experience" instead of dinner, so be it. But I had to warn those people away who might go in expecting a lovely meal for a special occasion. Those people who didn't have the luxury of dining out several times a week deserved the truth.

"Listen, Temp, I promised them a review. We have to come up with something nice to say. It's not like it's the worst place we've been to. Remember that 'Midwestern rustic' nightmare?"

"How could I forget? It was Cracker Barrel at five times the cost."

"Oh, come on, it was 'ironic,'" she said, unable to keep a straight face. "Haven't you been in New York long enough to know that?"

I shook my head. "If you think that was the low point, you're forgetting the table-to-farm fiasco."

Carol almost snorted Chianti from her nose. "What? You think a restaurant in Williamsburg where patrons can feed pigs table scraps in a pen out back is a *bad* idea?"

"Oh, it was brilliant until one of them escaped and ran into the restaurant and wreaked havoc on the place." I threw my head back and howled.

Carol was shaking with laughter at this point. "It's a shame the health department shut them down. I thought it was clever. Removing the distance between the diner and the source of their meal."

"I thought the whole idea of table to farm was to get people out into the countryside, not bringing the farm to the city."

Carol wiped a tear of laughter from the corner of her eye. "Such in-the-box thinking."

"The next thing you know, I'll be supporting the notion that restaurants should focus on feeding people. Madness."

"That sounds like a terrible business model if you ask me."

I took a bite of my humble cheese pizza and closed my eyes to appreciate the flavors. Fresh tomato, tangy cheese. Sweet basil that lifted the whole thing. "Crazy idea, I know."

"You aren't happy at the paper," Carol said. "I can smell an unhappy journalist from a mile away."

"Because they give up showering?"

"Ha ha, very funny. Listen, girl. You know I love you and we'll always be friends. But if this job isn't the right fit for you, let's find a solution."

I set down my pizza and took a sip of Chianti. "I know there are a million people who would love my job . . ."

"That doesn't matter. They may want it, but they don't have

your skills. You know the restaurant landscape in this city. For goodness' sake, you went to culinary school to learn the trade from the inside out when you got the job. Who does that?"

"It's the Luddington Way." I rolled my eyes at myself. It was one of the messages from Dad I'd taken to heart: whatever you do, put everything into it. And I had.

"That's great, but if this whole scene is making you miserable, as your friend, I'm telling you, you need to do something else. I can't stand to see you unhappy."

"And as my boss?"

"I would hate to lose you. You're one of my best. But there will be times we have to pull our punches on reviews, and I am powerless to stop that."

I exhaled slowly and found my eyes transfixed on the garnet hue of the Chianti before me.

"Listen, I can try to find you something else at the paper. You're too good to leave the business entirely."

"I appreciate that, Carol. More than I can express." And I knew she'd try, but it would be almost impossible to find me a gig that paid as well or got as much coverage as the restaurant beat. The paper, like all papers, was struggling and the staff shrank more each year. And the foodie scene was where I'd cultivated my skill set; she was right about that.

"Listen, you've just lost your dad. I know you weren't close, but it's still a loss. Why don't you take a break and jump back into the fray when your head is right? I'll hold your job for as long as I can."

I nodded. It wouldn't take long for whichever low-paid intern who took my place to impress Carol into a permanent hire, but the offer was a gracious one.

"I know this may not be my place, but you should go to France.

You've talked about it a million times, and your mom left you the means to do it. Take a few weeks. See where she grew up. Eat some amazing food that isn't served on repurposed industrial equipment. It will do you a world of good. And you can get some articles out of it too. Keep receipts and eat like a critic."

I'd been wrestling with that idea for the past week since the funeral, but to hear it from Carol's lips made sense. Made it seem like the logical next step in my life. I picked up my glass of Chianti and raised it to her. "I just might do that."

"You should. You'll thank me for it."

Later that night, in my studio apartment in Queens, I fired up my ancient laptop and clicked around the travel sites, determining how possible a trip might be. Plane tickets to Paris were easily found and not horribly overpriced since it wasn't high tourist season. Unfortunately, there was no train line to Sainte-Colombe, so I'd have to get creative on how to reach the village once I arrived in France. But it didn't seem to be an insurmountable problem. Lodging was the problematic part. There weren't exactly hotels in Sainte-Colombe, and a search for guesthouses came up blank. The only search that caught my eye was for real estate:

CHARMING MANOR HOUSE IN PROVENCE

If you're looking for the perfect getaway in Provence, your search is over. Spacious, fully furnished four-bedroom home on two acres. Will be lovely full-time or vacation dwelling once a bit of elbow grease is applied. Paradise is yours for the making.

I could spot an oversell without a second glance, but the fact remained that the price was reasonable, in a time when nothing seemed to be, and it was a way to reconnect with what I'd lost. A way to find out more about Mamà and her life before she'd met Dad. And maybe to find a place where I might fit in after so many years of feeling like I'd always been the outsider.

I snapped the laptop lid shut and shook myself for even thinking such a ridiculous idea could be possible. But after a few minutes, I opened the lid again. How impossible was the idea, truly? I had Mamà's nest egg now, and it was up to me to make something of it.

Chapter 4

ON THE ROAD TO SAINTE-COLOMBE

My heart thudded against my rib cage as I fought the urge to pull off to the side of the road and hyperventilate. I'd bought the little cactus-green Peugeot from the least sketchy-looking used car dealership in Aix-en-Provence, where I'd made base camp for a day or two before making the last leg of the journey to Sainte-Colombe. I just had to hope it was roadworthy even if I wasn't. The salesman assured me it was low mileage and reliable, though I knew less about cars than I did about quantum physics—which was precisely nothing.

I had kept up with the flow of traffic near the city, but even as traffic thinned out in the country, every muscle in my body remained tense. I was certain I would misgauge something and get myself, and anyone within a ten-car radius, killed. The farther I got from the city, the more the roads grew winding and narrow. If a car approached, I had to swerve off the road almost entirely to make room for it. The constant whir of cyclists on my right only added to my anxiety. My knuckles were eight massive pearls as my fingers clutched the steering wheel in a death grip. I forced my breath to even out and take the road one mile—or kilometer—at a time.

And to make matters worse, the legendary mistral winds beat against the side of my car, making the simple act of keeping the vehicle between two lines a far more challenging objective than it should have been.

I knew full well it wasn't just spontaneity but a dash of reck-lessness that led me to buy a farmhouse in Sainte-Colombe sight unseen, but the fact that there had been only one house in my price range available anywhere near the village made the choice for me. The part that was truly insane was buying a car, the cheapest auto-matic I could find, and thinking I could make the drive to Sainte-Colombe and arrive unscathed.

Dad had been an impatient driving teacher and my grandmother an unwilling one, so I had been proficient enough to get my license when I came of age, but never more than that. And then I had spent my entire adult life in New York, where owning a car would have been senseless and costly. Moving to a place that was inaccessible by train or most other public transport was perhaps not my finest decision, but I was committed now.

I reached the address the real estate agent had given me in less than two hours from Aix, but I was so grateful to park, my knees shook as I exited the tiny car.

I rested my hand on the roof of the little coupe to steady myself as I took in the building. According to the agent, the building was over eighty years old, but there weren't many newer in the area. I'd expected something that might need cleaning, perhaps some mini-mal restoration. What I saw in front of me was a ruin.

The exterior plaster, which had once been a warm vanilla color, was crumbling to dust. The windows were poorly sealed. More tiles were broken on the terra-cotta roof than intact. Even the shutters, painted a rather insistent shade of lavender, were peeling. I shuddered to think what the interior looked like, for it seemed no one had stepped on the property, much less inside the house, in decades.

I tore my eyes from the place and held my head in my hands. I could drive back to Aix and sell the Peugeot back to the dealership. I was pretty sure I had a few days' grace period there. I could back out of the house deal without too much fuss. It was always easier for the buyer to back out than the seller. I'd be out some money, but I could at least enjoy a couple of weeks in France like a sane person and go back to New York and real life. Carol could change my separation agreement to just a PTO request without any trouble if I called her immediately. I'd have money to put a down payment on a nicer condo, maybe in Brooklyn. Heck, maybe I'd even let Wal put it in whatever index fund he'd been talking about the day of the funeral. Through my fingers, I took in the sight of the heap of a farmhouse I'd bought and was ready to admit I'd made a spectacular blunder.

I took out my cell, outfitted with an international SIM card just before I left, and started searching for the agent's number. I had to be able to back out of this.

Before I could find the number, I smelled, then saw the plume of dust rising from a utility van ambling down the long driveway to the house. An odd choice of a vehicle for a real estate agent, but I was more concerned about how he managed to maneuver the hulking van down roads that seemed barely wide enough to walk on rather than why he didn't drive a compact car like most everyone else.

My shoulders sagged with relief when I realized I wouldn't have to manage the transaction in my substandard French over the phone. This would be easier to explain in person. What with roof tiles sliding off and shutters hanging by a hinge, the visual would be powerful enough.

A man with light brown hair kissed bronze by the sun and bottle-green eyes emerged from the van after it idled to a stop. He wore jeans and a T-shirt; a bit more casual than I expected in an agent, but the small towns of the South of France were less formal in dress than the major cities like Paris and Lyon. Or at least so I'd been told in French textbooks all through high school and college. I'd observed the same in French movies, which I watched frequently whenever I missed Mamà, and it seemed to hold up in the real world as well.

"You must be Ms. Luddington," he said, his English heavily accented but flawless. He extended a hand, but his smile seemed forced.

"Bonjour, monsieur," I said, remembering Mamà's stories about Sainte-Colombe. She always told me that at least a small attempt to speak French was always appreciated. And being flowery with the honorifics was always good form in small southern villages, even if their casual clothes might lead a person to assume that formalities weren't important. I extended my hand back to him. "You must be the agent, Monsieur Blanchet?"

"No, I'm the agent's friend who has been charged with bringing you your keys." He gripped my hand and released it quickly. "Tibèri Cabrol."

"Ah. That was kind of you to deliver the keys."

"Not at all. It's what friends do here. He's sorry he couldn't do it himself." He handed me a worn set of keys and a packet of papers we'd signed digitally. He didn't smile, though after the three days I'd spent in Paris and Aix, it didn't seem the norm here. "I expect it isn't the same in New York?"

I rolled my eyes at the presumption about standoffish New Yorkers. Though he wasn't really wrong. In a building of hundreds, I knew the names of four people. And the super, Jake.

"You've done your homework on me, I see." I held the folder of paperwork up to my chest like a shield.

"No. Matthieu—Monsieur Blanchet as you know him—just said a New Yorker was moving into the neighborhood. That's all he told me."

"I'm sure," I said, unable to keep the humor in my voice. "Your friend described the place as 'will be lovely, once a bit of elbow grease is applied.'"

"And so it will be." Tibèri, hands on his hips, turned to appraise the building, his stern face softening. "I'm sure she has good bones."

"'Good bones'? Isn't that real estate code for 'barely able to avoid being condemned by the local building authorities'?"

Tibèri finally cracked a smile. "Don't despair. I haven't been inside in ages, but houses like these were built to outlast doomsday."

"It looks like it already *has*. Perhaps twice." I resisted the urge to sit on the ground, bury my head in my hands, and cry for a solid half hour. "My brother is right. I'm impulsive. I'm an idiot. No wonder Matthieu didn't want to bring the keys himself. He was afraid I'd bolt on him."

"He has your money already. Not much you can do to his commission now," Tibèri pointed out. "But in truth, his mother is ill, and he had to go with her into Aix for treatment."

"Oh, I'm so sorry to hear that." I pried my eyes from the house and glanced over to Tibèri, whose expression had grown more solemn. He knew this woman and cared about her. "I just lost my father."

"Now it's my turn to be sorry," he said, his expression softening even more. He scanned the building for a moment before speaking again. "Listen, I can go over the place if you want. Assure you that it isn't a lost cause."

"You're handy?"

"Carpenter by trade." The corners of his lips pulled up in a small smile. He was proud of his work.

"Well, that's lucky, isn't it?" I laughed despite myself. "Let me guess, your real estate agent friend sends you out to all the fixer-uppers and takes a cut of your profits."

"That'd be rather clever." He chuckled. "But you give far too much credit to Matthieu for his cunning. He's the sort to double-check the math at a restaurant to make sure he isn't being *under-charged*."

"I hope that's true," I said, unconvinced that this Matthieu wasn't secretly dancing to have off-loaded a money pit. I forced my jaw to unclench and my shoulders to lower. "But yes. If you're willing, I'd appreciate you giving the place a once-over."

I almost divulged that I'd never been a homeowner before and knew next to nothing about repairs and maintenance but figured that it was best to keep that tidbit quiet. He'd probably deduce as much soon enough.

He led me to the door, a heavy wooden behemoth carved with various leaves, that was probably as old as the earth the house stood on. I used the key, a large, iron antique affair, and the door creaked in protest as it opened, as if the house itself was weary and had no desire to be disturbed. Every surface was covered in dust and grime . . . decades' worth. My eyes burned and my throat grew scratchy as the dust worked its way into my lungs. The previous owner had left behind their furniture, which might have been a boon to me, who no longer owned so much as a chair, but I feared that upon closer inspection, I'd find much of it was fit for nothing better than kindling.

"See, it's not so bad," he said. "It's just been a bit neglected, but nothing that can't be fixed."

"What do you mean? The paint is peeling off the walls, and it smells like rodents have been having a heyday in here."

"As long as they haven't gotten into the walls and chewed through the wiring, you're fine," he said with a wink.

"Rats in the walls? Oh, that's fabulous. I didn't need to sleep tonight. Thanks." I threaded the hair at my scalp through my fingers. "What a nightmare. I have to get out of this."

"Matthieu spoke the truth. It just needs elbow grease. Scrubbing and paint is easy. The important thing is that those exposed timbers you see? They're in fantastic shape. The tile floors don't show any problems from settling. The place just needs some attention."

"Why did it get neglected in the first place?" One of the many questions I should have asked Matthieu before signing on the digital dotted line.

"The previous owners died more than twenty years ago. From what I know they didn't have any family to pass it down to, so it sat in probate for ages. No one in the *département* was too worried about one vacant house so far out in the weeds, so it languished. It was Matthieu who fought to get the place turned over to the village so it could be sold and hopefully rehabbed. Though a rebuild would be fine too."

I mentally tabulated the remaining balance in my checking account. "Not happening unless I tear it down to make room for a forty-year-old RV."

"Rehab it is, then. And I don't think it will be as bad as you think."

He took the time to walk from room to room with me. The house had an open porch on the front and a screened one on the back, both in need of structural help. There were, as the advertisement specified, four bedrooms. There were also two sitting rooms—large and small—a dining room, a root cellar, a huge attic stuffed to the brim with heaven-knows-what that I didn't even want to ponder just yet. The three bathrooms were antique, and time had forgotten the kitchen altogether.

Tibèri stuck his head under the kitchen sink to examine the plumbing.

"Copper pipes, and I'd wager they're as sound as the day they were installed." He took a glass from the nearest cabinet, turned on the tap, and filled it. He inspected the water, holding it up to the light from the grimy window, and took a drink.

"Tastes just fine," he said. "The foundation and plumbing are in great shape. Everything else is trivial in comparison. No mold or pest damage; the roof only needs moderate repairs, which is a miracle. It's about as good as you could hope for, all things considered."

His words were meant to encourage me, but as I surveyed the wreckage of the house, I felt daunted. The visions of the old Tom Hanks movie with the horrific house renovation flashed before my eyes. I could see what was left of my modest inheritance floating away in the pockets of a series of contractors.

But there was no way on earth I could give Wal the satisfaction of coming home a failure.

It was what he and Grandmother expected.

Tibèri cleared his throat and snapped me from my reverie. "So did you buy the place as an investment property? Turning it into a B and B for rich Americans who want to get away from nonexistent problems? I have to warn you, more than a few have tried. Most of the time the owners find it isn't worth the trouble for the income."

I shook my head. "No, I'm going to live here." I sounded as unsure as I felt.

"Well, *that's* a relief at least." He punctuated his words by plunking the glass in the sink. I must have looked bemused at his adamance. Why would he care if I stayed here? He explained, "It's good for the village that the place won't become another project for a bored investor. Too many of them end up sitting vacant because the owner loses interest and moves on to the next thing."

"Ah. Plenty of that sort of thing in New York too. Entire high-rises owned by zillionaire investors sitting vacant, while none of the rest of us mortals can find a decent apartment we can afford."

"Some common ground. But I have to ask. Sainte-Colombe is a bit off the beaten path for most city folks like you. I'd have guessed Nice, Cannes, or Saint-Tropez to be more up your alley."

I wrinkled my nose. Those places reminded me too much of the glitzy sort Dad had hobnobbed with for work. "No. Not at all. My mother was born and raised here. She died when I was young. I guess I just wanted to know where she came from."

Tibèri's eyes widened in surprise. "Well, in that case, Mademoiselle Luddington, *bienvenue chez vous*. Welcome home."

When he left I turned to the largest of the drawing rooms and surveyed the mess. It would be a massive undertaking, but at least one person had the confidence I could handle it.

Chapter 5

I brought only my carry-on into the house that first night, as if unsure whether I'd commit to staying. Which was ridiculous because I was as committed financially as a person could be.

I had a dreadful dinner comprised of leftover airplane snacks and the remainder of a box of crackers I'd procured in Aix at the French equivalent of a bodega next to the seedy hotel where I'd stayed for two nights as I made my plans to head east to Sainte-Colombe. I then endured a horrific night's sleep, partly worried I'd asphyxiate from all the dust and wholly convinced I was the biggest moron to ever draw breath for diving headfirst into this foolish endeavor.

The next day, I stared at the mess for a solid ten minutes, not knowing where to begin. The first thing I needed to do was finish unpacking the car. I hauled my six overstuffed suitcases to the largest of the four bedrooms. The cases contained everything that had been in Mamà's tubs, and I was glad to have her things back in the village where they belonged. The rest of the cases contained an assortment of my clothes I deemed worthy of the trip, a few treasured books and knickknacks, and not much else. I gave away, sold, or donated everything I hadn't hauled with me. I paid the insane baggage fees—considerably more than the cost of the one-way ticket from NYC to Paris—to take extra cases on the plane, knowing that freighting the stuff would be expensive, time-consuming, and potentially risky.

But once I'd accomplished that, I was stuck. I wasn't sure how long I stared at the space, but I couldn't seem to urge myself forward and make a decision about where to start.

I could start by vacuuming the carpets.

I could start by removing everything from the shelves and attacking the dust.

I could start by scrubbing the floors.

I wrestled with arguments for and against each option, paralyzed, until it came to me: the windows.

I could start by opening the windows.

It was a small, concrete thing. It was a beginning. The house had been stagnant for so long, the very air was stale and needed desperately to escape into the hills to rejuvenate itself. I went to every room in the house and opened every window that would budge. A few would need to be replaced, and I hoped Tibèri's offer was genuine. But at least I had the funds to cover some improvements. I didn't have to live with things in the condition they were, and I had to adjust my thinking. It wasn't like my dingy apartment in Queens where improvements would be at the whim of the building owner or basically a donation by me to a property I'd never own. Every dime I invested in this home would stay mine.

I pulled out my notebook from one of my bags and started making a list, room by room, of what repairs were needed, but it would be hard to uncover it all when the place was coated in a few decades' worth of dirt, dust, and grime. I'd have to scour every nook and cranny first to figure out how good the "bones" really were.

There was so much to be done that as soon as I started cleaning one thing, I thought of another that was more urgent. I found some old rags and started wiping surfaces down as I came to them. After more than an hour of half-cleaning various parts of the house, I decided to focus on my most urgent needs: being able to prepare food and getting comfortable sleep. And since lack of food would make sleep impossible, the kitchen needed to be top priority. At least the antique bathrooms seemed in good repair, if in need of a good scrubbing.

The outdated kitchen was a sunny place, with a deep, enameled cast-iron sink, a refrigerator that belonged in a museum, and no dishwasher. Matthieu had the power turned on before I arrived and assured me that all the existing appliances worked, and miraculously, the refrigerator was among them.

The brightly colored tile backsplash was still pristine, if dusty, but the cabinets needed refinishing. I peered inside to discover the kitchen was still well stocked with pots and pans—the old-fashioned copper kind that cooked like a dream but would need a heavy polishing. I added ingredients to make copper polish to my shopping list, which was growing longer at every turn. The chipped dishes with the green leafy pattern would suffice, but there were only a few pieces of tarnished, mismatched flatware and a paltry offering of kitchen utensils.

It was approaching midafternoon when I got the kitchen to a state where I felt I could cook in it and not put myself at risk of a foodborne illness. The house no longer smelled like a mummy's tomb either, so I just might be able to sleep. But I'd have to go into town for groceries and essentials if I wanted to have a meal more substantial than airline snack mix and crackers.

My house was in the valley of rolling hills just below the village that was, quite literally, carved into the side of the mountain. The buildings were all the same shade of warm vanilla as mine. All the roofs were tiled with terra-cotta. The doors and shutters were where the owners showed their personalities. Bright azure, poppy red, forest green. The cacophony of color somehow made more sense to me than the uniformity of American suburbs with all their rules meant to ensure the houses weren't too similar, yet they all ended up the same.

The village had been there for close to a millennium, and it seemed like it would stand for several more. I drove up the narrow street to the main square where most of the local businesses were housed. I parked in one of the minuscule spaces, glad for the diminutive size of my car. I'd done my research before I'd left New York and knew there was an ancient church, a town hall that also housed the village school, exactly one café, one restaurant that served classic French home food, a bakery (naturally), a newsstand, a bank that doubled as a post office, a tiny grocery shop, and one solitary shop dedicated to kitchenwares. No clothing stores. No barber or hairdresser. Not even a proper pharmacy. There were any number of home businesses, however, where one could buy or barter for anything from honey to pottery.

It was worlds away from New York where any given neighborhood might have a dozen restaurants, just as many cafés, four bodegas, and a couple of upscale kitchen shops. And if they weren't what you wanted, there would be anything you could hope for within a few subway stops.

Chez Sarraut resembled an antique store more than any kitchenware shop I'd ever visited. There were no sleek Italian espresso makers, bulky countertop appliances of dubious utility, or piles of brightly colored silicone utensils meant to color coordinate perfectly with one's eight-hundred-pound stand mixer.

The aisles were narrow and the shelves laden with all manner of kitchen equipment, most of it several decades old, but all with plenty of wear left. Copper pans with a layer of patina that could be restored to a shine, mechanical appliances that most of the world had replaced with their electric counterparts long before, and a full aisle of antique dishes. There was hardly a speck of dust in the place, but neither were there customers browsing—much less purchasing—the goods.

In the single aisle devoted to new stock, I filled my basket with an assortment of wooden spoons, rubber spatulas, linen towels, and other basics, then moved to the used section to peruse the larger items. I scooped up a large, woven marketing basket, which would be a necessity for the weekly outdoor market, along with a tarnished silver French press that would get polished up and put back into daily use. I lingered at a deep-emerald-green Dutch oven and ran my finger along its smooth edge. I hadn't put anything like it on my shopping list, but it sang to me. I was single and didn't need such a large pot to cook in, but a single touch to the cool enamel took me back to the Connecticut kitchen of my youth.

Mamà made pesto soup in a pot just like this one. She would add herbs and spices to the bubbling mixture, and I would watch her, mesmerized, from the stool at the counter. I remembered the smell—herbs, garlic, and olive oil that seemed to permeate the very drywall of our kitchen. But slowly, the smell began to fade. Mamà's vibrant cooking was replaced by Grandmother's bland baked chickens and dry pot roasts.

The Dutch oven, even used, cost a small fortune, but then, it was meant to be something that would last. Something that could be passed down, even.

"*Allez-y,*" a woman coaxed me. She looked about my age and smartly dressed. It wasn't as though I'd expected the villagers to be dressed in simple dresses in rustic prints, straight out of *Jean de Florette* or something, but her clothes were stylish enough for any major city. Though she was perhaps fonder of color than New Yorkers or Parisians. She wore a simple turquoise tunic sweater, belted over black leggings, and mid-calf boots. Her accessories were simple, but she was effortlessly put together, in the timeless way French women had mastered so well. She was short and slight and had her almost-black hair cut into a sleek bob. "You won't regret it. It's a wonderful piece. We sell them as wedding gifts quite often."

"I imagine so."

"We can ship it wherever you like," she continued. "It would be a lovely souvenir from your travels. Far more practical than a T-shirt or a postcard, *non?*"

"I'm actually local." I wished my accent were better. My French was still decidedly "classroom French," owing to my lack of opportunity to travel, but it was as solid as I could have made it without that advantage. "Well, sort of. I just moved to town."

"Oh, in that case, welcome!" she said, her tone bright. "I promise if you learn to cook like a Provençale, you'll use it constantly."

"You're persuasive. Sold."

"That's my job," she said with a wink and extended her hand. "I'm Estèva. I'm glad to see someone new in town. It's been ages since we've had a newcomer."

I returned her smile. "A lovely name. I'm Tempèsta."

Her brow arched at the Occitan name, but she said nothing. "Let's get you rung up, shall we?"

She groaned under the weight of the Dutch oven, and I trailed her to the counter with the rest of my supplies in tow.

"*Papi*," Estèva called to an older man sitting at a desk in a small office off to the side of the register. She gave me a little wave and went back to straightening goods on the shelves.

"Bonjour, monsieur," I greeted the shopkeeper. He was a balding, rotund man—an appropriate look for one who ran a shop dedicated to kitchenwares. It showed he knew how to use the goods he sold. His eyes were downcast over his ledger book, his snow-white walrus mustache twitching as he read.

"*Oui, toute de suite*," he said, his eyes still lingering on the ruled sheets of paper. He finally pried his eyes from his ledger and the color drained from his very red face.

"*Bruèissa!*"

"Pardon?" I asked, not recognizing the word. "I'm sorry, my vocabulary in Occitan isn't what it should be."

"B-bruèissa, please leave this place," he stammered.

"I-I don't understand. I just want to buy these things—"

"Take it," he said. "Take it all and don't come back."

By now Estèva was back by my side, looking at her grandfather in alarm. "Papi, why would you act like this to our new neighbor? Especially one who is already such a good customer?" She gestured to the pile of kitchenwares on the shop counter.

He made the sign of the cross and stared at me, blinking. "You're back in the village?"

I blinked, uncomprehending. "I've never been to Sainte-Colombe in my life before today, monsieur."

The color returned to his face and deepened to a concerning shade of red. "God help us all. I asked you to leave."

Tears pricked at my eyes. Not precisely the warm greeting I'd hoped for, and I felt like a fool for hoping for anything at all. I left the kitchen goods on the counter and dashed for the grocery. I reached out to pull the handle only to realize the shop was closed. The sign indicated they'd reopen after the midday break.

I knew enough from my studies to prepare for lunchtime closures of an hour or two, but the grocery was closed for a full three and a half hours, from noon until the housewives came for their last-minute dinner ingredients at three thirty. It was only three in the afternoon now, so I'd have to go home empty-handed or wait for a half hour and feel like an ass the whole time.

Of course I hadn't checked hours. Of course I'd made assumptions based on what I wanted to be true. I lived in a place where there was always a grocery shop or bodega willing to serve me somewhere. I considered popping into the café for a sandwich, but I couldn't bear being in public just then. The cold winds blew right through the weave of my coat, so I sought refuge in my car. I jumped in the driver's seat and let the tears flow, mentally apologizing to the car for all the curses I'd uttered in its direction as I'd navigated the route from Aix to Sainte-Colombe that first morning, in thanks for providing me a bit of sanctuary from the outside world.

I knew, rationally, that everyone could see me, but there was at least the illusion of privacy in the car.

I'd let it all out and have plenty of time to compose myself. Once I felt human again, the shop would be open, and I'd run in for cheese and bread. And a decent bottle of Côtes-du-Rhône that I shouldn't indulge in. I didn't have to cook anything that night. And if I were lucky, they'd have a few basic utensils to tide me over before I could face the drive back to Aix or maybe a closer village to stock the kitchen.

Warm tears dripped off the end of my nose and I didn't bother to wipe them. I rested my head against the steering wheel until I heard knuckles rapping against the glass of the passenger window.

Estèva.

She moved gracefully, though she was laden down with kitchen supplies and struggling under the weight of them. I hopped from the car to assist her. She handed me the basket that contained the bulk of my intended purchases so she could better balance the heavy iron pot.

"I'm sorry about my grandfather. I've never seen him act like such a fool. He can't afford to offend a customer like this."

She went quiet, knowing she'd said too much. "Please take these things as an apology. I'm sure he'll be mortified when he thinks about how shamefully he acted."

"I can't accept this. It's too much. You have to let me pay you for them."

I reached for my wallet and handed her a pile of brightly colored euros. It was a little more than I owed, and I didn't feel I could afford to be careless with money in the face of all the repairs that were needed, but I was too embarrassed to be precise.

She accepted the money with a tinge of red in her cheeks. It seemed she couldn't afford to be too proud either. She squeezed my arm and ran back to the shop, bills in hand to add to the till, which I suspected wasn't exactly overflowing.

I rearranged the supplies, emptying the basket so I could do my grocery shopping. Before crossing the square, I paused a moment and sat on the bumper of my car, letting my breath even out before I entered the grocery store, which appeared to finally be opening. I didn't know if a cashier would hurl random insults at me in Occitan, not the French I'd have been able to parse well enough. All I needed were a few things for a simple dinner and breakfast and, saints above, please, some coffee.

I'd seen French markets in movies and read about them in text-books, but they were a marvel to see in person. Produce more vibrant and fragrant than I'd ever experienced, a small but pristine meat counter, and rows of dry goods that bore no resemblance to the artificially colored, preservative-ridden counterparts in the States.

Though the scene from the kitchen shop kept replaying in my mind, I felt my shoulders loosen as I walked the aisles and filled my small cart with essentials. Good coffee, several kinds of cheeses, pasta, some vegetables, butter, olive oil. An arsenal of cleaning supplies. It was therapeutic to envision slowly cooking meals instead of scarfing down yogurt before work or paying exorbitant New York prices for a deli sandwich at lunch.

The checker, who appeared younger than Estèva's grandfather by a couple of decades, was affable enough and I, mercifully, completed the transaction without trouble. I stowed the groceries in the trunk of the car and went to make my final stop. The boulangerie had a small line of people buying bread to accompany their dinners, and I joined the queue. When my turn came, I ordered one of the rustic *pains de campagne*, a little hardier than the traditional baguette and recognizable from its pointy ends.

The baker, an older woman with wisps of white hair, grew pale as she took in my features but thrust the bread into my hands and accepted payment wordlessly.

As I took the winding road back to my dilapidated little farmhouse, I tried to convince myself that I was reading too much into the baker woman's behavior; that I was being too sensitive after the exchange with Estèva's grandfather. But no matter how I persuaded myself to think otherwise, her expression was too much like the old man's for me to shake it off entirely.

Chapter 6

I sat at the wooden table, old and battered—no, careworn, like most everything in the house. While the contents of the house were not in anything resembling pristine condition, I was beginning to feel that every object here had known love.

I ate a modest dinner of bread, Roquefort cheese, salad, and wine with a chaser of dark chocolate. The assortment of kitchen supplies now cluttered my counters, waiting for the cupboards to be cleaned and space made for them. I'd have to do better than picnic dinners. A kitchen like this one demanded it. It *missed* being of use. But there was still much to be done before I could cook in earnest.

It was a bright room, and I could imagine the generations of families who lived here before me. The merry meals they shared at this very table. The moments of grief where they assembled around it and nourished their pain with the bread and jam of family and friendship. Each nick and scratch on the table had a history. I placed my hands on the rough wood and could almost feel it. It had absorbed more tears than it should have been expected to. It had known such great joy but also vast oceans of sorrow.

I cleared away the mess from the meal, admiring the green leafy pattern on the dishes that had been left behind as I washed the crumbs down the drain and wiped the plate clean with one of my new linen towels. The paint had faded with age, but the border of the plate seemed as though it had been painted by hand. Irregular, intricate; not one plate was identical to another. There was something comforting about the imperfections here. New York was all about sharp lines, minimalism, stark contrasts, uniformity. Here, the light, the color, the randomness of it all were celebrated.

I decided to move my new Dutch oven to the hulking gas stove, where it would spend much of its time, next to the copper kettle that would soon get a good polishing. The sun was getting lower in the sky, and I'd have to shut the windows soon against the evening chill. The thought of closing myself in with all the dust that remained made my lungs want to scream.

Sometimes Mamà used to simmer slices of orange and cranberries with cloves and nutmeg on the stove to clear the air in the house. I didn't have those things at my disposal and decided on a sprig of fresh rosemary from my grocery haul. I filled the kettle, and once the water boiled, I emptied it into the cocotte and pulled the needles of rosemary from the twig, pinching and releasing the oils as I dropped them into the gently bubbling water.

I was flooded with visions of Mamà. Her wrapping me up in a bright yellow quilt when I was maybe seven and quite sick. Her singing lullabies in French whose words I couldn't recall. Working with her at the sewing machine to make me a skirt in my favorite shade of purple for the first day of sixth grade. I gripped the back of the chair and had to fight to keep the tears from rushing down my cheeks.

I was about to force myself out of my reverie to move on to the bedroom to ready it for tonight's sleep when I heard a creak at the door and the *clump-clump-clump* of feet on the floor tiles.

A little woman who didn't reach the shoulders of my own rather diminutive frame entered the kitchen. Her hair, snow-white like the baker woman's, was coiffed carefully into a long braid that trailed down her left shoulder. She flouted the rules of "aging gracefully" that my grandmother so ardently ascribed to, which demanded short-cropped hair after the age of fifty-five. She didn't appear confused, as though she'd wandered into the wrong house, but neither had she bothered to knock. She held a wreath of dried lavender and regarded me solemnly.

"Bonsoir, madame. Is there something I can do for you?"

"I needed to see for myself that Nadaleta Vielescot has returned to Sainte-Colombe as Pau Sarraut told me over the telephone." There wasn't the same fear in her eyes as I'd seen in the others', but there was something akin to trepidation in them. "But you cannot be her. She'd be almost fifty years old by now, and you can't be but half that age."

I paused at the sound of my mother's name. "Nadaleta Vielescot was my mother. Though she was Nadaleta Luddington for the last fourteen years of her life."

"You are her daughter? This makes more sense. Old Pau is known for his dramatics." The woman shook her head. "You cannot go for a new ladle for the soup tureen without some ill tidings from him. But you say 'was' when you speak of Nadaleta?"

"She passed away fifteen years ago. We didn't know if she still had friends here to inform."

The old woman held a hand to her heart. "I am sorry to hear this. Your mother was such a dear girl. I was the best of friends with your grandmother Sibilia, and bless her, she was indulgent enough to let me love your mother as my own. She stopped writing when your grandmother passed, and I hoped against hope that it was because she was too busy doting on you."

A million questions popped into my head, all jockeying to become first in line. But my manners finally elbowed their way forward. "Madame, may I offer you some tea? Some coffee?"

She set the wreath down on the kitchen table. "Have you nothing stronger, my dear?" A glint of humor surfaced in the lines of her face.

I smiled and fetched the bottle of Côtes-du-Rhône I'd sampled with dinner, took two glasses from the cupboard, washed them, then served her a glass of the rich red wine.

"Dry the glass well, my dear. Even a few drops of water can spoil the bouquet of a good wine."

I obliged, taking extra care to dry the glass with one of my new linen towels. I placed the stubby, etched goblet in front of her and poured one for myself.

"Ah, the black currant sings in this one."

"I can taste the spices." I take a deeper sip, then hold the glass to my nose. "Nutmeg, maybe a hint of anise?"

"Well done. You have something of Sainte-Colombe in you. This is a good thing. Your mother named you Tempèsta, yes? Your grandmother treasured her letters from your mamà and the pictures of you most of all."

"Oh yes, I'm so sorry," I said, realizing I'd failed to introduce myself. "And you never told me your name, madame."

"Jenofa Peyronne. Though it seems strange to introduce myself to you. So much like your mother, it's unnatural that we should never have met."

"Well, I'm happy to be here now."

"Sometime you must tell me about your mother and what became of her in America," she said. "But this is not the night for ghosts. This house has seen more than its share."

I nodded in agreement, having sensed as much myself.

"You know this house," I said unnecessarily. It was a small village and Jenofa had been here her entire life; I was certain of it. There couldn't be a house in this village where she hadn't celebrated numerous weddings and births and mourned passings.

"Oh, *cara*. This was the house of Jacme and Liorada Tardieu. And their only son, Amadeu. Jacme was well regarded in the village. He had a talent with plants, which is why I brought you this humble wreath as an offering. This is a home that needs beautiful things. It is a cruelty that it has been left alone for so long. Lavender on the door is a portent of good luck. And it will keep the scorpions away."

I felt the burn of Côtes-du-Rhône in my nostrils. "Scorpions?" I asked, trying to recover my composure.

"Oh, they're little things. Not like the terrifying ones we see in movies about the American West. Not much worse than a bee sting, but better avoided, no? But if you hang the wreath, it will help. The house will do what it can to protect you."

She spoke of the place as though it were a living thing, but then again, I'd felt the same. "What happened to them?"

"Ah, I said tonight was not a night for ghosts, my dear. But it's only natural to be curious about your new home. Let it suffice to say that young Amadeu died under tragic circumstances when he was a young man, and his parents followed soon after too. Their grief was too much for their hearts to bear."

"Oh, that *is* sad."

"But we can hope you will make happier memories here. This place is not without hope, I don't think."

"I don't either," I agreed. "I had my doubts at first."

"Obviously you did. You're a person with a good sense of self-preservation." She barked out a dry laugh, then took a long draught of wine and surveyed the room thoughtfully. "This place looks a fright. But its cracks and scrapes don't go too far beneath the surface."

"You sound like Tibèri. 'Good bones,' he said."

"The Cabrols are good people. If young Tibèri says it, you can believe him."

I found myself hiding a smile. To be in a place where one could be certain of a person's character because of their lineage seemed quaint. But then I thought about the circles my father ran in and realized it wasn't so absurd. I was a Luddington and was expected to act as such. As though I owed something to a family legacy in which I never had a choice of taking part.

"So there is a question that is looming over you, my dear. It's following you like a rain cloud."

"Oh?"

"What is next for you? I can see the question on your face as plainly as if you'd written it across your forehead. In this, you are like your American family. Always so concerned about making a living, you never take the time to worry about making a life."

"It seems I'm an open book." I shrugged. "So much for being the mysterious new woman in town. I was hoping to keep ahold of my cachet a little longer."

I scoffed at myself. I was like the ridiculous kid at summer camp, thrilled at the opportunity to reinvent herself for a new group of peers for a few weeks. The awkward girl could pretend to be a social butterfly. The popular girl could allow herself the chance to fade into the woodwork for once. That was the appeal of new beginnings, wasn't it? The chance to try out being a new version of your own identity.

"Mystery can be a good thing, cara, so long as you aren't a mystery to yourself. There is no good to be had in spending so much time figuring out what it is you want to *do* that you don't have any left to figure out who you are."

I could think of nothing to say that was in any way equal to the wisdom the woman had offered. For Dad and Wal, those two things— what a person does and who a person is—were so inexorably linked, there was no telling the two apart. And perhaps that wasn't the wisest way to live a life.

"I think I have bothered you with this old lady's chatter enough for one night. I will come back to see you, if you don't mind. The walk is good for these old bones, and walking is always easier when you have a purpose waiting at the other end."

She rose and rinsed out her wineglass as though she were family instead of a new acquaintance. Then again, she knew the place better than I, and likely felt more at home in it.

"I'd love that," I said, realizing I meant it. "And maybe you can tell me stories about Mamà sometime."

"Ah yes. You would be eager to hear of her, wouldn't you? Perhaps over a nice supper one evening."

I smiled at the veiled hint. "I'm a fair hand in the kitchen, and I'm dying to play with the local ingredients."

"I would expect nothing less from Sibilia Vielescot's granddaughter." She cast her eyes to the stove and eyed my new green Dutch oven. "That cocotte was your grandmother's. I'd recognize it anywhere."

"Really?" I sputtered. "I found it at Sarraut's today."

And now the vehemence of his reaction made more sense. I bore a strong resemblance to my mother. He must have thought it was Nadaleta come back to reclaim the pot that had belonged to our family for ages. It must have felt like a visit from a long-forgotten ghost.

"Yes," Jenofa said. "She sold him a lot of her old kitchen things as she started to decline. When she sold him the cocotte, I knew she didn't hold out a great deal of hope to live much longer."

"I'd love to hear more about them both. It seems so strange to speak to anyone who knew my mother before she came to the States. It was like her life before she met Dad was just a fairy tale she'd talk about before bedtime."

"We will have this chat over dinner sometime soon. Hang that wreath in the meantime." She brushed one finger over the necklace of bronze herb leaves I'd worn for Dad's funeral and had worn most days since. "I didn't realize just how apt my little gift to you would be. The Bastida Èrbadoça is in good hands once again."

"Bastida Èrbadoça?" I stumbled over the pronunciation, which was at times more Italian or even Spanish sounding than French. *Bah-stee-dah Err-bah-doss-ah.*

"Yes, it's what this place has been called for generations. *Bastida* means 'manor house.' *Èrbadoça* means 'sweet herb.'"

Herbe doux in French . . . it made sense. House of the Sweet Herb. Though there was nothing seemingly *sweet* about the place in its current state, I could see how it had once been a place of light and laughter. I hoped it would be again in time.

"I had no idea. That's a beautiful name."

"I'm glad you like it," Jenofa said with an approving nod. "There is enough change in the world. It's nice for some things to stay the same." She kissed my cheek. "And don't worry about old Pau. He may be the mayor, but people know he's an old crank. He won't be a bother."

The mayor. Of course he is. I wanted to believe that Jenofa was being truthful, but given the vehemence of his reaction to seeing me in his shop, I wasn't convinced.

I stood at the door as she took her leave, and I watched as she walked down the red-dirt path to the edge of my property and turned down the lane toward her own. I noticed there was already a hook on the heavy wooden door and hung the wreath as she commanded. I breathed in the lilting scent and felt as though I were curled against my mother's chest once more.

It didn't matter if it brought good luck; it certainly brought back good memories.

I spent the rest of the evening running the exchange with the elderly neighbor over in my head, trying to make sense of it all, but I mostly failed. I found myself at loose ends, without the energy for deep cleaning and with too much for rest.

I pulled out a few pieces of the tarnished copper cookware and set about making a paste of flour, vinegar, and salt to use as a scrub on the careworn cookware. It took some doing, but bit by bit, the tarnish gave way with gentle prodding. I finished the process with a coat of metal polish and hung each of the pots and pans on the hooks where they'd once resided. They gleamed as brightly as the day they were purchased from the shop window, perhaps for Liorada, the day she married Jacme. Or perhaps they'd been purchased for her mother before her.

It was a small thing, but to see the shining copper pots hanging on the rack reminded me that there is joy in making old things beautiful again.

Chapter 7

T hough the late-winter wind was biting cold, I awoke the next morning to the sound of power tools in the backyard. For a moment I was certain I'd woken up in my apartment in Queens. But as I pried my eyes open, the cracked terra-cotta plaster of my bedroom walls brought me back to Sainte-Colombe.

As I became more aware of myself, and the effects a second glass of wine had wrought on my unaccustomed, no-longer-college-aged body, I remembered I hadn't hired anyone for any projects yet. There was plenty to be done, but I'd have to prioritize and be frugal with my funds. I'd have to do as much as I could on my own and hope I escaped the endeavor with all my fingers intact.

I hastily tossed on some clothes, descended the stairs, and headed out the back door to find Tibèri measuring some two-by-fours propped up on sawhorses. He stared with laser focus as he pulled a pencil from behind his right ear and made a mark on the board.

"Um, can I help you?"

"Sure. A glass of water now and again wouldn't be amiss. Wouldn't say no to a sandwich in a few hours either if you've had time to stock up."

"Okay." I brushed a mahogany curl off my forehead. "I know I'm the new girl in town and don't know all the local customs and all, but can you please enlighten me as to what's going on? Is it a special thing in Sainte-Colombe to wake up a newcomer at dawn with power tools, or am I just that lucky?"

Tibèri finally looked up at me and laughed. "It's not dawn; it's seven thirty. You've slept the best part of the day away. Madame Peyronne knocked on my door last night and told me your greenhouse was in need of repair, so here I am."

"And you always do what she says?"

"As a rule. There's little on this earth that scares me, but the wrath of Jenofa Peyronne is very near the top of that list. Right after venomous snakes and mice."

"Mice?" I raised an eyebrow.

"Creepy, dirty little buggers. Have never liked them, never will."

"Fair enough." I nodded. "So why the greenhouse? I mean, this is kind of you and all, but I would have focused on the house first." The idea of a whole greenhouse, when I'd barely had an adequate windowsill for an African violet back in New York, was enticing but felt indulgent given the list of other repairs needed.

"When Madame Peyronne gives an order, I don't ask questions. But she has a point. It's in worse shape than the house."

"I haven't even thought about the property yet," I admitted. "I was more worried about making the house livable."

"The first rule of repair is start where time is of the essence. If it's beyond repair or it's going to hold a while, you can leave it until those things on the narrow precipice between repair and ruin are taken care of. This greenhouse can be saved, but that might not be the case after one more winter finishes having its say."

"There's something of a philosophy in that, isn't there?"

"There's philosophy in all things, Mademoiselle Luddington."

"Can I lend you a hand?" I was mentally calculating how much I would owe this man, and if I could lower the bill by shortening the duration of the project, it seemed worth a try.

"Do you have any experience with carpentry?" He scanned my outfit. Like most everything I owned, it was black and formfitting. Black wool trousers and a thin black sweater with three-quarter sleeves. From his perspective I must have seemed like someone who didn't know one end of a hammer from the other.

"I helped build theater sets in college a few times," I said, knowing as the words tumbled from my mouth how moronic they sounded. "So I know a little more than nothing, maybe? But I can fetch and carry and follow directions as well as anyone else."

He appeared mollified by my humility in the face of power tools and relaxed his stance a bit. "You can help hold these new boards in place while I screw them in. It's easier to do with someone supporting them."

"That's true of a lot of things." I lifted one end of the two-by-four that had been cut to the correct length.

"It's your turn to be a philosopher." He hoisted the board to replace one of the studs from the wall that had snapped from years of neglect. A few more and the structure would have toppled. We'd need six new studs in addition to this one, and three new ceiling joists.

"You're sure this won't be too big of a job?" I asked.

"A few hours and cheap materials. The trick was the glass. I took care of it before you came down." He pointed to a pile of broken glass sheets he'd put in the back of his utility van.

"That was nice of you."

"Well, it had to be done first, and had the virtue of not needing power tools. I figured you were tired after your travels. I held off as long as I could."

I looked away from Tibèri for a moment, ignoring the stinging at the corners of my eyes. "That really *was* kind. Thanks."

"Listen, I heard old Pau was weird to you in town and the house wasn't what you were expecting. But having this place vacant and withering away doesn't do anyone here any good. It's winter and work is slow for the next couple of months yet. Consider this my investment in giving you a reason to give the place a fair shake."

I restrained an eye roll at the speed of the small-town rumor mill. "Deal. I overreacted about the house. Probably. I'm sorry I came off as a drama queen. I was giving in to a rare moment of pessimism."

"It happens to all of us. I can imagine you see buildings differently than I do. You see problems; I see potential."

"Right, because you have the skills to fix things without going bankrupt," I said. "It would alter your perspective, I would think."

"I'm sure it would. I'll do what I can to give you a hand around here."

"I appreciate that. Even just some advice on where to start would make it seem less daunting." I shook out my arms as I released the newly affixed stud.

"Happy to." He turned his attention back to the greenhouse frame that was slowly taking shape.

"You don't seem to like me all that much," I said. "But you're helping me anyway. Is Jenofa really that scary?"

"Not to put too fine a point on it, but yes. I've known since I was four years old not to make an enemy of that woman. But that's not why I'm helping you."

"Enlighten me." I crossed my arms over my chest.

"I told you, it's for the village."

"One empty house really makes that much difference? I'm missing something."

Tibèri looked back at me from the wooden frame. He placed his hammer back in the leather tool belt at his waist.

"Hop in the van and I'll show you why it matters."

* * *

Tibèri drove north, his hands firmly on the wheel, seemingly unfazed by driving a comparatively large vehicle on impossibly narrow, curvy roads. We didn't meet any traffic coming the opposite direction, and it was just as well because I had no idea how two bicycles could pass on this road unscathed, let alone vehicles of any size, without one careening off the steep cliff into the gorge.

Tibèri made no attempt at conversation, and I wasn't sure my efforts would be appreciated if I attempted it. I tried to appreciate the rugged scenery of Haute Provence with the craggy hills and scrubby-looking trees that seemed like they'd survived millennia of drought, wind, and epic fires but found myself too focused on the precipitous road and too curious about where Tibèri was taking me to be able to take it all in.

Eventually, the road became steeper and we found ourselves in another village with narrow streets and the quaint, beige plaster houses with terra-cotta tile roofs and bright doors and shutters. As in Sainte-Colombe, a number of small farms dotted the arable lands below, and the town lorded over them all from the rocky hill-top. Like many villages in Provence, it was built on high to protect against invasion from all manner of hostile outsiders.

But here, the paint peeled, the tiles were cracked, and there was an air of desolation in the village that Sainte-Colombe did not yet have. Tibèri parked the van in a spot at the bottom of the village. It was clearly not designed with cars—or even good-sized horse carts—in mind, so I was just as happy to leave the van behind.

"Let's go for a walk," Tibèri suggested. We wandered up to the top of the hill to the main town square.

"Welcome to Rocheville-en-Provence." Tibèri made a grand gesture with his extended arm to the town square.

"It's charming." And it was true; despite the state of disrepair, the charms of the ancient town hadn't been lost entirely.

"What do you notice?" He made another sweeping gesture to the town in general.

"It's empty, more or less." Opposite the square, an old man and woman, at least seventy-five years of age, were walking arm in arm. He held a cane in his left hand and his wife used him as her crutch. But apart from them, no one was around.

"And the businesses?"

I scanned the square. It once boasted the same sort of businesses we had in Sainte-Colombe. A café, a grocery, a bakery. But the café was shuttered permanently, and the signs on the grocery and bakery alerted the town to very limited hours. It was nine in the morning, the peak of French operating hours, and it appeared only the post office was open.

"Closed."

"Right. I come up here when I'm needed to help with repairs for the families who still live here. Because they don't have a carpenter here anymore. Fifty years ago, this town was twice the size of Sainte-Colombe."

"What happened?"

"Progress." He spat out the word as though it tasted of turned meat. "All the 'good' jobs are elsewhere. Aix, Marseille, Avignon. The kids all left a generation ago. And when I say *all*, I mean that *to a person*. There just isn't any opportunity here unless they want to live off the land. And let me tell you, the weather here can be capricious for farming."

"I've seen *Jean de Florette*," I quipped with a wink.

"An expert." He rolled his eyes good-naturedly at me. "But this is where Sainte-Colombe is headed. We've been a little luckier than most because we're stubborn."

"That I can believe."

His mouth twitched in a reluctant smile. "Estèva, Matthieu, and I stayed. A handful of others. But our kids—if we can afford to have them—won't. Not if there aren't more options for them."

"That's awful."

"At least Sainte-Colombe still has a chance. A lot of villages as small as ours don't have even a grocery or a café. All the residents have to drive to another town if they want so much as a baguette. But that could all change if the village continues to shrink."

"So what do we do?"

"We stay. We do what we can to keep the place in good repair and attractive. We try to lure in business where we can. It rarely works, but it's better than giving up altogether."

"It is."

"I don't expect you to truly understand, but I hope you will in time. There are villages like this all over France. Many without a single resident under the age of sixty. It's not just about one village.

It's about keeping all villages like ours alive. Preserving a way of life."

"I understand better than you think I do." My father's lectures about the Luddington Way and his litany of advice came to mind. Wal's sense of loyalty to Dad and his work. Grandmother's insistence on maintaining tradition and upholding the name. "I just hope you cling to this way of life for the right reasons."

"I just think there have to be more ways to live a life than cramming yourself into a tiny apartment and living shoulder to shoulder with people you don't care about and who don't care about you, all in pursuit of a job at a corporation that would happily replace you within two weeks if you died at your desk."

Dad's face flashed before my eyes for a split second. Wal had taken over at the helm even before the funeral. That had always been the plan—to never drop the torch. It still seemed wrong that the torch meant more than the person who bore it.

"Given where I lived just a few weeks ago and the job I left behind, I can't argue with you there."

"And I suppose I have to admit that if you've willingly given up city life, just maybe there's hope for you. Maybe."

"I feel honored by that small measure of approval."

"Don't crow too loudly. You've only just arrived. But I'm open to being pleasantly surprised."

"A bit arrogant, don't you think?" I shot him a scathing look of my own.

"Don't Americans think all Frenchmen are arrogant snobs?"

"Maybe so, but I'm trying to stay open to being pleasantly surprised."

"See that you do, Mademoiselle Luddington. Have you seen enough?"

I nodded. A cold winter wind blew across the square and I shivered. Sainte-Colombe was sleepy, but this place was a ghost town. We walked down to the cargo van, and Tibèri steered us down the narrow road back to our own little corner of Provence. This time, I wasn't as preoccupied with our certain death on the roads but rather what I might do to help improve the village's situation. It seemed a blink before we were pulling back into my driveway.

"I have other work to attend to for the rest of the day, but I'll come back soon to help with the greenhouse."

"Thanks." My eyes drifted to the village atop the hill as I opened the van door. A few people could be seen milling about the streets, and the sound of children's laughter could be heard from the area near the town hall as they enjoyed their recess. My eyes scanned the almost-empty town square. "Do you think Sainte-Colombe is like the greenhouse?"

To his credit, he didn't react as though my head were attached backward. "I'm not sure I follow."

"She's still standing, but do you think she'll hold for another winter?"

He glanced over at the half-demolished structure. "She will if I have any fight left in me."

I slid down from my seat in the van and looked up at him in the driver's seat. "I hope you have a lot of fight left, then. This place is worth saving."

His warm bottle-green gaze widened with surprise. "There *is* hope for you, New Yorker. I'll be back soon."

He left in a cloud of red dust, and I went back into the house, now determined to make sense of the smallest bedroom in hopes of turning it into an office. To what end, I wasn't sure, but one direction felt as good as another.

Chapter 8

I dreaded my trip into the village the following week. The potential stares and whispers. I considered driving into Valensole, but I refused to give in to that temptation. I walked into town, marketing basket in tow. I'd post letters to a few friends in the city who'd be charmed by the old-fashioned custom. I'd restock a few groceries. I'd hopefully be able to run a few simple errands without upsetting the peace of the village.

I was about to brave the grocery when a lilting voice called my name.

Estèva emerged from Sarraut's, a few wayward strands of her dark hair sticking to her face as she jogged to my side. "I was worried we'd frightened you off!"

"Oh no, I'm too brave to let that scare me away," I said, deciding humor was the best approach. "Or too foolish. But it seemed silly to stay at home all day."

"I'm glad. I'd hate for you to stay shut up. I tried to find out why Papi acted like such a fool when he met you, but he refused to speak about it."

"I'm sure he has his reasons." I stared at my feet a moment.

"Let's grab a coffee. The café here isn't bad at all." She gestured to a small establishment a few doors down from Sarraut's. Chez Arnaud was the quintessential French café. Tile floors, small tables, rattan chairs, and the bill of fare were all straight out of the French café guidebook that must exist somewhere. We both ordered coffees, and I was relieved the waiter didn't seem fazed by my presence.

"So how are things at the Tardieu place? I thought the house was in pretty bad shape."

"Not the greatest. But I've gotten over the shock. My neighbor Jenofa seems to have bullied poor Tibèri into helping me with renovations against his will."

"Yes, he has a soft spot for Jenofa. She's basically a *mamie* to everyone under forty in the village. She means well, but she can be overbearing."

"I can believe that. Though he doesn't seem to like me all that much. I'm surprised he agreed to do it, even for her sake."

"Duty runs deep here. Just . . . be patient with Tibèri. He's my oldest friend. Like a brother. I hope he'll be your friend too."

"That would be nice. Being new to town and all," I said.

She leaned closer as if to whisper a secret. "I have to ask, why would you leave New York for here? I dream of going someplace so . . . alive."

"Lots of reasons, really. Not the least of which is that even the best coffee in New York isn't this good. But also, sometimes the city can get to be too much." I refrained from mentioning Mamà again since the topic of her had been such a hot-button issue with her grandfather.

"Well, at least Sainte-Colombe has something going for it. But why not just take a vacation? Don't you think you'll get bored?"

"Honestly? No. I never felt at ease in New York. The new house . . . I don't know. It feels like a real home. Or it will when it's all finished. But I can breathe here."

"Americans have moved into town before. Occasionally Brits or Germans. They usually last a season or two and move on. There isn't enough to hold them here."

"I don't see why. It's such a beautiful place," I said.

"Beautiful, yes, but without much in the way of city comforts. People think they can go without, and they realize the truth after a few months."

"I don't think I will." I summoned confidence from somewhere I couldn't explain.

"I hope not." Estèva offered a smile. "It's nice to have someone new in town. You should come to the village meeting and finally be introduced to some people. There's one on Saturday. No better way to get to know how things work around here."

I hesitated, taking a sip of coffee as I considered, then nodded. "You're probably right."

"Estèva!" a voice yelled from the entrance to Sarraut's. Old Pau turned his head and saw us sitting together at the café table out in the courtyard. "Estèva, come see to the dusting!" His tone was gravelly and brusque. He didn't want her spending time with me. Didn't want her anywhere near me.

Her expression was exasperation and exhaustion in equal measure. "I probably should go or he'll be in a mood for a month." She fumbled for her purse.

"I've got the bill, don't worry." I waved her away. "He needs you."

Her expression softened to a smile. "Let's do this again soon. It's nice having someone to chat with."

"Absolutely."

"See you Saturday." She dashed back to Sarraut's, where old Pau grumbled so loudly, I could hear him even several shops away. Probably warning her away from me. Why the man loathed Mamà so much that he carried his animosity over to me, I didn't know, but there was no question that he'd borne a grudge for almost thirty years. Maybe more.

But more intriguing was Estèva's asking me to be patient with Tibèri's reticence. Something must have happened to make him wary, as he didn't seem the sort to harbor prejudices without reason. I shouldn't have cared, but I did. Did Pau's rancor play into Mamà's reason for leaving the village? She always claimed it was because Dad swept her off her feet, but I never believed that was the full story.

I paid for the coffees and trekked to the little grocery to stock up on a few essentials. I was distracted on the walk home, mulling over what might have been the cause of Tibèri's pain. I imagined a beautiful, sophisticated woman who thought she craved the quiet life, then realized how mistaken she was when she found there wasn't a single sushi restaurant within an hour's drive. I didn't understand that woman.

As I walked back home, I marveled at the sun kissing my shoulders and the crunch of the gravel underfoot. For all the posh restaurants, cultural landmarks, and sleek architecture, the city I left behind paled in comparison to the vibrance of these rocky hillsides.

Estèva described New York as *alive*, but the asphalt, cement, and steel were lifeless and faded compared to the soil beneath my feet that fairly vibrated with the potential to bring forth new life.

Chapter 9

*I*t's okay to be afraid, cara. But you can't let your fear make
decisions for you."

I heard my mother's voice as clearly as if she were
standing inches before me. I could see the furrow of concern in
her brow as she knelt in front of me and I pleaded with her not
to send me to kindergarten. The concern mingled with resolve
in her aqua-blue eyes told me she would not be deterred. Even
though I was terrified that I'd never make friends or find welcome in school, there was something comforting in knowing
Mamà couldn't be swayed.

And as I stood at the entryway to the town hall, it felt like the
first day of kindergarten all over again. Perhaps it was because
the municipal building doubled as the village school during the
day and was where, according to tradition, the children learned
Occitan in the afternoons three days a week. Children's drawings
hung on the walls, worn schoolbooks rested on cases at the front
of the room, and other telltale signs showed that the building was

the educational epicenter of the village. Perhaps it was the scent of chalk dust in the air that seemed never to settle that transported me so readily, but I was once again the trembling child on the school steps.

And I didn't have Mamà here to walk me inside and tell me it would all be okay. I'd have to take the steps on my own.

Every resident of Sainte-Colombe was gathered in the town hall, and though I knew intellectually it wasn't true, it seemed everyone was staring at me. At once I felt like I was suffocating in my charcoal wool trousers and heather-gray sweater, though the air outside still merited winter clothes in the evenings. That would be changing soon, but the mistral winds still blew, and there was still the danger of freeze for another couple of weeks yet.

Jenofa waved me over, and my shoulders dropped a few centimeters, but not enough that I could call myself relaxed.

Some of the children excitedly pulled their parents around the room to show off their artwork or to show them their report, which they pulled from desks that were neatly arranged on the west side of the building to make room for the metal folding chairs. Despite the handful of families, most of the heads in the room were shrouded in silver like Pau and Jenofa. Some were spry, others wore the signs of aging like battle scars. Two old men shot daggers at each other with their eyes, while the women with them, presumably their wives of many decades, rolled their eyes and sent sympathetic glances at their counterpart.

I got the sense that while seats were not assigned, there was a legacy to be respected. The Tessiyers always sat in the sixth row on the left-hand side, and so on. Thankfully, Jenofa waved me over to a place she'd saved for me so I wouldn't have to worry about stepping on the toes of a generations-long tradition.

Pau took his place at the front of the room at the center of a long table. Three people sat on either side of him, presumably the village council. Pau gently banged his gavel, and the people settled into their seats without delay. They watched him intently, and it was clear they were invested in what he had to say.

Pau stood, hands on each side of the lectern, and cleared his throat. The room wasn't large enough to require use of a microphone, and his confident baritone had no trouble soaring to the back of the room. "My fellow Sainte-Colombiens, it is good to have all of us gathered together once more."

Polite applause rose from the audience.

"As another winter comes to an end, let us be grateful that the village will live to see another spring, another bloom, that will yield great prosperity for our good citizens. But I will not insult the good people of our village by pretending this was not a winter of challenge and loss. Twelve of us have passed on. Eight have moved away to be with family. Two more businesses have closed their doors. And, as you know, there have been no families to move in and take their places."

I almost raised my hand to remind him that at least one person had done so, but I supposed I didn't qualify as a family so I kept my mouth shut. Though it likely wasn't an oversight. Pau wanted to ignore my very existence; pretend I was just the ghost of my mother come with the express purpose of annoying him.

Tibèri sat two rows ahead of me on my left, and his eyes flitted to mine so quickly, I wouldn't have noticed if I'd blinked at the wrong moment. He'd noticed Pau's omission, and I was glad at least for that.

"I don't need to remind you of what this means. With fewer residents and fewer businesses, we have a smaller base for taxes, and it means there is a higher demand on the *département* to provide our key services. They have assured me that as long as there is a soul living in Sainte-Colombe, we will have water, power, and the rest of our basic needs provided for."

There was a collective sigh of relief from the residents. Once the water and lights were turned off, the place would become a ghost town. But I could sense in Pau's tone there was a heavy "however" lurking in the air.

"The *département* has, however, raised the concern about continuing to fund our school here."

His eyes dropped to the lectern as if embarrassed or afraid to make eye contact with the people.

"We currently have twenty-three students, from ages five to eighteen," he continued. "And the *département* feels that it would be more efficient to transport those children to Valensole for their education next fall."

"What about Mademoiselle Langlois?" someone asked from the back of the room.

A reedy woman of about thirty-five with brown hair tossed up in a bun, whom I presumed to be Mademoiselle Langlois, the village teacher, shifted in her seat uncomfortably. This wasn't news for her, and she wasn't happy about it.

"It is my understanding she would be reentered into the teaching pool and offered a new position." What color there had been in Pau's face was now drained.

Jenofa leaned over to me, "In France teachers are assigned jobs and could be posted anywhere in the country where they're needed. The teachers can request where they'd prefer to teach but aren't guaranteed anything. The schools don't get a choice either. The teachers go where they're sent, and the schools accept the candidates they're awarded."

I nodded, remembering some of this from my studies, though the realities of the system and how harsh it could be never really set in.

Jenofa continued, "Nathalie—Mademoiselle Langlois—has family in the village. It will mean they'll all likely move out of the region entirely. It's a shame."

My hand went instinctively to my mouth. Another family gone. What was worse, without a school there would be even less enticement for new families to move to the village.

"This is a challenge for our beloved Sainte-Colombe," Pau said, his tone grave. "This village has lived through wars and famine and every sort of pestilence. We can certainly find a way through this."

"Is there anything that can be done?" a younger man asked. He had a child, perhaps ten years old, in tow.

"It is unlikely. They raised concerns over not only the expense of continuing the village school but also the condition of this building." He gestured broadly to the room. "We all know our hall is sound, if a bit worn, but they insist the children need access to a more modern facility. And though our students have scored beautifully on their examinations, thanks to the efforts of our excellent teacher, the authorities aren't convinced."

"The children need reading and mathematics, not computers and claptrap," a woman jeered. "Good books, not machines. They'll learn the rest on their own. We couldn't stop them from it if we wanted to."

"I couldn't agree with you more, madame, but the fact remains that it is the *département* and the rectorat that make those decisions, not me."

"What if we repair and modernize the hall?" Tibèri said, standing. "My offer to make all the repairs necessary if the village will raise the funds for the supplies still stands, Monsieur le Maire."

Pau nodded in Tibèri's direction. "For the sixth year in a row, Tibèri Cabrol has made this generous offer. Can we assume the materials have only gone up in cost since you last researched the matter?"

Tibèri's head inclined slightly to indicate the affirmative. My eyes scanned the room, and now that I had control of my childhood anxieties, I noticed the broken windowpanes, peeling paint, water-damaged ceiling, and a whole array of other wear that had been brought on by the passing of time.

"The matter has been brought up countless times, but the expense, even split evenly among the families, would be a great burden. Too great for some." Pau shook his head, and I could tell from his expression that the ledgers at Sarraut's would show that his household was among those who couldn't bear the cost of it.

"We sure can't afford it," a voice called out. "I've needed a new roof for three years myself. And I don't have children in the village to educate. Or grandchildren either."

"And that will be your defense when no new families move to town?" Jenofa rebuked. "We cannot think only of ourselves, but of the good of the village."

A general rumble of discord resounded through the crowd. Some were eager to contribute to the expense, while others protested. It wasn't that any of the villagers didn't want to contribute, far from it, but their meager means prevented it. Many were seniors who had to make every penny stretch. The younger ones with more earning potential were already strapped.

I'd imagined Mamà so many times over the years, it was a surprise to see a vision of Dad. Asking the mayor to consult the books and find some means of generating cash to help cover not only the bills and repairs that faced them but to create a nest egg for those sure to crop up down the line. I'd have given almost anything for a solid hour of advice from him.

While it was true I was my mother's daughter, I was still Luddington enough.

I stood and prayed my voice would carry. "Have we asked the authorities for any special tax consideration given the size of the village?"

"You have not been recognized to speak." Pau looked past me.

"No one else was and it didn't stop them." It was an old lesson from Dad: Don't afford courtesy to those who don't extend it to you. I'd thought it was harsh at the time, rude even, but now I recognized it as a power move. Deferring to Pau when he was dismissive would make me appear weak in front of the village. I didn't love it, but I saw Dad's point, at least when it came to business relationships. "Are there grants we can apply for to get money for the repairs?"

"We don't want help from the outside," Pau insisted. "We are not a desperate people. And we don't need meddlesome New Yorkers pushing their ideas in matters they don't understand and that don't concern them."

"I live here too, and this affects me and my property value," I pressed. Jenofa made a sound of approval next to me. "I'm not talking about begging for charity. I'm talking about negotiating with the government for a larger cut of the money we already pay in taxes. And better still, finding out if there are ways we can draw in more revenue to the village to make the place more sustainable in the long term." My finance courses came rushing back, and I itched to pore over the village's books.

A dubious buzz spread through the crowd, which I took to be a better sign than a hostile one. I could list a dozen actions we could take, not limited to asking for a reassessment of property values and applying for revitalization grants. Such things were abundant in the States, and I couldn't imagine the same sorts of things didn't exist in some form here as well. The French *département* was like a county in the States, and it was always in the interest of the county to keep the towns afloat.

"We will not grovel with the *département* to ask for crumbs. We will find a way on our own."

Jenofa stood up beside me. "That will be the death of this village, Pau Sarraut, and you know it. You're not being proud; you're being stubborn."

"The repairs would have been thousands of euros less if we'd sought out funding years ago when I started asking," Tibèri added.

Pau looked down at the lectern once more. "We may have no other choice but to let them close the school. It is better to face that reality soberly and with open eyes."

A roar of discontent surged through the audience.

Tibèri stood again. "So we will watch with open eyes as the school shuts down. We look on soberly as we become the next ghost village. This is what you want?"

The crowd stirred, angrier now.

"Obviously not, but I see things as they are. I am asking you not to panic," Pau said over the din. "I have been mayor of this town for thirty years. We have overcome adversity before, and we will again."

As if in reply, a massive clap of thunder cracked overhead, and the heavens opened up in a torrent of late-winter rains. Water began to leak from the roof, first in drips, and then more insistently, until the attendees dispersed unceremoniously.

Mademoiselle Langlois, used to the leaking roof, enlisted help to throw plastic sheets over the bookcases to protect the contents until the rains subsided before leaving with the rest of us.

I dashed to the parking lot along with several others who had driven from the little farms surrounding the village. Others rushed to their homes, many to tend to their own leaking roofs. I corralled Jenofa to give her a ride home and peered over the crowd to see if others needed assistance, but everyone scattered so quickly, I would simply have to scan the roads as I drove to see if others were stranded in the deluge.

As I pulled from my parking spot, only one person remained in view. Pau stood, drenched by the rain, staring up at the town hall where he had presided for three decades, his head shaking in despair. Did he curse the rain for adding to the damage they could already ill-afford to repair, or was he thankful it was there to cover his tears?

Chapter 10

SPRING

I drank in the scent of spring as I walked up the hill to the village for the weekly market. The season of rebirth emerged, not tentatively as it did in New York but with an enthusiasm I'd rarely seen. The harsh mistral winds of winter softened to warm, gentle breezes, and the trees were heavy with the buds of summer flowers yet to come. I'd spent the last few weeks of winter shoring up the house and making an uneasy peace with Tibèri, who was pleased I spoke up on the right side of things at the meeting two weeks before.

Friday, as tradition held, was market day in Sainte-Colombe. Even the name of the week, *vendredi*, "the day of selling," dictated that villages were meant to conduct their outdoor markets on Fridays. As the ties to certain traditions lessened, other villages had moved to having their markets on other days of the week, and sometimes specialized markets on certain days—I'd heard the gastronomy market with upscale foods in Périgueux was the stuff of legend. Sainte-Colombe, however, held its market on Friday and had no intention of changing that.

I pulled the large metal-and-canvas marketing cart that was popular among the residents for more serious shopping behind me. No one within a couple of miles of the city center bothered driving to town in good weather unless they'd be buying more than they could haul in a cart, and I was just as happy to leave the car in my driveway.

The town square was lively with activity as it had been on the evening of the town meeting, though I hoped the rains wouldn't let loose as they had that night. A dozen or more stalls were selling traditional fare—from artisan cheeses to cured meats to vibrantly colored seasonal fruits and vegetables, along with handmade goods and fresh-cut spring flowers. I filled my cart with cherries so plump with juice they seemed ready to burst, carrots harvested that very morning with dirt from the farm still lodged in their crevices, and the most resplendent bunch of spinach I'd ever seen in my life.

I perused the gorgeous produce. What should I do with the complete-but-still-empty greenhouse now that the weather was fine? I'd never kept so much as a spider plant before in the whole of my life, but it seemed a shame not to use the space. It wasn't a big enough structure to grow fruits or vegetables on any real scale. One of the vendors had a portion of his booth dedicated to selling seeds, so I considered the offerings. I passed over the lettuce, eggplant, and tomatoes, knowing the local farmers would do a far better job of it than I.

But as I reached the section of herbs—containing basil, sage, thyme, oregano, and all the other familiar contents of my spice drawer back in New York—I felt like this was something I could do. Even novices had herb gardens with some measure of success, didn't they? My hand wandered to my necklace and I felt a flutter in my core—the good kind—as I handed over the seeds to make the purchase.

The farmer inspected my choices as he counted the packets to tally my total. "A nice mixture, but you'll want some lavender too. It's good for keeping the scorpions away."

"I'll take all you have," I replied without hesitation, remembering the wreath and Jenofa's similar warning.

"That's a lot of lavender." Tibèri slid in by my side, shaking the farmer's hand before turning back to me. It was the first time I'd seen him in town, and he seemed far more relaxed than when he was focused on a project at the Bastida. Or maybe it was because he was in his element here and didn't feel so much at ease at my place. The idea bothered me, but I pushed it away. "Are you going to sell it? You don't have the land to compete with the major growers, but there's plenty of demand."

"I hadn't considered that. I was thinking more along the lines of planting a freaking perimeter fence around my house to keep the scorpions out."

He threw his head back in a full-throated laugh. "Not a bad idea. Start them in your greenhouse and plant them a few feet apart in a month or so."

"You have yet to officially introduce me to our lovely new neighbor, Tibèri." A woman ducked in beside him and clucked her tongue. She wore a simple but well-made floral dress. Her mahogany hair was swept back in a chignon and was all the more charming for graying at the temples. "Though you've spoken of her enough I feel like I know her already."

Tibèri shot the woman a warning look, but she seemed unabashed by his death glare. She wasn't cowed by him, and I liked her instantly for it.

"Mamà, our neighbor Tempèsta. Tempèsta, my mother, Audeta Cabrol." He let out an exasperated sigh. It was clear that my meeting his mother was *not* on the list of things he'd hoped to happen on an outing for spring artichokes and strawberries.

Unfazed by her son, Audeta leaned in to kiss my cheeks: *right, left, right* as I'd been taught in every French class since middle school.

"A lovely young woman come to town. What a pleasure for all of us. I can't tell you how happy we are to have you, my dear. Don't you think so, Tibèri?"

He rolled his eyes behind her back. Her meaning wasn't subtle, but with the dearth of single women of Tibèri's age in the village, she likely felt a direct approach might yield better results.

"Sure thing," he said, though his voice didn't convey the same enthusiasm as his mother's.

Audeta noticed the large supply of seeds I'd acquired from the merchant. "Oh, how nice. You're planning to do some gardening. I'm sure you'll find no finer place in the world than Sainte-Colombe to make green things grow."

"It seems a shame not to make use of the lovely greenhouse Tibèri rebuilt. I thought herbs were a good place to start."

Audeta nodded. "Indeed. Basil can be finicky, and rosemary is temperamental, but you'll get the hang of it. Tibèri will bring you some pots and starting soil from our shed so you get off on the right foot."

"I will?" Tibèri gazed at his mother with mock indignation. He might be annoyed by her volunteering his efforts, but he'd never complain in earnest about helping a neighbor.

"Yes, you will. I raised you to be a gentleman and a good neighbor, didn't I?" She playfully swatted his cheek. He snorted derisively in response, but he was probably already mentally putting the soil and pots in his van.

"I don't want to be a nuisance. I'm sure I can find a nursery somewhere to get supplies." I looked to Tibèri, whose gaze remained impassive.

"Nonsense. My husband has more pots and soil than he'll use in three lifetimes. You'd be doing me a great favor. And since your mamà was from Sainte-Colombe, no doubt she raised you to understand the importance of being neighborly as well."

I nodded. Indeed, Mamà had instilled the importance of caring for one's neighbors as though they were family. That kindness was rarely reciprocated in the snobbish suburbs, but she always said that was a reflection of *their* poor manners, not hers.

Tibèri turned to me, his tone less playful than the one he used with his mother. "I'll leave it all in the greenhouse later."

"That's so kind of you." One of the "rules" I remembered from Mamà was that it wasn't polite to turn down an offer of help, especially one so insistently given. It would be less awkward to accept Audeta's and, by extension, Tibèri's assistance and be done with it than to press my refusal further.

"C'est normal." Audeta leaned in to kiss my cheeks farewell again, and Tibèri followed suit, barely brushing his cheek against mine.

I set about finishing my marketing, itching to return to my kitchen and experiment with the lush ingredients the market had to offer. If there was an aspect of French culture I loved more than its reverence for good ingredients in cooking, I couldn't think of it. I focused on that, doing my best to ignore the whispers at a few stalls. People who recognized Mamà in my face or who remembered me from the village meeting. But the murmurings weren't followed with anything like Pau's rancor from our first encounter. I was beginning to feel a twinge of hope that I'd be able to make a few friends in the village, or at least feel like part of the community.

I'd never sought out a band of friends in New York, and aside from food tastings and social functions for work, I'd spent a lot of my spare time in my apartment keeping my own company. It wasn't particularly healthy, and I resolved to use this "life reboot" as an opportunity to try harder.

I wended my way down the hillside, wheeling my marketing basket and enjoying the reprieve of the shade from the majestic cypress trees that seemed to stretch all the way to the heavens, with their uniform branches almost regal in their bearing. How could Mamà have left this place? What happened that was so dire that she felt she had to trade a place she loved almost as much as any person in her life for the soulless suburbs of Connecticut?

* * *

The kitchen, without question the room I'd made the most progress on renovating, was becoming both my laboratory and my refuge from the world. I'd already spent hours and hours there concocting meals from the lush ingredients of the region. I'd delighted in strawberries that tasted of sunshine, carrots as rich as the soil in which they grew, and green beans a more vibrant green than I'd ever seen in my life. And the growing season was just beginning. Some of the dishes I made were laughably indulgent for a single person; others were beautiful in their simplicity. I didn't have to think about how I'd write up the braised carrots in an article for the *Tribune*. I could just cook for the sheer pleasure of it.

I unpacked my haul from the market, already pondering the culinary possibilities. The seed packets had worked their way to the bottom of the cart, so when the last of the produce and meat had been put away, I gathered them up to store in the greenhouse until Tibèri brought the planting supplies from his mother.

The greenhouse was already equipped with two huge, rough tables that ran the length of each side that Tibèri had fashioned from a few sheets of plywood and some two-by-fours repurposed from other projects. He'd rigged up access for a hose that was attached to the house water supply, but that I could control in the greenhouse to make watering easier.

I organized the seed packets by variety, deciding based on my limited knowledge which spots in the greenhouse would be more favorable to each sort. The ones that preferred more sun would be on the south end. Those that needed the most water would be closest to the hose, and so on. It was probably more elaborate than necessary since they could be moved easily as seedlings and the conditions didn't vary all that much. All the same, it was soothing to decide where things belonged and where they would best thrive.

I finally came to an arrangement that felt balanced. I was crossing back to the house to tackle one of the spare rooms when I heard a rustling in a pile of dried leaves and debris that I'd raked up when Tibèri had been working on the greenhouse. The rustling continued and was accompanied by a plaintive mewing sound of a cat in distress.

I approached the pile of leaves tentatively, not knowing whether the cat was friendly or feral.

"It's okay." I spoke softly, hoping to soothe the creature.

A kitten's head burst up from the leaves. It was solid black with huge ears and yellow-green eyes that took up most of his face.

"Can I pick you up?"

He sat, his huge eyes peering up expectantly and without any apparent hesitation.

He was skin and bones, in desperate need of nourishment. He seemed unfazed by the intrusion on his freedom. Likely, he knew that I was his best choice for a good meal. He tucked into a ball against my chest, and I could feel his little muscles relax as he realized he was safe.

The familiar rumble of Tibèri's utility van sounded in the driveway. He crossed the courtyard to me, holding a stack of pots, and appeared mildly annoyed to have been sent on the errand.

"Who have you got there?" He gestured to the black fur ball in my arms.

"A visitor, it seems. I wonder if his mamà is missing him. I haven't seen any signs of littermates." I held up the kitten so Tibèri could get a better look, and he gestured for me to hand him over for a closer inspection.

Tibèri assessed the little one, clearly with some expertise, and handed him back. "No, this fellow has been weaned. His mamà will have booted him from his happy home by now."

"Seems cruel if you ask me," I said, my tone deliberately waspish. "You're too young and too little to fend for yourself in the big bad world, aren't you? You still need your mamà."

"You're not one to leave your babies to make their own way after a couple of months, then?" There was something intimate about the question. The way he referred to my "babies" made me blush despite my resolve to remain aloof where Tibèri was concerned.

He must have realized the misstep; he cleared his throat and added, "Well, he certainly found an easy mark in you. You'll be feeding him foie gras out of crystal goblets by day's end, won't you?"

"Don't be silly. I have neither of those things. Probably roast chicken off an earthenware plate." I placed a kiss atop the kitten's head. He was filthy and would need a bath, but he seemed all too happy for the attention. I doubted he'd been around people too much, but he was smart enough to know he'd do better to befriend me than to be terrified of me.

Tibèri chuckled at the notion that the meal I proposed was somehow far more practical than the ridiculous one he'd suggested. He stroked the kitten's head, and the little black ball of fluff burrowed in closer to my chest, content.

"Cute little thing," he said. "Or will be when he's fattened up. But I'm afraid a black cat isn't going to help the rumors going around in town."

I heaved a sigh and felt the vibrations against my chest as the forsaken baby began to purr. "What rumors are those?"

"That you're a bruèissa. A witch."

Bruèissa. The word old Pau hurled at me. It made sense now. *Witch.* But why had Pau called my mother, the sweetest woman ever to walk the earth, such a thing?

Had it been Grandmother Luddington, I wouldn't have been surprised. It was the word the old woman had favored hurling at my mother when she was still alive. I remember my grandmother visiting on only a handful of occasions when I was a child, and it never went well. After one particular blowup, she stopped coming altogether. Dad would go visit her in her swanky Manhattan apartment. Wal would go with him. I did a few times, but it became clear that she preferred when I didn't. So Mamà and I would find adventures to fill our Sunday afternoons alone. Sometimes we'd drive into the country and ramble on hiking trails. Sometimes we'd putter in the kitchen together. Other times we'd go for ice cream and a movie. It didn't make up for the fracture in the family, but I was always happy for the extra time alone with her.

"A proper witch's familiar, I suppose."

He chortled. "That's the spirit. Just take the bait and run with it."

I laughed too. "It's like grade school. If someone makes fun of your eclectic fashion sense, you can either change the way you dress and still get made fun of, or you can up the ante and find even weirder clothes to show it doesn't bother you, and the idiots leave you alone."

"Something tells me you learned that lesson the hard way."

"I saw it happen," I said, not wanting to go into the boring wardrobe that Grandmother shoved me into, which had the sole virtue of being so uninteresting that there was nothing to mock.

"What will you name this little guy? *Minou? Chatouille?*"

"Nothing so prosaic. He's a good luck charm is what he is and deserves a fitting name."

"*Astre,*" Tibèri suggested. "It's the Occitan word for 'luck.'"

"I love it." The kitten regarded me with his yellow-green eyes and mewed.

"He approves." Tibèri tucked his finger under the kitten's chin and rubbed until he began purring once more.

"Astre." I tried the name on my tongue. "It's a lovely name. It sounds like something to do with the stars."

"That's where all luck comes from, doesn't it?" He gestured to the clear blue sky as though it were midnight of the new moon and the sky was alight with billions of flickering lights. "And don't worry about the Occitan. Your French is adequate; you'll pick up what you need soon enough."

I felt heat prickle my cheeks at the compliment but did a fairly decent job at keeping it subtle. His eyes scanned to the greenhouse he'd labored on for so long.

"How's the greenhouse? I hope you don't mind that I chose plastic instead of glass for the siding. The winds are fierce here," Tibèri explained. "My stepdad, Bernard, spent most of my youth replacing windows and glass panels on greenhouses. You'll be happier."

"Your stepdad is a carpenter too?" *Stepdad*. It explained why Audeta had mentioned "her husband" instead of "Tibèri's papa," though I'd thought nothing of it at the time.

"Yep. Mostly retired, though. I'm the fifth generation in the family. He adopted me when I was four, and the trade came with the surname, more or less."

A vision of Dad and Wal popped into my head. There was never any question that Wal would follow in Dad's footsteps. In his career and basically every other facet of life. We didn't talk much in the years after I left the house, but there was no doubt he was dating the right girls from the right families with the right connections. The sort of girls Grandmother had wanted for her son, until he'd disappointed her by marrying Mamà. I only hoped Wal would take better care of his health and not have the same outcome.

"Do you like it?" I asked. "Did you always want to be a carpenter?"

"Definitely not. I had my phase of wanting to be an astronaut, then it was a dinosaur breeder—"

"Let me guess, *Jurassic Park* was big here too?"

He nodded. "And obviously I'd never be able to claim French citizenship if I hadn't spent years on the pitch trying to make a spot on the national football team."

"What happened? Why didn't you pursue it?"

"Well, as it turns out, I'm a terrible footballer, so it sorted itself out. And the truth of the matter was that I was *good* at being a carpenter. Useful. I thought it was better to build a career where I had some skill and to leave kicking around a football with the guys as a hobby."

"Smart."

"Did you always want to be a journalist?"

"No," I admitted. "A novelist. Journalism seemed the 'serious' compromise to make my family happy."

"Did it?" He turned from the greenhouse to look at me.

"Nope. It was the great compromise that pleased no one. They wanted me to go into finance like everyone else in the family."

He shook his head. "There are times for compromise and there are times to be stubborn. That would have been one of the times for the latter, probably."

He was right, and his insightfulness was unnerving.

As if to break the uncomfortable silence, little Astre mewed again, this time rather insistently, so I knew I ought to get him inside for a meal. And a bath. I groaned inwardly at the prospect, having seen enough kitten rescue videos on social media to know what fun bathing a cat could be.

"You take care of your new friend," he said. "I'll unload the rest in the greenhouse."

I gave him a grateful smile and trotted back into the house, where I sought out anything that might be fit for a kitten to eat. I found some sliced ham, which I had to parcel out slowly out of fear he'd eat too much at once and make himself sick. He licked his lips eagerly, and he probably would have eaten the entire packet gratefully, but I made him stop after one slice to make sure he'd be able to keep it down.

I'd never owned a cat or a pet of any kind, even as a kid. Dad had persuaded Mamà to wait until we were older to be able to care for the pet ourselves. Then Grandmother claimed she couldn't abide animals in the house. And to be frank, getting through adulthood had seemed like challenge enough without the worry of keeping another innocent creature alive.

Thankfully, Astre didn't know this. He looked up at me, belly full, and jumped to my arms from the counter. He climbed up toward my face and nuzzled my neck as if to thank me for the meal. He trusted that I'd keep him safe. And it was truly gratifying to have someone believe in me that much. It didn't matter that it was a stray kitten. I placed my lips on his forehead and let him curl up in my arms.

"I'll do my best, little one. I'll do my best," I murmured.

Chapter 11

Under Astre's careful supervision, I spent the Thursday afternoon of his arrival planting the seeds in the soil and pots provided by the Cabrols. I researched online the best methods for starting seeds. Some required soaking overnight in water, which I'd done. Others could be gently tucked into the fine, nutrient-dense starter soil straight from the packet.

There weren't instructions on the seed packets, as one would find on those from a commercial seed producer. The farmer was used to dealing with locals who simply knew what conditions oregano or parsley would need to thrive. Thankfully, I found a book in the Tardieux' collection that provided a lot more insight for me to go on, beyond the help of strangers on the internet and my own intuition. Most of my reading mentioned seed trays, but Audeta had provided me with a huge number of plastic pots instead. I'd have to make do with this bounty if I didn't want to make another trip into Valensole.

It took a few hours to get the seeds all planted and organized. I labeled everything and took detailed notes in an unused, old leather ledger from one of the desk drawers about which seeds I'd planted and where I placed them in the greenhouse—anything to make the process methodical.

So much of it was my father's influence. To his mind there wasn't a detail about anything that shouldn't be micromanaged. I'd carried that compulsion with me. Sometimes it served me well, but other times it just kept me from making real strides on a project.

I honestly wondered if that wasn't half the goal of people like my dad. They wanted to appear as though they were working hard at accomplishing their big, lofty goals. Funding the arts, improving public school quality in the neediest parts of the city, reducing homelessness. They wanted to make steps to solve the problem. Enough that they would be lauded as heroes. But solving the problem? No. The steps needed would be too radical. Too unpopular. Too expensive.

Worse, if they actually finished what they set out to do, they'd find themselves without a purpose.

But this once I decided the recordkeeping could be a useful enterprise, so long as I didn't let it become unwieldy in its details. The ledger, however, would stay in the greenhouse so I wouldn't indulge in obsessing over it. The seeds were now carefully sown and cataloged, so that left nothing for me to do but wait. I scooped up Astre, who was now my constant shadow, and turned to leave for the house.

But before I put my hand on the door to leave, I felt a warmth in my chest.

"Rest well. I'll see you in the morning." I felt nutty, but there had been so many times I longed for encouragement when I was growing up, it seemed strange to deny it to these little seeds.

I went back to the house feeling more drained of energy than I had expected, given how little exertion the planting required. Back in New York, I'd have used a lazy afternoon like this to catch up on movies or to curl up with a good novel and a mug of herbal tea. Here in Provence, watching a movie would mean hunching over my laptop screen and streaming it over a subpar internet connection. As for books, I'd sold my meager collection to my favorite used book-shop in Queens and didn't feel equal to attacking any of the weighty French classics I'd found in the house.

Astre followed me as I aimlessly wandered the big, empty house. He meowed a few times, likely wondering what I was up to. I wished I knew. There were corners of the house I'd yet to explore, and while I didn't feel like taking on the dust bunnies in the attic or whatever sci-fi movie horrors might be lurking in the cellar, I did want to explore. After an apartment the size of a barely ade-quate broom closet in Queens, the house felt palatial, and there were any number of nooks and crannies I'd yet to see for myself, which seemed like an oversight given that I was mistress of the place. For a moment I fancied myself as Elizabeth Bennet on the first day after she married Mr. Darcy, when she was free to roam about Pemberley and discover the secrets of each room of the great house.

In New York I'd always rented. Restaurant critics of my stature couldn't afford to buy a shoebox in the farthest reaches of the city. Before that, it was dorm rooms. Before that, it was Dad's house. Perhaps, more appropriately, it was Grandmother's house. But this place, the Bastida, was my own. For the very first time I had a place I could paint whatever colors I wanted. I could use the rooms for whatever purpose I wanted. I could turn one of the bedrooms into a painting studio. I might have considered it, if indeed I knew how to paint, but it was enthralling to know I *could* all the same.

It was the opposite of the Luddington Way, in many respects. There was no one set path before me. There was no right or wrong answer. I was free to shape this house—and my future—however I pleased. It was exciting and terrifying in equal measure.

I rummaged in the closet of one of the larger bedrooms and found a reasonably modern boom box with a radio and CD player. The sort kids in the nineties coveted and would beg for at Christmas. It seemed positively anachronistic for the place and an odd reminder that there had been people living here as recently as thirty years ago. I didn't see any CDs in the nearby box, which seemed mostly filled with books and knickknacks I'd have to tend to later.

I took the stereo to the kitchen, wiped off the years of accumulated dust, plugged it in, and hoped it would come to life. The little red light flickered on, and I was able to tune to a radio station from Aix.

I didn't know the French music but was able to parse out most of the lyrics. The beat was definitely danceable, and I found myself bopping around the kitchen as I threw together a salad for lunch. My mood lifted, though it hadn't been low. My energy rebounded as I listened to music that felt as nourishing as the meal. I remembered reading that plants responded to voices and, in particular, music. The stereo likely had a battery compartment, so I could take it out to the greenhouse and let it play for a few hours each day.

Tibèri would think I was mad, playing music for seedlings. He seemed the ruthlessly practical sort who didn't suffer fools or waste time on idle projects. Given that my career was on hold, my life felt like one big, idle project, which was why, I was sure, he thought I was the human embodiment of a ceramic parrot. Ornamental but ultimately useless. Perhaps that was harsh, but I didn't think it was wholly inaccurate.

I wasn't sure why I thought of Tibèri as I found the supply of batteries I'd procured in town some weeks back, plunked them in the empty compartment of the boom box, and trudged out to the greenhouse. Perhaps because in helping to refurbish the place, he became inexorably linked to it in my memory. He was helpful and devoted to the town, but his manner toward me was mercurial. Helpful one moment, aloof the next. I'd have preferred either of those options reliably than the shift between the two.

What was it about me that was so off-putting to him? I wanted to tell myself it didn't matter what he thought, but I was too much of a Luddington to be able not to care at all. It felt at times like the whole village had sided against me, and I couldn't just ignore the sentiment. Popular opinion was the capital Dad had traded in, and I'd grown far too attuned to how others perceived me.

I placed the boom box on the sturdy table Tibèri built in the greenhouse and tuned in to a station. The classical seemed too lilting. The pop station was too cloying. I found a rock station that played hits from around the vintage of the boom box itself and cranked the volume. I didn't know if the seeds cared much about the music, but as I swayed to the rhythm, I knew the energy couldn't hurt.

And though I couldn't pretend the feelings of the village—and Tibèri—didn't matter, for at least a few minutes, they mattered quite a bit less.

* * *

"This is marvelous," Jenofa said a few days later as she inspected my potted seeds. I had tucked away the boom box, for fear she would think I was a bit mad for playing music for the nascent plants. I followed her with a watering can, gently watering a few of the herbs that preferred to grow in wetter soils. "I knew when I saw you that you and this house were meant to be together. You and young Tibèri have brought a part of Bastida Èrbadoça back to life. This is no small thing. *Deu meu*, but the family would be happy to see this." She gestured to the plants that rested on the long tables.

"I wish my mother had been given more time to teach me Occitan," I said, smiling at her exclamation. "I honestly didn't expect that it was still so common here. I spent years learning French but never found Occitan lessons. I have read some literature in Occitan, though." I thought of the poem "Mirèio" and almost heard Mamà's lilting voice wafting in the window on the breeze.

"That is more than most. Come, let us have something to drink, shall we? It is time you learned more."

We walked to the patio at the rear of the house, and she took her place on a rickety rocker while I fetched two glasses and a chilled bottle of rosé from the kitchen. Astre, dutiful as a puppy dog, followed me out of doors.

Jenofa accepted a glass, admiring the lovely shell-pink wine in the fading evening sunlight. "This is good," she pronounced after taking a sip. "I don't much wonder about not being able to find Occitan lessons. So few places outside of Sainte-Colombe really use it anymore. But we all speak French, and the younger ones at least a bit of English. You'll get by."

"Why does Sainte-Colombe still use it?" I asked, having been curious about this phenomenon since before I arrived. There were plenty of villages in Provence where street signs were labeled in Occitan below the French, but it was more of a quaint nod to the past than anything people relied on or actually used.

"Sheer stubbornness." She tapped her walking stick on the tile of the patio for emphasis, causing her long white braid to sway. "You probably never learned this in your studies, but before the turn of the century, the government tried to kill off our regional languages. They thought it would be better to have the country unified. We were no longer Provençal, or Norman, or Alsatian. We were French. Unified under the French language with all eyes on Paris."

"That's awful to force things. How did they manage it?"

"Changes like these always happen with children first. They insisted on French only in the schools. They'd send teachers from Normandy here. Send our teachers to Picardie, and so on. It didn't matter if a child of thirteen had never learned a word of French. One day a teacher would show up here from Lille or Nantes, and the child would have to learn their subjects in French, when they had learned them in Occitan just the day before."

Astre jumped on my lap, curled up, and began purring, seemingly just as interested in Jenofa's story as I was.

"As I was told, one of the young women in town, a lovely girl called Mirèio, held classes in secret." Jenofa took another sip of the wine.

"Just like the poem. Mamà read it to me repeatedly."

"It's good you know these things," Jenofa said, taking a long sip of her rosé. "Even if you weren't brought up here, your mother raised you to know your culture. This is very good. Young Mirèio was no doubt named for the poem. It is said the great poet Mistral loved our village, and her parents were adamant about preserving our ways. They were proud that their daughter taught the children to read and write in Occitan in the afternoons when the regular school was finished for the day. But it was not without risk."

"I can imagine." I wasn't an expert, but I didn't think the French government would have been kind to those who tried to subvert their programs. "How did she get away with it?"

"She made the children swear to follow all the rules at school. Never a word of Occitan on the school grounds. The older children would help the younger ones by supplying the French word if they were stuck. The teachers here constantly remarked on how compliant the village children were with the new laws. They never realized that we were compliant simply because we were quietly subverting them at every opportunity."

"Her plan worked," I said. "You all speak it fluently." I was a bit in awe of a woman who had left such an indelible legacy on the village.

"It's a point of pride," Jenofa said. "And all of Mirèio's descendants carried the torch and continued teaching our language. To this very day, we send the children for Occitan lessons as we have done for almost one hundred and forty years. But thankfully, we don't have to be secretive anymore."

"That is wonderful. Maybe they would let me take lessons too?"

"I don't see why not. You are of Sainte-Colombe and it should be your right. You know the teacher well enough. Estèva has done the job for the past eight years. Her mother for more than twenty before her. It passed to their family when the last of Mirèio's descendants left town."

"Oh? It must have been hard to leave the family legacy behind."

"I don't know whether it was hard for her or not." Jenofa's eyes were now fixed out on my empty land. "But your mother had her reasons."

"Mamà?"

"Your mother was the last of the Vielescot women born in the village. The last to serve as the Occitan teacher to our village children. But while your mother cannot return like the prodigal daughter, you have come to us."

"You know more about my mother's history than I do," I said, feeling envious. She'd had more time with her than I did, and it seemed, in a way, unfair.

"I was here for it, cara. I saw it from my own verandah."

"Why did she leave?"

"I think sometimes family expectations can weigh too heavy on one's shoulders," Jenofa said. "I think that carrying the legacy of a century of Vielescot women was hard for her. She was to be the torchbearer for our ways. Not just for her family but for the whole village."

I sat back in the decrepit chair, making a mental note to get a wire brush and some paint for the ancient patio set.

"She was unhappy to teach Occitan?"

"Not so much that," Jenofa said. "She loved the children. She loved her language. But it was the responsibility of keeping up old ways in a modern world that wore on her, I think."

I understood that. But in a strange way, I felt deprived. I was a Vielescot woman but was so far removed from my legacy, I felt none of that weight on my shoulders, but neither did I have it to root me anywhere. Perhaps that was her intent—to free me from expectation. But at the same time, it left me feeling unmoored.

And while she'd freed me, she'd not done the same for Wal and the pressures from the Luddington side. "I imagine my brother must feel the same. He's the fourth Walter Luddington, and it seemed he never had a choice in his career or anything else. It was all mapped out for him."

"That is a large burden to place on a child. And I wonder that we weren't wrong to pass the torch from generation to generation in one family instead of handing the duties off to whoever was the most capable and willing. Estèva loves her work. And it's an escape from the little shop that has been the center of her grandfather's world. She's too bright for that life."

"I spoke with her briefly. I think you're right about that," I said.

"Of course I am. And her family was so proud to take over these duties. But with this pride, will there be pressure for *her* daughter to pick up the mantle? If you have a daughter, would the duty rightfully pass back to her as a Vielescot? Or should we, when Estèva decides to retire, choose whoever wants the job?"

"I think so." I couldn't imagine doing to a child what my father and grandmother had done to Wal. Though I'd never had a relationship serious enough that I'd pondered having children in the concrete sense, I'd spent plenty of time making promises to any future children that they would never be made to feel as unwelcome as I had felt in the years after Mamà died. "A child should be born with the freedom of choice."

"You're wise for your years," Jenofa said. "If a little romantic. Choice is a luxury afforded to precious few. But I don't think we should limit the choices of the next generation more than we must."

"I think there is only one thing worse than forcing a child down one path and convincing her it's the only one that will please the family."

"What is that, cara?"

"Convincing the child that *no* path is good enough."

"No, that is a cruelty." She clucked her tongue. "I am so very glad Nadaleta's daughter has come back home. You belong here. You will come to the festival on Saturday. It's the Feast Day of Sainte-Colombe. I know you're a fair hand in the kitchen. Make something for the feast and mingle with your mother's people. It will be good for you."

She spoke it as a command, not a request. Anxiety bubbled up in my stomach. Even after attending the meeting, I still felt like a stranger here. But the whole point of moving to Sainte-Colombe was getting to know my mother's people, and that couldn't be done behind the closed doors of the Bastida.

Chapter 12

I paced my kitchen the next Saturday morning, deciding what to make for the feast day. Jenofa described it as a giant potluck / free-for-all with dancing, fireworks, and crafts-people selling their wares. I didn't want to attempt anything so grand that I'd fail and embarrass myself. I thought of the casse-roles and seven-layer dips and other concoctions the other moth-ers brought for such gatherings when I was growing up. Mamà's tapenade or daube would be met with skepticism and sometimes outright disdain. Too weird, too foreign. The reaction here would be the same if I dared to bring a corn casserole or a cheeseball.

Unable to decide on an offering, I wandered back to my green-house. I expected the pungent smell of damp potting soil and the trapped heat of the structure's siding. But the sweet smell of herbs nearly knocked me over as I walked in. Where I'd left random pots of seedlings buried in potting soil, I found the pots nearly bursting with robust plants. I knew such a thing was impossible, but it was hard not to believe what I observed with my own eyes.

It had been one week since I'd planted my seeds, and according to every website I'd checked, some of the varieties should just be starting to germinate.

Nothing should have been full-grown for weeks.

Yesterday, when I'd come to water, a few pots had shown little green sprouts. Just as I expected. Today, I had my own produce section in full bloom.

I rubbed my eyes. Had I been hallucinating from stress? But the plants were just as lush when my eyes came back into focus.

Maybe Provence's ideal climate for growing plants was more potent than I realized.

Maybe Tibèri was having a bit of fun, replacing my seeds with plants from a nursery in Valensole.

Maybe Audeta's husband had crafted a mixture of potting soil that was nothing short of miraculous.

Maybe the seeds *really* liked 1990s rock music.

But the truth was that my greenhouse was full of plants that looked weeks older than they were, and I had a dish to prepare. I'd solve the mystery of the rapidly growing plants another time and, in this moment, just be grateful for the possibilities they offered.

Pesto, I decided. It was easy enough to make but something familiar to the local palate. I took my shears, ready to trim the plants, but felt a cold pricking at my neck. Like I was five minutes late to an important exam I wasn't as well prepared for as I would have liked. Nervous but just short of panicked. I placed the shears on the workbench and the sensation eased. I picked them up, and it renewed.

Were the plants nervous?

Logically, I knew this was impossible. But the nervousness I felt wasn't imagined. Nor was it really *mine*. It was different from the anxiety I felt about mingling again in the village.

"I'll just take a bit," I whispered to the plants. Had I, in fact, gone bonkers? "I'll be as gentle as I can."

The sensation eased a bit but didn't go away entirely.

I trimmed one leaf from the basil plant in front.

"Is that okay?" The nervousness lessened even more. I continued to trim, slowly, methodically, until I'd gathered just enough leaves for the pesto. I took several from each of the dozen plants, careful not to overprune from any one plant.

"Thank you," I whispered to the plants as I gathered the leaves in a basket to take to the house. I rubbed some of the remaining leaves between my thumb and forefinger, very gently massaging them. Urging them to grow. One of the rosemary plants, a remarkably fine one, was so robust I couldn't help but rub the needles between my fingers. The tang of the rosemary oil on my fingers blended so harmoniously with the scent of basil, I decided to clip just a few sprigs of it to add to the pesto. It would be something different, something unexpected, but perhaps it was better than trying to do things exactly their way and not measuring up. I gave the rosemary a similar pep talk and returned to the kitchen with the trimmed foliage.

It was a ridiculous bounty for plants so young, but I tried not to think too much on it, repeating rationalizations in my head as I set to work in the kitchen.

I washed the herbs thoroughly in cool water in the sink and gathered the pine nuts I'd purchased at the grocery that seemed like a nice addition to salads, the large jug of olive oil I'd acquired, a couple of cloves of garlic, and a block of Parmesan from the fridge. I lightly toasted the pine nuts on the stove, minced the garlic, and grated some cheese. The closest thing to a proper food processor I could find in the kitchen was a manual food grinder that was quite possibly from medieval times, one that had been dug up in the back-yard after four centuries of neglect and half-heartedly refurbished.

I cleaned the ancient appliance as best I could and added the ingredients, the oil binding together the paste of basil, rosemary, and garlic. The scent of the herbs and nuts filled the kitchen with an earthy perfume so decadent, I wanted to bottle it and dab it behind my ears. I scooped the mixture into the earthen crock, covered it with a lid, and set it to rest in the refrigerator until the feast that evening.

"Just let them like me. Even a little would be nice."

I would serve it with slices of baguette I would buy and slice up beforehand. I found a platter and arranged everything so it would be perfect for that evening. I had no idea if the offering would go over well, but at least I wouldn't show up empty-handed.

* * *

When evening came around, I fretted about what to wear. My ward-robe seemed heavy for a place so filled with light and color, but there was nothing to be done about it now. I selected a black tank dress that was at least loose and flowy and tossed my hair up in a bun in an attempt to tame the wayward mahogany curls. The herb-charm necklace was at my collarbone, as it was most days.

I surveyed myself in the mirror and saw a woman who looked much as my mother must have, just a few years older than when she left the village. I saw Mamà's high cheekbones and well-sculpted nose. There was none of the Luddington ruddiness, nor did the blue of my eyes match theirs. My skin was maybe a little paler than my mother's Mediterranean, olive complexion. My curls didn't seem as rambunctious as hers had been. But there was so much of

Nadaleta in my face, I understood why old Pau had a moment of confusion.

I paced the room I'd claimed as my own. It was the largest in the house, with a private bathroom and a lovely view out to the rolling hills beyond the property. I was pretty sure the mattress was now stuffed with more dust than cotton batting, and I longed to replace it, but it would have to wait. The wooden bed frame with the hand-painted floral cartouche in the center of the head- and foot-boards would be a thing of beauty when it was properly polished. The room already felt like home, and I was tempted to stay home with Astre, who was napping contentedly on the bed, rather than face the village.

But my absence would cause more whispers than my presence.

I bid goodbye to the sleeping kitten, grabbed the pesto and my bag, and resolved that I would do my best to make some friends in the village that night. As I wrapped my fingers around the knob to the front door, I felt the pricking of knives against the inside of my stomach. My palms grew slick and my breath grew shallow. I wanted to slide to the floor and let the panic have me, at least for a while. But if I gave in to that desire, I'd never make it to the festival. I kept my hand on the doorknob and took deep breaths and let the aroma of basil and rosemary settle deep in my lungs.

With shaking hands, I turned the doorknob and shut the door to the house behind me.

I walked the mile into the village, cursing my proclivity for dark clothes in the warm weather and vowing to expand into pastels at the next opportunity. I shuddered at the thought. Perhaps jewel tones. Life was all about compromise, wasn't it?

The sun was sinking lower in the sky when I arrived at the town square. People were already assembling, filling the long tables with so much food I worried they might buckle under the weight of it. Someone had strung dozens of long strands of lights from opposite buildings across the square to create a twinkling canopy over our heads. Jenofa smiled at the sight of me but did not break her conversation with a gentleman of about her age to speak with me.

So much for that crutch.

I found a free corner at one of the tables and put my humble offering out with the intricate dishes like tian—which was a sort of casserole made with eggplant, zucchini, squash, baked tomatoes stuffed with bread crumbs, scallions, and herbs—and artfully arranged platters of braised chicken with vegetables. A table was laden with various bottles of wine and liqueurs, and quite a few of the villagers gathered there, still more thirsty than hungry given the warmth of the day.

The children, though few, were animated as they took to the corner of the square with their homemade kites. The wind obliged them with a gust, and the kites flew up, then dotted the sky in a patchwork of greens, purples, yellows, and reds. This was clearly an annual tradition and something of a competition to create the best kite, both aesthetically and functionally. They flew everything from traditional diamond-shaped kites to far more exotic offerings. The most impressive, in my view, was a large red-scaled dragon that took two children to control it. The tails of the kites danced wildly in the wind, like brightly colored serpents writhing in the sky.

Estèva and Mademoiselle Langlois sat at a table selling glasses of red wine—a fundraiser to help with the repairs to the school—to a modest crowd. But before I could cross over to purchase one, Tibèri arrived at my side and placed a glass in my hand. He was so eager to help, and bolstering the fundraiser was a quiet way to do it. But with the cost of the wine, I was sure it wouldn't raise enough money to repair more than a couple of windowpanes.

"You made it." He planted a kiss on my cheeks—*left, right, left*. "Welcome to our little festival. Something tells me you don't have potlucks quite like this in New York."

"No." It was clear that I was the only stranger here, and this was a gathering of families who had known each other for generations.

Tibèri seemed, if not exactly pleased to see me, happy that I was making an effort to meet people in the village. He might not care for *me* personally, but he seemed to think the presence of someone under the age of seventy was a boon to the village.

"There's someone you're long past due to meet." He ushered me over to a small group of people in their late twenties or early thirties who were gathered off to the side. "Tempèsta, you need to meet Matthieu Blanchet, your real estate agent and my friend and neighbor since birth."

"Pleased to meet you at last." I extended a hand. He laughed and approached for *les bises*. "I apologize for not being able to meet you before now. I've been remiss as your agent and your neighbor."

"I heard you had more important matters. Is your mother well?"

His expression went solemn for a moment. "Yes, I've been staying in Aix with her, and for once I am grateful that my work has been quiet so I was able to do so. The doctors in Aix are as diligent as I could wish for, but there may not be much more they can do for her."

"I'm so sorry."

"This is not a night to speak of such things. I have been missing home and my mamà made me promise to come and tell her all about the festivities. So we must, for her sake, enjoy ourselves. I trust you're getting settled in at the Bastida?"

"It's quite a project, but as Tibèri says, the Bastida has good bones."

"The very best. The new carpenters, they don't make them like that anymore." He jostled Tibèri in the ribs with his elbow.

"Nice way to speak to a man who will be fixing your roof tomorrow." Tibèri took a sip from a glass of wine he'd procured.

"You speak the truth. And go easy on the wine, will you? I don't want a shoddy roof because you're hungover." Matthieu sipped from his own glass.

"Only the best for my friends," Tibèri said. "And even the newcomers. Tempèsta here has the finest greenhouse in all of Provence thanks to me, isn't that right?"

Newcomer. Which was, in fairness, what I was. But I didn't quite fit in the category of friend. Not yet. Maybe I never would. This was his prerogative and no reflection on me, but I felt the sting all the same.

Though he was fishing for a compliment, he'd earned it so I nodded my agreement. "I've never seen plants thrive like this. In a week's time I had enough basil to make pesto for tonight."

"By all means, let's try some." Matthieu's eyes scanned the table, and I showed him where I'd placed the crock. He spread a spoonful on the sliced baguette. His eyes closed for a moment as he took in the flavor. When he opened them again, they were wide. "This is exceptional. Truly."

Tibèri sampled some as well. "I'm getting you more basil seeds. Also, I lied about payment. I expect a regular batch of this as thanks for the greenhouse."

"It's a deal." I mentally calculated how many batches of pesto it might take to convince him to shore up my front porch. Worth it.

Just then, I heard the grumblings of two old men, one tall and lean, the other short and squat. "She has gone riding with me every Sunday for two years," the taller one said. "You had no business to ask her to step out with you."

"She thought of you as a brother and nothing else. You know that, you old goat," the short one replied.

"I was hoping to convince her otherwise," the first responded. "She was on the point of it too."

"Stuff and nonsense!" the second decried.

I turned to Tibèri.

He shook his head. "The beverage table. Old Monsieur Tessiyer and old Monsieur Pujol have hated each other since they were boys. They manage to be civil most of the time, but they resurrect their old grievances every year at the feast once they've had too much of their Verveine liqueur."

I recognized the men from their contemptuous glares at the town meeting, which apparently weren't just reserved for that specific evening. "What are they arguing about?"

"A girl, of course. Long before our time, though. They both loved the same woman and neither forgave the other for not stepping aside. Sixty years and they won't let it go."

"What happened?" I asked.

"Legend has it she realized they were both idiots and ended up marrying a mason in Manosque."

I laughed, perhaps harder than was warranted. "Serves them right."

"Well, they both married lovely women and had four children apiece. They managed just fine without her. Their wives are the best of friends and find the whole thing idiotic, naturally. I think the old rivalry keeps them spry."

"But we should stop it before they get carried away. Last year, they knocked over the dessert table and my mother will never forgive them for ruining her famous *tarte tropézienne*." Matthieu turned to the bickering old men. "Messieurs, I don't believe you have met the most recent addition to our humble village. Mademoiselle Luddington has come all the way from New York and is living in Bastida Èrbadoça. Perhaps you will welcome her by doing her the honor of trying this lovely pesto she made for us."

The men regarded me warily, a flicker of recognition crossing their faces. But the taller of the two took a helping of the pesto. He nodded in approval and gestured for his nemesis to take his share.

"For someone not from these parts, you do well," the shorter one said. "I've had much worse."

"What a thing to say, you fool. This is some of the best pesto you've had in your life, and you know it. Just like you knew Izelda was with me," the other replied.

The other man's expression softened. "That Izelda was not good for you, Donat Tessiyer. She may have gone out with you, but she cast her eyes on every man that crossed her path. She would have made you miserable."

"So you allowed yourself to be one of them," the other one said. "I thought better of you. You were my best friend."

"I dated her so you would know how feckless she was. I didn't tell you what I was doing to save your pride. I wouldn't have married her for all the riches in Versailles. And it was worth losing you as a friend to see you spared the pain of an unfaithful wife."

Donat crossed his arms over his chest. "Do you mean that, Méric Pujol?"

"I do. I'd rather have you mad at me for the rest of my life than see you miserable with her for the rest of yours. I heard she left her poor husband and ran off with a banker from Lyon. Who knows what happened to her after that. But you loved her so much, there was nothing else I could think to do to break the spell for you."

"You are a good friend, Méric. I'm sorry I've been a fool all these years. Will you forgive me?"

"Of course, you old goat."

The two men embraced like brothers, and I found myself blinking back tears. The two men tottered off together, I imagined, to reminisce about the old days and to catch up on sixty years of missed friendship.

"It's a Feast Day of Sainte-Colombe miracle," Matthieu declared. "I was certain they'd end up dying of simultaneous heart attacks mid-quarrel at this very festival some year."

"What is *in* that pesto?" Tibèri took another helping and sniffed before he took a bite.

"Magic," said a voice from behind us.

Chapter 13

I suspected as much the moment I met you, but now I am certain."

Jenofa. She looked at me with serious eyes.

"What do you mean?" I took a few steps away from the crowd so that no one else, save for Tibèri and Matthieu, would hear.

"The women of your family have all had gifts, cara. Your grandmother was able to soothe animals and was more talented than any veterinarian in town. Your mother had a special affinity with embroidery."

"What do you mean?"

"If she embroidered a gift for someone—a skirt, a blanket, even a handkerchief—it brought with it all of what Nadaleta was feeling in that moment. If she was happy when she was sewing, the recipient would feel it whenever they used the gift. If she was sad, it was just the same. She learned how to control her emotions to be able to wield her powers intentionally. She was famous for giving newlyweds tablecloths. She would think about joyous family gatherings as she sewed, and the people in town swore that a meal served at a table dressed with her cloth would never be anything but harmonious."

Tibèri placed a hand on my shoulder. A steadying, comforting gesture I appreciated more than I could express. It was unexpected from one who hadn't been particularly warm, but I wouldn't shove him away now.

My eyes were locked on Jenofa's, but I heard Tibèri scoff in my left ear. "This sounds of people wishing something into being if you ask me. Nadaleta let people think a tablecloth was charmed and people went out of their way to be agreeable. And I suspect that somehow the tablecloth might never be used when a particularly difficult guest was coming to dinner."

"There is something to that," Jenofa said. "But that sort of thing has a power of its own. I for one saw your grandmother soothe a horse that even the most talented horsemen had forsaken. I myself felt your mother's tears when I wore a blouse she embroidered for me after her father died. It was how we discovered her gift. I couldn't wear the thing without feeling heartache, though she didn't tell me for many months that she'd made it on an afternoon when she was missing him especially."

"So you knew Nadaleta had just lost her father, and wearing the blouse made you think of her, which in turn made you sad to think of her loss." Tibèri didn't sound condescending in his explanation but definitely on the verge of exasperation.

Jenofa shook her head. "It was more than that, my boy. Stronger. I didn't feel sad for her; *I felt her sadness*. I am not one to fall into idle superstition either, no matter what you might think of me. What's more, Nadaleta embroidered an identical blouse, forcing herself to think only happy thoughts. She switched it for the one in my closet without telling me, and when I wore it, though I fully expected her feelings of grief to wash over me, the sensation was totally different."

Tibèri rolled his eyes.

"Mock me all you want, *mon gojat*, but the legends of the Vielescot women go back for generations."

I assumed the Provençal term was something like *mon garçon* in French, "my boy," endearing and slightly pejorative all at once.

"Tempèsta, did your mother ever make you a dress or something special?" Jenofa pressed.

"No. I don't remember her making anything except the quilt."

"Go on," she said.

"Apparently Dad had problems with insomnia, and she made it for him. I assumed it was just a kind gesture."

"Do you remember if it worked?"

"I don't remember Dad having sleep issues until Mom died." After she left us, it seemed like he never slept. But it wasn't three days after she died that the quilt ended up in a plastic tote in the basement.

But I remembered the few times when I was sick, or something was wrong, and Mamà would wrap me up in the quilt. I'd sleep the sort of pure, deep sleep usually reserved for those who'd run marathons and had unusually clear consciences. But charmed or not, it was something Mamà had made, and I was happy to use it now on my bed in the Bastida after it spent far too long moldering in a box. And while I'd attributed the good sleep I'd gotten since I'd arrived in Sainte-Colombe to the work I'd put in restoring the house, was there something more to it?

"I knew that our Tempèsta's gifts would have something to do with the garden. The necklace she wore. The fact that she chose to make her home at Bastida Èrbadoça rather than any other place in the village. These things all mean something."

My hand crept to my neck. I'd rarely indulged in impulse buys, but I'd not been able to leave the necklace behind in the thrift shop. But Tibèri had to be right. There wasn't anything more to it than my giving myself a small pick-me-up when I was feeling especially low after Dad had died.

"The Bastida was the only place I could afford within a hundred-kilometer radius of Sainte-Colombe." I felt Tibèri's hand on my shoulder, encouraging. My breath caught at the familiarity of the gesture, but I did what I could not to draw attention to it so I could focus on the conversation.

"Even so," Jenofa insisted. "You cannot tell me that the change in those two idiots was of their own doing. If they were going to forgive each other on their own, they'd have done it by now."

"You think that Tempèsta here has somehow made a magic pesto?" Matthieu asked, as incredulous as his friend. "It is some of the very best I've tasted, but I think your theory is a little far-fetched, don't you?"

"I don't know, exactly," Jenofa said. "None of the gifts have been straightforward. Tempèsta will have to experiment on her own and discover its true nature. It may take a lifetime to discover the extent of it. But if tonight is an indication, I think it is a powerful ability she will have when she learns to harness it. It is part of her legacy as a Vielescot."

"What is part of the Vielescot legacy?" Estèva joined our little circle, a glass of rosé in hand and a harried expression on her face.

"It seems Tempèsta has a way with herbs," Tibèri said. "Hardly surprising to have good luck with them in Provence."

"That's a bit of an understatement, don't you think?" Matthieu interjected. "Even if the old men's feud is a fluke, the plants aren't. My mother grew basil from seeds every year for ages before she was sent to the hospital. She's a dab hand at it, and she didn't have anything to harvest for three weeks. Tempèsta has a crop after a week? That seems pretty remarkable."

"There has to be a reasonable explanation." Tibèri scoffed, bewildered that his good friend was somehow buying into Jenofa's ideas about magic.

"No, I meant what does any of this have to do with the Vielescots?" Estèva pressed.

Old Pau came to join us, his expression sour. "Tempèsta's mother was Nadaleta Vielescot. No doubt she has come to take her mother's place."

Estèva's face drained of color for a moment. She had taken over my mother's place as the torchbearer of the traditions in Sainte-Colombe, and clearly the honor meant something to her.

I rounded on Pau. "Exactly how would I take her place?" I threw my hands up in exasperation. "Take Occitan classes from Estèva for ten years so I can boot her out of a job? Hardly." My limbs started to tremble. I wasn't used to standing up for myself. Anytime I'd tried it in the last ten years, it was met with disastrous results.

"Of course she doesn't mean to take Estèva's place. She couldn't possibly take over if she knows only fragments of the language and a few of our customs. Be sensible, Pau." Jenofa spoke like a mother chastening an unruly toddler. Estèva seemed mollified by the declaration, but Pau did not.

A few nearby villagers turned to gape at us. At me. There were a few murmurs from the crowd, and I distinctly heard the words "Vielescot" and "bruèissa." The faces grew from curious to vaguely hostile as the murmurs grew in intensity.

"We thought the village was freed from your family!" one bold voice finally yelled. "You'd do better to go back to where you came from."

Tibèri and Matthieu, two of the largest men in the village and among the most respected, glowered at the crowd. Their glares sent the onlookers scattering. I might have felt warmed by the gesture made in my defense if I hadn't been on the verge of breaking down into tears.

"Maybe it would be best for you to cut the evening short," Estèva said. "I can walk you home."

Pau opened his mouth to object, but one withering glance from Jenofa silenced him.

I picked up my pesto dish and muttered my goodbyes as Estèva wrapped an arm around me. "Well, that was an eventful evening, wasn't it?"

I rolled my eyes. "*Eventful* is one way to put it. Dumpster fire might be another. All I wanted to do was meet some people. Maybe make some friends?"

Estèva threw her head back in a laugh. "You left New York for Sainte-Colombe to make friends? That seems backward to me. There have to be a million more interesting people there than here. Several million."

"They're not interesting if they don't talk to you. You'd be surprised at how isolating it is to live in the city. Surrounded by people all the time, but no one who cares. It's where you go to find all the downsides of loneliness without the benefit of the solitude you'd get from actually being alone."

"We have plenty of solitude available here, I'll grant you," she said. "Though I am sorry people were rude to you."

We arrived at my house just then, and I showed her in. She nodded approvingly at the improvements I'd made and settled in at the kitchen table as though we'd been friends for years.

"I think this evening calls for a glass of wine, and I'd prefer to have company for it if you don't mind hanging out with the village pariah."

Astre chose that moment to jump on the table and mew his hellos to Estèva. She quickly won him over by rubbing his chin and scratching the patch of fur just above his tail.

"Oh, spending time with the village bruèissa seems like the most exciting social opportunity I've had in years. I absolutely insist on staying and drinking your booze."

I poured her a healthy glass of Côtes-du-Rhône and one for myself. Astre amused himself by batting at Estèva's fingertips as she flitted them about the tabletop for him.

"So how was it that you came to take over for my mother as the Occitan teacher? Once she left, what happened?"

"I was born a year or two after your mother left, so I really don't know the details. My mother took over at first. When she died, it was my turn."

"When was this?"

"It was about eight years ago? I'd just graduated high school and was going to go off to university in Aix. Cancer. The sort of tragedy that's as common as table salt from the outside, you know? Papi convinced me that he couldn't get on without me, and a few months became several years in the blink of an eye."

I was gutted for her loss, especially at such a pivotal time in her life. But it was some consolation to know that she knew what it was to lose a mother. It was a sad sistership to be a part of, but it was a comfort not to be alone in it.

"I see that look. Don't feel sorry for me. I do love teaching the kids. All five of them we have in the village, that is. And Papi needs me. He wasn't wrong about that. He refuses to run the store any differently than it was run in 1935, but he couldn't even do that without me. It may not be the life I dreamed of, but I have purpose. There's value in that."

"There is. Heaven knows I could use some of that."

"Well, let's go see this incredible greenhouse of yours. It may not be your purpose, but it might lead you there in one way or another."

We took our glasses of wine with us, and I showed her out to the greenhouse. The light was growing dimmer, but the days were long enough we didn't need the aid of flashlights to find our way.

I loved the earthy smell, the vibrant humidity of the greenhouse. In the fading light I could see that the basil plants I'd trimmed that morning were already more robust than when I'd taken my harvest. I could make ten more batches of pesto and not make a dent in them.

"This is incredible," she breathed. "Seriously, these were just seeds a few days ago?"

I nodded. "Yep. From the farmers market a week ago Friday."

"So, what, you whispered some magic words and *presto* you have an herb garden to make Jacques Pépin jealous?" She leaned over and sniffed the rosemary. Her eyes rolled back for a moment as though she were smelling the most delectable food instead of just an ingredient that would be sprinkled in the sauce.

"No magic words. I just listen to them and try to give them what they want." It sounded ridiculous, but I wasn't sure how to describe it any better.

"There are legends about your family in town," she said. "I always thought it was Papi trying to get me to sleep with stories, but now I wonder if they were true. Did you have any idea that you were good with plants before now?"

I shook my head. "I never had time for plants, really. It never occurred to me. I was once charged with caring for my grandmother's African violets when she went away with some friends to the Hamptons. They flourished so much while she was away, she accused me of killing her plants and replacing them. I just figured her generally awful personality was slowly poisoning them. She has that effect on most living things." I sighed and rubbed my eyes a moment. "I wish I knew. I wish I knew what any of this meant."

"I can't tell you." Estèva traced the outline of a mint leaf with the tip of her finger. "But I don't think anyone could. Not even your mother. This gift is likely one you have to figure out on your own."

I exhaled, hating that she was right. "I don't even know where to start."

Estèva leaned down to the basil to take a deep breath and sighed. "I don't know either, but I volunteer to sample any of your experiments."

I laughed, thinking of the two men who had put aside a feud that was older than Estèva and me together, over seemingly just a few bites of pesto. "I hope you don't regret that offer."

"Hey, I might end up inadvertently cursed, but I have a feeling it will taste amazing. Now get snipping and let's make something."

Chapter 14

Estèva and I took some cuttings—lovingly harvested—of thyme, basil, verbena, rosemary, mint, and sage. I took a few sprigs of lavender from my perimeter fence for good measure. We sipped wine and cooked as though the whole village hadn't made it plain just an hour before that I was unwelcome.

"It's a pity we had to leave the festival early," Estèva said as she gathered the ingredients for more pesto while I prepared chicken in a buttered-herb crust and lemon-verbena cookies. "But it doesn't mean we should forgo the Feast Day of Sainte-Colombe altogether. It would be like missing the Fourth of July for you."

"Ha, this will be my first one out of the States. I don't think I'll miss it much. My family wasn't one for fireworks and cookouts, so it was never a big deal."

"That's too bad. As tired as I get of life here at times, I like the times we all come together."

"It was enchanting tonight," I agreed. "To see families who

have known each other for generations gathering to celebrate something."

"It doesn't feel like there's much to celebrate, with fewer and fewer of us every year, but we still hang on as the world passes us by." Estèva chopped some basil leaves with a bit more force than was called for.

"Gentle with the basil," I coaxed her. "Well, the village is still here. It hasn't been abandoned or swallowed up by a nearby city. That seems like something to celebrate."

"Maybe, but sometimes I wonder if there is a point to it. Whether clinging to this way of life really serves a purpose. It's like my grandmother who insisted on using a manual food mill all her life even though Mamà had bought her an electric one. Was the extra trouble really worth it?"

I reached into the cupboard and removed the ancient food mill I'd used for the pesto just that morning. "You're about to find out. Unless you have your grandma's electric one in your purse."

She giggled. "Alas, no." She loaded the ingredients into the food mill and heaved a dramatic sigh. "Ancient kitchenware. My lot in life."

"Let me do it." I nudged her aside. "Who knows, maybe I'm the one who has to do it for any of this hocus-pocus to work."

"Be my guest." She gestured to the archaic device with a flourish.

I remembered when I made the batch of pesto that morning, wishing that everyone would like me. Clearly, that had been a failure, but the old men from the village liked *each other* again, which was something.

Was it as simple as that? Making a wish like you do over birthday cake candles?

I closed my eyes for a moment and tried to think of something worthwhile to wish for. The only thing that sprang to mind was wanting to feel like I belonged. Friendship, really. I cranked the handle of the food mill and concentrated on that thought.

And that night, we ate pesto and chicken, drank wine, and gabbed for hours. Astre had grown smitten with Estèva, and she with him. Whether it worked and I bewitched Estèva into becoming my friend, or if it was bound to happen since there were so few people our age in town, I couldn't be sure.

Should I be bothered by the idea? Scared by the strange gift I'd uncovered? Maybe, but that night, I wasn't. Estèva was free to decide whether I was worthy of her friendship or not, and I doubted the pesto could truly change that. Though the way Estèva ate the lemon-verbena cookies, those stood a decent chance of helping my case. But not through any magic; just the sheer power of good flavor.

"Do you really think you'll stay here?" Estèva asked between bites. "Don't you think you'll miss the excitement of the city?"

"Not hardly. I don't miss much of it, apart from a few restaurants and bookshops. A thrift store that I'm fond of." My hand flitted to my throat where the herb necklace lay. It had gone from a favorite piece to a talisman.

"Speaking of which, we need to get you out of those heavy clothes before summer. Half the town thinks you're in mourning. Not helping your cause. And you've barely had a taste of our weather. The sun here can be brutal."

I snorted. This was a part of the world that still respected mourning attire. No, people didn't dress in solid black for six months after the death of a loved one anymore, but the color was most often reserved for funerals, not everyday wear.

"You might be right. You'll have to direct me to a good second-hand shop."

"A girls' day in Aix, and soon. I don't trust you left to your own devices yet. You need training." Estèva, who was always put together, was dead serious. She took clothing seriously and was determined I'd not be known as the Fashion Victim of Sainte-Colombe.

"Agreed," I said, thinking it could be a pleasant way to spend an afternoon and a good way to make friends with Estèva.

"Tibèri is convinced you won't last all that long here." She spoke as if making a dire confession. "He thinks you'll get bored—which I would totally understand."

"Is that why he hates me?" He'd been friendly enough at the festival, protective even. But his gesture was likely just one of basic decency and nothing more.

"He doesn't hate you," Estèva said. "He's just leery of trusting you. It's not the same."

"I don't get it. Why doesn't he take me at my word? I might have panicked in the beginning, but I think I recovered from that pretty quickly."

"It's not my tale to tell, but suffice it to say, he's been burned by outsiders before."

I took a swig from my glass of wine and pondered what she might mean. Had a woman come through town and broken his heart? Unless it was last week, he seemed the sort to move past that type of disappointment quickly enough. I simply couldn't imagine him pining after a woman all that long once she'd moved on.

But truthfully, I didn't know Tibèri all that well. Perhaps there was a woman who had enchanted him and dashed his hopes. Maybe the ruthless pragmatism I saw in him was actually a *result* of his previous pain and a new defense mechanism against it, rather than something that had always been a part of him.

"Well, I don't plan on leaving. I hope he'll make peace with that eventually. I'd prefer not to have him glowering at me and expecting me to bail when we're in our seventies."

"Oh, by the time you're sixty, he'll be convinced you're serious enough. He's not as stubborn as some in the village."

"It seems to be a defining characteristic of the town," I said.

"You have no idea. And my grandfather is the worst of the lot." Her tone lost its humor and her expression darkened.

"What can I do?"

"About what?" She set her glass down and rubbed her temples.

"I don't know . . . the school? Your shop? The village? Everything?"

"Aside from bringing in a pile of cash or a huge vat of tourists who want to buy kitchen antiques? Not a lot. I'd ask you to convince Papi to modernize things a bit, but I don't think even your kitchen magic goes that far."

"No, there isn't a magic pesto in the world good enough for that," I said. "But I wish there were."

"I think you should continue to tinker in your greenhouse and your kitchen. I don't know about all the family legend stuff, but you *do* seem to have a knack, a gift, whatever you want to call it. Play with it. Explore and have fun. And feed me as often as possible from your trials. I'll still be trapped at Sarraut's, but at least I'll be well-fed." She took another cookie—I'd lost count after her sixth—and ate it with delight.

"It's a deal." It didn't feel like nearly enough, but it was definitely something I could do.

And if it helped her, even a little, maybe there was a bit of magic in the pesto after all.

Chapter 15

My mind raced all night, but this morning, haggard, I forced myself to focus on the sound of the bristles against the tile scrubbing back and forth: *swish, scrape, swish, scrape*. It left no room in my head for pondering Jenofa's revelations from the night before.

Bruèissa.

Witch.

I scrubbed to prevent those words from seeping deeper into my brain. To keep me from wondering how fond this region of France had been of burning witches.

But I couldn't, no matter how hard I tried, stop thinking about Mamà. I hadn't been fully honest with Jenofa; Mamà had indeed made me a garment once, when I'd tried to convince her that I didn't need to attend kindergarten.

Even now, my stomach lurched as I remembered my trepidation on the steps leading up to Susan B. Anthony Elementary School twenty-two years prior; the uncanny similarity of the sensation I'd felt on the evening of the meeting at the town hall. The buildings resembled each other about as much as a tabby cat resembled a daffodil, but my nerves at the meeting a few weeks ago were just as taut as they'd been all those years ago.

On the appointed morning, Mamà had driven me to the perfectly lovely, little blue school building with the well-manicured lawn and pristine playground equipment. But before she walked me to the school, she pulled my hair back with an elastic band and tied on a small yellow cloth that had little bits of embroidery all over it.

"This hair bow? It's not just any hair bow. It will give you the courage you need to face your fears and the confidence to know you are equal to them," she said. "I won't tell you that school is easy and that all the children will be kind. But hard as it is, you will make it through the day. And though some days will be harder than others, you will find that your courage will grow over time. You just have to trust yourself."

And, true to her word, I made it through the day. The teacher was fond of me. I even made a couple of friends despite my valiant efforts to blend in with the whitewashed walls.

I wore the embroidered bow in my hair every day for years. People recognized me by it, thinking it was a rather charming eccentricity of mine. When it grew tattered, I wrapped it around my wrist like a bracelet. When it grew even too ratty for that, I kept it in my pocket. When I was fourteen, my grandmother saw it and demanded I throw it away.

"Don't carry trash around like a hobo, girl. Put it in the bin this instant," she'd commanded. I didn't explain to her that Mamà had embroidered it herself; that certainly wouldn't have endeared her any more to the notion of my keeping it. I didn't try to tell her that

I'd carried it with me every day for nine years. I certainly didn't try to explain to her that I always felt a small jolt of confidence when I had it on hand.

I lied to my grandmother and hid it away. I didn't carry it around anymore in case she found it and threw it out. I kept it in the back of my nightstand drawer, my sock drawer, my desk drawers . . . moving it regularly so Grandmother wouldn't find it. I was certain she rummaged through my things when I was at school. What she was looking for, I wasn't sure, but I'd regularly find things out of place. It wasn't the "out of place" that was the result of tidying or putting away laundry. It was the sort of out of place from fumbling through desks and pawing through dressers. One day it went missing, and I assumed she'd finally been successful in her hunt, though I was never brave enough to confront her about it.

I always suspected that she was hunting for some sort of contraband—maybe an illicit wine cooler or cigarettes—that would give her a reason to persuade Dad to send me to some sort of boarding school for wayward girls. She would have loved nothing more than to have the house, Dad, and Wal to herself. But I never gave her an inch of reason to boot me. Perfect grades, never a complaint about my behavior from the school. I didn't even date because it felt like a minefield with her peering over my shoulder.

Though the cloth likely would have disintegrated by now, I wished I could have it back. What I wouldn't give to have an ounce of that courage again. From the day I lost it, I felt like that confidence had faded with each day that passed.

I shook my head from my reverie and returned my attentions to the Bastida. I crossed from the kitchen to the dining room that, like most of the house, was still in a sorry state of neglect. It was, or at least had been, a welcoming room. It was furnished with sturdy walnut furniture, and the peach color on the plaster walls was warm and inviting.

I determined the chandelier ought to be the first thing to be cleaned. It wasn't the sort that one found in the posh homes in the better suburbs of New York, with three tiers and dripping with crystals. This was a spindly, wrought-iron affair with a half dozen electric candles and a scrolled bowl-shaped base that had collected three decades' worth of dust, which sprinkled down like snow from the slits in the scrollwork onto the table when there was a breeze. It made no sense to clean the table or floor if the dust would continue to rain down on the rest of the room.

I climbed up on the table and quickly realized that the chandelier needed more than dusting. It would need to be removed and scrubbed. I clambered down, found the fuse box, removed the fuse for the dining room, located one of Monsieur Tardieu's old screwdrivers, and started to work.

"You could have called me for help, you know," Tibèri's voice called from behind me. It was still quite early, and he was dressed as though he stopped by on the way to a job.

"I think I can manage," I said, feeling the stress on my enamel as my teeth grated together. "I'm not all that handy, but it's taking out a few screws with a screwdriver. I'm not even using power tools."

"That thing probably weighs a ton. You don't want to hurt yourself."

I climbed down and plunked the screwdriver down on the table in frustration and pinched the bridge of my nose. "You don't think I can handle a simple household task without landing in the hospital, do you?"

"It's heavy and I don't want you to hurt yourself."

"This thing weighs maybe six kilos. Nine at most. I've got this."

"Tempèsta, I—"

"Listen, I know you feel obligated to help me because Jenofa is guilting you into it, but you're free. I hereby release you from any sense of obligation from Jenofa, your mom, or anyone else." I flitted my fingers like a genie being freed from a bottle.

"It's a chandelier. It's not a big deal. Why won't you let me help?"

I exhaled slowly. It was a good question, really. "Because I'm tired of being made to feel incompetent. People dismissing me without the slightest idea of my abilities."

And as I spoke the words, I knew how ridiculous I sounded. Three people I knew had acted that way: Grandmother, who never would have dared to entrust me with any sort of responsibility. Wal, who probably didn't think I could figure out how to make a simple bank deposit on my own. And Dad, who when he bothered to think about me at all assumed I was too flighty to follow through on anything and asked Wal to do it instead. But Tibèri hadn't acted that way, and it was unfair to cast him in with the others.

Tibèri's expression changed from annoyed to matter-of-fact. He grabbed the screwdriver I'd set on the table and handed it back to me. "Give it a shot." His tone wasn't challenging or defiant but calm and assured. "If you need help, ask, but I won't jump in unless you do."

Or if I fall and break my head open. He didn't have to voice that part. I was glad he didn't.

I worked slowly and carefully to remove the chandelier. I noticed the bowl was removable before I got too far into the process and took it down first, which would reduce the weight of the thing tremendously. I unscrewed the main part of the chandelier and, given the age and simplicity of the wiring, was easily able to disconnect it from the connections in the ceiling.

My black top was now a light gray from all the dust, but the chandelier, the ceiling, and I were none the worse for the efforts. Tibèri nodded approvingly.

"Well done. I shouldn't have doubted you."

"It's fine. It's just . . . I wish people didn't automatically assume that I'm useless, you know?"

"I'm sure it doesn't feel great," Tibèri agreed. Given his sex and profession, no one questioned his skills with a simple screwdriver. "Just like it sucks to have people assume you're all-capable and they get disappointed when they find out you're just a normal mortal. But I don't think this conversation is just about a dirty chandelier."

"No." I hoisted the dust-caked bowl of the chandelier off the table and hauled it to the kitchen, Tibèri following me. I dumped the bulk of the dust in the trash bin and ran the bowl under hot water in the sink. "I'm sorry I overreacted. I don't know what to make of everything that's going on. Having this strange gift. Knack. Whatever you want to call it. After years of being made to feel like I was unable to do anything for myself, it's weird, you know?"

"I can only try to imagine," Tibèri said. "I poked my head in the greenhouse and I have to admit, as much as the realist in me wants to come up with a scientific explanation, there is something extraordinary happening."

"Thanks for that." Given how hyperrational he was, having him acknowledge that something unusual was afoot made me feel slightly less insane.

"There's something else; it's not just the recent greenhouse stuff that caused that outburst. I know repressed anger when I see it." He crossed his arms as if daring me to contradict him.

I bristled. I hated it when he was so damned perceptive. "I don't know. Maybe having a future mapped out for me by my father and grandmother and then being criticized for not walking the straight and narrow quite as straightly and narrowly as they would have liked did a number on me. Then I move here to be free from all that and find I've inherited some legacy I knew nothing about. What am I supposed to do with all this? I am treated like I can't tie my own shoes by half the world and like some sort of freaking malevolent sorceress by the other half. I'm going to get whiplash."

"I don't think you're incompetent. And I don't think you're a bruèissa either. You're a woman with a unique talent. And sometimes a bit of a temper." He uncrossed his arms and took a few steps closer. "And I think the people in the village will come to understand that too."

"If they give me a chance. And I don't think that's a foregone conclusion."

"They will," he said. "In time. Meanwhile, just do what you can to be friendly and mix about in town. Maybe don't spike the food with forgiveness potion again for a while."

"No promises." I shot him an actual wink for perhaps the first time in my life.

"Good. Keeping them on their toes may be wise. But listen, we got off on the wrong foot, and that's mostly my fault. I'd like to try again and be friends if you're willing."

I studied his face a moment. His hair was lightening as the sun grew stronger in the weeks leading to summer. His skin was growing swarthier but didn't quite have the olive hue that others' did in the area. But as I scanned his even features and peered into his green eyes, I saw no trace of anything but sincerity.

I dried my hands and offered him my right one. "It's a deal. It's too small a town to refuse friendship when it's offered."

He took my hand in his enormous one and shook it firmly. His hand was warm and calloused, but not rough to the touch.

"So now that we're friends, I want you to promise me you won't take on projects you can't handle. I'm happy to help. It's not me being an overprotective jerk. Just wanting to help my friends."

"Thank you," I said, hoping he was sincere.

"I stopped by for a reason beyond making sure the village hadn't scared you off entirely. I just know there's a lot to do here, and I thought you might appreciate some help now that the greenhouse is done."

"Oh, well . . . sure." I tried to sound blasé, but I knew there were repairs far more dire lurking under the layers of grime. In a house this old, there had to be, and I sent up a silent prayer, on behalf of my bank account, that they weren't too extensive.

"Do you mind if I prowl around a bit? Get a closer look at the nuts and bolts of the place? The walk-through before was helpful, but there are a few more things I'd like to check out."

"Sure, go ahead." It seemed like a logical next step, though I had no idea what he'd be searching *for* exactly.

"Just go about whatever you're doing and don't mind me." He swaggered out of the room with a confidence I envied.

I spent the time rubbing the chandelier free from almost three decades of dust, and by the time Tibèri reappeared in the kitchen some time later, I was pleased with the result. There was something to be said for liberal amounts of elbow grease.

"Can I show you something?" he asked.

I turned from the sink and dried my hands, a flutter rising in my stomach. This could not bode well for the house or my finances. "Okay."

He motioned for me to follow, and I trailed him down the hallway that led to the back porch. The open fuse box was admittedly a far more complicated mess of wires than the more civilized, modern breaker boxes with their neat, labeled rows of switches I'd been accustomed to. Some of the wires were a bit frayed, and all of it seemed about a thousand years out of date.

"Oh, I left it open when I turned off the power to the dining room. I didn't want to fry myself having a metal screwdriver so close to live wires."

"Smart, and yes, you did, but that's not the end of the world since it's not raining. But there is no way wiring like this would pass any kind of inspection," he said, not mincing words. "If you ever wanted to expand the place or do any sort of major renovation that would require permits, this would all have to be redone."

"Well, thankfully none of that is going to happen imminently. The place is growing on me as it is, and I certainly don't need a new wing just for me."

"But you may want a new HVAC system when summer kicks in. This place doesn't have AC, and with the climate doing what it is . . . you may want it sooner rather than later. You'll need a permit to do that. Not to mention that this could become a serious fire hazard at any time."

I rubbed my eyes with the heels of my palms and exhaled slowly. "What are you saying?"

"If this were my place, I'd rewire it. Room by room, before it becomes an emergency situation and you have to do it all at once and the place is uninhabitable for weeks. And before a shoddy wire shorts out and sets a fire."

"That sounds expensive and inconvenient."

"Like I said, one room at a time so it'll be less of a hassle for you. But it will mean tearing out the plaster and replacing it with modern drywall. Will probably be a good idea to get rid of the lead paint and other nasty stuff they used in old walls anyway."

"Expensive and inconvenient," I repeated, pinching the bridge of my nose. "But it sounds necessary."

"I think so," Tibèri said. "If not now, soon."

"Fine. We might as well."

He patted my shoulder, and the little tingle I felt at the warmth of his hand annoyed me. It was a simple gesture from a man hoping to help a neighbor and get some work out of the deal. Nothing more. But that sensation wasn't new. Since Mamà died, I'd experienced so little in the way of affection, I reacted strongly to positive touch. But after a couple of bad relationships, I'd become better at taming my reaction to such innocent gestures.

"Listen, I know it's not the news you wanted, but you'll be glad you did it. I'll do what I can not to be in the way." His eyes met mine and it was clear he meant what he said. And he was good at his job, from all accounts, and wouldn't steer me into senseless repairs I couldn't afford.

The part of me I wasn't proud of wanted to scream or punch the wall. Thankfully, I was usually in control of those baser instincts. "And you think I'm going to hire you without a second opinion?" I arched a brow. Sarcasm was always better than a tantrum, if slightly less satisfying.

"If you can find a carpenter willing to come all this way to do a job, he'd charge you twice as much for the inconvenience of having to drive so far. We French aren't like you Americans who commute an hour from the suburbs into the city. And he wouldn't be willing to work room by room either."

I smirked. "I knew I was my mother's daughter. I felt like I spent my life on filthy commuter trains when I worked in the city.

Good for reading or taking notes for an article, bad for anything else."

"Glad our culture isn't totally lost on you." He returned the smirk.

He walked me from room to room, explaining what he'd have to do to get the house rewired and other repairs he thought were in order. A few windows would need to be replaced, the bathroom updates would be fairly extensive, and the wiring work would take weeks and require that almost every square inch of the place get repainted, but overall he had been right: the Bastida had good bones.

But my shoulders sagged with the immensity of it all. It would be weeks with Tibèri coming and going. With me having to clear out one room for wiring while painting the one that was just completed. Not to mention I could see the rest of my nest egg from Mamà dissipating before my very eyes. Tibèri couldn't help but see how daunted I was in the very furrow of my brow.

"It will be a clean slate for this house," he said. "Fresh paint, some new fixtures . . . You'll be able to make the place your own."

I forced a smile. "I like that idea. The house does deserve a clean slate."

"Just please promise me no stark New York minimalism or neon colors or anything horrific," Tibèri pleaded.

"No. The Tardieux loved this place and I don't want to change it entirely. Just restore it to its former glory in most cases. Though bringing the bathrooms into the twenty-first century doesn't sound awful."

"That I can agree to." Tibèri extended his hand. "Shall we get started?"

Chapter 16

Later that week, I sat down at my laptop, which I'd placed on the antique desk in the smallest of the bedrooms, and tried to come up with words. Some way to describe what life in Sainte-Colombe was like. Carol's request to submit an article for the Travel section of the paper weighed heavy on my shoulders. The offer wouldn't be valid forever, and I had to submit something before she forgot altogether that she had extended the invitation. And it was the gig I'd always wanted. It wouldn't be a huge paycheck, but it might lead to others. It would do something to refill my coffers, which wouldn't remain flush for long with all the renovations the house needed.

I didn't begrudge a cent that I'd spent on the house or improvements to it, but the lack of income was unsettling. But try as I might, the words to describe Sainte-Colombe wouldn't come. Astre sat on the desk's upper shelf, peering down at the blinking cursor and blank screen. He emitted a meow that sounded questioning.

"I know, I know." I scratched under his chin. "You don't

understand why I'm sitting here staring at this infernal box instead of playing outside with you."

He meowed again but circled around and curled into a ball and began purring.

So easily contented. How lucky for him. And though he'd been my pet for only a short time, I was comforted by his presence in a way I'd never experienced. He followed me from room to room and was rarely more than a few feet away from whatever I was doing. While dogs got the credit for being the loyal species, I couldn't imagine even the most faithful golden retriever who was more attached to his human than Astre was to me.

As he shifted position and curled up on my desk, my eyes drifted back to the screen. The idea of putting anything into words about rebuilding my life in Provence seemed impossible. How to describe the colors, sounds, and smells that were so beyond what I'd ever experienced back in New York? It felt like a task that was bigger than I was.

I snapped the laptop shut and picked up the snoozing kitten so we might explore the greenhouse together. He loved batting at the leaves, and the plants somehow seemed to enjoy his carefree presence, provided he wasn't too exuberant.

Estèva had told me to explore my gift, and she was right. I'd felt the lure of the greenhouse since I'd planted the seeds, spending far more time there than the plants really required, and I still couldn't parse out a reason for it.

I grabbed my "greenhouse notebook" from where it rested on the workbench and took a new set of measurements to chart the growth. The basil was now six centimeters larger than it was two days before. It was a quick-growing annual—I'd read as much many times—but it was already larger than the average fully grown basil plant and should have needed another week or two to reach full maturity. The lemongrass, verbena, rosemary, sage, and thyme were already growing at similarly impressive rates.

It was a magnificent bounty of plants, to be sure, and I had to think of more uses for them. Certainly, I could dry them and make blends of herbs de Provence. I could freeze some for use in winter, but it seemed like I could do more.

I heard a rapping at the greenhouse door and saw Jenofa standing there. I waved her in.

"What a crop you have, cara. And so early in the season too."

I didn't bother playing it down with her. While Tibèri would offer up a rational explanation for it all, Jenofa would be open to other, less obvious explanations. "They're growing much faster and larger than they should." I tapped my notebook with the tip of my blue ballpoint pen.

"It is your gift," she said. "Like your mother, and her mother before her. And even before."

"A curious gift." I rubbed the bridge of my nose and exhaled. "A pile of herbs, far more than I could ever use in five years' time."

"I doubt they're meant for you to use, at least not for you alone. Your mother embroidered dresses and such for herself, but the gift didn't manifest for her own garments. Only the ones she made for others."

"Estèva says I need to explore my gift. But I can't even begin to think of uses for it all."

"She is right. Why not experiment? Tisanes, infused oils, balms, and ointments. Listen to them, my dear. Let them guide you." She gestured to the plants with her walking stick.

Could she possibly know that I could feel the energy of the plants? That I could read them as plainly as any book?

She and Estèva were right. If I was given any sort of gift, I might as well test it out.

"Would you care to stay awhile? I can get you something to drink if you like."

"Of course. I'd love to sit with you." She patted my arm and I felt a surge. She had an ache in her fingers. The calendula began to hum softly.

She needs a salve. Calendula with some rose oil.

"Jenofa, can you tell me where to get beeswax?"

"Why yes, cara. What for?"

"Salve for your fingers."

"Don't trouble yourself over that, child," she said, absent-mindedly rubbing her joints.

"Your fingers bother you." I swallowed back my hesitancy and admitted, "The calendula will help. It *wants* to."

"And you worry about what to do with your crop." Her lips turned upward. "It isn't for you to decide. They will tell you what they want."

"Some of these herbs are annuals. The basil, the parsley, the coriander—the calendula—will live only one season. What if I misuse it? It has such a short time to live."

"So have we all, my dear, so have we all. The oregano, the mint, they are lucky and have many chances. The rosemary and thyme are luckier still to be evergreen and last to see much of our comings and goings. But it was never their choice. Like us, they must do the best with the life they are given. But you are wise to want to make their lives count. Perhaps it's why they chose to make you their steward."

"I don't know. But I can make you a salve. It might help."

"Very well," Jenofa said. "It would be wrong of me to refuse a gift. Just as it would be wrong for you to refuse yours. I will help you, but first, you'll do as you promised and sit with an old woman and have a drink."

We walked to the back porch, and I fetched some iced tea I'd brewed with some of the verbena left over from the cookies. It was crisp and refreshing on a day when the temperatures had taxed us all.

"You know, cara, I was around when your mother discovered her gift. She was perhaps ten years younger than you are now. It scared her, too, even though she still had the guidance of her mother. But she learned how to master it well. The way the calendula called to you? It was the same way your mother knew how to use red thread or blue. Whether to embroider a sunflower or a bird. She learned to trust herself. You will do the same."

"Mom never embroidered much when I was growing up." I thought of the hair ribbon and the quilt, but there were few other examples.

"She had her reasons, I suspect. I think it was something she preferred to leave behind," Jenofa said. "And that is your right too. You don't have to keep a single plant in the house. Your sweet grandmother stopped keeping animals after your mother left. It became too much of a burden. She preferred to help others with theirs from time to time. Like so many things in life, it will go through phases. Phases where your gift is the center of your being and phases where it wanes in importance. And neither is better than the other."

"But why? Why our family? What makes us so different?"

"That is an impossible question to answer, my dear. Some say that the women of your family were blessed because you willingly took on the burden of teaching our ways. Others say it was a curse from the French for defying them, but that it backfired. The truth has been lost to legend, I'm afraid, but the origin of your gift matters far less than what you do with it."

Jenofa finished her tea and gave me the names of an olive farmer and a beekeeper who could see to my needs. I trundled out in the little green Peugeot to collect the beeswax. Later that afternoon, I took a large cupful of olive oil and let it soak with cuttings of calendula and a few drops of rose oil I'd found a week before at the pharmacy. I added in a small sprig of mint on a whim and let the mixture rest. I melted the beeswax, then added the oil mixture and poured it into little jars to harden.

As I worked, I focused on wishes for good health and a respite from pain. The end result smelled divine, and though I wasn't sure if it would truly do Jenofa any good, at least the scent would distract her for a few moments. And it was a small step toward figuring out what purpose, if any, this gift might serve.

Chapter 17

Estèva, curious to see my progress, met me at the Bastida the following week for the promised shopping excursion rather than having me join her in town. She walked from room to room, exploring with the same attentiveness one might use in a world-class museum. "You've done a lot already. It's an amazing transformation, really. The house has been empty since I was a toddler. It grew creepier and creepier as time went on. We made up ghost stories about the place."

Tibèri had wired two rooms already: the master bedroom and the kitchen. So the spaces I used most often were back up and running. I'd rejected out of hand the idea of painting each room the same shade of beige or taupe as was standard in many suburban homes in America. Sure, it made sense to turn the house into a blank slate when you were selling it, but why not *live* in the space when it's yours? I'd chosen a soft green for the kitchen, which suited it beautifully. For the bedroom I matched the existing terra-cotta fairly closely, and it looked far better for the fresh coat of paint.

As each room was completed, I'd decide on the color that seemed to best fit the space. Tibèri had been exceedingly helpful in securing paint samples from Valensole and gallons of the stuff once I'd selected a color. He didn't have time to paint, and I'd save considerable money doing it on my own, but he did lend me some of his painting gear and took the time to give me pointers on how to paint well and efficiently. He'd praised the job I'd done so far, saying I did as good a job "cutting in" the ceiling as he'd ever been able to do.

I snapped out of my thoughts to respond to Estèva. "It's coming along, and I am really starting to love the place. But it *does* feel a bit haunted sometimes," I admitted. "And with the town bruèissa coming to live here, a whole new generation of children will have fodder for their stories."

"Do you really hold any stock in what they say about the women in your family? Papi loves to tell all kinds of folk stories about the village, but I never thought he believed them."

I had a greenhouse full of rosemary, thyme, basil, and all manner of herbs that seemed to be defying the laws of nature, but I felt strange voicing my feelings aloud. "I don't know. I've never considered myself to be either a believer or a skeptic of such things. But the place does feel special."

I unlocked the doors to the little green car and, to my relief, Estèva asked for the keys.

"Where are we going?"

"You'll see." She handled the car with a confidence I envied, and we toured the winding roads from Sainte-Colombe down to Aix-en-Provence. It was still early in the tourist season, so the place wasn't totally overrun with visitors. I imagined in another month the place would be packed elbow to elbow with travelers. But even so, the place buzzed with midmorning energy. People, even the laziest of the jet-lagged tourists, were up and enjoying the peak of their espresso buzz.

Estèva's face glowed as we left the car behind and merged with the people walking along the sidewalks.

"This place is so . . . *alive*," she said, though I couldn't be sure it was to me and not just to herself.

"I only spent two nights here after I flew in from New York. I should have taken more time to explore the place, but I was eager to get to Sainte-Colombe."

"Few people have ever said that," she snorted. She must have noticed my expression drop slightly. "I know the place is charming and idyllic, but . . ."

"I've spent a couple of months there. You've been here your whole life. I understand."

We ducked into a clothing shop, not in one of the more upscale parts of town but on one of the narrow side streets that tourists rarely bothered with. Estèva held up loose flowing dresses against my frame, soft tunics, loose gauzy pants, and featherlight skirts. Yellows, blues, greens, pinks . . . Not a hint of black on any of them.

"The trick, you'll find, to beating the heat in a place without air-conditioning is actually to cover yourself as much as you can, but in light fabrics. Desert people wear long caftans. Shorts and tees won't protect you."

"Sound reasoning," I said. "It's lovely stuff."

"You came with an expert. I know where the locals shop. And what will serve you best."

Estèva made me try it all on, and it felt as comfortable as walking around in nightgowns and pajamas. No wonder the Provençaux were so laid-back. No constricting cuts, no itchy wool. It was like being able to breathe more deeply than I'd been able to in years. I spun for her in a cotton dress that had a bold pattern in colors that ranged from turquoise to aqua to teal. She nodded her approval.

"It's lovely. We just need to add a belt."

She returned with a thick belt in a light brown that gave the look a bit more definition. She added some light scarves and a couple of pairs of sandals to my pile, along with a big floppy hat. She spoke with the shopkeeper and insisted I wear the blue dress out of the shop along with the belt, sandals, and hat.

"You'll look like one of us," she proclaimed.

"Well, I certainly don't look like a New Yorker."

I was surprised at the modest total when the shopkeeper rang up my purchases and carefully arranged them into three large bags. Even in a fashionable town like Aix, the prices didn't compete with the sticker shock in New York.

We returned to the car and Estèva heaved a sigh as I shut the trunk after stowing the bags. She held up her hands as if she expected me to lob the keys at her. She was used to running to Aix for one or two errands and rushing back home to run the shop or teach her classes.

"We don't have to go back just yet, do we?" I asked. "You don't teach for another few hours, yes?"

"Not until tomorrow," she said, her face brightening.

"I'm no expert, but I've never heard of a ladies' shopping expedition that didn't involve a decadent lunch. Which will be my treat. And you need to show me around. All I know of Aix is the train station, the car dealership, and a less-than-amazing hotel."

She beamed. "Sounds great to me."

We meandered around the streets of Aix, admiring fountains and quaint buildings in the old town. We stopped in to marvel at the architecture of the cathedral and enjoyed the quaint tree-lined Cours Mirabeau. We chose a little place for lunch that was tucked in along one of the side streets, hoping to find one of the hidden gems, rather than the busy hot spots.

The little restaurant specialized in seafood, so Estèva chose a *salade niçoise* with fresh tuna while I opted for mussels steamed in a white wine and butter sauce. The notes of shallot, bay leaves, and parsley played on the dryness of the wine and the creaminess of the drawn butter. Each bite was more flavorful than the last, and I couldn't help but wonder if there wasn't something that made everything taste *more* here. It wasn't just that the food tasted better here . . . There was simply more flavor to it. The same with color. I'd never seen a bluer sky, or the earth a more vibrant shade of red, than in Provence.

And for once, I had a meal in a restaurant and didn't feel compelled to critique it. That was almost as freeing as exchanging the heavy woolen *New York Tribune* clothes for the gauzy dresses.

Provence took every ounce of what was good and somehow made it . . . *more*.

"Thank you for this," Estèva said. "It feels good to be someplace different for a while."

"I already love Sainte-Colombe. But I don't think it's healthy for you to chain yourself to it. Let's make a promise to come to Aix, or some other little jaunt from the village, once or twice a month. A trip to Marseille or the beach, whenever we can manage it. You'll be of more service to your papi and the students if you're not burned out all the time."

"I'd really like that," she said. "Since you do seem set on staying, can I ask you something?"

"What's that?"

"What are your feelings for Tibèri?" She didn't quite make eye contact as she fiddled with her napkin.

My stomach lurched. "Oh, are you and he . . . ?"

"Oh no, no, no. It would be like dating my brother. No."

I felt a wave of relief and it annoyed me intensely. "Oh, that's good." I fumbled for words. "We've had a truce. Agreed to be friends. It's a good thing."

"So you like him then?"

"I mean, sure I do. He's one of the nicest people I've ever met, once you get past the bristly first impression."

"He is," Estèva confirmed, tucking a lock of her brown-black hair behind her ear. "He's a good man. One of the very best. And he deserves the same in a woman."

"And you don't think—?"

"I think you're lovely," Estèva interjected, her brown eyes not meeting mine. "Smart, funny, kind. All the things I would want for one of my dearest friends. But I also think you've been through a lot recently. I'm just asking you to treat his feelings with care. Take things slowly and don't break promises. That's all."

There was something she wasn't saying. Something about Tibèri. A secret? A past heartbreak? It was hard to say. But that she felt the need to protect her friend spoke volumes about both. "That seems entirely fair. You have my word."

"I *am* glad you've come to town. I didn't realize how much I needed a friend."

I reached over and patted her hand. "I didn't either."

Later, as we headed back to the car, we passed by a kitchenware shop. It had flashing gadgets, gleaming pots and pans, and even more importantly, a steady stream of shoppers. Estèva's mood fizzled like a depleted sparkler at the end of the Fourth of July parade. The glimmer that had been in her eyes during our excursion went out with a sputter, and I felt the weight of her worries creep back.

There had to be a way to make their little kitchenware shop profitable again. And a way for Estèva to regain a sense of purpose. There had to be a way to persuade the rectorat to keep the school in Sainte-Colombe so those efforts wouldn't be wasted on a doomed village. But the question was . . . how?

Chapter 18

SUMMER

Tempy,

I hope you've had a good time in Sainte-Colombe. I'm sure it's every bit as beautiful as Mom described it when we were kids. I know that things didn't end on a great note between us, or between you and Grandmother either, but it's time to put all that in the past and come together as a family. You belong back here with us. It's what Dad would have wanted. I'll arrange for a flight home next week as soon as I hear back from you.

All my best,
Wal

All your best? Was that really your best, Wal?

Tempèsta

I slammed the Backspace key to delete the passive-aggressive response to Wal's email and snapped the laptop lid shut, though slowing my force before the lid made contact with the keyboard. Replacing the archaic laptop would have been a headache. An expensive one.

Wal's email was a thinly disguised order to return home, likely issued by Grandmother Luddington. And it was perplexing too. Why would she even want me back? She'd spent the last fifteen years of my life making it abundantly clear that she wanted nothing more than for me to be as far from her as I could manage. I spent my teen years banished to my room when she couldn't think of someplace out of the house for me to be. Long summer camps several states away, after-school activities that kept me out of the house until bedtime. Once I left for college, there were always excuses as to why I should avoid coming home for the holidays. Dad often made those calls, but I could always hear the sound of Grandmother pulling the strings while he danced for her.

"Hey, kiddo. You must have loads of friends you're dying to spend time with over break, don'tcha? Things are just so crazy with work, I don't think I'd be able to spend much time with you. I'd hate for you to miss out on a good time."

So fall break, Thanksgiving week, and spring break were spent alone in the dorms. I didn't mind it, for the most part. I enjoyed the solitude after weeks of forced socialization. I took courses over the summers to keep up with my triple major, but winter break usually meant an awkward Christmas on some college friend's parents' couch.

It wasn't ideal, but it was fine. Except the year that Wal screwed up and posted a picture on social media from the Bahamas. Dad's arm was wrapped around his shoulders. I suspected the picture was taken by Grandmother. As good as I was at controlling my temper, I couldn't help but send a scathing text to the three of them that time.

Don't be so sensitive, Wal had texted back. It was a spur-of-the-moment thing. We figured you already had plans.

But they couldn't be bothered to ask. They couldn't be bothered to wonder if I *wanted* to be included. And likely because Grandmother convinced them it was better that I wasn't. And despite their claims to the contrary, Christmas was booked months in advance at any resort Lucille would have deigned to visit in the Bahamas. They planned it with every intention of excluding me.

She'd have been clever. *"Oh, I'm sure with good grades like hers, she's working too hard to take the time to come home. Best leave her to work."* Or *"She's likely quite popular. I don't think we ought to pressure her to come along. We'd hate to put her in the awkward position of turning down an invitation."*

It was the way she did things with Dad and Wal. Manipulating to get her way.

With me she was more direct. *"Don't you have anyplace to be aside from under our feet? If you tried harder, you'd have more friends, you know."*

But no matter which tack she took, the meaning was the same— she didn't want me around.

So why now? Why did she want me back all of a sudden? There had to be a reason, and that reason would have nothing to do with me and my best interests. I decided to ignore Wal's message altogether and hope he'd get the message.

He didn't ask how things were going here. He didn't ask if I was okay.

He didn't know I'd bought a home and was laying down roots here.

And to be fair, I never volunteered that information either, but the audacity to assume I'd come running back at his beck and call . . . My face grew tight and the blood rushed to my cheeks.

I decided it was dangerous to be in the same room with any device that I might use to communicate with my idiot brother, so I sought refuge in the greenhouse. I watered and pruned, not bothering with measurements or my usual slow puttering at the tables as I spoke with the plants. I didn't stop to *feel* as I usually did.

I cut back the blue hyssop, which was growing unruly. I tossed the cuttings on the kitchen counter with more force than was necessary. It was no fault of the hyssop plant that my brother was an insensitive tool, but the motion of flinging down the cuttings was just a bit therapeutic.

I decided to make a hyssop lemonade by chopping up the hyssop and letting it steep in boiling water with some honey. It was a lovely honey, the perfect shade of golden amber, bought from the beekeeper who had also sold me beeswax for Jenofa's salve. The aroma of the honey-and-hyssop infusion filled the kitchen like notes of lilting music as I juiced lemons. I strained the juice and added it to the hyssop infusion and put the lot of it in a jug in the refrigerator to chill and to enable the flavors to develop further.

I heard a knock at the door and found Tibèri, grubby from a day on the job.

"Hey, I came to get started on wiring the third bedroom," he said by way of greeting. "I had time this afternoon, so I decided to come by."

The truce was working. He was affable. Neighborly. I'd take that improvement over the bristly resentment I'd felt from him before. "Of course, but you must be parched. Let me get you some lemonade first."

"That sounds wonderful. I hope you don't mind me coming over unannounced like this."

I paused to consider. Perhaps I should have been more insistent about keeping him at arm's length. I thought about Estèva's warning and didn't want to string him along if she was right and he was somehow hoping for more than friendship. But the truth was that he, Estèva, and Jenofa were the first people who'd ever felt comfortable enough for such familiarity. When I searched my feelings, I realized how nice it was to have people in my life who felt like they didn't need an invitation—or even a reason beyond seeking my company—to drop by.

"I don't mind at all." I led him to the kitchen where I poured two glasses of the hyssop lemonade. "But something is bothering you."

He shrugged. Clearly something *was* bothering him, but he was trying to remain stoic about it. "Matthieu is moving to Aix."

"Oh, I'm sorry. That will be a loss for Sainte-Colombe."

He glanced up at me as he accepted the lemonade. "Thanks for that. It's not about losing a friend. He's too good a friend for an hour's drive to make a real difference. But . . ."

"He was one of the few young ones left in town."

"Right. I knew it was coming. And it makes sense for him. And for his mother. But it doesn't make it easier. And if the rectorat makes good on the threat of pulling the school, his business will dry up entirely. Better he start networking in Aix sooner rather than later."

"No. It's a lousy situation."

"It is. But this is delicious." He raised his glass to mine as we settled on the back porch. And indeed it was. The honey was less cloying than plain sugar and the hyssop provided a floral flavor somewhere between mint and lavender.

The second sip wasn't quite as satisfying as the first, but I passed it off as my palate adjusting to the new flavor.

"Blue is a good color for you." He indicated the dress. It had been a few days since the shopping excursion, and he'd yet to see me in any of my new clothes. I tried to ignore the little thrill that he'd noticed and been bold enough to say so.

"A bit of color is refreshing," I said. All my black clothes were relegated to the back of my wardrobe now, and I had already considered putting them in a different room altogether.

"Why did you wear so much black before if you don't like it?"

"Fitting in. I wanted to look the part of a sleek New York journalist. They tended to wear a lot of black at my old paper. A lot of people in New York do."

"I would think in a field like that, standing out might serve you well."

I cocked my head, considering his words. "Perhaps you're right." I'd been so conditioned to try to blend in that I never attempted anything else.

Tibèri took what was perhaps his fourth or fifth sip of the lemonade. "I'm not sure why, but the taste is growing overwhelmingly bitter."

I tasted from my own glass, and it was all I could do not to spit it back out again. "Mine too. Let me get some more honey."

We both added several spoonfuls of honey, but it was even more bitter than before we added it.

"You haven't poisoned us, have you?" he asked, the tone of his voice still mostly humorous.

"Unless the plant was belladonna labeled as hyssop, no." I ran off to the greenhouse to hunt down the offending plant. The hyssop I'd pruned had wilted and was on its last legs.

"This plant was healthy two hours ago." I examined the leaves. "Resplendently healthy."

"I wonder if some sort of fungus or insect got to it. Though I don't know of that sort of thing happening so quickly."

"No, there isn't a fungus or a parasite harming this plant," I said, sure of what was ailing the poor thing. Whereas the plants usually welcomed me and encouraged my attentions, I got the distinct impression the hyssop was *afraid* of me.

I'd scared it. Hurt its feelings. Poured all the negativity I was feeling toward Wal into it. And it was suffering from that negativity just as certainly as if it suffered from blight or aphids.

It was all my fault.

"I'm so very sorry, little one. So very sorry."

I rubbed the wilted stalks, the penitence radiating from my fingers. I offered it fresh water and spoke soothing words as Tibèri looked on, baffled.

I just hoped it would be enough to save it.

Chapter 19

It's so great of you to come help around here," Estèva said as
I wiped dust from an old cast-iron kettle and helped to tidy
the shelves. More distressing was the dust that had accumulated on the small selection of new products. I ran a mental
inventory of all the things in my own kitchen. Almost everything
there was half a century old, mechanical rather than electric, and
still functioned perfectly.

"Happy to help." The rag I used had quickly transformed
from bleached-white and pristine to dingy gray. Estèva cleaned
constantly, but the inventory simply wasn't changing out. The
dust settled on these once-useful, once-prized kitchen imple-
ments, and I couldn't help but feel like they were sorry for being
passed over.

Wal would have shaken his head at the whole thing. The
kitchen in his Manhattan bachelor pad, though rarely used, was
stocked with all the trimmings an avid kitchen-gadget enthusi-
ast would long for. The sort that did all the mundane food prep

tasks in a fraction of the time but broke within a couple of years. "Designed obsolescence," he'd called it. I called it wasteful. He had told me I was being naive, and that not "overengineering" products had helped the economy surge for decades. Gone were the days of refrigerators that would last for two generations or cocottes that could be passed down from mother to daughter like the one I'd purchased here.

To make peace with him, I admitted that his Italian espresso machine was a marvel. It had cost the equivalent of three months of my rent, but I didn't begrudge him that particular luxury. And of all the things he had in his kitchen, it was the one that would last for a decade or two and was worth the expense. It seemed a better use of money than dropping five or six dollars on a to-go coffee on the way to work, if one had the money to invest up front. If I managed to come up with some ideas and sell a slew of articles, I'd consider having Estèva order one in for me. Or she'd suggest a quick overnight girls' trip to Tuscany to buy one in person, which, given the expense of such a machine, didn't feel like that much of an additional extravagance. Of course, I'd have to start with a first article before I could reach anything like a "slew," but there was no use in reminding myself that I'd hardly written a syllable since I arrived at the Bastida.

Estèva had me to the shop when old Pau was having his nap. He still wasn't comfortable with my presence, but she hoped I could win him over. I thought about offering him some of my pesto, but there was no chance he'd sample anything I made.

Estèva looked defeated as she wiped the dust from a set of mixing bowls. How long had they been on the shelves? Five years? Ten? How many dozens of times had she wiped the dust from them?

But she didn't toss down her rag in despair as she cleaned them once again. She didn't even sigh in discontentment. She was several years beyond that.

Just then, we heard the bell ring as the front door opened. Estèva nearly jumped from her skin in surprise. "Hello, Jenofa," she said, when she regained her composure. "Wonderful to see you. Can I help you with something?"

"I was actually looking for our Tempèsta. When she wasn't at home, I thought she might be here with you." Her face was bright as though she carried good news, though Estèva was crestfallen for the briefest of moments when she realized she hadn't come to shop.

Jenofa turned to me. "The salve you have made is a wonder. I haven't been free of pain in my hands in so very long. I was able to paint without discomfort this morning for the first time in a decade."

"Oh, Jenofa, I am so glad." I put aside the French custom of the *les bises* and took her into a hug *à l'américaine*. "I hoped it would help."

"More than any doctor has been able to. They told me it was just the nature of growing old. Something to accept and cope with. And for years I told myself that the pain I felt when I was painting would help sharpen my art. Would make me more deliberate with every stroke of the brush. But no, it merely caused me to think far too much about each one instead of going with my instinct in the moment."

"I know something of that." The way my instincts let me feel the hum of each herb in the greenhouse. The way I knew which branches to prune and which to leave alone. Which plants needed more water and which should be left dry for a few more hours.

The poor hyssop plant was still recovering from the other day. I'd mollified it by giving it preferential placement on the greenhouse table, nearest the window it preferred. I added rich soil to the pot and massaged its leaves between my thumb and forefinger as I whispered a few especially kind words. She still didn't trust me fully, but I could sense she wouldn't remain mad forever. I wouldn't prune that hyssop again this season unless it was necessary for her health. I wouldn't use her in any recipes until she bloomed anew next year. We would have a chance to try again then, and that gave me hope.

"Cara, your gift is a powerful one, and yours to use as you see fit, but I hope you will use it for the betterment of others as best you can."

Estèva's face grew stormy for a moment, as she clearly pondered unpleasant thoughts. Perhaps she was jealous that it was my family who'd been blessed—or cursed—with this weird gift and felt somehow left out.

"It's not as spectacular as you think." I desperately wanted to downplay Jenofa's grand pronouncement, sensing how ill at ease it made Estèva. "I have a knack with herbs. It's just a green thumb and a bit of intuition."

I flashed a look at Jenofa, who caught on to what I was trying to do.

"You have seen her plants for yourself, Estèva. She has a remarkable green thumb, just as you have a remarkable gift for language. We all have our talents, do we not? But I think you can help each other. Tempèsta, you should make a few things for Estèva to sell here in the store. I can spread the word that the Sarrauts are experimenting with some new offerings in the shop."

"It's an interesting idea," Estèva said. "Though I'm not sure Papi will approve."

"You leave Pau to me. It's more than interesting, and you know it. It will give Tempèsta an outlet for her talents, it will bring a new vitality to the shop, and hopefully it will result in a bit of income for both of you."

Estèva arched her brows, expectant. "Well, what do you think?"

I exhaled slowly. Would I be able to supply them with enough products to make the venture worthwhile? It might be worth trying.

And as I thought of the neglected laptop that Astre was increasingly viewing as a preferred napping surface, I certainly didn't have any better ideas forthcoming.

"Let's try it. No guarantees, but it can't hurt."

Estèva's face brightened, but then she became hesitant. "*Deu meu*, where will we put things, though? This place is a jumble. Papi won't let me get rid of this old stuff to make way for anything new."

And suddenly, my Luddington roots kicked into action. "He's right. We don't need to get rid of it. We need to sell it. To city dwellers who are tired of buying the same cheap kitchen gear over and over again. We need to appeal to the home cooks in Aix, Marseille, Montpellier. Those who want things that will last and who can't afford to buy new at a premium."

"No one will see all this old stuff and think of it as anything other than a collection of antiques. No one wants to cook with this stuff anymore. They want shiny new pots and pans and fancy gadgets. They might want a few of these pieces for decoration . . ."

"Some of them will, sure. And some of these pieces would be safer as decorative statement pieces, and we'll sell them that way. But I think serious cooks will love this stuff. In the States some people scour yard sales and flea markets for this sort of thing. I'm sure there's a similar sentiment here in France too. Newer isn't always better."

"But how will we lure the city people here?" Estèva wasn't shooting down the idea, just thinking of the logistics.

"We don't. Though that may happen, too, and we'll make it a lovely shopping experience for them. But even more important, we're going to get you a website and rebrand this place. It's not 'used kitchen gear.' It's 'premium, heirloom-quality kitchen goods.'"

"This is very smart." Jenofa thunked her cane against the tile floor to punctuate her sentence. "I never thought I'd say this, but I think it is a good thing you brought a little of New York here to Sainte-Colombe, cara."

"Even New York has its virtues," I agreed. "And marketing prowess is one of them."

Estèva twirled me around in a hug. "It's brilliant."

"It just might be. It may flop, but it won't cost much to try. And we'll become well acquainted with the post office staff. I'll do something nice for them to thank them."

"Those lemon cookies," Estèva said, remembering our little feast on the night of the festival.

"Lemon?" Jenofa asked.

"Lemon and verbena . . ."

"What did you do to them?" Estèva asked. "I've been dreaming about them for weeks. You *are* a bruèissa, aren't you?"

"Nothing nefarious. All I did was *hope* you'd be friends with me. It wouldn't be right to change your thoughts or even influence them much . . . I just hoped for you to have an open mind."

"Well, that was always going to happen, but you should bring me more of those cookies on the regular to make sure of it," she deadpanned, causing Jenofa to laugh. "So you know how to make a website and all? I can barely run a computer. The local schools didn't even get computers until about fifteen years ago, and they're not exactly state of the art."

"Absolutely," I said. "Nothing fancy, mind you. But we want

a fresh design with clean lines anyway, which means it'll be easy enough to do. What we need to start are some great photos."

For the next few hours we used my phone to photograph the fifty most valuable or interesting pieces from the shop. Vintage copper, cast iron, and brightly colored ceramics. Antique appliances that would outlast any of their electric counterparts. Thankfully my phone was one of my few high-end indulgences, necessary for the job, and boasted a better camera than most stand-alone devices. And thanks to my work at the paper, I'd learned how to use the right settings to get a professional-looking photo.

"The Analog Kitchen," I said. "That's what we call the site. The Analog Kitchen, hosted by Sarraut's of Provence."

"Clever." As an artist, Jenofa had a good eye for helping us compose the photographs and use the light to show the wares at their best advantage. "Ah, you see this painted tureen here? With the roses? Isabèu Fabre was given this as a wedding gift from her mother-in-law. Maria Fabre hand-painted it just for Isabèu, but she never used it out of spite. From what I hear, Isabèu overheard a comment Maria made about her wedding dress and never forgave her. And so this pretty tureen, so lovingly made, has never served a bowl of soup in all its days."

"How sad!" I snapped several pictures of it, fiddling with some settings in hopes that they'd turn out well enough for editing on the larger screen back at the Bastida.

Estèva giggled. "You speak as though simple objects have feelings."

"Don't they?" I asked. "Even if we imagine them. Jenofa, what other pieces in the shop do you know about? We should include this on the website. People will love it."

Estèva rolled her eyes, but Jenofa seemed to have an anecdote for most every piece we photographed that day.

Later that evening, energized by the thrill of a new project, I sat at my desk and insisted that Astre let me reclaim the warm clicky-box he'd grown so fond of sleeping on. He happily removed himself to my lap and watched the screen as I edited photos and tinkered with website templates, seemingly enraptured by the colors and shapes on the screen.

Eventually, he curled up and purred on my lap, content to sleep where he knew he was safe and protected, while I picked away at the website into the wee hours of the morning, his purrs spurring me on. And though I was bleary-eyed in the morning, I was gratified to feel like I had a real purpose.

Chapter 20

For two weeks I was immersed in two endeavors: enhancing Estèva's website and developing products for the shop. The former project was in decent shape after a few days, but adding in the anecdotes about the pieces and the provenance of some of the more valuable antiques took longer.

Going out to the greenhouse in my bare feet, shears and watering can at the ready, was the perfect counterpart to hours in front of the laptop screen. I also stopped every few days to paint a newly wired room and clean up after Tibèri had updated another space.

Silly though it was, I told the herbs what I was doing. I wanted to make things, whatever they were, to help people. Like the salve for Jenofa, I wanted the herbs themselves to give me the ideas for the things we should make for the store.

I made a few more salves and lotions. I dabbled with making some lavender candles with the leftover beeswax. I made dressings and jellies. I dried some herbs to sell in packets so the customers could use them as they saw fit, but I included some ideas on the labels Jenofa designed.

As soon as the website went live and we began moving some of the inventory from the kitchenware shop, I'd have the stock we'd need to fill the shelves. Things that people would consume and need more of. It was a lot more sustainable business for Estèva, and while I tried to keep my emotions even while I crafted products for the shop, I couldn't help but instill the wish that the endeavor would be successful.

The familiar knock sounded at the greenhouse door. "And what is our friendly village bruèissa working on today?" Jenofa asked.

"Some tea blends. Yerba, mint, and hooded skullcap to help with sleep. Verbena and sage are invigorating." I showed her the blends I was drying, and she waved a hand over them as though she were preparing to taste a fine Bordeaux.

"Exquisite," she said. "Perhaps you'll send me home with a bit of the yerba blend to try tonight."

"Of course. Free product for you, always." I put a few of the tea bags I'd already prepared in her marketing basket that she had hoisted on one arm.

"Thank you, cara. I haven't seen Estèva this happy since she was a girl. It warms my heart to see her so. And the plants are not the only thing blooming in this greenhouse."

"I needed to be replanted," I said, flashing a grin. "Not enough sunshine in New York."

Jenofa chuckled in turn. "Well put. I think your mother felt the same way before she left. The pot that suits one plant is too cramped for another."

"I've been meaning to ask you. You told me weeks ago that the house where she grew up isn't here any longer. Would you be

AIMIE K. RUNYAN

willing to take me to the site at least? Do you think the owners would mind?"

Her gaze dropped to the earthen floor of the greenhouse, and she exhaled slowly. "Not at all, cara. We can go now if you wish. It isn't far."

"Great. If you navigate, I'll drive."

"No need for the car. We can walk from here. Follow me."

We left the greenhouse and walked along the dirt path that led from the Bastida to Jenofa's house. Before we reached her house, we turned on a little side path that headed south, parallel to where my property ran. We walked for a few minutes and came to the foundation of an old house that had burned many years before.

"This was your grandparents' house," Jenofa said quietly, reverently, as if we were in church. I half-expected her to make the sign of the cross.

"What happened?"

"Your grandmother grew tired and sickly soon after your mamà left to marry the American. She became forgetful and clumsy, though she'd been robust and healthy before. One day, there was a fire and she barely escaped with her life."

"Oh my goodness, how awful." I couldn't take my eyes from the rubble that had been the house where my mother grew up.

"Your grandmother sold the property to a developer who never did anything with it. That money was what your mother passed to you. And, after all this time, it was that money that brought you back to us."

"Mamà rarely spoke of her parents. Though when she did, it was lovingly."

"Your mamà probably had only whispers of memories of your

papi. She was so young when he passed. But your grandmother, Sibilia, was a resourceful woman and gave your mamà a happy girl-hood. When Nadaleta left, something in Sibilia's spirit broke."

"Where did she go after the fire?" I imagined the frightened woman running from the burning building right where we stood. I felt an involuntary shiver knowing the terror she must have felt.

"She came to stay with me. She was my very best friend and clos-est neighbor my whole life. I couldn't let her go anywhere else. I hoped I might be able to nurse her back to health, to help her regain some of her vitality under my care. But it wasn't to be. She died a year later."

"Was she much older than you?" I asked.

"Six months younger, cara. She was only fifty-five years old when she died. But she aged so quickly . . . it was like caring for an eighty-year-old woman. To witness it was one of the great tragedies of my life," she said. She didn't bother wiping the tears from her eyes or stilling the quaver in her voice.

"Why did Mamà leave her? Surely she couldn't have known how her mother would react."

"No. Your mother had her reasons for leaving, but Sibilia never let on how she was failing. When they spoke, Sibilia made herself sound as strong and vibrant as she always was. She forbade me from letting your mamà know how bad things had gotten. We did tell her of the fire, but your grandmother made it sound like a small thing. As though coming to stay with me was like a pajama party from your American movies."

"But why would she hide such a thing? I'm sure Mamà would have come home. Dad had the resources to make it happen."

"I think your mamie wanted your mother to settle into her new life without the burdens of the past. As much as your grandmother missed her, she wanted Nadaleta to have a happy time in America and to spend her energy on her new family."

"That's sad. Mamà wouldn't have wanted that. She would have brought Mamie to Connecticut or found some other way to help. I think she ended up hurting Mamà more than she shielded her from anything."

"What a wise lesson from one so young." Jenofa finally wiped away her tears. "I walk by this place every day and always offer a prayer for your mamie. And now your mamà. I remember the past. I honor the past. But I try not to let it take away from my present joys and future happiness. I don't always succeed in that, but I do well enough."

I wrapped an arm around Jenofa. "Thank you for being so good to Sibilia. I wish I could have known her."

"As do I, cara. But I am honored that I get to see the woman her granddaughter is becoming. I think she would be proud of you."

I could think of no words equal to the compliment she'd just paid me, and I wiped away tears of my own.

"It seems fitting that you bought Bastida Èrbadoça with the proceeds from the sale of your family land, Tempèsta. Though it's a shame nothing has been done with it."

"Tibèri is right. Every empty parcel is a wasted opportunity for the town."

"And a reminder," she said. Of what, she didn't clarify.

I walked Jenofa home. Though I'd planned to spend the heat of the afternoon in the comfort of the house working on the website for Estèva, I found I couldn't sit still. I went back to the greenhouse, Astre in arms, to continue plotting out new products for the store.

I concocted cologne with rose oil and thyme. I infused each blend in alcohol and hoped in a few weeks, some of the blends would make for pleasant-smelling perfumes and colognes. The honest, woody scent of thyme would suit Jenofa; the delicate rose would be perfect for Estèva. For Tibèri I combined rosemary with cinnamon and cloves. I tried, with some success, to emulate the delicate perfume Mamà wore. The last remnants remained in the crystal bottle in a place of honor on my dresser, which I uncorked from time to time, trying to remember her scent.

For Wal I made a clean-smelling blend of citrus and vetiver. And I knew, though I wanted to deny it, that I couldn't leave his emails unanswered forever.

Chapter 21

"C ome in quickly," Estèva beckoned, her eyes scanning
the street. "He'll be back soon."

I walked into Sarraut's, my laptop in tow, prepared
to show Estèva and Pau the final draft of the website I'd created for the shop. I'd also made printed copies of short versions
of the stories, which Estèva promised to translate into French
and Occitan for display in the shop. The idea was to remind
the locals of why these pieces were special. While selling to the
wider world was a sound financial plan, it would also be nice
for some of the pieces to stay in the village where they had been
loved for so long.

In addition to my laptop case, I also lugged a large plastic crate
with all manner of creations from my greenhouse, all designed
for sale at Sarraut's. Everything from herb mixes for cooking to
skin creams, and a bit of everything in between. Estèva wanted
to make a display of them to see whether it would increase traffic
to the store.

"Pau doesn't know that I'm coming?" I asked, setting the crate at my feet.

"Not yet," she admitted. "I thought it might be better to catch him unaware so he wouldn't find a reason to stay away."

A lump formed in my gut. How would Pau react to our plans for the website and modernization? *I* knew Jenofa was absolutely right about Estèva, but convincing the good mayor would be another thing entirely. Even if sales went through the roof, I could see him being opposed to the website out of sheer stubbornness.

I took a breath and remembered something my dad used to say: "*You don't always need to win people over to your side right away. Persuading them that an idea is worth a chance is often enough.*"

It was one of the maxims he'd spouted over dinner, and one I'd taken to heart. Wal probably had it tattooed on his forearm. At the very least it was transcribed in one of the many leather notebooks Wal had filled with such pearls of wisdom from Dad.

"Do you know what you want to do if he says no?" I clutched my ancient tank of a laptop across my chest like a shield. As if Pau might come in at any moment and hurl one of the ancient steel meat axes at my chest if he saw me trespassing in his store.

It was ridiculous—or so I hoped.

"Come on now, have some faith!" Estèva cried. She scanned the printed copies of the stories and thumbed through them, nodding as she read.

"Oh my word, Estèva, speak!" I finally burst out. "What are you thinking?"

"I can't believe it, but you make *me* want to buy this junk. I've dusted that stupid teapot one hundred seventy-four times if I've dusted it once, and now I want it for myself."

I walked over to the shelf where an ivory teapot painted with pansies had resided—perhaps for fifty years or more—and handed it to her. It had been a first wedding anniversary gift to a woman in the village from an impoverished aunt, who had wanted desperately to give her favorite niece a proper silver tea service. But it had been the best she could manage. The niece had treasured it and grown pansies each year as a tribute to her beloved aunt, whom many suspected was actually her mother who had been forced to give her love child to her married sister for the sake of appearances. "I'm sure your grandfather owes you back wages."

She laughed and held it to her bosom. "I might hate it less if it were mine and not something to unload. These stories are magnificent."

"Thanks to you and Jenofa. I just merely took them down for you."

"No, you cast a spell with words, you bruèissa. This is just brilliant. People will be clamoring for this stuff, and I won't have to dust the same pans over and over again until the end of time."

"Like the culinary equivalent of Sisyphus," I supplied. "But instead of a giant boulder on your shoulders, it's soup tureens and cast-iron pots."

"And they're just as heavy, let me assure you."

"I know." I patted her sloped shoulders, knowing it wasn't their actual weight that troubled her. "I hope this helps, but even if it doesn't, it's worth trying. The setup didn't take too long because I know my limits as a web designer and used templates. If you can manage the site fees to take it live, I won't charge you for my time if you don't mind me using the shop as idea fodder for some articles."

"Not at all. It needs to be good for something."

"This place will be. It is already."

"You know, it's a shame Papi is so stuck in his ways. You're the only one who seems to believe in this place as much as he does. The difference is that you just might be able to turn this place into a viable business, and he refuses to change."

The pit in my stomach returned. "You're sure he won't mind about the website?" I asked.

"There's only one way to find out: we'll show him. Offline first, with these." She indicated the printed pages.

I heaved a sigh. "I hope you're right. I just don't want him thinking the website is some form of black magic sent to undermine him or some such nonsense."

Estèva laughed. "Oh, he will, but I'll handle it. And when he's ready, we'll put some of your stock on the shelves. You did bring some, yes?"

I nodded. "I hope I didn't haul this in only to fail."

She didn't offer platitudes; just nodded.

The tinkling of the store bell sounded, as if to punctuate her nod, and a cool trickle of sweat formed at the nape of my neck.

"Estèva, you need to remind Tibèri about the faucet in the kitchen!" Pau bellowed, not yet having seen me. I flinched at the sight of his rounded frame and the wisps of hair on top of his head, but he'd retreated into the shop office, so I remained hidden from view.

"I did two weeks ago!" she hollered back, shuffling things on the shelf. Clearly this mode of conversation, yelling between the two rooms, was normal for them. "He'll be here Thursday when the parts come in."

"Why so long?"

"He can't make the mail deliver the thing any faster, Papi. They didn't have one in Valensole that would work, so he had to special-order it from some place in Marseille. The sink isn't a standard size, and it would be a bear to cut new faucet holes in it. It's designed to survive German artillery fire after all."

"You have that right. Made to last. Not like the flimsy new garbage." Pau grumbled more and I caught something about "back in my day."

Estèva rolled her eyes.

Yes, back in his day, the plumber could have gotten a faucet from Valensole in less than an hour that would have worked with their sink without a problem. But back then, his archaic cast-iron sink was the norm, not the exception. And that was, perhaps, the root of his frustration. He didn't see why he should have to get rid of a perfectly functional sink in order to get replacement parts in the immediate region. I sympathized with him, but the world had changed while he was poring over his ledgers.

"We have a guest," Estèva announced, finally prompting Pau to lift his head. He locked eyes with me and shook his head.

"You can help her with her purchases and see her out." An improvement—Pau wasn't casting me out immediately. Either he was softening to me or he was in control of his faculties enough to recognize how dire his financial situation was and was willing to take my money. Either way, it might make him more agreeable to our ideas.

Estèva led me to the office area, and I felt like I was entering a sacred shrine. Worse, it was Pau's sacred shrine and he wasn't pleased to have me encroach upon its sanctity.

"Actually, Papi, we have something to show you. Tempèsta has been working on a website for the shop so we might be able to increase our reach. If we move some inventory, we could have more shelf space for new products with a good profit margin. It could really help us out."

"New 'products' indeed. They will help our pocketbook because all the modern junk breaks in a week. Not at Sarraut's." Pau shook his head emphatically and cast his eyes back at his ledger.

"You're right, Papi." Estèva's admission caused Pau's head to snap up in surprise. He clearly wasn't used to hearing these words from her. Not recently. "Sarraut's stands for quality, and that's what we want. Solid-quality kitchenwares from the best names."

I dared to chime in. "And if there's enough interest with the website, we can continue to seek out the top-quality antique cookware. You said it yourself: they don't make things like they used to, and we can find more treasures all over Provence and make sure they're not going to waste in an attic or, worse, in a landfill."

I could envision Estèva scouring estate sales throughout the south and even beyond. It could be an opportunity for her to get outside of Sainte-Colombe regularly and to shift the direction of the shop into something that might challenge her.

His brown eyes looked like they wanted to bore a hole in my soul. Estèva rescued me by handing him the stories.

"Tempèsta has written up the stories about all the pieces in the shop. Jenofa and I talked her ear off. Sharing them will entice people to bring a piece of Sainte-Colombe into their homes. She'd include them on the website and we could display the stories in the shop, once I translate them."

Pau's eyes scanned the sheets Estèva handed him, but after a few moments, he handed them back. "I never was much for English. Top marks in Latin and Occitan, though."

I smiled. "I wish I'd had the chance to learn Occitan. My mother recited the poem 'Miréio' to me, but not much else."

Pau looked at me and said:

"Tu, la perleto de Prouvènço,
Tu, lou soulèu de ma jouvènço.
Sara-ti di que iéu, ansin, dóu glas mourtau

Tant lèu te vegue tressusanto?
Sara-ti di, vous gràndi Santo,
Que l'aurés visite angounisanto
E de-bado embrasssa vósti sacra lindau?"

"That's when Vincen realizes Mirèio is going to die and curses the saints for allowing her to suffer, isn't it?" I asked, remembering it was one of the passages Mamà repeated often for the beauty of its language. *"You, the pearl of Provence, the sun of my youth . . ."* One could hear the anguish in Vincen's pleas, and in Pau's.

"Very good," Estèva said, always the teacher. "Your mother didn't neglect the classics."

"She was a Vielescot," Pau said with grudging respect. "She might have lived in America, but she never would have been able to truly leave Sainte-Colombe behind."

I paused. "I think you're right about that. Whenever I saw her staring out a window or with a faraway look in her eyes, I think her heart was here."

"You speak the truth. Her specter will never leave us be. I see evidence of this standing before me in my very office."

I turned to Estèva, not knowing how to take a further step on the minefield of Pau's temper, which was clearly growing more dangerous.

"She wants to help us, Papi. *I* want her help. I want to make Sarraut's a real business again. If you search your heart, you know we need to make some changes."

He waved his hand in dismissal. "Put up the stories if you must. Though there isn't a soul in this town who doesn't know them all."

"It's for those who don't, Papi." Estèva rushed around the side of the desk and kissed his forehead. *"Gramàssi."*

"You're welcome, stubborn girl."

He actually smiled, very faintly, though it vanished when he saw I was still in his office.

"Estèva, spare your papi's old knees and fetch me a coffee and a *chocolatine* from the café like a good girl, will you?"

"Yes, Papi." She clearly didn't want to spoil what little bit of good graces he'd bestowed on us.

"I will have a word with Tempèsta before she leaves," he added.

Estèva and I exchanged looks, and I was not keen on what word Pau had waiting for me, but she obeyed and ducked out of the shop to the nearby café.

"I appreciate that you want to help Estèva. She has modern ideas and she sees in you a willing collaborator in turning some of those ideas of hers into reality."

"Th-thank you—" I stammered.

"It wasn't a compliment," he barked.

I forced myself to breathe and allow my pulse to slow. "I hope you know my intentions are only to help your business, to no benefit of my own, and to make Estèva happier."

"Every Vielescot woman has intentions as pure as the snow on Mont Ventoux in the first light of the new year. That is what makes you so dangerous. Just because actions are founded in good intentions doesn't mean they won't lead to disaster."

I felt the marrow chill in my bones. Not knowing what else to say, I mumbled a goodbye and left the shop. I didn't wait for Estèva to return. I considered telling her what he'd said about the Vielescot women, but she'd dismiss it all as his silly superstition.

But even if they were just silly superstitions, he believed them, and that made them every bit as dangerous as if they were true.

Chapter 22

I put on a gauzy red dress with flowers and the wide belt
Estèva had helped pick out during our excursion to Aix.
I'd prepared a dinner for Tibèri, a small thank-you for the
many projects he'd taken on around the Bastida. He worked for
minimal pay, so a meal seemed like a small way to begin to show
my appreciation for all he'd done. And it seemed appropriate to
thank him with food that had, in part, been grown thanks to his
efforts.

There was a lot left to do—rooms that were still a clutter of
antiques, windows that needed to be replaced, and miles of
walls to paint—but room by room it was becoming a home.
And the kitchen was the heart of it. I had chicken simmering
in a red sauce with onion, garlic, oregano, thyme, and sage. The
vegetable course was a small tian, more elegant than my usual
ratatouille, with carefully arranged layers of green zucchini, yellow squash, red pepper, and purple eggplant. I had baked a rosemary focaccia before the day got too hot and rounded the meal

out with lime-and-mint margaritas with a splash of orange liqueur, and lemon-basil sorbet for dessert.

I'd had a carefree afternoon in the kitchen, cooking as soft classical music lilted through the speakers of the ancient boom box I'd moved to the hub of the house. I twirled barefoot on the tile floor as I moved from pot to oven and as I mixed the small pitcher of margaritas and added the little sprigs of mint. The summer was growing hotter by the day, and the tartness of the freshly squeezed lime juice, mixed with a bit of tequila, balanced with the sweet, orange Grand Marnier and mint so robust it seemed like it was still growing, would be the perfect refreshment.

He entered the house, knocking on the doorway but not pausing before he entered. He was long past such formality, and there was something comforting in that.

"You smell wonderful," he said.

"Lavender perfume with orange and spices. One of the new products for Sarraut's if Pau warms to the idea. Perhaps a bit premature, but I wanted to try it."

"Estèva is beside herself over what you two are doing. I don't know that I've ever seen her so happy, aside from when she's teaching."

"Me too. It's been so fun acting like a mad scientist in a laboratory."

"Sainte-Colombe's own Madame Curie," he said.

I blushed at the compliment, wishing I could be a bit more suave, but I never would be without a personality transplant. But we were building a friendship, and my acting like a lovesick teenager was not going to earn me points with him.

I willed the color in my cheeks to subside and screwed on a smile. "The food needs a little time. Come see the website. It's nearly finished."

I led him to the room I'd claimed as my office and fired up the laptop, much to Astre's chagrin. Tibèri scrolled through the site, which I'd kept sleek and black so the photos would pop on the screen. He clicked on several to see the details and the little anecdotes provided by Jenofa.

"I really hope this helps," he said, not pulling his eyes from the screen. "But even if it doesn't move a single mixing spoon, you did a kind thing for her. She's been stuck in a rut for too long."

"It was nothing. I'm surprised she didn't come up with the idea herself."

"I'm not at all. Sarraut's has been run in the same way for generations. People get stuck in their ways and it's hard to change. I love my village and I love our ways, but there is no sense in clinging to traditions that do not serve us."

"Especially when it comes to business. She deserves better. And if one business improves, it could help bolster the others in town."

Which could save . . . everything.

"You're a good friend." Tibèri finally looked up from the laptop. There was an expression on his face I couldn't read, and I pushed it from my mind.

We went back to the kitchen and served up the food on a platter and took it to the back porch so we could eat while we enjoyed the breeze.

"If I believed in magic, I'd be forced to believe all the rumors about the women in your family," Tibèri said after his first bite of chicken. "This is incredible."

"So you don't believe what Jenofa says about me? You don't think I'm a bruèissa?"

Jenofa seemed to believe it all without question. She would have been shocked if I didn't have a gift, given what she believed about my family. Estèva seemed willing enough to believe it, though she wasn't as enthusiastic about it as Jenofa, almost tentative when the subject came up.

Tibèri was the only one who truly doubted that there was anything extraordinary about what had happened.

"No, I think you have talent in the greenhouse. Probably because you're so enthusiastic about your new ventures and you don't have the day-to-day slog to pull your attention from it. You're talented in the kitchen too," he said as he sampled from each of the dishes. "You have an understanding of how the flavors work together. But I would hate to dismiss your talent as some mystical gift when it's something you're working to . . . well, cultivate."

I ignored the pun and leaned back in my chair. "So you don't think I have magic?" I wasn't sure how I felt about it. I was self-aware enough to know that I did enjoy the notion of being special. Even more, I enjoyed the idea of the connection with my mother. Did it matter what Tibèri thought? Perhaps. But it didn't have to change how I felt.

"I never said that. I absolutely do think you have magic. The magic to make Estèva believe in herself again . . . The magic to bring this place to life when none of the rest of us could."

Tears pricked at my eyes. "Do you really mean that?"

"I make it a habit not to say things I don't mean, Tempèsta. I have a feeling, deep in my soul, that you may be one of the best things that has ever happened to this village since Mistral visited almost two hundred years ago. You could be our saving grace."

He reached over and, so gently I wasn't sure if I was imagining it, stroked my face with the back of his finger.

"I want to help. It seems like the least I could do for my mother's memory. It's what she would have wanted."

"I don't doubt that," Tibèri said. "But don't forget to figure out what *you* want in the process. You matter too. And I worry your family forgot to remind you of that."

"More than you know." I turned away to glance at the vibrant hues of violet and ochre on the horizon as the sun began to fade from the sky.

"That isn't fair to you," Tibèri said in a tone that was somehow both soothing and seething in the same breath.

"No, it wasn't. But life rarely is. Isn't that how the old axiom goes?"

"I think so. But it isn't how things *should* be. Not for someone as kind and giving as you." His expression changed from pensive to something else. "Has anyone ever told you how amazing you look in red?"

I tried my best to ignore the heat in my cheeks that was, quite likely, serving to make my face the same shade as the featherlight dress. "No, I don't believe so," I sputtered. "I haven't worn it in a while."

"I'm glad Estèva got you out of those heavy things. You were dressed for a funeral instead of the market."

"Gee, thanks." I playfully punched his shoulder. "I appreciate that."

"I'm serious. You're too beautiful to hide behind dark clothes." He reached over, played with a tendril of my hair for a moment, and tucked it behind my ear. First the caress with the back of his finger, now this. He'd never attempted such familiar gestures before, and as much as I enjoyed these gentle touches, I felt something drop in my gut.

I sat back and studied his face. He didn't appear to have indulged in too many margaritas, but there was a softness in his expression

I'd only seen when he was looking at his mother or occasionally Jenofa.

"Tibèri, I am so glad we've decided to forge a friendship. The village is a lonely place without you and Estèva. So please don't take this question the wrong way: Where is all this coming from?" I gestured between us.

Tibèri exhaled slowly and locked eyes with me. "I don't know, really. I just feel like I'm getting out of my own way."

"I-I'm not sure what you mean." My voice rose an octave and acquired a bit of an adolescent squeak. And then the panic in my gut grew more insistent. He'd cleaned his plate, but his glass still had an inch of the green cocktail remaining. I slid it from his reach.

"All I know is that nothing in this town was going to change before you arrived. I don't know if things will now that you're here, but for the first time in my adult life, it feels like they might. And that's a pretty incredible sensation after ten years of feeling like I was trying to push a stalled car with the emergency brake on, if you know what I mean. Maybe a train would be a more apt metaphor."

"I think I do," I said, thinking of all the times I'd tried to elicit some sort of emotion—any emotion—out of my family.

"You *are* magic, Tempèsta. Don't let anyone tell you different." And then he leaned over and brushed his lips against mine. At first it was soft, tentative. Then he grew bolder and pulled me into his arms.

Alarm bells rang in my head. People didn't downshift this quickly. We'd been on a slow road from what was just a few steps away from open hostility to a budding friendship. Then, in the space of the flap of a hummingbird's wings, he was kissing me.

And heaven knew, I enjoyed it . . . but something felt off.

I pushed myself away, gently but firmly, and tried to catch my breath. "Tibèri . . ."

"I know. I don't know what came over me, but . . ."

I looked at the food, mostly consumed. And the half pitcher of margaritas that remained. I picked it up and sniffed it, as if I'd be able to detect its magic through scent like I would soured milk.

Tibèri shook his head as though coming out of a trance. "You didn't use your little magic herbs on me, did you?"

There was basil and oregano in the chicken. And mint—lots of it—in the margaritas. But unlike the pesto, when I had focused so much of my energy on the people of Sainte-Colombe liking me, there had been no intention when I made this meal for Tibèri. I had simply been . . . happy.

I shook my head. "No, I don't think so. Really and truly. I don't think it would happen unless I *tried*."

"That's what I'm worried about," Tibèri said. "Would you deliberately try to . . . ?"

"Drug you with a love potion? No. Even if I wanted . . . that. How would I feel knowing I had to dupe you into caring about me with some plants? It would be pretty hollow, don't you think?"

He sat back, thoughtful. My words seemed to ring true for him, but he didn't seem completely mollified either.

He looked as though he was on the point of a response when we both received a flurry of texts on our phones. I pulled mine out from the pocket of my dress and saw they were all from Estèva, sent to both Tibèri and me:

Come to the shop as soon as you can. Papi has gone mad.

Chapter 23

Tibèri, Estèva, and I stood in the entryway to Sarraut's to find the small sampling of my products Estèva must have finally decided to display strewn all over the floor. Old Pau was pacing about the office area ranting in Occitan. Something told me the vocabulary he used was not the kind that Estèva taught the children.

Tibèri spoke a few words to him in Occitan, which only resulted in him pointing a finger at me and muttering more angry words, the only one of which I recognized was *bruèissa*.

I stood there, helpless, as Tibèri spoke firmly to the old man and Estèva fought to control her tears as she tried to reason with him. I considered helping to clean up the mess he'd made but was worried it would just set him off more. Whatever spell Tibèri had been under had been broken, and he was as frosty as he'd been weeks before. I was pretty sure we'd lost whatever progress we'd made toward building a friendship, but at the very least, he wouldn't tolerate any of the abuse Pau was hurling in my direction.

"What's going on?" I finally whispered to Tibèri.

"Oh, the old man's finally gone dotty, that's all." He heaved a sigh and pinched the bridge of his nose. "Nothing for you to worry about."

"He keeps pointing to me and calling me a witch, so I think it is."

"He thinks you're trying to bewitch the town with your potions." Estèva stood shaking, her arms folded over her chest. She shot her grandfather a withering look.

Tibèri shot Estèva an exasperated look of his own.

"What? She deserves to know what he's saying. She's not a child," Estèva retorted.

I tempered a scream of frustration. "It's fine, Tibèri. I'd rather know what he's saying."

Tibèri just shook his head and gritted his teeth.

Pau spoke a few more words and Estèva finally snapped. She took one of the drinking glasses that had been on the shelf since before she was born and smashed it to the ground. Pau gestured to the shards of glass and, I assumed, chastised her for breaking merchandise.

"*J'en ai marre!*" She switched from Occitan to French, which meant I could actually understand what she was saying. "I've had enough. You want to keep everything the same. You don't want to even try the website that might actually move some of this junk. It's not 1952 anymore. We can't keep this up. Tempèsta graciously offered to help save this business, and you act like a spoiled child."

"How dare you speak to your grandfather like this," he replied. "After all I've done for you."

"Oh yes, you've done so much. You kept me tethered to a tiny village with no opportunity and a dying business. Papi, we sold less than a thousand euros in merchandise last year. We can't keep going like this."

"Sarraut's has been in business for over one hundred years. We never needed a website or this garbage"—he gestured to my products on the floor—"to stay afloat before. We didn't need it then; we don't need it now."

"You stubborn old man. Times have changed. You've seen the books. We're not running a business; we're curating a museum no one wants to visit. We're sitting in this musty old building day after day, watching sixty-year-old pots and pans tarnish and rust. I am tired of living like this. If it weren't for the little bit of money the parents pay for Occitan lessons, we'd be without power and water."

"Estèva, I didn't raise you to be so disrespectful."

"And my mother didn't raise me to live a life like this." Estèva threw her arms up in the air.

"Don't you dare invoke your mother's name in this conversation. She lived and died for this shop. For this village."

"She died for it, yes," Estèva spat out. "She ran herself so ragged she didn't know she was sick until it was too late. And she didn't want the same for me. She told me so before she died, but you guilted me into staying. You know what? Do what you want. Run this business like your customers are coming in on their horse-drawn buggies for all I care. But I'm through. Sarraut's will die with you."

She let out a long breath and her shoulders lowered several inches. I didn't know if she meant it, but she'd wanted to say it for a long time.

"You can't mean that," he said. "You would drop the torch just like that?"

"There's nothing left to carry, Papi. If you let me modernize the place, there might be something worth saving, but I won't spend another day here to no purpose, surrounded by a pile of junk. I'm not going to waste my life carrying a torch that went out thirty-five years ago."

The old man went purple in his plump face. "I won't hear you speak like this to me, Estèva. Not as long as you live under my roof."

She rolled her eyes at the tired rebuke. "I don't want to spend another night under this roof. I'll get a job in Aix and never step foot back in this damned shop or this miserable village again."

"Estèva!" He slammed a fist on the counter.

But she had already bounded up the stairs to the apartment she shared with her grandfather. I could hear her thudding around upstairs as she gathered her things. Tibèri began gathering up the products I'd made from the floor.

I felt hesitant to move, given how vehemently Pau opposed my being in his shop, but it was better not to let him think I feared him. Thankfully very little was seriously damaged, but without an outlet to sell it, it mattered little. All the same, I hated to waste the products I'd made from the herbs I tended so lovingly.

Tibèri shoved past Pau to collect a few of the bags that eagerly awaited patrons who didn't come so we could haul what was salvageable back home.

Estèva retuned with a suitcase and a few duffels. Likely all her worldly possessions.

"Good luck with the shop, Papi. You're going to need it. Tibèri, Tempèsta, if I might trouble you for a ride."

Tibèri took her suitcase, and I one of her duffels. We crossed the square to his utility van, stowed Estèva's things, and clambered inside. I sat in the back with her to provide a bit of comfort.

"Where will you stay?" Tibèri asked as Estèva shut the door.

She turned to me. "Can I stay at the Bastida? At least until I find a job?"

"Absolutely. I'd love to have you."

And as we pulled away from the square, Estèva dissolved into tears. I rubbed her back but made no attempt to quiet her.

Tibèri was less able to accept that she needed to have her tears. "I'll talk to Pau, Estèva. He can be made to see reason. You won't have to move to Aix."

She shook her head. "You don't understand, Tibèri. For the first time in my life, I am free of that wretched place. I couldn't be happier."

Chapter 24

T ibèri managed not to make eye contact with me at all. He was still convinced I'd slipped a love potion into the margarita and was nowhere near ready to process any other truth. He'd have to simmer for a while before I could reason with him, and I'd have to learn to cope with the stony silence until he came around again. I couldn't shake the sensation of loneliness that pricked at my neck at the realization.

But to Estèva, he was kinder. "You are going to land on your feet." He scooped up Astre and handed him to Estèva. "If you need lessons, just ask this little guy."

The kitten meowed his approval and burrowed into Estèva's arms.

"Faithless cad," I said with a wink.

Tibèri seemed about to make a snide remark, but he swallowed it back. His expression seemed pained as he turned to Estèva. If she was serious about moving to Aix, it would be another blow to the village. And more, it would be a blow to him personally.

Tibèri gave Estèva three *bises* before departing. He merely nodded in my direction, and I suspected that was more for Estèva's benefit than mine.

"I am so sorry to have ruined your evening," she said as Tibèri drove away. "If I'd known you two were having a date, I wouldn't have barged in."

"Don't worry about it. You needed help. It was a good thing Tibèri was here. Don't spare it another thought. Let's figure out a place for you to sleep." *And it wasn't a date, no matter that for a few minutes, at least, it felt like one. A good one.*

The second-largest bedroom had been rewired and tinted a soft blue and was thankfully outfitted with a comfortable bed and freshly laundered linens. Chances were, she wouldn't land a job in just a day or two, and she'd need a comfortable place to stay. Thinking of the death-trap sleeper sofa at Dad's house—Wal's house now—I certainly knew how important it was to have a nook where I felt welcomed.

Estèva ran her fingers through her dark hair and rubbed her eyes once we got her things stowed in the room. She examined her face in the mirror, with dark circles under her large brown eyes that her skillful application of concealer and mascara couldn't hide entirely, and sighed in defeat.

"I'll try to get out of your hair as soon as I can. It's so good of you to take me in."

I wrapped an arm around her and gave her a side squeeze. "No more of that. I hope you'll stay awhile. I have plenty of space. Don't feel like you have to rush into anything. You can take your time and decide what's the right path for you to take next. I'll be glad for the company."

She wrapped me in a hug. "You're a good friend, Tempèsta. Thank you."

"Listen, you've had a crap show of an evening and you are officially taking a weekend off. I have all sorts of herbal spa products made by yours truly, not to mention food and drink. We are going to enjoy the dickens out of the 'scratch-and-dent' products, courtesy of one Pau Sarraut."

Estèva giggled. We went to the kitchen and organized the products that Tibèri and I had scavenged off the floor and sorted them into two piles: salable and nonsalable. I'd concocted face masks, foot scrubs, and shampoos in addition to the teas, dressings, and marinades, and we could have a weekend as grand as at any fancy New York spa that Grandmother Luddington enjoyed so much.

"Let's do masks first," she said. "Marshmallow and licorice root in oat flour. Sounds like a dessert for the face. It'll be decadent."

"It will be once we add in the pitcher of margaritas and the sorbet that Tibèri and I never finished." I regarded the pitcher skeptically. Had my concoction really bewitched Tibèri beyond the usual powers unleashed by the fickle gods of tequila?

"I'd say again that I feel bad about spoiling your evening . . . but I'll be honest, right now I don't. Booze and dessert sound like heaven."

"Good." I set a kettle to heat for warm water to add to the mask powder and fetched glasses and bowls for the margaritas and sorbet. We settled in around the kitchen table, applied our masks, and sat back with our refreshments as they hardened.

"This stuff is incredible." Estèva touched the goop on the side of her face. "Better than the pharmacy masks they sell in tubes."

"Not bad. I have a ton of it if you want more." A laugh escaped my lips. "Be sure to tell your friends."

"It just isn't fair. You put in all that hard work to supply the shop with new products, not to mention the website."

"I finished the website just this afternoon." I knew it was likely a waste of time, given Pau's reaction to the idea, but I couldn't help but finish it. Estèva never had the chance to see the draft, so I grabbed my laptop to show her. She scrolled through the sleek page, admiring the photos and reading the stories.

"Oh, the stories," she said on a breath. The forsaken soup tureen. The copper cake mold that had passed down through four generations of women as part of their trousseau on their wedding days. It fell into old Pau's hands when the last family member left town. A cast-iron kettle that had been brought in because the owner didn't like wrestling with the nine-pound beast of a teapot when she got older and arthritis set into her hands. Her home was tiny, and she didn't have room to keep an extra kettle lying around, but as it had belonged to her mother, she couldn't bear to put it out with the trash.

"This is so beautiful," Estèva said, her masked-up face glowing from the computer screen. "You make all that junk seem like treasures."

"Because they are. Each dish, each pot, each pepper grinder was once a prized gift to a young couple or a valued investment that a couple scrimped and saved for to help run the heart of their home. Things people cared about so much that they entrusted them to Sarraut's when they could no longer take them with them."

"You understand Papi's mission more than I ever did." She wiped a lone tear from her cheek and smeared her mask. I tossed her a warm washcloth to wipe it off. She admired her clean face in a little mirror that hung in the kitchen, presumably there so the lady of the house could quickly check her hair and the state of her lipstick before answering the door when she was expecting company. Her skin was fresh and dewy. "Amazing." She rubbed the back of her finger against her cheek.

"He doesn't quite have it right, though," I said. "If he fully understood the value of Sarraut's, he'd know that he's not honoring the memories those items represent by letting them collect dust in the shop. He'd do better to honor them by making sure they ended up in homes that would appreciate them."

"He needs to see this for himself," Jenofa called from the kitchen doorway. "You'll forgive me, I let myself in."

"Come join the party." I stood to pour her a margarita.

"I've been to see your papi." Jenofa accepted the glass and raised it to me in a silent toast before putting it to her lips. "I don't go out at night much anymore, but my telephone lit up. Most of your neighbors overheard the fight."

"Of course they did. The joys of village life. You can't poop without everyone knowing what color it is." Estèva took a long drink from her glass, which I refilled from the pitcher. I slid some of Jenofa's special salve across the table to Estèva. She opened the can and exhaled with pleasure as the tension eased from her joints.

"Don't be crass, Estèva," Jenofa said, her tone uncharacteristically sharp. Then she broke into a mischievous smile. "Even if you're right."

"What did Pau have to say?" I asked.

"That Estèva is the most ungrateful, wretched girl to ever draw breath. And that you, Tempèsta, have turned her away from him. Poisoned her with your concoctions and your ideas."

"Of all the asinine . . ." Estèva swore under her breath.

"Precisely what I told him." Jenofa gently clinked her glass against Estèva's. "You're a good girl. You've sacrificed so much, especially when your mamà died."

Estèva turned to me. "I was studying political science at the university in Aix. And I was good at it too. I hoped to go on for an advanced degree at the Sorbonne. Mamà was so proud. But she died in my second year. The cancer hit hard and fast. One minute she was feeling a little run-down; the next she was gone."

I reached over and touched her hand. It wasn't unlike my mother's story. Though Estèva did get a few more years with hers, it was still far too soon.

"Papi begged me to come home and stay with him. He claimed he couldn't go on without help in the shop. Mamà never told me how bad things were there. From the way Papi spoke, you'd have thought Sarraut's was outselling Galeries Lafayette. It wasn't long before I realized that there was nothing for me to do in the shop but wait for the dust to collect so I could wipe it all down again. But Papi always convinced me to stay."

"Stubborn old fool," Jenofa said. "I've never met a man as resistant to change as Pau Sarraut."

"Mamà reorganized the place once." Estèva's eyes glazed over as she reminisced. "He yelled for a week straight. When he finally calmed down, he realized how much easier it was to find things, but he never once apologized."

"He is the most exasperating sort of man," Jenofa agreed. "The kind that makes me glad I never married. But I do hope you will be able to mend things in time."

"You think I should go back? Apologize and smooth things over?" The color drained from Estèva's face.

"Heavens no, child. If you go back now, things will return to the way they always have been within a quarter of an hour. No, you must wait for him to come to you. If he does, you don't give in. Not an inch."

I agreed. "You can't go back to that."

Estèva's tears rolled down her face unrestrained, but she smiled. She smiled because she knew she wasn't alone.

"I do hope Pau will see sense. As much of a dunderhead as he is, I hate for him to lose you."

"He doesn't have to," Estèva said. "But it's up to him to mend the fences. After ten years wasted in that wretched store, I'm simply fresh out of nails."

Chapter 25

I
t was obscenely early on a Friday morning, and my hands shook as I set out the products fit to sell after Pau's temper tantrum. Estèva had arranged for me to have a space at the weekly Friday market, and Tibèri had scrounged up a folding table from his mother's garage for my use. I found a hand-embroidered tablecloth in one of the closets at the Bastida that was a riot of flowers and greens that would pull together the display. It was beautifully done. Was it Liorada's handiwork, or perhaps one of her predecessors? In any case it felt like a much-needed good luck charm as I faced the village. I'd salvaged herb mixes and infused oils for cooking, which fit in well with a farmers market, and I added a selection of salves, perfumes, and soaps to see how they sold at such a venue.

"It looks great," Estèva said, returning from a chat at one of the neighboring booths. "It'll be good to have something different. Having the same dozen tables peddling their stuff week after week gets boring, and people will be happy for a little change."

"I'm not sure this village is all that enamored with change. Even small ones. This feels like a mistake." My table was in a prominent spot, no doubt owing to Estèva's and Tibèri's influence, and I felt exposed. I could imagine other people reacting the way Pau had done, and I was terrified.

"I may regret saying this, but give the people a chance to surprise you. I truly hope they will."

I wanted to share her faith, but I found myself unable to voice the same enthusiasm.

"Listen, even if these old cranks don't bite, we can take the show on the road to a few other towns to see if we fare any better. The only thing we stand to waste today is a bit of time."

I put my hand on the table and forced myself to breathe. The tension eased slightly. "You're right. It's going to be fine. It won't even be time wasted. We'll get a sense of what works and what doesn't. Market research for next to nothing."

"You're starting to sound like the New York City businesswoman you swore you aren't," Tibèri said, approaching the table. He was supremely annoyed with me. I could tell he was trying to conceal it, but he was failing at the endeavor rather abysmally. He wasn't dressed for work but was dressed in shorts, a relaxed short-sleeved button-up, and sandals—dressed for a day of marketing in town.

My hopes to make a bit of profit from the market amped up even more. He was able to make a better living than most in town, but I could tell he had more leisure than he wanted. Even if he despised me, I still wanted to see his business thrive. I wanted that for all the Sainte-Colombiens.

"I was raised by a New York businessman and have a degree in finance," I said. "Some of it was bound to rub off, no matter how I tried to resist it."

"Well, let's put all that business acumen to work and make enough so we can retire young and wealthy, shall we?" Estèva nudged me with her elbow.

"I'm going to stick close," Tibèri said. "Just in case you need me."

The steel band around my nerves loosened further still, and my face split into a smile. "Thank you," I managed to squeak.

He would be there, and I found the idea of his watchful presence so soothing it was, oddly enough, almost unsettling. Estèva slid me a sideways glance and subtly shook her head. Now wasn't the time to get distracted with an analysis of Tibèri's gallant gesture or my idiotic reaction to it.

Within a quarter of an hour, most of the villagers who weren't involved in running a booth came to do their weekly shopping. The local grocery shop supplied the people with the bulk of their dry goods and pantry staples, but most of the people in town preferred to buy seasonal products from the outdoor market. There was something to be said for a round of cheese from the woman who tended the cows and sheep that produced the milk to make it. Something to be said for shaking the hand of the man who grew the tomatoes you'd later turn into sauce.

I loved that there was a closeness to the food here, which I didn't feel in New York. Sure, there were wonderful markets there, and the farm-to-table movement was so immense it was almost passé, but there was a real difference in eating products grown just minutes away and cultivated with generations of knowledge of the land.

Jenofa strolled about the market, chatting with friends and buying some greens for her salads. She smiled but, like Tibèri, was keeping a bit of distance to allow others to approach. To my great astonishment the first to approach my table were Méric and Donat, the recipients of my infamous pesto, along with their wives,

Anne-Laure and Rosalinde. The women walked two paces behind their husbands and seemed to be lost in happy conversation after too many years of having them cut short by the feud between the men.

"It is good to see you taking part in things." Donat extended his hand to mine. "Your mother and grandmother were important in teaching about our heritage and would be proud to see you here."

"Oh, thank you. I hope you're right."

"Of course he is," Méric chimed in. "Though it still pains me to say it. It was a shame when your mamà left, but we're thrilled to have you back with us, even if she cannot be."

Something akin to warmth filled my chest as I helped them select some basil oil and a mix of dried herbs. Rosalinde was delighted with my lavender soap and Anne-Laure chose some salve for her hands that troubled her, much like Jenofa's.

They were just about to settle up when Pau stormed across the square from the shop. He strode right up to the booth, ignoring me completely, and stood to his full height in front of his granddaughter. "Estèva, there are matters in the shop that require your attention."

"I no longer work for you. Those matters are your own affair now."

Donat emitted a low hiss; whether it was disapproval or surprise, I couldn't quite tell.

"We will discuss this in private," Pau insisted, pointing with his cane.

"We won't discuss this at all. Not after what you did to Tempèsta's things." Estèva gestured to the products on the table.

At this point Tibèri and Jenofa approached, both wearing expressions of concern. Tibèri crossed his arms over his chest in his trademark "I am not in the mood for this" pose.

"What did he do?" Rosalinde turned to Pau with a pinched face and arms akimbo.

"I invited Tempèsta to create a small display with some of her things as a gesture of welcome to the village. And to liven up the shop a bit," Estèva said. "And my grandfather made a mess of her products and acted disgracefully."

"Pau Sarraut, did you really do such a thing?" Méric asked.

Pau refused to look his neighbor in the face. "Estèva, I forbid you from associating with this woman," Pau barked. "Get back to the shop. Now!"

Estèva raised her face from the products she'd been arranging and now stood to her full height. She raised a finger and jabbed him right in the chest. "I told you when I left, I want no part of the shop anymore. You can run it yourself or close the doors. I am finished letting you order me around."

"Pau, you ought to be ashamed," Jenofa interrupted. "Your job as mayor of this village is to protect the livelihoods of the residents, not destroy them. You had no call to damage Tempèsta's goods that she worked so hard to make."

The crowd murmured their agreement. There wasn't a body among them who hadn't suffered the loss of a crop, a fire, or some other disaster that caused them great hardship. It was hard enough to accept when they happened naturally, but to inflict such a loss deliberately on someone else was unforgivable.

I heard someone in the crowd mutter the word *Ugolin*, a reference to *Jean de Florette*, the famous Provençal novel and film. The villain, Ugolin, destroyed a neighbor's farm by blocking his well.

The insult caused Pau to again turn a worrisome shade of purple and begin to shake. "You quiet down, woman. You always took up with the Vielescot women. You're as much of a bruèissa as they were.

And good riddance to them." He turned to me. "It was a blessing the day your mother left this village."

"How dare you," I said, finally finding my voice. "I've hardly exchanged a few dozen words with you, and you act like I poisoned your well and set fire to your fields. You can keep my mother's name off your filthy lips, you nasty, bitter old man."

He raised his walking stick over his head with both hands, and Estèva and I jumped back. He moved to bring it crashing down on the table, but Tibèri stayed his arm.

"Stop it, Pau. Now. Go back to your shop and leave the girls alone before you say or do anything else you'll regret." Tibèri's face was white with rage, and he pulled Pau several paces away from the table before releasing his grip.

"You watch out for your boy, Audeta Cabrol," Pau said, seeing Tibèri's mother in the crowd that had surrounded the booth. "Men don't last long when they get involved with the Vielescot women. You don't want your boy to be next."

"Go back to your shop, Pau Sarraut." She seemed almost as menacing as Tibèri. "We've had enough of your crazy talk for one day."

He stared at the band of villagers, none of whom considered him with much sympathy. He was their mayor, and they'd treated him with respect for decades, but in damaging my products, threatening me, and disrespecting the memory of my mother, he'd gone several steps too far.

But then the all-too-familiar lump in my stomach formed, hard and icy as ever. What had he meant about men not "lasting long" once they formed relationships with Vielescot women? Was it part of the reason why Tibèri was so distant?

Jenofa came behind the booth and wrapped an arm around me. "Don't listen to the old man. He's just upset the world isn't what it once was."

"It never was," Estèva interjected. "He might think the village was a thriving hub of commerce fifty years ago, but it was draining even then. He concocted a Sainte-Colombe in his mind that never existed, and it's that fictional village where he presides as mayor. Not the real world."

Jenofa's expression was contemplative. "It's the danger of dreams, isn't it? They can be beautiful, but they can do more damage than good if they obscure reality too much."

"Well said," Estèva said drily. She rubbed her eyes and addressed the crowd. "Listen, Tempèsta is new to the village, and we've been remiss in welcoming her as we should. That isn't the Sainte-Colombe way, is it?"

Heads shook and a few grumbles rolled through the crowd.

"If you want to welcome her, consider buying some of her products. If she doesn't have what you want, ask and she might be able to make it for you. She has a gift with herbs unlike any we've seen in the village. Do your part for her as she and her family have done for us for generations. She is trying to bring new life to the village, and the least we can do is support her little enterprise."

A line formed behind Méric and Donat, who finished paying.

"Pay him no mind, dear girl." Donat patted the hand I'd extended in thanks for his purchase. "You are a Vielescot and you belong here as much as any of us."

Within twenty minutes the table was bare and I had a list of commissions, carefully noted by Estèva, that would take weeks to fill. I knew that once those orders were filled, many in the town wouldn't have need of my goods for quite some time and I'd have to find other markets and outlets at which to sell, but the show of support was far more valuable than the money in my pocket.

As I folded the embroidered tablecloth, the only thing left and the one item I'd refused to sell, I couldn't help but think about Pau's cruel words. He called my mother's departure a blessing, and I couldn't fathom what a nineteen-year-old girl possibly could have done to invite such wrath from a man more than twice her age.

Whatever the reason, it was clear his anger had transferred to me. For today, the village was on my side, but he was their mayor, their friend, and their neighbor. He would do his utmost to turn the tide against me again, and I'd have to be prepared when he did.

Chapter 26

Temp,

Haven't heard from you, so I wanted to check in. Am worried. Plane ticket home is waiting for you. We want you home.

Please let me know you're okay.

~Wal

I felt the urge to throw the laptop through the open window but thought better of it. Every time I saw Wal's name in my inbox, I clenched my jaw. Grandmother had convinced him that I was somehow beholden to them, despite having been ignored for years.

I'd tried to respond a few times over the past couple of weeks. I had drafts saved. Some thoughtful and well expressed. Others were expletive ridden and, frankly, counterproductive.

But I had to respond. I didn't owe him much, but I supposed

some reassurance that I was alive was perhaps on the list of things I did owe him.

I stared at the blinking cursor and willed it to write my reply for me. That it would know the appropriate words for Wal.

> Dear Wal,
>
> Before I disrupt my life, just a couple of quick questions: Why on earth do you want me back in New York when you never showed the least interest in seeing me when I was there? Furthermore, why does **Grandmother** want me back when she spent most of my life trying to ship me off to second-rate boarding schools in Nepal?
>
> Kind regards,
> ~Tempèsta

A bit too passive-aggressive.

> Wal,
>
> Um, no thanks.
>
> Happy summer!
> ~Tempèsta

It was direct. Effective. Concise. But also would likely be taken as a smidge rude. Pity.

I opened up the web browser and admired the beautiful, gleaming website I'd created for Chez Sarraut. I was sad that the beautiful pieces would remain in the shop, simply moldering away. Sadder still that their stories would end.

But did they have to?

My editor, Carol, was the only one besides Wal who emailed

me. Well, apart from the department stores reminding me of their "best sales of the year" once a week, news bulletins from various papers, newsletters I didn't remember signing up for, and the usual reminder about my extended car warranty that long predated my tenure as a car owner. She usually sent quick messages to say hello, update me on the newsroom drama, and ask how the Bastida was coming along.

And she always ended her emails with the same question: What have you been cooking?

Pau Sarraut might not allow the Analog Kitchen to go live, but at least Carol could enjoy the stories.

Dear Carol,

Sainte-Colombe is enchanting, as always. The fennel is especially robust lately, and the lavender is at its peak. If only you could smell my yard. It's so pretty, one almost forgets that I planted it as a perimeter fence to guard against scorpions.

If you were here, I would cook you a fabulous bouillabaisse with all the right herbs from the greenhouse and make a mojito with the freshest mint you've ever tasted. I'd serve it in earthenware bowls that have been sitting for half a century in a kitchenware shop called Sarraut's. A young farmer, Bénéʒet Gabas, was, as legend has it, courting a woman by the name of Aliénore Durand. She was from a wealthy family from Marseille, and they met when he'd gone to the city to sell stock. The two became besotted with each other and exchanged letters for months. He visited her when his work on the farm allowed.

One day when he'd gone to Marseille to visit and they

were strolling the streets together, she admired a set of fine china in a window at one of the department stores. It was far too expensive for the young farmer or his family. She knew that he was of modest means, so she didn't give the beautiful china another thought.

But Bénézet adored Aliénore and wanted her to be his wife. But more than this, he didn't want her to go without the luxuries she'd grown up with. He was very aware of the sacrifices this refined city girl would have to make if she came to live in a small village like Sainte-Colombe, and he didn't want her to make this one. So he learned how to make dishes with the help of a local potter and replicated the pattern on the china, painting each dish by hand. His attempt was admirable, though I'm sure nothing as refined as the fine artisanal china from the store window. Instead of giving her a ring, he presented her with the earthenware dishes, bent down on one knee, and asked her to be his bride. Apparently, the bride's family was not impressed by the gesture and urged her to refuse his proposal. They thought it was shameful that he wouldn't spend money he didn't have on an extravagant gift and that the handmade dishes were a sure sign that she would spend the rest of her life as a pauper's wife. But Aliénore, disgusted by her family and so moved by this grand gesture from her beau, ran away with Bénézet, and they eloped that very night.

They settled down on his family farm in Sainte-Colombe and had six beautiful children, all of whom have moved away from the village to different parts of France. I expect those children are now doting on their darling grandchildren in Bayeux, Strasbourg, Tours, Nantes, or wherever they landed in this beautiful country. None of them likely knows of this beautiful gesture that has been left behind, but they were all born because of the love it represented. And in Sarraut's, there are a thousand more forgotten stories just like this one, all hoping to be remembered.

So yes, Carol, all is well in Sainte-Colombe, and I can't wait for you to visit.

With love,
~Tempèsta

I breathed a sigh of relief . . . release . . . as I heard the *whoosh* of the email zooming off to New York. At least someone would read about Bénézet and Aliénore, and it felt good to know that at least one of the stories would live on a little longer.

Invigorated by sending the story to Carol, I clicked back on Wal's email and hit the Reply button.

Hi Wal,
All is well here, no need for alarm. Sainte-Colombe is beautiful, and I've never been better. No need to send a ticket, brother dear. I *am* home.

All my best,
~Tempèsta

Chapter 27

In addition to the fun of having a sister-figure in the house, Estèva proved to be as industrious as a housemate as she was at running Sarraut's. Other than teaching a few hours a week and job hunting, she had little to occupy her time aside from helping to get Bastida Èrbadoça back to its former glory. She helped attack the dust and grime in all the spare rooms, making order out of chaos, until we couldn't avoid the most dreaded task of all: the attic.

Though the rest of the house had been a mess in varying degrees, the attic was by far the worst, and I'd yet to do more than take a cursory glance at the space until the rest of the house was in better order. It was nearly as large as the rest of the house and was stuffed full of antique furniture, boxes of varying vintages, and tremendous quantities of dust. There were boxes of records from the 1940s and '50s that appeared to be in playable condition if the turntable could be made to work. Hundreds of books of every possible description along with photos and correspondence between people I didn't know. It was hard to know where to begin, the project massive in scope.

"What will we do with all this?" Estèva lamented at one point as she sorted through a box of old paperwork that was older than either of us. "There's so much."

"I'm hoping there might be a few pieces that might fetch a price to help with expenses, but Jenofa seemed doubtful. The Tardieux were frugal people. I'll probably use what I can downstairs, though. It seems wrong, somehow, to get rid of it all. These things represent generations of Tardieux memories."

"You sound like Papi." Estèva scoffed like an affronted teenager. "The Tardieux are all gone, God rest them. To keep all this seems like a waste of space. If it were me, I'd have Tibèri call in a dumpster and be rid of anything that didn't set my soul on fire."

Tibèri. The mention of his name bothered me more than it ought to, but I shoved it aside in favor of the job that needed doing.

"Some of it will end up in the dumpster, obviously. No one needs seed receipts and tax forms from 1975. But I'm in no rush with a lot of this. I want to take time to figure out which things are beautiful and useful and which I can part with."

"I think our mothers somehow swapped us at birth. You're Papi's granddaughter through and through, and I'm the one who should have ended up in New York."

"Ha ha." I stuck out my tongue. "Unfortunately, your grandfather hates me, so it's just as well I'm not his granddaughter. He'd be a great match for my grandmother, come to think of it. They'd bond over their mutual hatred of me."

She giggled. "Romeo and Juliet have nothing on them." But then she paused in her movements and tossed her broom aside.

"He's an idiot," Estèva said, her shoulders slumping. "He's the mayor of a dying village, and he can't accept that things need to change. He won't even speak to the rectorat to try to change their minds."

There was a crack in her voice as she swallowed back tears. I wrapped an arm around her, wishing I could tell her he'd come around. But I wasn't one for empty platitudes, especially when I didn't believe it was true. She slumped down against the side of a bookshelf, curled her knees to her chest, and buried her head in her hands.

I sat beside her and wrapped an arm around her shoulder. She was exhausted by Pau, but he *was* her only living relative, and it killed her to be estranged from him.

"I wish things were better for you," I said. "Pau may love this village, but he definitely loves you more. That doesn't mean he's acting in anyone's best interest, even if he's doing it with the best of intentions."

"Thanks for that," she said, her breathing uneven. "I'm so tired of people sticking up for him. Even Jenofa and Tibèri in their own way."

"Their philosophy is different. They see him as an unmovable object blocking your path, and they don't see any use in trying to make him budge, which is fair. But in their minds, the only options are to try to push against a brick wall or to stay put on that blocked path and make the best of things. I happen to think there's a third option." I squeezed her shoulder. "If he won't get off your path, carve your own around him. And that's exactly what you're doing."

"You make it sound so easy." She laughed.

"It isn't, but you're strong and smart. You'll find what it is you want to do. And it'll be up to Pau to accept it or not. Either way, you'll be fine."

She leaned her head against my shoulder and exhaled. Just as quickly, in true Estèva fashion, she wiped the last of her tears from her cheeks, ran her fingers through her short crop of brown-black hair, and stood. "Let's get through this mess, shall we?"

"You've got it. And I promise I won't just keep stuff up here to molder away, and I'm not going to cram the downstairs full of junk either. Honest."

"Good," she said. "This house has plenty of old memories to get by on. It deserves some new ones."

We cleaned and sorted in companionable silence for about an hour before I found myself face-to-face with the massive wardrobe that might be nineteenth century or even older. I took a cloth to wipe away a layer of the dust and found it was a beautiful thing made of dark walnut with light chestnut inlays.

"Look at this," I said to Estèva, continuing to wipe the wardrobe clean.

She crossed the room and ran a finger along the intricate wood-work. "Wow, it's a great piece. I won't even yell at you for keeping this one."

"That's good, because it's going in my room." It was possibly the most beautiful piece in the whole house, and I'd have to find a way to bribe Tibèri and several of his friends to take it downstairs to the main bedroom to replace the much plainer one that currently housed my clothes.

"Open it," she said. "Maybe you'll find some vintage Chanel or Dior."

"Or Narnia," I quipped.

"A little black dress or Mr. Tumnus. Sounds fun either way."

I tentatively pulled on the handle, not wanting to abuse the antique hardware. I was relieved when it opened easily and didn't release a roving band of moths, like something out of a cartoon.

Estèva, ever the clotheshorse, dove into the contents voraciously. Most of the clothes were classic and well cut, if a bit staid. Were these Liorada's things? Perhaps even her mother's? Maybe Jenofa would know, but for the moment, my eyes as well as Estèva's were drawn to a pristine white garment bag in the back.

"Ooh," Estèva breathed in excitement. "A gown? Maybe designer. Let's find out."

"Not here with all the dust. Let's get it to my room."

We bounded down the stairs, excited to discover what might be inside. It could be a fancy vintage designer gown I could sell to keep myself afloat for six months, a tattered old coat, or the linen table-cloth that Liorada had used every Christmas of her married life, which had no value other than sentimental.

Once in the dust-free safety of my bedroom, I slowly lowered the zipper of the garment bag. It wasn't the tablecloth or the moth-eaten sixty-year-old coat but a gown of sage-green tulle. The skirt, though rumpled from almost three decades crammed in a garment bag, was full and whimsical. The bodice was structured, with little vines of lavender embroidered up the boning.

I peered inside the back seam of the gown's bodice. "No label. It looks hand stitched."

She peered inside. "I'd bet my last euro on that. And expertly done at that. It's not Dior, but the quality is just as good."

"Pity it won't fetch Dior prices, though."

"All the better. It'll make you less hesitant to keep it," Estèva said.

"Says the woman who was at the point of calling for an on-site dumpster an hour ago," I muttered.

"Not for clothes like this. You have to try it on."

"Why not you? It's a perfect shade of green for you."

"No, this feels more like you. And besides, this is your house. Your things." Estèva gingerly removed the dress from the bag and inspected it before she removed it from the hanger. "It needs a good steaming, but I don't see any damage offhand."

I stripped to my underclothes and allowed Estèva to help me into the gown. It fit as though it had been hand-tailored just for me.

"It looks incredible on you," Estèva said.

I turned to see my reflection in the mirror and stifled a gasp. My skin had taken on a bronze hue. My hair was shinier. I was glowing.

But not just visibly. I felt as though I were floating. Giddy and light, like a child at a carnival after too much candy floss.

But deeper somehow, as though that feeling were entrenched in my heart.

Like I was in love.

"You have to keep it," Estèva said. "It's enchanting on you."

I almost insisted she try it on, to know whether she felt the same elation I did when she put it on, but something kept me from sharing it just then. It seemed too precious to let anyone, even Estèva, partake in. But also like I was witnessing someone else's joy.

I removed the dress, returned it to the bag, and hung it in my wardrobe. I wasn't equal to figuring out the mystery behind it. Not yet.

Enchanting had been Estèva's word, and it seemed more than apt.

* * *

Summer was at its peak, and the herbs in the greenhouse bristled with life. Most of the herbs would need to be harvested and used very soon, or else dried or frozen for use in the winter. I'd purchased a dehydrator to aid in the drying process, which would yield some wonderful flavor for the colder months. Estèva had secured an interview for a job in Aix and would be gone for most of the day, so I busied myself in the kitchen, ensuring that none of this year's harvest would go to waste.

Jenofa was good friends with an olive farmer who sold me a massive vat of olive oil that I could put into smaller bottles and infuse with herbs. Basil oil was potent and prone to bacteria growth, so I was especially careful to research that one and bottle it properly. I made blends of rosemary, sage, and oregano with garlic that was flavorful and classic. One batch I infused with lemon zest and verbena that would be a nice touch for salads. I tried some more creative combinations such as oregano with turmeric and blood orange with thyme.

I was beginning to understand how the herbs worked together; which paired well and which herbs would overpower their counterparts. Rosemary was a bit domineering, while oregano could pair well with many others. They all had personalities, and making blends was much like coming up with a seating arrangement for a black-tie dinner. You had to know who could be seated together and who would be better off separated from each other. Infusing the herbs in oil would only intensify those effects.

I imagined the lovely labels Jenofa could design if the oils were to be sold at Sarraut's, but as old Pau hadn't come around and made any effort to mend things with Estèva, that wasn't likely to happen. Some had long enough shelf lives I could hold on to them for a while. Others would spoil quickly, and I would have to sell them at the weekly market.

I admitted to feeling a sense of grief when I thought of the herb season coming to an end. Certainly the growing season was long here, and the greenhouse made it possible to keep certain plants going all year long, but my gut told me the magic would always be strongest in the spring and summer, when life was at its most vibrant and the herbs were flourishing.

But in that moment of grief came the balm of knowledge: I would be here next spring to sow more seeds. Next summer to tend the crops. Next fall to cull the harvest. I would feel the soil under my fingernails and mulch between my fingers another year. And there were always fall crops to help bide the time.

The last of the oils were cooling, not quite ready to be corked, so I left them on the counter to cure for a while before storing them in the cellar.

I peered up at the ceiling and drooped at the prospect of all the work that remained in the attic. Estèva had done so much, it seemed only right to try to make progress without her to spare her the chore later when she returned from her job interview. So I made my way back to the attic.

Not quite as breathtaking as the wardrobe but charming all the same, I came across a wooden headboard, inlaid with painted green herbs, that I absolutely had to use in my room. It would play up the colors in Mamà's quilt beautifully, and the whole thing would be a dream with some crisp white sheets and sage accent pillows. I'd enlist Estèva's help to haul down the headboard when she returned. I dusted it off so it would be ready to take its place back in my bedroom.

I finally reached a large stack of boxes labeled *Amadeu* in the far corner of the attic that must have belonged to the son of the house who had died young. I imagined that his parents packed up his belongings at some point, unable to cope with seeing the memories of him all over the house, but equally unable to part with them.

To peer inside felt like trespassing in a way that none of the rest of the renovation had. Furniture was largely communal. Something the Tardieux had shared with family and friends. The kitchen was a place to welcome the outside world. But this was the first of the items I'd come across that was truly personal.

There were scads of books, French classics mostly, in fine leather-bound editions. Some, like *Les Misérables*, *l'Immoraliste*, and *Madame Bovary*, were well-known titles I'd read many times in school. Others were more obscure but looked just as captivating. He'd been of the age to be finishing university when he died, so I wondered if he'd planned to become a literature professor or even a writer himself. Each leather-bound tome was inscribed to Amadeu from his parents with a date and a small note in Occitan. I parsed out that most were given to him for special occasions such as birthdays, his saint's day, graduations, and more. They seemed like loving parents who invested quite a lot in their son's love of the written word. He seemed a young man after my own heart.

I decided to take these down to the room I'd set aside as my office and create a small library with them. I hoped Amadeu would be happy to know that his beloved books were being cared for and read rather than crumbling to dust in the attic.

There was a box of trinkets, the sort of treasures that teenagers held on to, that seemed incongruous with a house that seemed suspended in the 1950s. There were tickets to movies and sporting events—a framed ticket to see the French national football team play Brazil in 1989 appeared to be a prized possession. When he came back around to talking to me, I'd have to ask Tibèri to explain the obsession that European men had with soccer, but I doubted I'd understand it any better for having asked.

I fought back the lump in my throat that emerged when I thought of Tibèri. He still hadn't accepted that I hadn't tried to bewitch him, and I could think of no way to prove that I hadn't. He'd have to trust me, and I sensed that trust wasn't his strong suit.

I turned my attention back to the box, which contained a shoe-box full of snapshots from an old Kodak. The first photos I went through were of a pack of boys in their late teens—all clad in foot-ball jerseys, arms around shoulders—who looked on top of the world. There was one with a boy, I presumed it was Amadeu, who was shaking the hand of an older man and accepting a plaque for some honor or other. He was tall, olive-skinned, and dark-haired like so many of the people in Sainte-Colombe. Handsome too. One of the last I saw was another shot of Amadeu, this time with his arm around a young woman.

A woman with soulful blue-green eyes and untamed mahogany curls. A woman whose face was so ingrained in my memory, I knew it as well as I knew my own.

It was my mother.

Chapter 28

I took a bottle of the olive oil I'd infused with rosemary, sage, thyme, and garlic and decided to walk to Jenofa's little house down the dirt lane. In a moment of inspiration I grabbed the green dress as well. If anyone might have a clue as to the origin of the dress, it would be her.

Given the frequency of her visits at the Bastida, I hadn't taken the opportunity to visit her home yet, which was definitely a breach of etiquette. Dropping in was the neighborly thing to do, even though I was going armed with a small gift in one hand and an ulterior motive in the other. I knocked and entered before she had a chance to come to the door, as she did so often at my own home.

The house was much as I'd pictured it. Small, but not oppressively so. Rich terra-cotta tile floors and creamy-white plaster walls. She had vibrant paintings on the walls, but the furniture was muted. The house served to highlight the art, like a skilled ballroom dancer all in black, enmeshed in a tango with his brightly clad partner, who made sure with every step across the floor that all eyes were on her.

I hung the dress on the coatrack in the entryway, figuring I'd wait to spring that question on her until I'd had the chance to ask about the photo. I found Jenofa on the back patio, canvas on easel and palette in hand. I watched for a few moments as she dipped the tip of her brush's bristles in a splotch of paint the color of rose madder—a warm and peachy pink, at home in a land so full of light. I saw her streak the vibrant pink across the brilliant sky on her canvas as she tried to capture the glory of a Provençal evening. It was hours before sunset, but Jenofa had seen the spectacle of color over the western hills thousands of times. She wasn't painting one sunset: it was a lifetime of them.

"You've finally come," she said at last, smiling at my arrival, though she didn't turn from her canvas. She spoke as though I'd been living next door for years rather than a matter of months.

"I brought you something." I showed her the bottle of infused oil I'd brought.

"Ah, I must sample your handiwork." She set down her brush and palette and wiped her hands on her paint-spattered apron. Her face twinged with discomfort as she rubbed her hands, and my heart ached. How hard it must be to have one's greatest joy inflict pain. I made a mental note to experiment with more herb blends to find a more potent solution for her.

She led me to her kitchen where she pulled out plates and glasses, tore us each a large piece from a baguette, and poured two goblets full of sparkling water.

She poured the oil directly onto the plate, ripped a chunk from her portion of the baguette, and dipped it into the oil. Her expression was reflective as she let the flavors settle on her tongue.

"This is very good," she said. "Good oil, better herbs. Just the right amount of garlic too. And given that your oil contains sage, I suspect you come wanting information."

"You know the language of herbs all too well for my liking," I said, not entirely insincere. I pulled the faded photo from my bag and placed it in front of her.

A sadness flashed across her face as she saw Mamà gazing adoringly at the boy in the picture. Jenofa took a sip of her bubbling water and looked off into the distance before focusing back on me.

"You chose to buy Bastida Èrbadoça. I wondered if it was chance or family history luring you back home without your knowing it."

"Family history? My mother never lived there. You told me she lived next door before the house was destroyed."

"No, cara. She didn't live there. But your father did," she said, not quite looking me in the eye.

"*What?* My father was born and raised in Greenwich, Connecticut. He never even came back to France on vacation after he married Mamà."

"That man was the one who raised you. A good man, I am sure, but not your father. Your blood father was the boy in the photo: Amadeu Tardieu, the heir to Bastida Èrbadoça. He was your mother's sweetheart from the time she was a girl in pigtails."

I felt the brightly painted tiles of Jenofa's kitchen swirling around me as I tried to make sense of her words. I put a steadying hand on the kitchen table as though I was afraid I might slump from my chair. I shook my head, trying to force the world back into focus. When it didn't, I cradled my face in my hands.

"That can't be," I said, speaking through my hands. "My mother never would have lied to me."

"No. Your mother was honest, like her mother before her. But she might have been careful to withhold the whole truth until you were old enough to accept it. You were very young when she died, after all."

"You know this for sure?" There was enough Walter Luddington in me to run through the logistics of it all. How it could be proven. What it all might mean.

"Yes, my dear. I loved your mamà as I would have loved my own daughter and tried to protect her just as I would have done if she'd been mine. There was hardly a day that she and Amadeu didn't spend together. The whole village had them matched from the time they were five years old."

"What happened?" I asked. "Why didn't they marry and raise me here?"

I thought of that alternate existence: Being raised in a tiny village where everyone had known me since birth and my family for generations. Knowing the love of grandparents. Two parents who loved me without trying to mold me into something else. Would I have been content to stay here and take my mother's place, the torchbearer of all the village traditions? Or would I have resented the inherited responsibility and longed for a more exciting life in Paris or Marseille or even Aix or Avignon?

"Oh, cara. The unthinkable. Young Amadeu went to Lac Sainte-Croix with your mother. They would go often, children of the sun that they were. He was a confident swimmer and went out too far. A cramp pulled him under and no one was able to get him out in time, though your mother tried swimming after him. It was a miracle that she didn't drown as well and take you along with her."

"My God, how terrible." I felt a million questions forming on my tongue but couldn't find a way to voice any of them.

"It was," Jenofa said. "She was inconsolable. I sat with her for days. Your grandmother too. We wondered if your poor mamà would survive the heartache. Had she not realized a week after Amadeu was gone that she was expecting you, she might not have. I always thought that you saved her."

My heart stopped a moment, too heavy and painful to beat.

"But why did she leave?" I repeated. "Certainly she had other choices."

"Cara, your mother was sick with grief. I think she couldn't bear the thought of being here and raising Amadeu's baby alone and everyone looking at the pair of you with pity. Your grandmother took your mamà to Nice one day, to get her some air a month or two after the tragedy. The man you knew as your father was there on vacation after finishing college and before beginning his job. He met your mother and claimed that he knew he could not live without her as soon as he set eyes on her. I think she accepted him because she thought it was the only way she could escape her pain."

I was sitting in the chair, arms wrapped around my midsection, as if trying to hold myself together. How awful for Mamà. How . . . unexpected that Dad . . . Walter . . . would have married Mamà knowing that I was along for the ride. So many things began to make sense. Why had she never told me? But then it occurred to me: all those nights when she read "Mirèio" to me, she was.

She was, in her way, trying to tell me the story of the star-crossed lovers whose love had been denied by the fates, just as her own had been. And it was clear why she made more of an effort to share the story with me instead of Wal. I was her connection to Amadeu in a way he couldn't be.

"What about Amadeu's parents? And Grandmother Sibilia?" I asked some time later when I'd gathered my thoughts. "What happened?"

"Amadeu's mother was always a sickly woman. When her only child died, it weakened her heart. A bad bout of the flu took her a couple of years after Amadeu died. Your grandfather tried to carry on. The Tardieu men were proud, and he wouldn't have the village think that grief could best him. But there was a hollowness in his eyes after Liorada passed. If she'd lived, things might have been different."

"It seems like so many things could have been different."

"But they weren't." Jenofa dipped another piece of bread in the oil. "No good can come of wishing we could change the past. All we can do is work to make the best future we can by respecting the present."

"You're right," I said. "About everything. I just feel like the world isn't the same place I knew this morning."

"Because it isn't. But I think you will find this new world of yours will make sense, once you get used to it."

I hoped she was right, because in that moment nothing, absolutely nothing, added up.

"But why didn't *you* tell me, Jenofa?"

"Because, cara, it was for your mother to tell you, not me. I knew that with you living in the Bastida, the truth would come out soon enough. Forgive me for that, but I knew it wouldn't be long."

And it was true, the Bastida shared her secrets in her own time.

I grabbed the garment bag from the entryway and unzipped it to show her the green gown. "I thought you might know something about this. I found it in the attic."

"That was your mamà's gown." Jenofa confirmed what I hadn't yet been able to acknowledge. "I saw it in progress all those years ago. It was the loveliest gown I ever saw. She made it with your grandmother Liorada, who was a great seamstress herself. It was a project for them to become better friends before they became family."

"That's lovely. Mamà and Amadeu were engaged?"

"Yes," Jenofa said firmly. "Your mother loved Amadeu, but she was raised in the old ways and wouldn't have allowed him liberties if there wasn't a wedding in the making. That dress was to be her wedding gown."

It wasn't white or traditional in any way, but Mamà hadn't been one for following such rules. It made perfect sense for her.

And when I put it on, I felt the love she'd felt for Amadeu. My father.

I felt humbled by such an incredible gift.

And, perhaps for the first time in my life, the thing I wanted most was to speak to my brother.

Chapter 29

Hey Wal,

You won't believe what I just learned. Mom was pregnant with me when she met Dad. No wonder Grandmother Luddington always hated me. Send her my regards, will you?

~Tempèsta

I sighed and deleted the words. He couldn't find out in such a flippant way. He deserved better than to find out that I was his half sister in an email. He might have been the golden boy, the favored child and all that, but it was never *his* fault. It was Dad and Grandmother—Lucille's fault.

There wasn't a single thing Walter ever did for me that he was obligated to do. He loved Mamà so much that he was willing to take on the burden of raising another man's child just to be with her. But Lucille took advantage of Dad's grief and made me feel like a leech sucking resources from the family.

No . . .

That wasn't right. If Dad had truly loved Mamà that much, he *never* would have allowed his mother to treat me that way. If he loved her so very much, he never would have wanted her daughter to feel like a burden. If he'd had trouble keeping Lucille in line at first, while he was deep in mourning? Fine. But fifteen years of him allowing her to deliberately exclude me from the family wasn't something I could forgive.

No child should have to spend their teens, their most vulnerable years, feeling unwanted by her own family. A girl grieving the loss of her mother should not have been forced to face her grief alone.

And yes, Lucille was most certainly the architect of that misery for me, but Dad never once stopped her. And Wal never stood up for me. Even when he was old enough, he should have been able to face her wrath like an adult.

She might have been the mastermind, but Dad and Wal were complicit.

I shut the lid to the laptop, scooped Astre into my arms, and set him on my lap. He put his paws up on my collarbone and stretched. He kneaded the flesh of my thighs for a few moments before curling back up in a ball.

"Such a good boy," I cooed to him. He let out a little meow of agreement and went back to sleep.

I lived for these moments.

I lived for Astre brushing against my legs while I cooked.

I lived for my late-night chats with Estèva while we used up the last of the products old Pau had damaged.

I lived for Jenofa's impromptu visits that usually ended up with plenty of village gossip and one cocktail more than I intended.

I lived for Tibèri's presence in the house that was now so rarely bestowed. I missed him, and I no longer hated to admit it to myself.

Because, for the first time since Mamà passed away, I felt like I was actually part of a family, and he was meant to be part of it.

And I had to face the truth that there was no reason I should have been made to feel like I wasn't part of one for the last fifteen years. But of the three of them, Wal was the least to blame. And he deserved to hear the truth from me.

I stood up from the desk and placed Astre back on his favorite perch with a kiss on the head. I wasn't sure where to go next. I couldn't think of a thing that needed my attention in the kitchen or the greenhouse and felt a momentary resentment at my own industriousness. Estèva might be another hour or two yet, and I didn't feel like I could face Jenofa again today.

What I wanted was Tibèri.

And he was probably as eager to see me as he would be for a tax audit.

He was probably on a job, but I decided to take the risk and walk to his property, just beyond Jenofa's, anyway.

His parents were away for a few weeks, visiting with some of Tibèri's aunts and uncles in cooler climes, so the main house, a farmhouse not unlike Bastida Èrbadoça but in much better repair, was empty. But the little house, the miniature version that Tibèri had built for himself on the corner of the land, had lights on and Tibèri's utility van was parked in front.

I took a breath and knocked on the front door. He opened it, still wet from a shower and wearing a fresh T-shirt and shorts with bare feet on the cool tile floor.

"Tempèsta." His eyes widened in surprise. "Are you okay?"

"Yeah, I'm fine." I knew it sounded stupid; I clearly wasn't.

"Come in." He gestured me inside, closed the door, and grabbed some clothes that were strewn on the furniture. "Forgive the mess. I wasn't expecting company."

"Please don't worry. I honestly thought you might be out at a job or something. I was just hoping I'd catch you on the off chance you might be here." *I wanted to see you, but I didn't think you'd be home. Smooth, Temp. Real smooth.*

"I finished early." He went to the kitchen and reappeared with two glasses of sparkling water. Even if he was furious with me, Audeta's son and a good Provençal lad would never let a guest go without refreshment. "Sorry I don't have much else around here. Bachelor living and all."

I waved a dismissive hand. "I shouldn't have come by unannounced. It was rude of me. I have a bad habit of it today, apparently."

"Oh?"

He motioned for me to sit on the worn sofa—a hand-me-down from the main house, I suspected—and I told him of the photo and the resultant visit with Jenofa. He was the first person I'd confessed the truth to, and it felt like a release. But it also felt like a rehearsal for telling Wal.

He listened to every word, and when I was finished, he rubbed his eyes in the same way a college student does when they've been up all night studying. Just like a scholar, he was trying to process a lot of difficult information all at once. "How are you doing with all this?"

"I really have no idea. I need to tell my brother and our—*his* grandmother, but I don't know how. I tried a dozen times to write him, but it's too big of a thing to put in an email."

"I see your point," he said. "So you'll go back to New York?"

His putting it into words made it uncomfortably real. "Yeah, I suppose I should. I don't think a phone call will be much better than an email. This seems like face-to-face material."

He nodded. "You're right." The words were affirmative, but he sounded morose.

"Listen, I know I probably shouldn't be bothering you with this given . . . well. I'm just sorry that things happened the way they did. I really wanted us to be friends. I wouldn't have risked that with a silly love potion. You might never believe me, but it's true."

"I do believe you, Tempèsta. I don't think you meant to entrap me or anything. But I do think your herbs were at work that night, even if you weren't aware of it."

"What do you mean?"

"Just as I said, something in that drink of yours helped me to get out of my own way that night. I care for you, Tempèsta. A lot. And it scares the hell out of me."

I looked at him quizzically, urging him to continue.

"We've had foreigners in and out of the village since before I can remember. They come with grand plans and always end up running home when they realize that Sainte-Colombe isn't Cannes or Nice."

"And one of them broke your heart," I supplied.

"They all did, in a sense. Every time one of them left, they left a home that was only half-renovated and often spread the word that we were a tired little backwater with little in the way of . . . anything. But one in particular stung worse."

"A girlfriend?"

"My father," he corrected. "He was Australian. I mean, still *is* as far as I know, but I assume he's still alive. I never met him. He came to Sainte-Colombe with great hopes of turning the place into a resort town. He met my mother when she was young and naive and convinced her that he was the answer to all of her and the village's woes. He didn't stay a full year before he went jetting back to Sydney. Lucky for Mamà that Bertrand came into the picture not soon after and was mad for her. He was happy to raise me as his own and he's been a great dad. They couldn't have any more kids after me, so I don't think he resented me as much as he might have otherwise."

I considered his hair, bronze where most everyone else here had dark. His skin was more golden than olive. He was tall and muscular instead of slight and lean. It made sense. And I could imagine his physical differences made him feel like a bit of an outsider despite generations of connection to Sainte-Colombe.

My chest constricted. Our stories were, on the surface, quite similar. Both raised by men who were not our fathers. But my father hadn't chosen to leave me behind. Tibèri's did. His adopted father loved him and accepted him. Mine had not. These things made all the difference in the world.

Tibèri wrapped an arm around me. "I hope this is okay," he whispered.

I leaned into his chest and nestled in. "More than okay."

He stroked my hair, for how long I didn't know. And it didn't matter. Being in Tibèri's arms felt good and *right*. Was this how Mamà felt in Amadeu's arms?

I had so many questions for her, but I'd never be able to ask.

I raised my head and peered up at Tibèri. His expression was one of questioning and concern. I leaned in and pressed my lips tentatively against his.

He didn't pull away. He lingered but he didn't seek to deepen the kiss.

When we pulled apart, he stroked the side of my cheek and cradled me close. "You've been through a lot. As much as you tempt me, we probably shouldn't confuse things more today. But I'm sorry

I was such an ass the other night. I've always been guarded with outsiders, and I was supremely annoyed with myself for letting you get over the walls I've built around myself."

"You're a great carpenter," I said with a laugh. "They're hard to scale, those walls of yours."

A smile caused the corners of his eyes to crinkle, and I felt the whole room lighten. "A good craftsman never shirks, even metaphorically."

"I care about you too, Tibèri. And I don't want to hurt you. I may be an outsider, but I wouldn't have been if just a few things had gone differently."

He mused, "If your parents hadn't gone swimming that day, we'd have grown up as neighbors. You and I would have known each other all our lives."

"And I'd be holding a grudge against you for sticking gum in my hair in the middle of Mamà's Occitan lessons when we were eight, or some such nonsense."

He laughed. "You can't blame me for trying to distract you from getting top marks. I would just be trying to level the advantage that you'd have with your mother as the teacher and all."

"She would have been impartial, and you know it."

"Of course, but when are children ever rational about such things? She'd have been beloved by the whole village, and we'd have all been jealous of you. But I'd have tried to win your forgiveness eventually."

We chuckled at our little exercise in make-believe for a moment, but then I closed my eyes and focused on the beating of his heart. I wanted to rally at the injustice that we never got to live that version of the past. It seemed so grossly unfair. But then I thought of Jenofa's words:

"No good can come of wishing we could change the past. All we can do is work to make the best future we can by respecting the present."

And I knew what I had to do.

"Tibèri, I have to go to Connecticut." The truth of it gave me an ache in the pit of my gut. It was the last place I wanted to go, but it had to be done.

His arms clamped tighter around me. As if his embrace could keep me from leaving. I wished so very much that it could.

"Just a few days. I'm not leaving Sainte-Colombe forever. Just long enough to tell my brother what Jenofa told me."

His muscles relaxed ever so slightly.

"I'll come back," I promised. *To you.* But I wasn't brave enough to say the last part out loud. Not yet.

Disregarding his own advice, he lowered his lips to mine again, kissing me gently. In his arms, I could feel a future. A future in Sainte-Colombe, living in the Bastida Èrbadoça, waking up in Tibèri's arms each morning. Raising beautiful children. Building a life together.

I felt the glorious freedom of realizing what I wanted and the absolute privilege of knowing I just might be able to have it.

I might not be able to keep it forever. In all things, there was always the looming threat of tragedy, but Tibèri and I could enjoy happiness while the fates allowed it.

And I would be grateful for every moment we were able to enjoy it.

I could have lost myself in his kisses for the rest of the day, and I was tempted more than I ought to let on, but after a time I did force myself to pull away.

"When I come back . . . ," I began to say.

"We'll have a lot to talk about. Good things."

We fell back into kisses for a few more minutes before I finally gathered up enough resolve to go back to the Bastida.

I scooped a sleeping Astre off the laptop, hugged him to my chest, and twirled around the room before kissing him on top of the head and sitting down to fire up the laptop once more. The kitten was not amused by my antics, but he seemed to forget soon enough and settled in to sleep on the desk shelf and was content to accept the occasional scratches and pets as I typed. He was simply pleased I was in the room. After years of feeling the inverse in my father's home, it meant more than the stars.

The little orphan kitten was the first being to let me know I was worthy of being loved other than my mother.

I opened a browser and clicked to the airline's website and sorted out a ticket for the following evening. All the tickets to New York were exorbitantly expensive, but I managed to find one to Boston with a layover in Iceland with a sticker price that didn't give me heart palpitations. I'd ask Estèva to drop me off at the train station in Aix so she could have the use of my car, then I'd head off to Paris by train. And I'd have to figure out the schedule for the commuter train from Boston to Greenwich. But that could all be arranged later.

I saved the e-ticket information to my phone and clicked over to my email.

I popped my fingers and clicked Reply to Wal's last message.

Hey Wal,

I have some news and will be coming back for a short visit. Let me know if the sleeper sofa isn't available, and I'll find a place to stay in the city. See you very soon. Flight info below.

~Tempèsta

I cut and pasted the info from the e-ticket and included it with an approximate time of when I expected to be in the Greenwich train station.

I then composed a message to Tibèri with the information for my return. I knew seeing proof of the return ticket would give him solace. I knew it did for me.

I took one of my smaller duffels and filled it with a few changes of clothes and necessities. Unlike my last trip where I was laden down with all my worldly goods, I'd be able to stow a bag under the seat in front of me and be done with it.

And there was a lightness in that, which had nothing to do with my luggage.

Chapter 30

Wal was waiting at Logan Airport in the Arrivals area past security, his arms crossed over his chest. He was in his uniform: an expensive, navy pinstriped suit, a red power tie, and an annoyed expression. He'd come from the office and likely planned to return for a few hours before the day was over.

"Why did you fly in *here* instead of the city?" he asked by way of greeting.

"Because it was five hundred dollars cheaper and I told you that I'd planned on taking the train to Greenwich," I retorted, keeping my tone even. "Nice to see you too, by the way."

"I'd have paid for the ticket. I had to take most of a day off work for this."

"I didn't need your help. And I'm taking *several* days off work to come see you. And I didn't ask you to drive your idiot self up here to get me. That was your choice. So stop playing the martyr and let's go."

He was as stunned as if I'd whacked him upside the head with a cast-iron skillet from Sarraut's. Pity I hadn't brought the one that had belonged to Magdalena Fabre, gifted to her on the occasion of her wedding in the early 1920s by her older sister, Loïsa. It seemed Loïsa mistrusted her future brother-in-law's honor. And if legend was correct, she was more than justified. Several village babies of uncertain parentage seemed to bear an uncanny resemblance to him, though I never learned if Magdalena had the chance to use the skillet for its intended purpose.

I paused in that reverie to realize that Wal was still gobsmacked at me defending myself. He probably thought my outburst at the funeral was a one-off, fueled by grief. I let that sink in for a moment, and the corners of my mouth turned up like the Grinch's when he'd finally foiled Christmas.

"Let's get your stuff." He glanced at his watch in consternation.

"It's right here." I patted my duffel.

"That's all you brought?" His tone was intensely annoyed, and I hated how much that pleased me. "How much did you leave behind in France?" I could tell he was tabulating the cost of having it all shipped back.

"I told you I'm only staying a few days. Did you even read my email?" I urged him toward the exit, and we quickly found his sleek electric car that was charging in one of the stations. It was the high-end sort that cost a normal person's annual salary but was, in Dad's words, an important symbol of commitment to environmental causes. I'd personally chosen public transport as my green option, but I doubted Dad had ridden the subway since his twenties. Wal unplugged it and we climbed in, me tossing my duffel in the back seat.

"When did you get to be so difficult?" he asked.

"About the same time I stopped being beholden to you and Lucille for anything. I don't know why you think I have some obligation to come running at your beck and call, but I don't. I know you fancy yourself lord of the manor now—heir to the Luddington throne or whatever—but you need to get the notion out of your head that you have the right to tell me what to do."

Wal set his jaw and I could actually hear the enamel of his teeth scraping together. Perhaps the quiet of these new electric cars wasn't such a virtue. It was an awkward drive back to Greenwich, dotted only with the most superficial of small talk. Mostly it was Wal filling me in on the gossip from the circles he and Lucille moved in and of which Dad had once been the center.

We finally pulled into the drive. The house was the same, not that I expected much different.

"Grandmother's in the city, and I've got to take a meeting on Zoom from the study," Wal said. "Why don't you clean up and get some rest. Help yourself to anything in the kitchen. We were thinking of ordering in from Giacomo's for dinner."

Giacomo's was a great little Italian place nearby that I loved. There always seemed to be ample evidence—by way of not-at-all-concealed branded take-out containers in the fridge—that Lucille went to great lengths to order it right before the rare times I had come back during a school vacation. One of her countless little barbs. That he persuaded her not to this time was not a small gesture.

"That sounds great." I tried to sound amenable.

I went to the room that used to be mine to see it transformed. Not into my old room, of course. All of my childhood paraphernalia that still existed was in Sainte-Colombe. The space was now a guest room with an actual bed. I wasn't sure if the sleeper sofa had been relegated to the fifth circle of hell where it belonged, nestled among stickers that didn't come off the front of books, take-out chopsticks that splintered, and erasers that smudged, but it had been replaced by a queen-size bed that boasted a reasonably comfortable mattress. The room was decorated in white and a shade of green that wanted to be sage but wasn't fully committed to the endeavor. The room was almost offensive in its sterility, but at least I didn't feel like I was infringing on Lucille's precious sitting room.

Though I wouldn't be here long, I unpacked my clothes and arranged my toiletries in the bathroom. Small things to give me a sense of control before I faced Wal and Lucille again. The shower was soothing, and I was glad to wash off the layer of grime I always felt I'd accumulated after a long day of travel.

While Wal's meeting droned on and Lucille was still off elsewhere, I sat outside on the back porch for a while with a book and a glass of some unimpressive iced tea concoction from the fridge. It was warm—almost unpleasantly so—but the sun didn't feel the same here. Less sincere and enshrouded in an oppressive mugginess I'd forced myself to forget.

I noticed a little peace lily on the patio. It was overwatered and in a spot that was too shaded. I moved it into the full sun and stroked its leaves as I did in the greenhouse back at the Bastida. I felt the slightest twinge of the familiar tingling in my fingers, but it was an echo of what I felt in Sainte-Colombe. It was a reminder of where I belonged. It was also, in turn, a harrowing reminder of what Mamà had given up when she came to the States. If her gift was anything like mine, it was merely a shadow of what manifested back home.

Home.

I sent off texts to Tibèri and Estèva, alerting them that I'd arrived safely and was already looking forward to my return. Both responded warmly, and I felt the eastward pull at my heartstrings

THE MEMORY OF LAVENDER AND SAGE

with each *ping* of my phone. I also rattled off a quick note to my former boss, Carol. I hoped she'd be able to squeeze me in for a coffee in the city before I headed home. I tried to concentrate on the book, but I couldn't help but rehearse the story I'd heard from Jenofa so I could recite it to Wal.

I had the photo of Mamà with Amadeu with me, and I would show him when the time was right. And a packet of my dried herbs—basil, marjoram, thyme, and a healthy clipping of my best oregano—that we could sprinkle in oil and use for dipping bread. Italian food wasn't quite the same as Provençal fare, but the two married well. It was a blend of love, harmony, courage, and joy. If any mixture could help make the evening run smoothly, it was this one.

I'd taken care to keep my temper even as I'd prepared the herbs and lovingly attached one of Jenofa's labels to the package. A bit of Sainte-Colombe to keep me moored, even though I was so far from home.

By the time dinner rolled around, I was on edge. I'd hoped to talk to Wal about Mamà before Lucille came home, but it was looking less likely as the minutes ticked away. I decided to funnel my nervous energy into setting the table, pouring some wine, and mixing the herbs with the oil with a quick wish for a pleasant meal as I swirled it with a fork. The meals from Giacomo's always came with a short loaf of savory Italian bread that would pair well enough with it.

"You didn't have to go to all this trouble," Wal said, emerging from his office into the dining room. He'd cast off his suit jacket and tie and had undone the top two buttons of his dress shirt. It had been Dad's official signal that he was off the clock for the evening, and it appeared to be Wal's too.

"No trouble. I just wanted to make myself useful."

I heard a muffled harrumph, hastily covered, from the hallway. Lucille entered seconds later with two large take-out bags.

"Shrimp fra diavolo and Caprese salad, right?" she said by way of a greeting.

"I'm impressed." I leaned in to kiss the air above her proffered cheek. "After all this time."

"You've been gone less than half a year, Tempy," Wal pointed out.

"And probably five years since I came home and you hadn't *just* eaten at Giacomo's a night or two before." I saw no sense in hiding the fact that I knew very well what she'd done so many times over the years.

Lucille hadn't been home that particular visit five years ago, which explained why Dad and Wal didn't balk at my meal suggestion. I swore the woman remembered my order out of sheer spite.

"Such unlucky timing." She forced her lips into a smile that must have been uncomfortable for her. We transferred our meals onto plates and put the appetizers—stuffed mushrooms and fried calamari—on a communal platter.

"So unlucky." I returned an equally contrived smile. "But look, oil for the bread with herbs from my own greenhouse. Try some."

Wal obligingly ripped a piece of his bread, dipped it in the oil, and swirled it before eating. "Really good, Tempy. You said you have a greenhouse?"

"Yes. A big one. My neighbor—" I faltered a bit. I didn't feel the need to disclose Tibèri for what he truly was just then. That could happen later if things went well. "My neighbor and I restored the one on my property, and I've had a great crop this year."

Lucille's bread remained untouched.

"You'll have to get a balcony greenhouse when you come home," Wal said. "You're good at this."

I gritted my teeth to the point I felt the muscles in my jaw seize. "I'm not coming back, Wal. Not permanently."

"Then why are you here, if not for that?" Lucille said. "I assumed your brother had convinced you that your scheme was foolish and it was time to come home."

"I have news."

Lucille set down her fork. "Walter Luddington, you're not going to lay down one dime to get this girl out of a mess, do you understand me?"

"*Grandmother!*" he barked. "We spoke about this."

"Very well." She turned to me with an expression of saccharine sweetness—the sort of sweetness that caused cancer. It was fitting.

"Everything in Sainte-Colombe is amazing. Not that you asked, but I bought a house. I have friends. I have a cat . . . It's incredible, really. But I learned something important about Mamà that you need to know."

I tried to do better than just blurt out Jenofa's story in one incoherent ramble. I wanted to do justice to Mamà's history and remember the details. At the right moment, I produced the photo of Mamà and Amadeu.

"So you finally learned the truth." Lucille tossed back the photo after Wal had seen it. "We had to keep it quiet, naturally. For appearances. Though everyone whispered about the whirlwind wedding and the baby that arrived *so soon* afterward. Once . . . *she* . . . died, I told Walt to tell you, but he promised . . . *her* . . . he wouldn't when she was dying in the hospital. He promised to continue to raise you as his own. Sentimental fool."

She knew. Of course she did. Mama would have been about three months pregnant with me when she and Walt came back to the

States. Even if Lucille hadn't known about me when Mamà and Walt married, my early arrival would have given away the truth. I hadn't considered that she'd known, but then again, I tried my best not to consider her at all.

"Too bad he didn't honor that promise," I spat out.

She rounded on me. "You ungrateful sow, what do you mean?"

"Oh sure. Food and rent money until the end of college. Which, hey, thanks for that. It's more than most kids get. But I wasn't invited back here on holidays almost ever, rarely got so much as a phone call on my birthday, and there was the matter of you contriving every possible method to ensure I didn't feel welcome within a ten-mile radius of you, Walt, this house, or even my own half brother."

"Why, you vicious little—"

"*I won't say it again, Grandmother. Hold your tongue!*" Wal had never, in his life, spoken to Lucille in such a way. It suited him. "Listen, Tempy. That's all going to change. We want you to come back. I'll handle everything."

"You haven't listened to a word I've said, have you? I have a life there. I *love* it there. For the first time in my life, I feel like I belong somewhere. Why would I give that up to come back here and be made to feel like the black sheep again?"

"Listen to your brother," Lucille prodded.

I shot her daggers, which silenced any further rebuttal.

"You belong *here*, Tempy. I'm sure your time in the South of France has been incredible for you. You look healthy and rejuvenated. But that's not real life. You had a job and connections here. You can rebuild from that. And I'll help you. I'll get you a nice condo in a better part of the city. It wasn't right to let you fend for yourself like that all these years."

This was him trying to fix things, in his clumsy way. Logically, I knew this . . . but I wasn't ready to forgive him.

"Do you hear yourself? You honestly think any life that doesn't center around New York and your values isn't *real*? The arrogance of that statement is almost awe-inspiring, Wal. But you know what, I've had a talent for one thing my whole life—detecting BS from the pair of you and Walt. At any other point in my life, if I'd moved four thousand miles away, Lucille would have been dancing a jig and you'd have been too wrapped up in yourself to notice. What gives? And no more crap. Give honesty a shot."

"People are talking," Lucille said. I could see she was using every ounce of control she had not to seethe. "People are saying you left because of . . . well, the disparities you mentioned before. There are rumors that the will was unfair to you. And worse, donations are drying up. We can't afford to let all your father's work go to waste because of some bad PR."

"Well, the man I spent my whole life thinking of as my father did cut out his oldest child from his will. And that's how it looks to everyone else," I said. "And I'm sure you had something to do with that decision."

"Wal is the rightful heir as the only biological Luddington child. It would not be fitting for my husband's legacy and the work of generations to pass out of the family—"

"Grandmother . . . ," Wal said, his tone warning.

"That said, to provide you with nothing was, perhaps, short-sighted," she finished.

"So the optics are bad," I said. "But I hate to tell you, they always have been. Ever since I started trying to get a foothold in New York, people noticed. When people found out who I was, they assumed I was climbing up the ladder with the Luddington powerhouse behind me. When they found out I was on my own, at first I let them think that Walt wanted to give us the chance to sink or swim on our own. But they weren't blind. They could see the advantages Wal had that I didn't."

"Well, all that's in the past now. Wal is offering you a very nice condo in the city, a generous allowance, and he's certainly willing to make calls wherever you need in order to reestablish yourself at whatever paper you choose. Or a new endeavor altogether if you prefer."

"Whaddya say, Tempy? A gorgeous place overlooking Gramercy Park? All the best people nearby?"

"Seriously, Wal? Have you met me?"

"Or a little garden condo in the West Village? You'll love it."

A "little garden condo" that would be the size of one of my closets at the Bastida and that would cost Wal a fortune. Sure, it would be nearer to the paper and all the trendy restaurants that I had to review. And it was as appealing as a Brazilian wax followed up by a root canal. I had no desire to go back to the rat race. To spend my time tearing down the life work of talented chefs who came to New York too early in their careers. Who might have been the best thing ever to hit the restaurant scene in Topeka, Kansas, but who weren't ready for the big leagues. I couldn't fathom going back to a cubicle and trying to pretend like I enjoyed the Manhattan scene I'd worked so hard to be a part of. France felt like home in a way New York never could.

"SoHo? Tribeca? God help me, even Williamsburg if you want to be with the hipsters. I won't judge," he continued when I didn't reply.

Like hell he wouldn't. "No. And I still don't get it. Why do you need me back here? Surely you can smooth things over with the right words. You two always manage it."

"It's not good for Wal's career for people to talk as though he pushed you out of the way," Lucille explained. "And it isn't good for the family reputation."

"Of course he didn't. *You* did. So take the fall on your own to save Wal's image if you want. I don't see why you're bothering me with this."

"Think of the good of the family," Lucille pressed. "You may not be a Luddington by blood, but whatever you become, you owe it to this family."

"That's where you're wrong. I became the woman I am and will become *despite* this family." I stood, leaving my meal largely untouched. "And you seem to overlook the fact that the great Luddington family is now officially just the two of you. There isn't some grand clan to protect. So good luck to the pair of you."

"Tempy, come on," Wal said. "Being this difficult isn't like you."

"Maybe it is. But you never took the time to find out. Feel free to spread whatever rumors you want about me. Let them think I'm off on an early life crisis. Went off on a culinary tour of Europe and got mobbed by angry restauranteurs when they found out I'm a food critic. Whatever you want. But I will not be coming back here. Sainte-Colombe is home, and that's where I'll stay. I only came because I wanted you to hear the truth about Mamà and Dad from me and in person. But I don't owe either of you one more iota of consideration."

I pushed away from the table. Lucille hadn't touched the oil and herbs, and a smile tugged at my lips as I realized a hard truth. Even an offering of love, harmony, courage, and joy could not work its magic on those who refused to partake of it.

Chapter 31

I took the commuter train from Greenwich to SoHo where Carol lived. She agreed via text to host me for the night on the understanding that I'd have to explain everything in person and over quantities of wine that would probably be inappropriate for a work night.

She buzzed me into her loft. It was chic and bohemian with splashes of loud color to contrast the exposed brick walls and wood beams in the ceiling. It was a fabulous space, and she'd done a marvelous job with every inch of it. Wal would buy me a place just like it. Heck, he'd probably try to buy *this* place from Carol if it meant I'd stay. But, where once I'd have jumped at the chance, I found no appeal in city life at all.

"What the hell are you doing back in New York?" she asked, taking me in for a hug. "You're supposed to be cooking for me vicariously in the Bastida Herba-whatever."

"Èrbadoça, Err-bah-doss-ah," I supplied. "It's a long story. And I'm going back tomorrow."

"Good, because if you come back, you're fired." She poured me a glass of a bold red and gestured to a small platter of cheese and crackers, for which I was grateful, thinking forlornly of the uneaten food back on the table in Greenwich.

"Fired? I'm not really employed, am I?"

"Oh yes, you are. I just got it all worked out. You're our new travel food columnist. You're writing on location from Sainte-Colombe. I want more stories like the one you sent me about the dishes. You had me, a hardened New Yorker with not an ounce of discernible sentimentality in my body, openly weeping in my office over a set of dishes. I'll be sending you a new contract next week."

I spun her around, nearly knocking over her coffee table.

"I take it you accept?" She wiped tears of laughter from her cheeks as I righted her.

"Yes, and I know just how to celebrate: a bit of the Bastida for us both." I pulled out the leftover herbs from my bag, and she rummaged for some oil and bread.

Her face lit up as she tried the herbs. "I have to come visit. All of New York does."

"I only have three spare bedrooms." The wine was a feisty, peppery red that did its best to overpower the herbs, but they ended up harmonizing on the palate after a while.

"Spare bedrooms? Three of them?" She threw her head back in a full-bellied laugh. "After that place you had in Queens?"

"I know, I know. I've come up in the world."

"But seriously, New York *will* come to see you. What you sent me is incredible, Tempèsta. The column is going to be a hit. I see cookbook deals and the lot of it for you."

I blinked. "Really?"

"There is no doubt in my mind. And that website of yours will be huge."

"Would have been," I corrected. "The proprietor of the shop thinks I'm a witch."

"Oh, you know how to play nice. Charm him."

"I mean more in the literal sense. Let's just say I have some interesting family history back in Sainte-Colombe."

"Sounds like article fodder to me."

"Or therapy fodder," I said with a snort.

"Those two things overlap way more often than you think. Basically that Venn diagram is a circle. But an actual witch? That *is* an angle I haven't heard."

I told her, in the least sensational way I could, about my talents in the greenhouse, Mamà's talent with embroidery, and what little I knew about Grandmother Sibilia's skills with animals. I admitted it was all a little preposterous, and that imaginations were often as vivid as the colors in the landscape in Sainte-Colombe, but that the legends had shaped the village's opinion of me before I showed up.

"'The Kitchen Witch of Sainte-Colombe.' That's your column title. You love it, don't you? Tell me you love it."

"It's fantastic." I smiled at the moniker. "I suppose if I have a reputation, I might as well lean into it." I thought of Tibèri's assessment of Astre adding to the whispers about my being a bruèissa and smiled. I absentmindedly pulled my phone from my bag and sent him a text. I realized too late it was almost three in the morning, but at least it would be waiting for him when he woke up, and a smile tickled the corner of my lips.

"Too right. It's a great hook. People will love you. You are going to do it, right?"

I sighed. Mamà's money wouldn't hold out forever. I had to think of some long-term way to make my path forward. I wouldn't need a huge income, but it would be good to do the sort of things Walt had always droned on about, like investing and saving for retirement and all the things I'd never had the resources to do before. But it was a tie to New York when I had wanted to sever them.

"I will. And I'll send art and everything. But the pay had better be stupid."

"It's a midsize newspaper in the age of the internet. It's not stupid, but as stupid as I could talk the head of editorial into. You'll be fine."

"You're amazing, you know that?" I wrapped an arm around her. "I'm lucky to have you as my boss. And my friend."

"Oh, you're so freaking lucky. This"—she made a sweeping gesture indicating herself—"is not the sort of person everybody gets to be friends with. Welcome to my entourage."

We laughed until the downstairs neighbors thudded on their ceiling with a broom handle to demand quiet.

"And they call *you* a witch," Carol said. "That woman is pure evil. She loves leaving nasty little notes for everyone in the building."

"I bet she and my—Wal's—grandmother would get along so well! We should introduce them."

We tried to compose ourselves with very mixed results.

"You know that the column is all about your skills, right? I've got a zillion people pitching columns to me all the time. If I'd seen that piece come across my desk with a stranger's name on it, my reaction would have been the same. I pushed it forward because it stood out. And that's because you're writing about things you care about. People you care about. I saw you try for five years to give the restaurant review gig a real shot, but your heart wasn't in it. You weren't ever going to be great at it because you didn't want it. You *could* be great at this."

"I appreciate your vote of confidence. It's nice to know someone believes in me."

"Now what about that carpenter you've been mentioning? Surely he believes in you."

"I think he does. Which is why I need to get back as soon as I can. It'll go a long way in helping him to trust again."

"Oh, he's not the only reason you need to go back," Carol clarified.

"I know, I know. I have a column to write."

"That, yes. And you also have to mail me Aliénore's dishes. I don't care if it costs twice the national debt to ship them to me. Their love story deserves a second reading."

Tears trickled down my cheeks. Pau didn't have to know who had bought the dishes or that I had anything to do with it. I could convince Estèva to handle it once she and her grandfather were speaking again. It would get Sarraut's a bit closer to the black.

But without the website, Sarraut's didn't have much of a chance. And even if *I* was doing okay financially, the village as a whole was not. It was better, but it wasn't enough. September loomed large on the village calendar, and though the rectorat hadn't officially closed the school, it seemed the announcement couldn't be far off.

I lamented to Carol about the state of the village, explaining my concern for the fate of the artisans who were without enough customers, and the flight of the younger generations.

"Your column will help," Carol assured me. "I can't promise a huge influx, but you'll get more than a few New Yorkers coming to town. But you're not wrong. You need a real tourism campaign."

"Pau would never allow it."

"Why does that matter? He sounds like a massive grump. Surely you can get it done without him."

"Not really." I took a long pull from the glass of heady red wine. "He's the mayor, and he pulls all the strings in the village. If I don't get him on board, it simply won't happen."

"Well, crap. Of course he's the mayor. He probably got elected by the very virtue of being the oldest, grumpiest man in the place."

"Without a doubt," I said, unable to contain a dry laugh.

"So find a *French* tourism program that already exists. It'll seem less like an outside invasion to him. And less work for you and the rest of the village than reinventing the wheel."

"I think you're on to something." I leaned back against the plush sofa. "Truly."

"I always am." She took out her phone, nestled her PopSocket between two fingers, and began typing with one hand, never setting down her glass of wine. "Here."

She thrust her phone at me after a few moments of scrolling. She'd pulled up a glossy bilingual website from the French tourism board:

VISITEZ LES PLUS BEAUX VILLAGES DE FRANCE.
VISIT THE MOST BEAUTIFUL VILLAGES IN FRANCE.

"Look into this program," Carol urged as she patiently listened to me extol the virtues of the program. "I bet they have grants and all sorts of government programs to help preserve the place. And even if the village isn't chosen, the people who live there will get to enjoy the facelift. And they *will* choose it because you're smart and know how to pitch it. You'll turn Sainte-Colombe into a center for gastro-tourism without ruining the place."

"I hope you're right." A tingle of electricity prickled my fingers as my brain whirred with possibilities. If it was just enough that we could repair the school and convince the rectorat to keep Mademoiselle Langlois at her post, it would be worthwhile.

"I am. Just remember, Sainte-Colombe may be your own little corner of paradise, but that brain of yours has plenty of New York cunning left in it. Don't shun it; use it to save the place."

Chapter 32

The next afternoon, I was back at Logan Airport after ducking into the office with Carol to sign contracts and squee with a few of my colleagues. I endured the long train ride north from the city by pulling out my laptop and making notes on my plans for the village and trying to contrive a way to get Pau on my side. Or at least out of the way. It was hard to focus, but I managed to channel the torrent of ideas into a single document. The dread I'd felt upon leaving had been officially replaced by the thrill of anticipation of returning home.

Home.

I'd snapped a photo of myself at the boarding gate that read *PARIS* in big, bold letters and another from my seat on the plane and texted them to Tibèri. It wouldn't be long before I'd be back in Sainte-Colombe and I could share everything with him. I worried he'd think my plan was too much like the one his own father had concocted almost thirty years ago, but I'd have to find a way to convince him that I didn't want to change the village. I wanted to save it.

The flight was direct, and I felt like death in a chafing dish when I stumbled off the plane. I'd have to get to the airport's TGV station and procure a ticket to Aix. I'd be back in the Bastida within about four hours if I was lucky and hit the window right. If I didn't, I'd have an hour's wait for the next high-speed train.

I was following signs for the train station when a hand gripped my bicep.

Tibèri pulled me into an embrace, and I allowed myself to linger there for a while.

"I told you I was coming back," I mumbled into his chest.

"And I mostly believed you," he said with a smile. He took a step back and lowered his lips gently to mine.

I fell back into his arms for one more embrace. "Shall we go home? I miss the Bastida."

"The Bastida will have to wait until tomorrow. I want to show you Paris before we go back. You haven't been here apart from the airport as I remember."

"That's right."

"As a food reporter, this is a vital part of your education. I know you're dead on your feet, but we can just wander the streets, eat some good food, and leave in the morning."

"That sounds . . . incredible." I slid my hand in his and we took a regional train to the heart of town. He showed me hidden corners of the city I'd never read about in any tourist book. We didn't sit to have a full meal anywhere but bought offerings from any bakery or street vendor that seemed interesting. Coffee, copious amounts of strong espresso, helped fuel me through my jet lag.

The Eiffel Tower and Arc de Triomphe were as impressive as

they seemed in photos and movies, but there was far more charm in the little winding side streets in Montmartre. There was a delightful little bakery with a dark green façade that claimed to date from the 1870s where we had delectable *tartelettes au citron* and cool Perrier water to refresh us. We watched artists paint in the Place du Tertre while tourists ate in nearby cafés, and wandered in one of the oldest churches in Paris, which was only a few meters from the famous basilica that lorded over the whole city.

At last Tibèri led the way to the rental apartment he'd secured for the night. I indulged in a long shower, dressed in the nicest outfit that I'd taken to New York—a gauzy red dress I'd bought with Estèva—and freshened up the best I could.

When I returned from the shower, Tibèri was effortlessly elegant in a way that only European men could master. He wore a simple button-down and trousers but looked as though he'd stepped off the pages of *GQ*.

"I don't have anything fancier. I didn't pack for a night out in Paris."

"You will be perfect. Nothing as fancy as the *Tour d'Argent* or a Michelin Star restaurant for us tonight. I want to show you a little place where the people who actually *live* here like to eat."

The evening was settling in, and we descended to the street. He laced his fingers in mine, and I was perfectly content not knowing where his hand began and mine ended. We entered a small restaurant tucked in on a side street. There wasn't a word of English, German, Spanish, Japanese, or Hindi being spoken. They were speaking Parisian French. More, they were speaking the French of Montmartre and *this* neighborhood.

A waiter, not clad in the traditional black and white of the white tablecloth–style restaurants in the heart of the city but rather casually attired and with a smudged apron around his waist, came to wait on us. Tibèri ordered steak with fries and warm chocolate cake, while I had duck breast with baked potatoes and crème brûlée. In true food-critic fashion, we split our entrées so we could sample a bit of everything. It was classic French fare, not unlike that which could be found in the nicer restaurants in New York, but somehow it tasted better.

Maybe it was the water. Maybe it was the well-seasoned copper pots. Maybe it was a chef who loved his work. But each dish was prepared masterfully.

"I didn't think I'd be able to eat a full meal after all our sampling today," I said, surprised to see our plates cleaned.

"We walked a lot, and you've been traveling. Easy to work up an appetite. I thought you might like this place." His hand was on mine as we sipped our after-dinner coffee and watched people walking by on the narrow street outside.

"You know Paris well. I'm a bit surprised. When I think of you, I have a hard time envisioning you outside of Sainte-Colombe."

"Oh, I went through my rebellious teenage phase, the same as many in the village. I lived here for a few months with some school chums until we ran out of money. The difference was, I came home."

"Are you glad you did?"

"Every day. When I got back, I couldn't imagine why I'd left. Don't get me wrong—I love Paris. I love Aix and Marseille and Lyon too. I have a special soft spot for Florence and Salzburg. I enjoy getting out and seeing the world, but Sainte-Colombe is home. And I confess I was worried you'd feel the same way when you got back to New York."

"There are plenty of things I love about New York. The restaurants, the theater, the museums, the interesting people you watch but never speak to. Honestly, though? It's big and impersonal. It never felt like home. Neither did Greenwich. Not after Mamà died anyway. I felt like a freeloading guest in a hotel until I left for college. My apartments were better because I felt like I at least had some control over the space. But the Bastida is the first place that ever felt like it was *mine*. I couldn't give that up."

He took my hand and pressed his lips to it. "You deserve to feel at home. You deserve to feel like you belong. Like you're valued."

"A part of me always thought it was too much to ask. You spend so many years convinced that you're unlovable, unworthy . . . you begin to think it's true."

"I'm glad to know that's changing for you. You have Estèva, Jenofa . . . me. The rest of the village too. They see you as one of our own now, or are starting to. And I've watched you bloom there. I've seen you become more assured and confident. And I've loved watching it happen."

I swallowed back tears, not sure of how to respond.

"And you have turned the Bastida back into a beautiful home." He stroked the side of my face with the back of his finger. "It deserved the new life that you've given the place. I am honored you let me help you with that."

"Well then, I can't begrudge you the opportunity to help shore up my roof before winter," I said with a wink.

"It will be my privilege. But I expect payment in mint margaritas, pesto, and whatever else you can conjure up in that kitchen of yours."

"It's an accord," I said. "And no witchery, I promise."

"I don't think it matters. I've fallen for your spell, and I don't care to wake up from it."

I took his glass of Burgundy and playfully sniffed at it. "Magic more potent than mine." I returned it to him.

"Oh, the magic of the vine? We French would say there's nothing stronger."

"Tibèri, since the wine has you in such a pliable mood, I did come up with an idea when I was in New York."

Every muscle in his face tensed, but I launched into my hopes to include Sainte-Colombe in the Most Beautiful Villages in France program and what it could mean for the revitalization of the village we both loved so much. I emphasized how the whole project would center on keeping Sainte-Colombe the way it was, but with a few coats of paint and perhaps some new shutters here and there. How the local tradespeople would be able to sell their goods in volumes like they had in times past. In fact, the plan really depended on Sainte-Colombe retaining its essence.

And the grants might be enough to rebuild and modernize the town hall so the school could continue. Tibèri could design it to be the building he'd always envisioned. And if all went well, the increased revenue could make it all sustainable in the long term. As I explained, his face grew less and less strained and more thoughtful. I could almost see him mentally scribbling a list of supplies he'd need from Valensole and beyond.

"So what do you think?" I said, finally pausing for breath. "I just want people to have the chance to fall in love with the place like I have."

"I think it's brilliant, but you'll have to get the whole village behind you. And I warn you, they've convinced themselves that any attempt to change is a waste of time. You'll have a slog ahead of you—*we* will," he corrected. "I'll throw my support, and my time and tools, behind the project."

"Thank you." I reached over to squeeze his hand. "I think I can do this. If I could just convince them to give it a fair shot, it could change everything."

"I know you're right, but Monsieur le Maire will be harder to convince."

Chapter 33

The next morning, we took the métro to the Gare de Lyon and hopped aboard the southbound TGV. I was glad that Tibèri had chosen to take the train to Paris instead of driving. It allowed us to enjoy the countryside and each other without the stress of maneuvering the roads. Tibèri was a far less nervous driver than I, but it would have been far riskier to steal kisses if he'd been driving.

I'd been in a fog of jet lag and nerves the last time I'd taken the train from Paris to Aix, and I barely remembered the blur of scenery. Now, I had the certainty of knowing where I was going and how to get there. And with whom. There was beauty in the unknown but grace in certitude, and I felt comfortable finally embracing the latter.

We found Tibèri's utility van in the train station parking lot three hours later and trundled back on the winding road from Aix to Sainte-Colombe. The tenor of the conversation changed from the beauty of the French hillsides to more prosaic matters, such as the improvements we wanted to make to the Bastida.

"You'll eventually need a bigger office," he said. "And built-in bookshelves. Maybe we'll build you a little cottage-office for your work so you can separate work from home." He reached over and patted my thigh.

"I love the idea of a separate office." I filled him in on my project as the newest food columnist at the *Tribune*.

He loved the idea of the column and how it would keep some of the village's old memories alive. And I was bursting to tell Estèva as well.

When we arrived at the Bastida, Estèva was inside. I could hear the sounds of her crying from the spare room she'd claimed and the sounds of her throwing her belongings in a case. Tibèri waited in the living room while I went to check on her.

"Papi had a heart attack last night," she announced as she opened the door to me. "I just found out. It took them this long to find me because he was unconscious."

I enveloped her in my arms. "Oh my God, is he going to be okay?"

She shrugged. "They don't know much yet. He's alive, but he isn't awake. I was at the hospital with him in Valensole all day. I can't even see him tonight because visiting hours are over. They may have to transfer him to Marseille. It's all my fault."

"No, sweetie." I stepped back and held her biceps with my hands so she was forced to look at me. "No matter what happens, it's not your fault. And blaming yourself won't help him. It will just wear you down. Let's just focus on doing what we can to support him."

She dissolved into tears, and I held her close. "I'm so sorry it happened. But please, please don't blame yourself."

She nodded against my shoulder, but I wasn't convinced she really meant it.

"I'll come with you to the hospital tomorrow," I said, rocking her gently.

"But Papi doesn't like you."

"I'm not going for him. I'm going to support you."

Her response was just more tears.

"Come, have you eaten?" I asked.

She shook her head.

I led her by the hand to the kitchen and gestured for Tibèri to join us. I rummaged around in the pantry and the fridge and cobbled together an assortment of cheeses, meats, and bread to ensure Estèva had something in her system, along with a glass of verbena lemonade to keep her hydrated.

I broke the news to Tibèri so Estèva wouldn't have to do it a second time. He consoled her, wrapping a brotherly arm around her, and spoke words of kindness as I tried to throw together a proper meal. I settled on pizza, as I'd made some flatbread before I left and could make a passable one with marinara that I'd made and jarred, good mozzarella, and some of my last fresh basil of the year. A simple meal, but these were the moments that called for simplicity.

"If he dies, I'll be alone," Estèva said bleakly.

"Are you alone now?" I gestured to the room.

She shook her head.

"And that won't change, no matter what happens to Pau," Tibèri said.

"It isn't the same and you know it," she said.

"Estèva, I have no family left in the world, save one half brother who will probably never speak to me again. I lost the only family member I had who cared about me when I was thirteen. I found my own family. You already have."

She grew silent and thoughtful. It was a hard truth, but Pau wasn't going to live forever, and even if he did pull through, this was a reality she would have to confront before too many years passed.

I coaxed her to eat and drink, which she did without protest. She was practically nodding off at the table by the time the meal was finished, so I hauled her off to her room and hoped she'd be able to sleep.

"Do you think she'll be okay?" Tibèri asked as I walked him to his van.

I glanced back at the house. "I don't know, but I'll do what I can for her. I just hope he pulls through, for her sake."

"The Sarrauts are sturdy stock. I wouldn't count old Pau out just yet." Tibèri pulled me into his arms for a last embrace before going back home.

I kissed Tibèri goodbye and watched until the van had turned off down the road.

I soon found Astre, who had made himself at home on my bed, and was greeted with the plaintive mews of a cat who hadn't fancied being without me for a few days, even with Estèva here to dote on him.

"What are we going to do about Pau and Estèva?" I asked him, hoping he had answers. He locked eyes with me and blinked a few times slowly.

"I don't know either."

As ornery as the old man was, Pau meant the world to Estèva. Healing him was far beyond the scope of my gift, but I hoped he would wake up long enough to mend fences with her. But truly, I hoped he'd make a full recovery and live to see Estèva find her path in life and support her along it for a bit longer.

I went to the greenhouse, the air still warm with the promise of late summer. It was the fever of those last golden days where children begged for one last beach trip before they found themselves back in the schoolrooms for another year. The cicada song floating on the breeze entwined with the heady perfume of drying lavender.

I would make a gift for Pau. I wouldn't try to feed him anything in case it would be against medical orders. But there wasn't a hospital-bound person who couldn't use a good salve for their hands and feet. Yarrow was the traditional choice for healing, but it also represented protection and everlasting love. The kind he had for Estèva and she for him.

I was about to take the yarrow to the kitchen to infuse with oil and beeswax for the salve when I saw the poor, butchered hyssop plant that had never quite regained its strength after my shearing some weeks back. I stroked its leaves and asked if it might, just this once, be willing to allow me to take a cutting for a very important cause.

I felt its hesitance, but then the tingling sensation radiated up my fingers when it offered its blessing. As gingerly as possible, I snipped a single stem of blue flowers to add to the yarrow salve. Hyssop was an herb that represented cleansing, so I hoped it might mean a fresh start for Pau and Estèva.

A start that would allow him to maintain the dignity of Sarraut's that he'd clung to for so many decades, but that would not shackle Estèva to her family legacy for the rest of her days to make it happen.

Chapter 34

Estèva drove us to the hospital the next day just before visiting hours were set to start. The hospital in Valensole was not a large, gleaming state-of-the-art thing like I remembered from some of my darkest days in New York when Mamà was clinging to life after the accident. It was a small municipal hospital that was always three nurses and two doctors short of the ideal staffing.

Estèva was pale as we exited the car. I knew she was expecting the worst, though surely they would have called her mobile if he'd passed in the night. I passed her some lip balm I'd infused with thyme. The herb of courage. "Your lips look a little dry."

She eyed me warily. "The bruèissa is up to her tricks again."

"Always. Trust me. It's just a little boost. And a lot healthier than day drinking to cope with the stress of it all, right?"

"I suppose," she muttered and applied the balm. She glanced down at the tube and looked wistful. "Nice stuff. It would have sold well at the shop."

"Maybe someday. But for now, let's worry about Pau."

We checked in and found his room in short order. When we entered the room, nurses were bustling around, changing machines and changing fluids. And Pau was very much awake.

"Papi!" Estèva was ready to launch herself into her grandfather's arms. She might well have done it if he hadn't been surrounded by machines and busy nurses.

"He just woke up a half hour ago," the head nurse explained. "We were at the point of calling you. All his vitals are good. We're keeping him here for a few days for observation, but he should make a good recovery if he follows orders."

"He will." Estèva shot a warning look at her grandfather. He appeared incredibly weak but nodded.

I retreated to the hallway so Estèva could speak with the nurses while they prepared Pau for life among the living after he'd been so perilously close to crossing over to the other side. I was grateful for reasonably comfortable chairs in the hallway, and more still that I'd had the foresight to bring a book and a notepad in my bag to keep me company.

It was over an hour later when Estèva finally emerged. "He's napping. I'm going to use the loo and grab a coffee. Do you mind sitting with him?"

"Of course not."

She padded off down the hall and I took her place by Pau's side.

As I sat, he began to stir a bit. His eyes opened. "Bruèissa . . . ," he said in a weak voice.

"Shhh. You shouldn't try to speak. Just rest." I took his hand that wasn't encumbered with an IV, and he was too weak to pull it away. I pulled the yarrow and hyssop salve from my bag and began working it into his dry skin. "There, doesn't that feel better?"

He nodded, barely able to move his head. I worked on his hands, then his feet, for a while in silence. He seemed less agitated by my presence, which was about as much as I could ask for.

"You won't believe me, but I do understand why the things in the shop are so important to you. So much of life happens in the kitchen and at the dining room table. Those items that produce our meals become precious. But it's not about pots and pans and old relics. It's the stories. You don't want them to be lost, do you?"

He gently shook his head.

"I agree with you. I know now it's why I came to Sainte-Colombe . . . to hear the stories of my mother's village. They're too beautiful to be forgotten."

He didn't speak but blinked thoughtfully.

"A friend of mine in New York wants to spend a fortune to buy Bénézet and Aliénore's dishes. Not because they are elaborate or made by some exclusive manufacturer. It's because they *aren't*. It's the story behind the dishes that made her want them."

He nodded.

"You understand the importance of those stories. I do too. So does Estèva; more now than she did before. And if you let Estèva and me tell those stories, we can find new homes for all the beautiful things you've been safeguarding for so long. And make room for new treasures and stories as well. Don't you think that Bénézet would like to think of the dishes he so lovingly made being used again?"

Another nod.

"I'm glad. Estèva is a good and kind granddaughter, and she deserves to be happy. I think you want that for her too."

He nodded.

"Think about letting her use the website. It's a change, but it doesn't necessarily follow that it's a bad one. Please just consider it."

I let him drift back to sleep, and I hoped he'd keep his word. Estèva would have a lot on her hands, contending with his care when he got home. The income from the website would take away one worry.

She came back within another five minutes, coffee in hand, ready to continue her vigil. I rose to reclaim my spot in the hallway.

"No, stay, Tempèsta," he rasped. Estèva blinked in surprise but took the other chair in the room. "Estèva will be easier with a friend nearby."

"Just save your strength, Papi," she urged.

"I'm strong enough to talk for a bit," he insisted. "I'm sorry we quarreled. I'm a stubborn old man and I brought this on myself." He gestured to his chest.

"Don't blame yourself, Papi. I should have listened to you. Just get better."

"I'll do my best, *mon lapin*."

She took his hand in hers and kissed the small patch of skin that wasn't obscured with an IV. I thought it funny that Pau referred to an assertive and ambitious woman like Estèva as his "rabbit," as though she were a little plush bunny, but it was what he'd always expected of her: to be sweet and compliant. I hoped he'd come to see her the way I did one day.

We stayed with Pau until the nurses kicked us out for the day and then returned to the Bastida.

"He's so frail," she said as we were driving home. "I've never seen his skin so gray and pasty."

"He's been through a lot. He has a lot of healing to do."

"Yes," she said. "I'm moving back to town tonight so I can get the place ready for him when he's discharged."

"You don't have to rush off tonight. You can go in the morning."

She shook her head. "No, I'll be going back to Valensole to spend time with him. It won't take me long to collect my things. Do you think I can borrow your car to visit him until he's discharged?"

"Of course."

Estèva set her jaw in determination as we turned onto the road that led to the Bastida. And not just because she was focused on the road. She was feeling guilty for her grandfather's health and was blaming herself, despite what Tibèri and I, and even Pau himself, had said.

And I worried that all the progress Estèva had made would be for nothing once Pau returned home.

Chapter 35

I 'm sorry, buddy," I called in response to Astre's plaintive
meowing on the other side of the door. I hated to shut him
out, but the idea of scrubbing mint-green cat prints off the
hardwood floors in the second guest room didn't seem like the
most enjoyable or profitable use of an afternoon. Tibèri had just
finished wiring the room, and there was only the smallest bedroom and a hallway left for him to do.

A few months ago, or even weeks, I'd have been filled with
dread at the idea of the repairs being complete and mad at myself
for harboring such feelings. But now I didn't have to worry about
the absence of Tibèri in the house or my life. And that knowledge gave me peace as I freshened the lovely little room with
the new paint and love it deserved.

Lost in that reverie, I felt my phone vibrate in the pocket of my
work shorts. I pulled it out to see I'd gotten a message from Wal:

Just landed in Aix. On my way to you.

I blinked several times, wondering if I'd read the message properly. What? Do you even know how to find my place? I typed out, then wiped an errant smudge of paint off the screen with a self-disparaging mutter. I dashed to the bathroom to scrub my hands free of the offending green so I could reply without permanently damaging the device.

You gave me your address when you moved and I'm pretty sure Google is a thing in France. I'll find it.

I shook my head and shoved the phone in my back pocket. I felt a dozen emotions at once concerning Wal's impromptu visit, and all of them called me to the greenhouse.

I surveyed the growing collection of plants I'd amassed, all so lush and verdant you could practically watch them grow. Should I dabble with anything for Wal to make his visit more pleasant?

But I didn't want to meddle with him. I didn't want to manipulate him with herbs to stop him from quarreling with me. If he was mad, I wanted him to cast it in my face. I wanted him to be forthright.

Because if I was going to have a relationship with my brother, it had to begin, like all other relationships, with a foundation of honesty.

That wasn't to say that the conversation with Wal couldn't use a little boost. I found the heartiest thyme plant and rubbed its tiny leaves with my fingers and whispered sweet words to it before pruning a couple of sprigs. Thyme was for courage. And we would *both* be in need of that. Before leaving, I turned to the hyssop, which was growing stronger with each day, and murmured a few encouraging words before leaving it to heal.

I took strawberries from the fridge and cut them into slices, then tossed them into a pot with water, sugar, and thyme to make syrup. I thought encouraging thoughts. Hopeful thoughts. But nothing that would interfere with him making up his own mind about things.

Together with lime juice, a bit of soda water, and a few ice cubes, the strawberry syrup would make for a lovely late-summer drink. A splash of vodka to top it off seemed wise. Not much, as we needed to tackle some hard topics, but a dash of liquid courage to help us through. I left the mix to chill in the fridge and rushed to tidy up and shower.

I heard the hum of a rental car and a knock at the door an hour later, just as expected. I had the cocktails and a modest charcuterie board with what I had on hand already set up on the back porch. Astre had very solemnly promised to be on his best behavior, but I had my doubts.

I opened the door to find Wal in a white button-down and khakis that somehow, even after a full day of travel, were without a solitary wrinkle.

"This place is ten miles past the middle of nowhere," he said by way of greeting. He took me in an awkward one-armed hug.

"Then it must be ten miles closer to *somewhere*," I quipped.

"Fair point," he said.

I took his bag—a small leather overnight bag that intimated he didn't plan on staying long—and set it on the sofa before escorting him to the porch. A workaholic like Wal never took an impromptu extended vacation. I honestly thought the idea of more than a couple of days away from the office would be the opposite of relaxing for him. Astre observed Wal with curiosity but wasn't quite brave enough to approach.

"This is . . . quite the place you have here." He took his seat on the restored patio chair. He eyed the drink suspiciously, but the summer sun had him warring between his thirst and a deep mistrust of any food that was so unapologetically pink.

"Thanks," I said. "It's come a long way in five months. Still quite a bit to do, but the wiring's nearly in order and the rest should be easier. She has good bones."

"That sounds like real estate doublespeak if ever I heard it." Wal finally took a tentative sip of the strawberry-pink beverage and raised a surprised brow in approval. "It seems like an awful lot of upkeep to me."

"Jargon or not, it's still true. They don't build houses to last like this anymore." I gestured to the vista before us. "It's lovely here."

"Listen, Tempy. I didn't come all this way to fight. I want to make things right. They haven't been for a long time."

"No, they haven't been. Though I'm surprised after my visit back to Connecticut that you even wanted to see me again. Let alone so soon. It's been less than three weeks."

"Neither Dad nor Mom would have wanted us to stay estranged. You know that."

"Right. Lucille is perfectly fine with it, though."

"Perhaps, but I'm not. I was sincere in my offer back home. What I want is for you to come back and work for the foundation. I want us to fill Dad's shoes together. I know it's really what he would have wanted. I'll keep Grandmother at heel. I control the purse strings, and she'll be in dire straits if she crosses me."

I swallowed back a scathing remark. He meant what he said, but she would find a way to sneak in the barbed insults when he wasn't listening, and going to the mat for me every time she stepped out of line would get tiring. Were it just Lucille's pettiness, I probably could have moved past it. But it went far deeper.

"Wal, my place is here. I'm trying to help Sainte-Colombe not slip into oblivion. Mamà loved this place, and I think my being here is what *she* would have wanted. Like you said after the funeral, Dad's legacy is yours; Mamà's is mine."

Wal rubbed his eyes and looked as though he were gathering his words like so many wildflowers from the field. "I wanted to get into this a little later, but I suppose we might as well get it out now. I learned some things while I was dealing with Dad's estate shortly after you left. Things you should know about."

"Okay," I prompted, hoping the drinks were potent enough to help coax the words from him.

"Well, first, it was clear Dad knew Mom was expecting you when they married. She never kept it a secret."

"I'm glad she didn't. It doesn't seem like her, but people have been known to do rash things when faced with grief or unexpected pregnancy. At the same time, it's a lot to handle."

"She was always ruthlessly truthful," he agreed. "But they did celebrate their anniversary a few months early each year for appearances' sake."

"Seems a small price to pay to appease Lucille."

"True. She told people they were already married when they came back from France and that the wedding in the States was just a gesture for Dad's side. But Dad knew. And so did Grandmother and Grandpa Wally."

"I can only imagine how she seethed," I said, unable to contain a Disney-villainess laugh. "I can't imagine Grandpa Wally was exactly happy either."

"No, he forced them to sign a prenup so the Luddington fortune wouldn't 'leave the family.' Their words, not mine."

Grandpa Wally always seemed so jolly; this news surprised me.

He also seemed fond enough of Mamà. I tried to consider things from their perspective. As Lucille had said, their fortune was the work of generations. I could wrap my head around their attachment to it. But their animosity toward me before I was even born was harder to justify.

"Dad wasn't happy about the arrangement, which is why he wrote the will the way he did. He saved all Mamà's money that came to her after her mother died in a trust for you. He added every dime that he was legally permitted to and said it was Mom's 'allowance' that could, under the terms of the prenup, be passed on to you. He added in some of his own discretionary funds and invested the whole lot so you wouldn't be left with nothing after he died. One of the terms of the prenup was essentially a nondisclosure clause. They couldn't tell us about it. If I weren't executor, I wouldn't have found out either. It's probably why he named me to the post."

"Dad had a genius for finding loopholes. He wanted us to know," I said, taking a hefty drink from my glass.

"Of course they both expected to live longer than they did, especially Mom. They would have had more time to add to your fund. He didn't give you as much as he wanted to, but he gave you every penny that he legally could. I wanted you to know that. And I, selfishly, wanted to be the one to tell you."

I reached over and grabbed his hand. "I'm glad you did."

"He loved you, you know," he replied after a few long minutes.

My silence spoke volumes.

"Don't confuse affection with love, Tempy. He might not have been affectionate with us, but he did love us. He just didn't know how to show it. Every time he offered us some little pearl of wisdom, he was saying 'I love you.' He wanted us both to have the best, whether it felt like it or not."

"I believe you. I just think it's tragic that Lucille smothered all the human emotion out of him."

Wal shook his head. "Just the outward appearance of it. Which is sadder, if you think about it. I think Dad was a deeply emotional person who was simply forced to bottle it up at Grandmother's insistence. She saw it as weakness."

I set my glass down on the table with a forceful clunk. "She's wrong. Showing emotion and vulnerability? That's strength. That's power. Putting on a façade is just putting a dime-store Halloween mask over the problem instead of facing reality and working through it."

"You're right. It took me a long time to see it, but you are. Her approach to life and business is emotionally lazy. Worse, it's destructive in the long term. Look at Dad."

"What do you mean?" I asked.

"Otherwise-healthy fifty-one-year-old men don't die from heart attacks. It was five decades of bottled-up stress that took him out. Grandpa Wally got seventy-five years, but he was a wiseass and it probably helped him cope."

I laughed, remembering his penchant for practical jokes. "Do you remember the Easter luncheon, back in maybe 2003 or so, when he slipped a whoopee cushion under Lucille's seat at the table?" My shoulders shook at the memory of it.

"Like it was yesterday. She was mortified." He raised his voice an octave. " *There was a Vanderbilt in attendance for crying out loud, Walter. How will I ever show my face in Manhattan again?* "

Tears spilled onto my cheeks at Wal's impersonation. "Spot on. Oh, she was livid. One of my favorite childhood memories."

He was laughing nearly as hard. "Not for nothing, but if *that* is one of your favorite childhood memories, it sort of makes sense that she doesn't like you that much."

I brayed a bit louder. "Well, it's not like there wasn't some lead up to that point," I said, still laughing. "She'd done a pretty good job of letting me know she didn't like me before then. Don't you remember the way she'd buy me a dress, I'd think I looked fine, and then she'd bemoan that 'she just couldn't find the right colors to suit my complexion' when I modeled it for her? Constant little digs and jabs."

"I know. I think it was *her* way of coping too. When Dad married Mom, she thought she'd lost him forever to some pregnant French girl from God-knows-where who was only after his money. Dad was her only child, and she didn't want to see everything pass to some obscure third cousins."

"I'm glad the family money meant more to her than I did."

"I'd try to spare her some charity," Wal said. "Grandpa Wally was a hoot, but he was a workaholic in a way that puts Dad and me to shame. She spent most of her life alone. She lived for her causes . . . and for Dad. She sacrificed her marital happiness on the altar of the Luddington Foundation, and she couldn't bear for that loss to be for naught."

"I suppose I understand. But I wish she'd tried to talk to me about it. I wish she hadn't blamed me for a tragic outcome that never came to pass."

"I wish that too," Wal said. "You deserved better. But she's still alive. You're still here. You could come back home and fix it."

"Not a chance. This is home now. This is my life."

"It's a nice vacation, but is it a life? Can this really make you happy long term?"

"Yes," I said without an instant's hesitation.

"You say that now, but what about three years down the line when the charm wears off and you've lost three years of career development?"

"This may be anathema to you, but I don't care about a career. I don't care about some posh Manhattan lifestyle. I want a *life*. I've pieced together enough work that money isn't an issue. It's not building an empire like you and Dad, but it makes me happy."

"But Dad's empire needs you. I can't do it alone. The stress of Dad's position is worse than I ever imagined."

"You thrive on the adrenaline from it all. Just like Dad. You don't need me."

"Tempy, do you not remember what happened to Dad?"

I took in a deep breath. "So do better than he did. Ignore Lucille's horrid advice. Our generation knows a lot more about stress management than Dad's did. Take up meditation and yoga. See a shrink. Eat vegan."

His face, that of a dedicated carnivore, fell at that last suggestion. "Okay, be vegan a few days a week. Whatever."

"Yes, meatless except for steak, fries, and beer on Friday nights?"

I laughed. "Like Mamà always said, life is all about balance. Very French attitude. 'Once a week won't kill you' seems to be a national motto. Especially with food indulgences. Not like in the States where once you hit a drive-through, people act like a recovering alcoholic who fell off the wagon."

"There's wisdom in that," Wal allowed. "But all kidding aside, I need you, Tempy. I was in the hospital last week."

I sat up straighter and set down my glass. "What happened?"

"I was in the office until late, as always. Finishing up a proposal for a donor Dad had been hoping to land for years. I'd been living on vending machine food and antacids for days, trying to get it done to Dad's standard. One minute, I'm focused on the proposal; the next minute, the room is spinning and I later woke up in the hospital."

I felt the blood drain from my face, and I reached out to take his hand in mine. "Did they find out what caused it?" A million possibilities, from a stroke to cancer, whirled in my brain.

"A bleeding ulcer. A bad one. If the janitor hadn't come to empty my wastebasket, I might have been unconscious in my office for another seven or eight hours before anyone found me, and I might not have made it."

I felt an ache in my own gut at what that phone call would have been like. "Wal, you're way too young for something like that. What does the doctor say?"

"It's stress. I can manage the ulcer with diet and limiting booze, which is fine. Cutting out ibuprofen will be harder. But ultimately, it'll all be a stall if I don't reduce my workload."

"Lucille must have been beside herself," I said. It was true. With Dad gone, Wal was the sole beneficiary of her fretting. The thought made me shudder.

"She was. She was at the hospital in tears when I woke up." He gazed out over the expansive field that was my yard, not meeting my eye.

"But?"

"Once the doctor told her what was wrong, she blew it off. She doesn't 'believe' in stress. As far as she's concerned, I was just overtired and need to eat better. She isn't wrong about that entirely."

"So stress isn't 'real' and it was just Dad's time?" I shook my head. "Sounds like her."

"She's from a different time, Tempèsta. You can't expect her to change."

I thought of the village where I lived, so mired in tradition, and the changes I was planning to ask of them. I believed they could do it, and she jolly well could too.

"I absolutely do expect her to change, Wal. The Luddington family has always prided itself on having high expectations for their own. That should go double for the matriarch, shouldn't it? And I do expect people to evolve and adapt to new information. Even the Great Lucille."

"Good luck with that," he said with a snort. "You might as well ask the *Venus de Milo* to smile while you're at it."

"Apt. I always thought of Lucille as being made of stone."

"It's all the Botox. But I'll pass along the compliment. She'll send her plastic surgeon a bonus."

We both burst into gales of laughter. Lucille's fondness for her "treatments" was something we all knew of, but about which we were forbidden to speak.

"Come back with me, Tempy. We can do this thing together. We can make it even bigger and better than it is now and make Dad proud because we did it as a team. I can't do it alone. I'm not as strong as he was."

"You're stronger. Dad forged on even though his body couldn't cope. You're strong enough to ask for help before it's too late."

"So you'll come?" The hope on Wal's face was almost heartbreaking.

"Wal, I can't. This is my home now. I have responsibilities here. To the village, to the Bastida. I can't leave. Mamà left this place to mend a broken heart and that was her right, but the place has never been the same."

Astre chose that moment to hop on my foot and meow triumphantly as though he'd felled a lion.

I looked down into his huge yellow-green eyes. "And, yes, I have responsibilities to you too."

He seemed satisfied by this and crawled up into Wal's lap. Wal was uncertain about the little fur ball who'd made himself at home on his khakis, but he seemed to relax after a few moments of purring. Astre was remarkably good at making people relax despite themselves.

"Is it more important to you than I am?" he asked.

The air squeezed from my lungs. Wal was never one for dancing around an issue, but it was rare that he asked a question *quite* so pointed.

"No, but those things *are* more important to me than Walt's foundation." I felt a hard question deserved an equally blunt reply. "You have choices, Wal. You can quit the foundation and find a line of work that won't kill you. If you stay on, you could hire more help that isn't me. You probably have the means, if you invest well enough, to quit altogether and spend most of your time golfing with diplomats and ex-presidents if you want. Current presidents if you're really savvy with the market."

Wal smiled wryly at that for a moment, then leaned forward. "I guess it was a lot to ask. I'd just clung to the foolish hope that you might want to come back and take the place that I think Dad always wanted for you."

"If it makes you feel better, I'm taking the path Mamà would have wanted instead, and it feels right. At the best of times I felt like a fish swimming upstream. I finally get to go with the current and see where it takes me."

He slumped in his seat, a mixture of defeat tempered with dignified resignation. "I'm glad for you, Tempy. You deserve that for once."

"There's more. I met someone." I tried not to blurt the words like a confession. I had no reason to be worried about his approval of my relationship, but so many years of seeking approval that was never granted had taken their toll.

"Figures. There's always a man involved," he scoffed. I playfully punched his arm. "What sort of guy is he? Butcher, baker, candle-stick maker?"

"A carpenter."

He raised a brow. I think he'd expected an investment banker or at least a classically trained chef. Did Wal even know any carpenters back in the city? Likely, someone else had gone to the trouble of hiring one when there was need, and his only duty was to admire the handiwork and write the check.

"What? Handy to have one around given . . ." I gestured to the vastness of the Bastida and the grounds. "And he loves me." It was the first time I'd said as much aloud, and I let the weight of the truth wash over me.

"Well, that's a foundation to build on, I guess. Pardon the pun. I just hope he'll make you happy."

"He does, Wal. He really does."

Wal, for the first time in my memory, leaned over and pressed his lips against my forehead. "He damned well better keep it up, or he'll have me to answer to."

Chapter 36

Wal, just as I remembered from our childhood days, was nothing like a morning person. He staggered out to the living room in shorts and a well-worn Yankees tee.

"My word, for once you don't look like you're going to sell me a used car." It was the first time I'd seen him in anything less than business casual since he was in college. His sandy-blond hair was disheveled, and it suited him. He stuck his tongue out at me, and I called truce by handing him a cup of herbal tea in a heavy earthenware mug. He sniffed at it dubiously, pleading for his caffeine with plaintive eyes.

"I know coffee is one of the main tenets of your religious belief system, but not on my watch, sir. It's not good for ulcers. Try the tea. It's mint with ginger and just a bit of lemon for flavor. But not too much because the acid is bad for you."

He rolled his eyes. "One internet search and she's an ulcer expert."

"Not mixing acid and ulcers seems like a no-brainer. Just try it."

He took a tentative sip, then widened his eyes in surprise and took another.

"See, I told you France wasn't half bad."

"They have great coffee, from what I remember," he said, grousing. The brew, admittedly, wouldn't give him the same caffeine boost.

"'Remember'?" I asked. "You've been here?"

"Not here specifically, but Paris," he said as though it were a reminder of something he'd told me countless times. "I came for two weeks in college. London and Paris. How do you not know that?"

"Um, probably because Dad floated you the trip money and didn't want to make me cry in my fifteen-cent bowl of ramen," I reminded him.

"Good point. Listen, if you're serious about staying, I might as well change my ticket. I planned that we'd need a couple of days to pack your stuff. I might as well go back a day sooner if I can. Can I get your Wi-Fi password?"

I bit back a rebuke. It was presumptuous of him to assume he'd be hauling me back to New York on such short notice, but his reason had been compelling enough that he wasn't out of bounds in thinking he'd be able to persuade me. And I had to admit, it hurt to tell him no. It was also no surprise that he'd lugged a Luddington Foundation laptop with him on vacation.

The truth was, he did need help. He embodied the best of Dad's traits—his drive, his ambition to do good in the community. But like Dad, he hated asking for help. That he'd come to me had cost him a lot. I wanted so badly to help him, but I couldn't give up my dreams for his. Once upon a time, I probably would have done so, but I wasn't going to revert to being that version of myself.

"You don't need to rush off, you know. Stay. Breathe fresh air. Eat good food from my garden. Go for walks."

"I have to get back to the office, Tempy. You know how it is."

"I know you're still healing. You have to have weeks of sick leave built up. Just because you're in France doesn't mean you're not recuperating. The foundation won't crumble if you take a week off to get your strength back."

He averted his gaze. "I know you're right, but it doesn't feel right to let things slide at work."

"Just like Dad. Look, you've been ill and you flew all the way here to see me. Going back so soon won't be good for you. You have to take better care of yourself, Wal."

"I know."

"Then it's settled. You're not changing your ticket unless it's to stay longer. And anyway, don't you want to take some time and see the town where your mother grew up? There are people here who knew her. I know you were always a chip off the ol' Dad block, but Mamà was still your mother."

He grew a bit pale and became deeply interested in staring into his mug of tea rather than at me. "I suppose. It feels weird after all this time, ya know?"

"No, I don't really know. I can't imagine not wanting to reconnect with my memories of her. But it's different for you, maybe. You had Walt and Lucille to take her place. I spent every day trying to remember what she looked like. How she walked. What she smelled like."

"Listen, I—"

"Lavender and sage," I said. "She smelled like lavender and sage no matter what perfume she wore or soap she used. Always."

His eyes met mine at last. "You were so much like her it felt like

I was infringing on your territory when I tried to remember her, I guess."

I crossed my arms over my chest. "She loved you every bit as much as she loved me, no matter what Lucille might have convinced you of otherwise. I hope you know that."

"I know she did, but we weren't the kindred spirits that you and she were." His eyes glazed over a moment as if he were trying hard to recall a memory. "I remember her making calissons one time. I thought they were the most wonderful thing I'd ever tasted. Citrus and almond . . . I think about them sometimes. I remember when I was thirteen, I saw some at a fancy little bodega in the city with Grandmother. I asked for some and she realized *why* I'd chosen those over some name-brand American cookies most teen boys would eat by the sleeve. She got me a box of Chips Ahoy! and told me 'You never can tell what's in some of that imported stuff. Better to eat what you know.' She knew it wasn't about the sweets for me."

"And it sure as hell wasn't about the sweets for her. We'll get you a boatload of calissons in town. I bet the market has plenty. We can go soon. I was going to take some soup to Pau Sarraut, the kitchenware seller in town."

"Let me guess, this old man is also the police chief and the dog catcher too."

"Don't be silly." My grin turned devilish. "He's the mayor. And he's been in the hospital and needs soup. The village takes care of their own, and it's my turn to help."

"You've gone rustic, haven't you? Borrowing a cup of sugar and taking over a lasagna for the new moms and all that?"

If only we had new mothers in Sainte-Colombe these days. I brushed off the thought and smiled. "'Going rustic,' as you call it, seems nicer than never knowing your neighbors and not knowing something happened to them until their apartment starts to smell weird."

He laughed and scoffed. "Like I said, *rustic*. I'm surprised you don't have chickens in the backyard."

I arched a brow. "Not the worst idea I've heard. I love fresh eggs."

"You've not just gone rustic; you've gone full-on Farmer in the Dell." He threw his hands up and shook his head in defeat.

"Come on, Farmer John. Let's go be neighborly. It'll be good for you." I grabbed a crock of soup from the fridge.

"Yee-haw," he replied amiably, holding the front door open for me.

I rolled my eyes and led him down the drive and on the path that led to town.

"Not driving?"

"No, it's only a mile and it's not that hot. I may have gone rustic, but you have gone *soft*, city boy."

"Brat," he muttered.

While the mood was light, I decided that perhaps I might take advantage of the levity to let him know what was said about me in town.

"Bold of you to insult me. I'll have you know there are those in this village who think I'm a witch. They wouldn't dare tempt my wrath."

"What, have they seen you adding Adder's fork and blind-worm's sting to a bubbling cauldron?"

"*Macbeth* quip. Nice. But no. That's Scotland. This is Provence. I ended a sixty-year-old feud with my skills." I pointed my nose in the air for effect.

"What skills might those be?"

"Pesto skills. With the herbs grown from my own greenhouse."

"So enchanted pesto? That's a thing here?" Incredulity fairly seeped from his pores.

"That's right. Let's just say, I'm better than a fair cook."

"So those herbs you brought to the house, were they . . . meant to trick Grandmother into being kind to you or something?"

"Not really. I'm nothing more than a common kitchen witch, not some sorceress out of a fairy tale. I can influence and coax. I can promote harmony where I wish and truth where it's needed. But like with any plant, I can't cultivate a thing without a seed, can I? I can't make her love me more if she doesn't love me at all."

"Tempèsta . . ."

"Don't give me platitudes, Wal. It's true. And it's fine. I'm trying to make peace with it. But it's easier to accept it as an absolute. It's easier to admit that she doesn't love me at all than to try to cope with the idea that she doesn't love me *enough* to matter."

"I guess I can understand that. So this Pau is a friend of yours?"

"His granddaughter, Estèva, is, more accurately." I gave a brief rundown of the past few weeks' drama with Estèva's departure and stay at the Bastida as well as Pau's heart attack. As well as his less-than-courteous welcome to town.

"It's kind of you to do this sort of thing. It's exactly the sort of thing Mom used to do."

"People in Greenwich thought she was nuts because she came bearing 'weird' stews and soups whenever someone was ill or needed a lift," I said, unable to contain a chuckle. "But she didn't care. She just wanted to help people, even if they thought she was the loony who didn't make lasagna like the rest of the moms. I'd give anything to be that strong."

"You don't care that I think you're weird."

"You're my kid brother. You'd think I was weird no matter what

I did. Pretty sure you signed a contract to that effect when you were born."

"In utero," he corrected. "The Kid Brother League doesn't allow for slipups."

"You're vigilance personified."

"Semper Fi. Or something like that."

"Semper annoying. We're nearly there," I said as the town square came into view. I directed him to Sarraut's, which was closed while Pau recovered.

I rang the bell to the apartment abovestairs and soon Estèva came bounding down the steps. She smiled at the sight of me through the glass, but then her brow furrowed when she saw Wal, yet another newcomer to the village.

"My brother, Wal," I explained as I went in to kiss her cheeks. She accepted the soup and led the way up the stairs to the apartment.

The flat had been transformed into a makeshift hospital room for Pau, who still seemed as though he had much healing to do. Estèva's face was drawn with concern as she took the crock to the kitchen to reheat the soup.

"Another American come to see us?" Pau said. "If I'd known, I'd have had Estèva help me smarten up a bit. This young man doesn't much resemble the Nadaleta I remember, but he has her nose. And the broad shoulders of the Vielescot men." Pau was wearing pajamas, and his wispy white hair wasn't as neatly combed as it usually was.

Wal cleared his throat, perhaps unused to being compared to Mamà instead of Dad.

"He looks like his dad." I realized the adjustment from "ours" to "his" probably should have been more difficult than it was.

"Oh, you two look more alike than you realize." Pau gestured for us to sit on their faded old sofa. "You remind me greatly of your grandfather Frédéri, rest his soul."

"What was he like?" I felt like I ought to have the question tattooed on my forehead as often as I asked it.

"Quick to laugh and quicker to help his neighbor. There was never a better man who drew breath than Frédéri Vielescot. Well-liked by everyone. A wonderful husband to Sibilia and a good father to Nadaleta. I'm sorry you two never got the chance to meet him."

"There are a lot of people I would have liked to have met. My grandparents and my father."

Pau grew solemn.

"That sweet Tardieu boy. That was a tragedy. It nearly broke your mother. And me, to be honest with you. Amadeu was my godson, and I loved that boy as if he'd been my own. And I must admit, I wasn't kind to your mother after it happened. The rest of the village wasn't either."

"Why?" Wal asked, finally finding his voice.

"For myself, I blamed her. Perhaps because she was lucky enough to survive when he did not. The village followed my lead, perhaps because they resented her talents and gifts. Your grandfather died young, too, and some began to whisper that it was the curse. Nonsense, given that your great-grandfather lived to be ninety-four. And when I saw you enter the shop all those months ago, I thought certainly it was your mother's spirit coming back to haunt me for my lack of compassion. It's no wonder she ran off with the American. It was an escape for her."

"She wasn't the sort to hold a grudge," I said. "I don't think you have much to worry about."

"Cara, I am indeed haunted. Not by your mother, though, but by my own conscience. Your mother didn't deserve my reproach and neither did you. I'm very sorry for how I've treated you."

"Monsieur Sarraut, you don't need to apologize."

Estèva entered with her grandfather's soup. "Apologize for what?"

"For being a right fool, that's what. I let my old grief for a boy taken too soon allow me to treat Tempèsta and her mother before her terribly, and it's only right to apologize. You've been a good neighbor. A good friend to Estèva. You've tried to help her make the business thrive again. And I was ungrateful for all you tried to do for us. I'm embarrassed it took a heart attack for me to see it."

I took his free hand in mine and squeezed it. He ate some of the soup at Estèva's urging.

"You make the finest *soupe au pistou* this village has ever seen. And I include my late wife's in that assessment, even if I will have to answer to her for that in heaven." He took a few more bites of the soup. "And I need to apologize to you too, Estèva. I've been a brute to you. I never should have made you come home from school when your mamà died. And I should have listened to you when it came to managing the shop. The pair of you have good ideas, and I should have let you run with them."

"I still think the website is a good idea. My boss in New York got Bénézet and Aliénore's dishes and has sent me a dozen pictures of her table set with them. She couldn't be happier to have a bit of their story as part of her life. We could make sure all your treasures are loved and useful once more."

"I think it's a wonderful idea. I know you and Estèva will do brilliantly."

"We can talk about all this later, Papi. Don't strain yourself," she said.

"I won't strain myself, cara. This heart trouble taught me a lesson. I'm going to retire. The store is yours to do with what you will. Modernize it. Sell it. Turn the place into a cabaret if you wish. But whatever you do, I want you to be happy."

Estèva pressed her lips against her grandfather's forehead. Tears glistened in her eyes.

"And what's more, your young man has come to see me. My greatest triumph in my final term as mayor will be to recommend that the town council apply to be counted among the 'Most Beautiful Villages of France' with the tourism board. I don't much like the idea of the place being flooded with tourists, but I will trust you to manage to do this without destroying the soul of Sainte-Colombe."

My jaw dropped. In a million years I never thought he'd agree to it. "You have my word," was all I could think to say. I didn't know what Tibèri had said, but I'd have to find some way to thank him, though there wasn't a meal in the world equal to what he deserved for bringing this about.

"I know my trust will not be misplaced. You may be American, but you are also Nadaleta and Amadeu's daughter. You know what we have here."

Wal and I excused ourselves, but before we left, I showed him a few of my favorite pieces in the shop and told him the stories behind them.

Just as we were about to leave the town square, Estèva bounded down the stairs and out onto the street. She threw herself into my arms and planted a kiss on my cheek. "Thank you," she murmured.

"Of course."

"Why don't you come to dinner tonight?" Wal suggested. "You need a break from granddad detail."

She nodded at Wal and wiped the tears from her cheeks. She managed a smile and returned up the stairs.

"You're learning." A smile tugged at the corner of my lips.

"I hope you don't mind that I invited her over. She's obviously been through a lot, and it seems like she could use a night off."

"Not at all, brother dear. Not at all."

Chapter 37

I decided to turn the dinner into a little party, so I invited Jenofa and Tibèri as well. Both were more than interested in meeting Wal, and it wasn't likely they'd have another chance to anytime soon. Wal would leave the following day, and I couldn't imagine that it would be easy to lure him back to Provence. Once he was back in New York, just like Walt, he'd become absorbed with work and wouldn't surface again for months. And I hated that for Wal. Getting Walt out of the tristate area was as complicated as an act of Congress because he couldn't bear to be away from his work, even if it was, quite literally, killing him.

I set Wal to work as a sous-chef, chopping and measuring as I put together a vegetable tian with eggplant, tomatoes, zucchini, and onion. The main course would be a roasted chicken with tarragon and sage, with couscous on the side and a classic olive oil cake flavored with just a hint of lemon and served with raspberries.

"I knew you were a food critic. I had no idea you were so handy in the kitchen," Wal said.

"It seems poor practice to judge a craft you can't perform yourself," I said. "I'm no Michelin Star chef, but I went to culinary school in the city when I landed the gig at the *Tribune*. I didn't want to be a hack."

"It shows," he said as I corrected the way he held the knife.

"It's all about good ingredients. No amount of talent and cunning can make up for shoddy ones. I never thought to be a food critic, but it turned out to be a fantastic plot twist," I mused.

"What's it like, having a life where you actually get some choices in your career? Where a plot twist is possible?"

"It's unsettling at times, but I feel like it's all turning out. I felt like I was out of place for so long."

"You seem happy here, Tempy. Glowing even. You belong here."

I wrapped an arm around him, careful not to get cake batter on him. "It makes me happy to hear you acknowledge that. But, Wal, I want you to glow too. You can have all the plot twists you want."

"Please, I don't get plot twists. My life isn't a novel; it's a tech manual. Once I finish step four, step five is laid out for me on the next page, and you know that step six is as sure to follow as the sun is to rise in the east. And day after day, I'm reminded that if I don't follow the instructions just right, it'll all come crashing down."

"How to Build a Successful Career the Luddington Way," I quipped. "It sounds like dull reading."

"It'll never be a bestseller."

I shook my head, realizing that it very well might have been a bestseller if Dad had penned it. There were thousands of people in New York alone who would have loved his advice about how to get ahead in the concrete jungle. And there was still a part of me that wondered if I wasn't a little broken for not being one of them. But there was no use in pretending, and far less in letting the same handbook claim Wal just as it had the man who raised us.

"Chuck the whole damn thing and write your own. You get to be the author of your own life story, Wal. There are only two people in the world who think otherwise. Lucille and you. There's no convincing Lucille that there's any way but 'the Luddington Way,' but you don't have to live your life to please her."

"I wish you could understand that it really isn't that simple."

"And I wish you understood that it *really* is. You have skills, an education, and plenty of money. You're luckier than most. If you have a different dream, go chase it."

"Therein lies the rub. I've been so busy trying to be Dad, I never took the time to figure out what *my* dreams are."

"Well, you've come to the right place. The Bastida is a wonderful place for dreams." I made a mental note to switch the guest quilt for the one Mamà had made for the duration of Wal's stay. He needed the sleep even more than I did.

Wal and I set the table and arranged the food, chatting more companionably than we had in years. I had always known that the tension that existed between Wal and me was the product of Lucille's vindictiveness and Walt's preoccupation, but I was glad we'd come to a point where we could relate to each other just a bit better.

* * *

No one in Provence would dare come to a dinner empty-handed. Estèva came with some silver salt and pepper shakers from the shop I'd admired, along with well wishes from Pau, who was resting comfortably in the company of Méric and Donat. Tibèri arrived with some late-summer wildflowers, and Jenofa with a photograph of Mamà in a silver frame. She was perhaps eighteen when the photograph was taken in the village square. She was wearing a red embroidered dress and dancing. Her partner, Amadeu I assumed, had his back to the camera, and we could see only his gleaming black hair and the edge of his profile. He held Mamà in his arms as if she were a treasure. And to Amadeu, she had been.

"She was beautiful." Wal handed the photograph back to me.

"Just like you," Tibèri said, glancing at the photo and rubbing the small of my back with his hand. The little frisson of delight at the contact warmed my cheeks.

"How are you enjoying your time in Sainte-Colombe . . . Vahl?" Jenofa asked.

"Wal," I corrected gently.

"I'll never get my mouth around that sound," she said, waving dismissively, her long white braid jostling as she shook her head.

"I'm enjoying it more than I ever thought possible," he replied. "It's a lovely place and Tempèsta has made a lovely home here."

"She has become a valued part of the village. Like your mother was for many years. It feels right to have the Vielescot children back in Sainte-Colombe." Jenofa raised a glass of rosé and we all followed suit.

"I hope you're staying awhile," Estèva said to Wal. She wasn't fully able to conceal her enthusiasm. "Though I expect our sleepy little village isn't as exciting as New York."

"Another two days, I think." Encouraging. For once he didn't have a concrete plan. "Have you been to the city?"

She chortled. "I've only been as far west as Brittany. And that was years ago." A cloud passed over her face for a moment.

"You ought to come sometime. It's worth seeing with a native," Wal said.

Subtle, brother, subtle.

"I don't see how, with Papi unwell . . ." Estèva bowed her head remembering the heavy tether that kept her in Sainte-Colombe.

"The time will come for you to spread your wings, cara," Jenofa interjected. "You'll be able to gad about to your heart's content."

Estèva turned her attention to the food on her plate, though I sensed she was just moving it from one end of the china to the other with her fork.

"But now, what I want to know is what our Tempèsta has planned for Sainte-Colombe now that Pau will make his wishes known to the village council." Jenofa looked to me expectantly, and I suddenly felt like I was presenting at a meeting of the board. And given the influence Jenofa, Tibèri, and Estèva had over the town, it wasn't entirely untrue.

Wal folded his fingers and rested them on his midsection, seemingly curious as to how I'd respond. "Well, the first thing we'll have to do is meet with the village council again and hope to rally some real support for it. Pau's blessing will help a lot, but we can't assume everyone else will automatically agree that it's a wise course of action. There has been so much blowback against any sort of change, I'd be shocked if all hearts turned overnight."

"So how do you propose to win over the hearts and minds of the good people of Sainte-Colombe?" Wal pressed. He was in CEO mode and was in the mood to test my mettle.

"By appealing to their sense of community and self-preservation in equal measure. Keeping the school from being disbanded is something they can rally behind. They know what it would mean if we lost it. And, of course, that all ties in to having a healthy economy and steady population to justify having a school in the first place. Saving their individual businesses may be their immediate concern, but that won't happen unless we have a healthy collective of businesses to draw in some crowds."

"Avoid using the word *crowds*," Tibèri warned. "That's the very thing small-town folks are afraid of."

"Visitors," I corrected. Tibèri nodded, approving.

"Guests," Wal prompted. "It's more welcoming *and* it implies agency on the part of the villagers."

"Brilliant." Estèva beamed at Wal. "That is exactly how we have to think if we're going to convince the biggest curmudgeons."

"Guests," I affirmed. "We need to convince the village businesses to invest a little in a facelift of their premises. A coat of paint, a new sign. I can give plants to put beside the doors to anyone who wants them."

"A lovely idea. And I will make pots so it will all look unified," Jenofa offered. "I have enough clay sitting in my studio to make a dozen pots for every business in Haute-Provence. It will give me something to do."

"Not too unified," Estèva mused. "We want them to be unique and typical of the region. You'll have a booming trade if this works. People will come to eat and will want a souvenir to take with them. Your pottery will be just the thing."

"Just the thing. Colors and shapes that harmonize, but not too uniform." Jenofa's expression was distant as she designed a new line of terra-cotta *jardinières* in her head.

"If you want, we can carry your pieces in the store so you don't have to rent space," Estèva offered. "We'll move a lot of the antique inventory when the website takes off. I've actually been scouring the surrounding towns for new stock. And your herbal goods too,

Tempèsta. Papi promised me he was finished with temper tantrums."

"I'd wager twenty euro that's because her salve soothed his arthritis." Jenofa smiled as I reached onto the shelf behind me where I kept my store of handmade lotions and potions to hand her a pot of the salve. Remembering my experiment with fragrances, I took the bottle of citrus and vetiver cologne I'd concocted for Wal and passed it to him.

He unscrewed the cap and breathed in the aroma. "Nice. What's this for?"

"It reminded me of you. Fresh, clean, vibrant . . . sophisticated without trying too hard. Eau de Wal, if you will."

He sniffed again. "This is great, Tempy. You'd probably make a fortune with bespoke scents in New York."

"And where would I grow the ingredients? My balcony?" I gave him a wry look but didn't feel the same rancor as I used to when Wal was needling for his way. He couldn't truly come to terms with the idea that the world outside of the greater New York area wasn't an elaborate work of fiction—but he was trying.

"This is all perfect, though. We need the businesses of Sainte-Colombe to collaborate just as you all are. We have limited space in the village proper, where we want the bulk of our guests to focus their visits. If we encourage the artisans to collaborate with the shopkeepers and restauranteurs, it will lessen the need for new buildings. And for the cost of paint and some plants and pots—and a donation of my labor for a few weeks—it just might work," Wal added.

We discussed the merits of suggesting partnerships or letting them happen organically. In the end we felt it was better to drop some hints about which partnerships might be beneficial to those involved, letting them think the ideas were their own. Old rivalries and bad blood would naturally keep some of the worst partnerships from forming, which was just as well. I couldn't rely on pesto to sort it all out.

I turned to Wal. "This sort of thing is your bailiwick. Any other suggestions?"

"I think this is all great, Tempy. You've nailed down that the most important part is getting buy-in. But be sure to show them your vision of what Sainte-Colombe can be. It's easier for people to latch onto an idea when they can see what they'd be working toward. I've seen more fantastic projects die in a boardroom because the person pitching couldn't convey their dreams to the decision-makers than for any other reason."

I sat back in my chair and exhaled slowly.

"Wal is right," Estèva said. "We have Tempèsta to come up with stories and an impassioned speech for the village council, but from last time, we know that isn't enough. Jenofa, we need you to paint Sainte-Colombe as it *could be*. The fresh paint, flowers, pots . . . and a small but lively presence on the streets. Show them what we hope for. After a million years running the shop, I can dazzle them with numbers and give them a reason to vote with their pocketbooks. And we have Tibèri to lend a hand with the facelift, which will be a show of support. We don't expect them to do it alone. This time, we're going to back up Tempèsta so they can't say no."

Wal turned to Estèva. "I should hire you for the foundation."

"Don't you dare steal her away until after this goes through," I hissed, narrowing my eyes on him. "Wasn't it Dad who said that stealing talent in the middle of a deal was a lowbrow move?"

He held up his hands in mock surrender. "I was kidding. Honest."

I crossed my arms, mollified for the moment. But how big of a grain of truth was at the heart of his jest? And if it weren't for Pau, Estèva would have her bags packed before the offer was out of his mouth.

Chapter 38

Aweek later, Estèva chose a dress for me, flowing and turquoise, from among the clothes we'd purchased in Aix. The village council was meeting that afternoon, and we knew that we had to be flawless in our presentation if the Sainte-Colombiens were going to agree to put forward an application to the tourism board. It was no different than when Wal made his big pitches for donations. He wore a suit that cost more than I used to make in a year at the newspaper, a power tie, and a take-no-prisoners attitude. The uniform was different, the approach was different, but the rules were just as rigid.

Surprisingly, Wal was still here, despite two impassioned calls from Lucille that the office was "simply going to fall to pieces without him." In reality they would function perfectly well without him. And the golden rule of high-powered jobs like Wal's was never, under any circumstances, let anyone see how dispensable you are. Lucille knew the inner workings of the foundation and had seen it countless times. An employee who'd been central to the organization found herself unofficially demoted after maternity leave. Or someone would be transferred to a less desirable department after using up some accrued vacation time. And no one, not even Wal, was completely immune to it.

I often wondered if it was why she interfered in our lives so much. If she allowed Wal to lead a life without her trying to steer his course, he'd learn in short order how capable he was of doing the steering for himself.

Wal assessed me as we prepared to venture to the town hall for the meeting. "You're ready to knock 'em dead," he said. "You'll have them eating from the palm of your hand by the time you're finished."

"You make them sound like feral cats." I examined myself in the hall mirror, almost shocked at the differences Wal must have seen since I moved from New York. I wasn't the waif clad in black trying to be invisible.

"I think that's a healthy expectation for meetings like these," Wal said. He'd changed since coming to Sainte-Colombe too. Somehow he seemed less *crushed* under the weight of the world. Or the foundation. Those had been synonymous for Wal for a long time.

I nodded in reluctant agreement, squared my shoulders, and got behind the wheel of the Peugeot. Jenofa and Tibèri were already waiting for us at the crossroads so we could all ride together. My hands no longer gripped the steering wheel like a life preserver while marooned out at sea in a tropical storm. Progress.

The town hall was filled largely with the same people as were present at the last town meeting I'd attended months before. Matthieu's absence was glaring, as were the seats of two villagers who'd passed on since spring. Their time had come, and it was sad to see them go, but the reality that there were no young people to fill their seats in the council meeting brought the problem to even sharper relief. I hoped others would notice and that it might soften their hearts a bit.

Pau, still not fully back to health, looked tired as Estèva helped him to his place at the center of the head table. It might be the last time he presided over a village council meeting, and though I'd been in town for less than a year, it seemed like the end of an era. He cleared his throat and the room fell to a hush. He opened with lavish thanks for the outpouring of support since his hospitalization.

"For several months, I have been remiss in one of my most important duties and greatest honors as mayor. I want to, in my official capacity as mayor, welcome Tempèsta Vielescot-Tardieu as a new resident of our fair village."

It was the first time I'd been formally addressed by my parents' surnames and, not for the first time, I felt a pang of loss for the life that might have been if my father had survived.

I glanced sidelong at Wal, his blue Luddington eyes fixed on Pau, and thought that perhaps some good had come of the winding road that led Mamà to New York.

As if reading my thoughts, Pau continued, "Tempèsta has not spent her life here but is a daughter of this village, and I am grateful she has returned to us. And I also wish to welcome her brother, Wal Luddington, also a son of this village. Though his home is in New York—God help him—we all hope your visits will be frequent and of long duration."

A polite round of applause followed, and I was shocked to see color in Wal's cheeks. He hadn't expected to be mentioned at all, but he didn't grasp the depths of Mamà's and her family's lineage here. I hoped he might in time.

Pau's tenor turned serious. "My friends, either you have known me for my whole life, or I have known you for all of yours. I think it's reasonable to say that I do not have the reputation among you for being a man who easily changes his mind. Stubborn. I used to think it was a virtue. That it showed firmness of mind not to yield to new ideas. That changing course showed a lack of resolve. Perhaps it is my recent health troubles, the blessings of old age, or the kindness of our prodigal daughter who has come back home to roost, but I no longer believe that my intractableness is a badge of honor to wear proudly."

A few murmurs circulated through the crowd, but his iron gaze quickly hushed them.

"For a man not to change his mind when presented with new and relevant information shows a lack of imagination and courage. For too long I have clung to the beautiful past that we all remember. When Sainte-Colombe was a vibrant village filled with joy. The laughter of children filled the air. The sound of families, not just the shuffling of old men. I spent many years in grief for that way of life and in denial that there was any possibility of things return-ing to the glory days of old. In the latter part I was right. There is no returning to the past, sad as that may be to accept. But we can improve Sainte-Colombe for future generations by being better shepherds of our town in the here and now. We may never be the bustling village we once were, but we could once again be a village where our grandchildren and their children will be able to find work and build lives worth living."

I had no idea that old Pau could be so eloquent. From the stunned look on Estèva's face, it was a surprise for her as well. He appeared somewhat revived as he spoke, and I allowed myself to feel the slightest twinge of optimism.

"Retaining our school is of primary importance. I have used

every ounce of influence I have to persuade the rectorat to give us a one-year extension to implement changes in the village. One year to show them the potential for growth and to renovate the facility. They have agreed, but they have made it clear that they expect real change, not just promises. Our newest resident, Tempèsta, has a solid plan to help revive Sainte-Colombe, and as your mayor and your friend, I humbly ask you to listen to her with open ears and open hearts."

Estèva and Tibèri applauded Pau's words. Audeta and Bernard too. Then several of the other villagers who had come to be friendly to me in our interactions during the market and in the village soon joined in. Heat rose in my cheeks, but I kept focused on Pau so I wouldn't become distracted from the purpose of our meeting today.

It took everything I had not to walk over to Pau and kiss his cheeks in front of the whole village, but given that he wasn't an effusive man, I didn't think a public gesture would be welcomed.

I scanned the crowd and hoped my jitters weren't too visible. I thought of the tricks that people suggested for finding oneself at ease in front of a crowd, like picturing the audience in their underwear and all that. But I decided it would be better to think of them as they were: the people who had loved my mother.

"I am humbled by Mayor Sarraut's words, and I will strive to be worthy of such a gracious welcome to our beautiful village. I do not pretend that the events surrounding my mother's departure from this village were not the cause of suffering for many. I can only imagine the pain that losing a beloved native son must have caused. Amadeu Tardieu represented the best of Sainte-Colombe, and to lose him must have been unendurable. I, too, wish that my parents' story had a happier ending. I wish I could have known my father, but that simply wasn't to be. And so, I must make do with the memories that you, his friends and neighbors, have of him."

The hum of whispers from the audience, now more excited, called to mind the buzzing of bees. It was the first time that Amadeu Tardieu had publicly been acknowledged as my father. Mamà hadn't been visibly pregnant when she left the village, but anyone who knew my age could have deduced the truth.

And to name Amadeu Tardieu as my father was to give the Sainte-Colombiens no choice but to acknowledge that I was wholly of this village, and they couldn't deny my place in it. Or my voice in its future.

"I had only thirteen years with my mother. Many of you had more than that. But I am certain that she missed Sainte-Colombe each day she was away. She told me stories about Sainte-Colombe so often that the streets of this village seemed as familiar to me as the ones I grew up on. If her life had gone the way it should have, I expect she'd be the one up here trying to persuade you all that we cannot allow Sainte-Colombe to fade away into obscurity, as so many other villages have. She would have fought to make sure our way of life survives the challenges of a changing world. She understood, even better than I do, that the businesses in our village don't just represent the hard work, sacrifice, and talent of one person but oftentimes that of generations. She knew how precious Sainte-Colombe was, and she would have done everything she could to help usher our village into a new age. And since she cannot, I know she'd want me to do the same in her stead. I believe applying to the 'Most Beautiful Villages in France' tourism board program will be a clear path forward for all of us."

Tibèri, soon followed by Jenofa, Audeta, and Bernard and several other villagers, stood and applauded. Pau, aided by Estèva, did the same. I could have broken into sobs on the spot, but I needed to keep my resolve intact a bit longer. I could dissolve into a puddle of tears—those of gratitude, relief, grief, and probably a dozen more varieties—in Tibèri's arms when we were alone. There was a job to be done.

Jenofa started off the next part of the meeting by sharing her vision for the facelift, so the villagers could see what we envisioned before they could conjure images of some Disney-fication of their beloved town. Dad had always said the worst thing you could do with stakeholders was to let their imaginations run wild.

Estèva then showed them our estimated costs for sprucing up the village, followed by the rather impressive financial data from other villages that had joined the association. Her presentation was as professional as any Wall Street executive's, and Wal was enthralled. Impressed, even.

I then launched into our specific ideas for how to leverage the village's charms to become a center of food-based tourism, which was a rapidly accelerating niche in the market, but one that was unlikely to create unruly swarms of tourists.

Most of the questions were pragmatic. How much would inclusion cost? If the whole idea flopped, what would be our next step forward? What was our time frame for the application process? They were intelligent questions made by people who were genuinely, miraculously open to being persuaded. And we had one year to prove that their faith in us was well-placed.

Chapter 39

T o Sainte-Colombe." Pau raised a glass of Côtes-du-
Rhône that glistened a velvety red in the waning
evening light on the back porch of the Bastida. "To a
bright and prosperous future for us all."

"And to Tempèsta," Tibèri added. "Who had the vision to
bring it all about."

"Hear, hear," Estèva and Wal said, raising their glasses.

"In all my days I have never seen the village agree on anything so quickly," Jenofa said. "I thought it would take several
more meetings and a vat of Tempèsta's pesto to make things come
about, but the motion passed handily after a single vote."

"I'll win over the dissenters too," I said. "Just give me time."

"Take my advice as mayor, Tempèsta. You will never win uni-
versal approval." Pau helped himself to a serving of the lemon-
tarragon *daurade*—a fish popular in the region—so delightfully
flavorful it hardly needed embellishment.

"Pau's right. You don't need unanimity; you need a majority," Wal agreed.

"Maybe not at first, but I want the whole village, in a few months' time, to know this was the best possible move. To a person, I want them all to see how this will save our way of life. Naysayers will only undermine what we're hoping to do."

"You sound like Dad," Wal said. "When he had employees who didn't share his vision for his campaigns, he personally won them over. He didn't like it when winnable hearts weren't convinced."

"The Luddington Way isn't all bad. And each one of the objections raised was valid. How to cope with more traffic. Where people would be able to stay in the area. How to make the city more accessible without a train connection. But none of them are insurmountable. It's not often in life that we can please everyone, but in this, I think we have a shot at convincing them that this will work out in their favor."

"Marie Binoche says she can't afford to fix her roof. I can at least help with labor for that," Tibèri said. "It needs repair whether or not we participate in the program."

"Gilles Langlade is worried we'll force him to paint his shutters some color he hates," Jenofa said. "We need to let him have a nice shade of green. His neighbors won't mind letting him choose first."

Jenofa, ever with the artistic eye, had hoped to have residents repaint their shutters from a preselected palette of colors, alternating so that no adjoining houses were too uniform in appearance. It wasn't unlike how American suburbs sought to have new developments vary the façade of each house so they didn't look too cookie-cutter from the outside. But if your neighbors chose a color scheme first, your choices would be fewer.

"All easily handled. We know which residents will be more particular than others, and we can handle the color choices delicately. By next spring the village will be fit for a postcard," I said.

"Fit to live in." Estèva took a drink from her glass. "Whatever happens, at least the people of the village will have the benefit of the repairs."

"And the Luddington Foundation will help with the school," Wal interjected, his head down, scrolling his phone with intent.

I turned to him, my mouth gaping in astonishment like a codfish out of water.

"I emailed the board." He brought his eyes to mine. "I told them about your project. Usually we focus on the arts in New York, but given your ties to the *Tribune* and the pieces you've been running, they were persuaded to let me use some of my discretionary educational funds to help. It's not a lot, but it's enough to do a solid renovation. And once you have everything running at full speed, you'll be able to sustain the upkeep."

I leaped from my seat and wrapped my arms around Wal's neck from behind. "Really?" I managed to squeak.

"Consider it your inheritance from Dad. The one he should have left you." He reached up and patted my arm.

"Does Lucille know about this yet? Has she blown a gasket?"

"She's on the board, so yes. She isn't thrilled, but she thinks we can use it quietly as PR for, well . . ." He waved a hand dismissively.

"The chatter about me being cut out of the will. I honestly don't care. She can spread the word all she likes."

"It won't help as much as she thinks. People will think we're throwing money at you to keep you from publicly shaming us for everything. And, more to the point, it's not why I did it."

I took my place back at the table. "I know. You did it for Mamà." I leaned back in my chair and picked at my fish. "Because deep down you *are* a mama's boy."

"No, Tempy. I did it for you. Because I want to be a better brother."

"I appreciate that, Wal. More than I can say." I reached over and squeezed his hand. "You know what? I can even mention the foundation in one of my articles for the *Tribune*. Why shouldn't the foundation see some good press from all this?"

"Because not every good deed has to be done for press." He folded his hands as he did when making a point in board meetings.

"Who are you and what have you done with Walter Luddington IV?" I made a show of reaching over to feel his forehead.

"It's still me. Grandmother thinks I've gone mad, but at least now she's more on board with the idea of my taking more time off," Wal said with a chuckle.

"You are?"

"I thought I might stay around a bit longer. If you can stand to have your pesky kid brother around for another week or two."

"You can stay as long as you like. Months if you want."

Wal laughed again. "I haven't changed that much, Tempy. I can manage to keep abreast of things from here for a little while, but I don't want to give up on Dad's vision either."

"No," I said. "But make sure you don't forget to take some time for your own either."

He shook his head. "I promise. You didn't get all the creative genes in the family. You got some Luddington business acumen, and I managed a smidge of the Vielescot charm, if I do say so myself."

"I am sure that's true," Estèva said. "One will help the other flourish."

"Cheers to that," Tibèri said. "But Tempèsta is right, Wal. You should spend more time here. It would be good for you. And we like having you around."

Tibèri's encouragement meant a lot. It conveyed that even if things between him and me progressed and Tibèri moved to the Bastida, Wal would still be welcome. Tibèri and Wal seemed like unlikely friends, but I couldn't be happier for it.

"Well, the food is better, even than New York, though it pains me to say it. But I promise I won't be a stranger. So long as you all manage to pull yourself out of paradise for a few days and come to the city every once in a while too."

"Absolutely," Estèva said with enthusiasm. I'd have to figure out how to angle a ticket for her to New York courtesy of the *Tribune*. Surely the woman who ran the shop that inspired the column had a reason to see the offices?

"My granddaughter will have to bring my warm wishes with her. I have seen too many winters to venture so far from home. I will content myself with her stories of its wonders," Pau said. "But I will be with you in spirit."

"Well, I might just come too," Jenofa said. "There are galleries I'm dying to see there, and I've never had such an excuse to go."

"And some of the best urban architecture in the world for you, Tibèri," Wal said. "You'd love it."

"Oh, I probably would." He slid me a sideways glance. "If I were offered a tour from a native."

"Native expatriate," I said. "But sure. Playing tourist will be fun."

Everyone began dreaming up a trip to New York that sounded like it would take three months to accomplish. The Neue Galerie, shopping at Bloomingdale's, going to the top of the Statue of Liberty . . . I couldn't say for sure if the trip would ever happen, but for the first time, maybe ever, I felt more excited than dread-filled at the prospect of a visit to New York. And even if Lucille wasn't keen to see me, Wal would be. And more than any endowment he offered to Sainte-Colombe, that was a precious gift.

I was about to serve dessert when a clamor of voices came around from the front of the property.

Audeta was there, along with a large swath of the village. They carried food, drink, tables, chairs, gifts, and musical instruments. My jaw dropped as they began to set up a massive party in my own yard that rivaled the Fête de Sainte-Colombe of late spring.

"What is all this?" I finally managed to ask.

Audeta came to my side, kissed my cheeks, then wrapped an arm around me. "Tibèri said the Bastida was finished last week. It seemed high time that we throw you a housewarming party, don't you think?"

Estèva beamed and Wal looked goggle-eyed as the band began to play their music and nearly every resident of the village came to offer me their best wishes. Pau seemed to light up with an energy I hadn't seen in him before. This was the Sainte-Colombe he remembered, and the one that could be once more if we worked hard enough and the stars aligned just right.

I turned my eyes heavenward and hoped Mamà and Amadeu could see the scene that unfolded at the house that would have been their own. There was so much I didn't know about them, but I couldn't help but think that to have the village here, celebrating their daughter as one of their own, would have given them some much-deserved joy.

Chapter 40

W al had stayed for another two weeks and returned at Christmas for a shorter visit. He was welcomed, not just by Tibèri and me but by the whole village, when he returned. We celebrated with a sumptuous Christmas Eve feast, complete with the table laden with the traditional thirteen desserts that the Provençaux prepared for the occasion. It was far different from the black-tie Christmas galas he used to attend, but I think he found the gatherings here far warmer than those back home.

Wal was used to a cheerful reception when he returned to the office after an absence—which were becoming more frequent, thank goodness—but it wasn't the same as being welcomed into a community. I sensed that Wal loved it almost as much as I did.

Thanks to the efforts of the villagers, some grant money, and Tibèri's expertise, the village was cleaner and more vibrant than it had been in fifty years, according to Pau and Jenofa. The broken terra-cotta roof tiles were mended. The exteriors of the homes and businesses were freshly painted the creamy white once more, when for so long they had been a dusty gray. But that was where the uniformity ended. The shutters were a riot of color, and in the end there had been no real conflict over the choices, as Jenofa offered them a huge palette to select from. Her pottery was seen everywhere in the village, gracing nearly every front stoop and windowsill. And in each of them were herbs lovingly selected from my greenhouse.

For the Sarrauts I chose rosemary for the remembrance of all the stories of the items in the shop and the love they represented.

For the café I chose chamomile for comfort.

For the town hall, which boasted the four largest urns of all, I chose thyme for courage, mint for protection, chives for harmony, and laurel for victory. And Tibèri's remodel of the space was a wonder to behold.

For my own house, though tourists would rarely venture this far, I filled the pots Jenofa gave me with lavender and sage. Devotion and wisdom. They flanked the front door on the porch that Tibèri had rebuilt and that I'd painted a shade of green to complement the lavender shutters.

The Luddington seed money had provided Jenofa with the clay and paints she needed, and it subsidized the cost of running her kiln night and day as well. Her time, though? That was a gift she gave freely to the village she loved. The same for Tibèri, who worked from dawn until past sunset each day, systematically painting and mending his way throughout the village. He even convinced some carpenter friends from Valensole to donate some time as well, which helped speed along the renovation process.

It was a cool morning in March on the day that the committee was to appear to inspect the village for consideration. I felt steel bands constrict around my stomach. It was true that even if the tourism board didn't approve our application, the town would still be better off for the efforts. But when I thought of the long hours Jenofa put in at her pottery wheel and the hours Tibèri toiled all winter in the bitter mistral winds, I couldn't bear the thought of the project not being successful.

Not just because of Tibèri's and Jenofa's heroic efforts, though that was enough. But also for shopkeepers and artisans like Estèva and the others whose livelihoods would be improved so dramatically by greater tourism activity. And I was equally nervous, along with most of the village, that we *would* be successful. Too successful. We didn't want the place overrun with obnoxious tourists for months of the year, gawking at the quaintness of the place without really participating in it.

I had no worry that the place would become a hot spring break destination for the college crowd, but there was risk enough that the tourists could overwhelm the place like locusts, who would devour everything of value and leave only traces of the village's soul in the wake of their destruction.

Tibèri and I walked to the village to be on-site as the committee walked the village. Pau and a couple of members of the town council would accompany them on their inspection, but neither of us wanted to be left waiting on the outskirts of town. We decided to take a table at the café so we could casually watch the tourism board and try to gauge their reactions.

When we arrived, it seemed we weren't the only ones with the idea to spy on the proceedings, and we snagged the last table at the place. Benoit, the café owner who was not a day under seventy, walked with a spring in his step that made him look closer to twenty. When was the last time he'd seen his tables full? The last time he had to call his wife, Jeannette, down from the apartment to lend him a hand in the kitchen to keep up with the orders? The two of them would be kept hopping, but the Sainte-Colombiens were perfectly content to wait a little while for their coffee, pastries, quiche, and sandwiches, as they were the secondary concern, far less pressing than overseeing the wanderings of the committee.

Benoit practically bounced from table to table, serving each cup, glass, and plate with a practiced grace that would suit any fine restaurant in Paris. Tibèri and I both ordered typical French breakfasts: baguette and croissants with butter and jam accompanied by strong coffee and served with an infectious smile.

It was just a sample of what could happen here. And while Benoit and Jeannette could keep things going for their patient friends and neighbors, they'd need a waiter or two to help if—*when* our guests arrived. Jobs that might keep some of the younger generation from fleeing town. Better still, that would attract new families. Such hopes, and the strong coffee, did nothing for my nerves, but I tried to appear relaxed as I slathered the rich cherry preserves on the crusty bread.

Two sleek black Mercedes pulled into the small village parking area that had been swept impeccably clean by Pau himself, who was reinvigorated under Estèva's care. It seemed like everyone assembled held their collective breath as the committee members emerged from their cars. Three men, two women, all appearing to be approaching middle age. Dressed more stylishly than anyone in the village but with the casual grace of Paris rather than the honed edges of New York. Pau was animatedly welcoming the committee and ushering them to the sidewalk where they'd begin the tour.

We all tried, and largely failed, to appear nonchalant as they wandered from shop to shop, taking notes on their clipboards and occasionally whispering to one another. What any of us wouldn't have given to have superhuman hearing or the ability to read lips, but we did our best to surreptitiously read their body language and facial expressions.

These people were savvy enough to keep both things neutral, but there were small tells. One woman stopped in front of the window display at Sarraut's that showcased various copper pots, pans, cake molds, and other pieces. Each one had been polished to gleaming, and even in the emerging light of early spring, they shone like Christmas baubles. Their provenance and a short history had been added to the display with signs penned in a whimsical calligraphy by Jenofa that had replaced my computer printouts. The woman lingered awhile, long enough to read the display in its entirety, even pausing to take notes on occasion.

I wasn't sure if Estèva could see the woman's intense scrutiny of the display, but I'd have to tell her all about it when the Mercedes finally rolled away that afternoon.

I could feel the tension radiating off Tibèri as the leather soles of the visitors' shoes clacked along on the cobblestones. He'd not only put his hard work into the restoration of the village; he'd put his soul in too.

I rubbed his arm, and he pulled my hand to his lips for a quick kiss, and I knew we were thinking the same thing:

This has to work.

It seemed like the committee spent the whole day wandering the village, when in reality they were only there just over an hour. I saw little old women muttering prayers under their breath, and the air crackled with electricity when any member of the committee paused to linger in a shop or scribble down notes. When at long last the black Mercedes wheeled away, the entire village seemed to exhale in relief, along with years of worry, in one mighty breath.

Pau, armed with his walking stick, approached the crowd assembled at the café. Estèva burst from the shop, hard on his heels.

"They must deliberate, of course," Pau said. "But they were pleased with what they saw. The village is neat and well-preserved. The quality of the artisanal goods, exemplary. And they were impressed to see so many of us sharing a midmorning coffee together as a village. They find the custom rather quaint."

With that the entire crowd burst into laughter. I got the impression that if a ten thirty coffee break was what was needed to earn the favor of the tourism board, it would become a village tradition in no time.

"My friends, I cannot promise anything. I don't know what other factors may be at work in their decision-making, but I feel it safe to say, we have a good chance."

"Papi, I don't think I've ever heard those words come from your lips," Estèva said.

"Well, cara, all I can say is that it is a wonderful change to have cause to use them."

With this, Benoit passed around a massive tray of pastries and kept the coffee flowing for the next hour as the village chatted excitedly about their plans when—not if—the committee selected the village to participate in the program. Amalie, the beekeeper, wanted to experiment in more floral honeys and asked me to help cultivate some flowers and herbs for her to use. I readily agreed, suggesting several plants she hadn't considered.

Benoit hoped to lure his grandson, Fabien, back to the village with the prospect of a job, and potentially the whole business one day. Estèva hoped to go to Marseille in the coming weeks to find more antique kitchenware for the shop.

And at once, the terra-cotta tiles seemed redder, the shutters more vibrant in their rainbow of assorted colors. The coffee was more aromatic, blending with the butter in the pastries to create a decadent perfume over the café. And all because there was, for the first time in so very long, room for optimism.

Chapter 41

SUMMER

T he first days of June were mellow as butter and crisp as thyme. The greenhouse was thriving even more than the previous year, which seemed impossible. The basil was resplendent, the rosemary was stout and fragrant, and the dear hyssop plant had forgiven my misdeeds and was now the picture of health and vitality. I would prune from it only sparingly this year in hopes it would grow stronger yet.

I harvested bunches of mint, sage, lemongrass, and oregano for the grocery, which had begged me to help supplement their stock. Between this new enterprise and the products I made for Sarraut's and the weekly market, I'd have to plead with Tibèri to build a second greenhouse to house it all. The idea was enticing . . . more quantity, more variety, and more options to play with. Though he was so busy with the renovation of the town hall, it wasn't something he would be available for anytime soon.

I tied the herbs into neat bundles and placed them in my

massive marketing basket to deliver to the market in town on top of some product and potted plants and other odds and ends that had been ordered in the past two days. The sun would be relentless later in the day, so I prodded myself to make the trek up the hill before it grew any hotter.

Not far from the Bastida, there was now a row for parking for those who couldn't find a coveted space at the top of the hill. There were already two cars taking up spaces, so driving wasn't really an option unless I left the car idling and dashed into the store and out like a madwoman. Which, admittedly, sometimes was the right option when I needed to focus on my column for Carol or had products in the making that needed my attention. But today I had some time. I'd walk so I could linger.

Some tourists pulled up and locked their cars at the bottom of the hill upon which rested Sainte-Colombe. When they saw me walking by, looking very much of the region in a flowy green dress and carrying a basket brimming with herbs, they waved and shot toothy smiles my way, probably thinking I was a charming native.

I returned the waves out of habit. Americans, obviously. No one else would wave and smile at strangers. I wrestled between scoffing internally and missing the automatic, if somewhat superficial, warmth that small-town Americans showed for others. The States didn't feel like home anymore, not that they had for some time, but I had to admit that Americans had their virtues.

Wal was due to visit soon, and the prospect delighted me. I'd set aside a guest room at the Bastida as "his" and let him keep a few things there to make his travels more streamlined. Though he spent more time at the Sarraut house visiting with Estèva than he did with me at the Bastida when he was in town, I was still pleased he had a place in my home to call his own.

The village was, despite the early hour, already milling with "guests." Though tourists were notorious for sleeping in, it seemed there was always a healthy flock first thing in the morning. They had leisurely breakfasts at the café or one of the two restaurants, one of which was new. The chef, Giselle, was young and from Valensole, which was close enough that she was welcomed even by the stodgiest of locals. She'd devised a clever menu, seasonal and replete with local produce—including my own herbs—and successfully married the traditional Provençal palette with modern tastes. She even deigned to make a heartier breakfast for the American and British visitors, though the locals stuck with their coffee and pastries until lunchtime.

I snuck into the kitchen and left a bundle of herbs on the prep station with a note as I usually did when Giselle was busy. I also left a small vial of perfume with notes of orange blossom and vanilla with just a hint of oregano and calendula that she might enjoy. She caught my eye as I slipped out, not breaking her cadence with her sauté pan but mouthing *Merci* as I scooted out.

"And thank goodness for you." I was greeted by René, the proprietor of the grocery. His trade had always been the safest in town, as there would be demand for groceries in Sainte-Colombe until the last resident left town, but his business was growing with the alacrity of my own herbs. He took the bundles from the basket and placed them on the refrigerated shelf in the produce area. "I can't keep them in stock. I've already had three people asking for your basil this morning."

"Basil is love," I replied as if that were common knowledge. "Who among us can ever have enough?"

"Wise girl." René placed a kiss on both my cheeks. "If you can bring more by Wednesday, I'd be grateful."

"I'll see what I can do. But it's up to the plants, really."

He squeezed my elbow and smiled. "They love you; they can't help but grow."

I slipped him a small jar of moisturizing cream infused with sage and thyme for his dry hands in thanks.

Pau was flipping the sign from Closed to Open. It was painted by Jenofa, who'd made one for all the businesses in town with designs that reflected the wares in each shop. Sarraut's had artistically stacked pots and pans, the grocery had verdant produce, the honey shop had beehives, and so on. The script was in French *and* Occitan, which pleased Pau to no end. And the tourists found it charming, which was a nice bonus.

Pau saw me crossing the square to his shop and waved cheerfully. "Well, bruèissa. Back with your magic herbs again, are you?"

"Three times a week without fail," I said with a wink. "Any less and you'd all grow immune to my charms."

He chuckled. "I think it would take longer than a few days for that, cara. Come in."

Estèva was at the computer in the office, deep in thought.

"We sold the silver tea service," she announced to no one in particular. "Full asking price and within France so we don't have to take a hit on shipping."

"Well done," I said. She looked up, surprised to hear my voice instead of her grandfather's.

"It's the very last piece we had in the shop when the website opened." Her face split into a wide smile. "There isn't one single item in this place I've dusted more than twice."

"And may it stay that way." Pau rolled his eyes heavenward. "I can't believe people will buy things over a computer without seeing them with their own eyes, but I am grateful people are trusting fools."

"They trust *us*, Papi. The Sarraut name means something," Estèva replied.

"And not just in Sainte-Colombe. You have quite the following all over France and in New York too. They know Estèva vets your products with an eagle eye," I said.

"Your boss keeps sending me hunting," Estèva said with feigned annoyance. "I'd think she'd have enough to outfit three kitchens by now."

"She likes to entertain and regale people with stories of her fancy cookware. I bet she prints out the stories and keeps them out for handy reference. And, heaven help us all, she's taking cooking lessons at my old school, so naturally she thinks she's the Julia Child of the twenty-first century."

Estèva chuckled. "She sounds like a character. I'd love to meet her someday."

"I'm sure you will. She's been talking about coming out here for ages. And Wal would love for you to come to New York."

Her lips curled into a smile. "He's been asking me weekly for ages now. It's just so hard to get away from the shop with . . ." She gestured broadly to the ordered chaos of the office.

"I can help in the shop whenever you need it," I offered. "You should go. It could be good for business as well as for *you*. Meet with Carol. She'll have a zillion contacts for you with ideas on how to expand." I could see the flurry of fancy dinners at all the best restaurants where Carol would introduce Estèva to prominent antique dealers, kitchen suppliers, and even a few celebrity chefs. Sarraut's was gaining clout, and I had to note with pride that my column about life in Provence was certainly good publicity for them.

Pau sidled up to me and placed a hand on my shoulder. "You should go, cara," he said to Estèva. "Our Tempèsta could manage the computer nonsense for a few days. You've always wanted to see New York, and it would make me happy to see it happen. Just bring your Wal back with you for a nice long visit."

Estèva made a face like she was in pain. "Fine, consider my arm twisted."

"Email Wal. He'll be delighted. I'll email Carol and tell her you're coming when you have dates." I felt a twinge. I knew that once Estèva got a taste of New York, life in Sainte-Colombe would seem impossibly small for her. She'd stay close to home for as long as her grandfather lived, but once Pau was gone, I could see her falling in love so easily with Wal's life in Manhattan.

I only hoped Lucille would be more welcoming to Estèva than she'd been to my mother. But Estèva wouldn't be going into the relationship with a baby that wasn't Wal's, which had to make it easier. And unlike Mamà, Estèva was a savvy businesswoman and would be keen to integrate into their society. She'd be a boon to Wal as well as ambitious in her own right. Mamà had wanted nothing more than to be a good mother to Wal and me, take care of Dad, and keep a lovely home. And she'd done an amazing job at all three, but Lucille had seen it as freeloading.

I tried, very hard, to imagine what it would have been like to have been put in Lucille's shoes, having her only son marry a girl from another country who was pregnant with someone else's baby. With Walt fresh out of college and from a wealthy family, Lucille couldn't help but suspect Mamà was a fortune hunter who found Walt to be a prime target for ascension into an easy life. Walt was naive, wealthy, and ready for love after long years studying and living up to familial expectations.

Lucille had been wrong about Mamà, though I had to admit her suspicions had been warranted at first. The prenup Grandfather had insisted on was probably wise too. But Mamà had proven herself to the Luddington family over and over again. Lucille simply refused to change her behavior based on that new information.

It was that which I found hard to forgive, but for Wal's sake, I was trying.

I emailed Lucille on Sunday afternoons. At first, nothing too deep or meaningful, but I extended the olive branch. Later, I told her what I'd learned about Mamà. About my own father, Amadeu. Explained what had happened in case it helped her to make sense of why Mamà had jumped at the chance to leave Sainte-Colombe and be with Dad.

The truth was that Dad had fallen in love with Mamà at first sight. And, though maybe not as quickly, Mamà had come to love Walt with the sort of Vielescot ferocity that made the cold welcome she received everywhere irrelevant.

Lucille replied to my emails with short missives. She was glad I was well, her arthritis was playing up, but not too awfully. She included a few social updates about people I knew only by name, but with whom she thought I'd be terribly fascinated. Estèva would be, and I hoped it was enough to gain her acceptance.

Estèva clicked her mouse a few times and began smiling at the screen as she typed. I turned to Pau. "That didn't take much convincing, did it?"

"No," Pau said with a chuckle. "But if she is going to take up with an American, at least he has roots in this village."

He had a point. Whether they were strong enough to keep her here very long, I wasn't sure. But she still taught Occitan classes three days a week, though it took a lot of work to schedule her life around it these days. I sat in the back of the classroom when I could and did my best to teach myself from Estèva's books when I could not.

I felt an arm encircle me from behind and recognized the familiar scent of the cologne I'd made for Tibèri. Sage and sandalwood with a dash of cloves, all mingled with his own natural aroma that always seemed to have a tinge of sawdust he couldn't scrub off. I loved it. I drank in the warmth of him for a moment, melted against his chest, before breaking the trance with words.

"I didn't think I'd get to see you this morning," I said, not opening my eyes. "I thought you had work at the Tessiyer farm."

"I did, but I finished early and came into town to repair Madame Pujol's steps. I'll be working at the town hall the rest of the day."

"Bravo," Pau said. I could feel a jostle as Pau patted him on the back. Between the Luddington Foundation seed money and the increase in commerce, the village had enough money to restore the town hall to its former glory, and Tibèri had thrown himself into the project like he'd been commissioned to design a great cathedral.

"I hate to say it, but I do have a project in mind for the Bastida when your nonexistent free time rolls around," I said.

"Let me guess. An authentic Swedish sauna with cedar planks and all the trimmings?" He squeezed me closer.

"No, another greenhouse."

I could feel the rumble of his laughter against my back. "You Americans and your obsession with work. I may build the sauna anyway and insist you use it."

"I'm more of a jacuzzi girl. But you're not wrong about the work thing. It's just so wonderful to see the village come to life again, I can't help but obsess over work."

"And she's not American," Pau interjected. "She's a Sainte-Colombienne."

"True, that." Tibèri placed a kiss on my cheek. "A new greenhouse it is, if you let me put in the jacuzzi as well."

"If you come use it with me, it's a deal." I turned to kiss his cheek in return.

"There's nothing I'd enjoy more." He cradled me to his chest. I could hear the low rumble of Pau's chuckle and Estèva clearing her throat noisily, as if offended by the display of affection.

I had more rounds to make in town, lavender plants for the bee-keeper and some personal orders for a few of the older folks in town who needed some extra basil or thyme before the Friday market and didn't want to make another grocery run. But it was a different world now. I was greeted with smiles and welcomed in for coffee when I came to make a delivery. I was greeted on the street as if I'd lived there my whole life.

As Pau had said, I was a Sainte-Colombienne.

Like my mother.

Like my father.

And all the generations before them.

All the way back to a girl named Mirèio who had loved and lost . . .

And left a legacy that I hoped would last for generations more.

Chapter 42

FALL

"E at," Jenofa ordered as I sat before the antique vanity in a silky robe that Estèva had procured from somewhere for this occasion. I'd never seen the need for a dressing gown before today, but I was glad for Estèva's forethought. She and Jenofa were my self-appointed bridesmaids and bridal entourage and were charged with preparing me for the big church wedding that Audeta had been agonizing over for months.

The public vows had been exchanged at the *mairie* the day before. Pau was delighted to perform his duties as mayor and officiate a wedding for the first time in many years. French law dictated the ceremony at the mayor's office had to be open to the public, and it had been astonishingly well attended.

"It's fine, I'm really fine." The butterflies in my stomach, seemingly coated in steel, rattled within me, which was ridiculous given that I was, in the eyes of the law, already married. But somehow this seemed far more official than the legal vows.

The thought of eating caused the acid to rise from my core, and I couldn't imagine swallowing a bite.

"Eat," Estèva echoed. "If you pass out in the church, Audeta will murder us all."

Jenofa set a plate of sliced bread, three kinds of cheese, sliced ham, and tiny squares of chocolate on the vanity and gestured insistently. I sighed and took a portion of the bread, Emmental, and ham. This was not a battle I'd win.

"Good," Jenofa said once I'd eaten two slices of the bread and toppings. "I wasn't going to give you this on an empty stomach."

She produced a bottle of champagne and three flutes and poured generous measures for all of us.

"Jenofa, you're a treasure." Estèva took her glass with breathless enthusiasm.

"Let's drink to our sweet Tempèsta, returned to us after far too long an absence, shall we?" Jenofa raised her glass.

"And to many happy years with the kindest man this village has ever known," Estèva added.

"Cheers." I lifted my own glass and clinked it against each of theirs.

"You deserve this, Tempèsta. And Tibèri too. I know you'll make each other very happy."

"No," Jenofa said. "That is something they cannot do for each other. Two people can add to each other's happiness, they can help it grow, but each must bring their own to the marriage, or it will never flourish. Even the greatest love cannot make happiness bloom where there is no seed planted."

"Well, it's a good thing that Tempèsta has such a green thumb, isn't it?"

"Indeed." Jenofa clinked her glass against Estèva's a second time.

I finished my champagne and took them both in my arms. "I'm so happy I have both of you. You're the family I always needed."

"Okay, you need to stop before I ruin my mascara. Let's get you dressed."

Jenofa agreed and both set to work on my hair and makeup for what seemed an eternity until they commanded me to stand and slip into my shoes and dress: Mamà's beautiful gown from the attic that she should have worn to marry her Amadeu. The green of Mamà's dress suited my complexion just as it would have hers.

The tension eased from my stomach as I examined myself in the mirror. Mamà knew a baby was coming when she sewed the gown and perhaps hoped this very day would come. The day her daughter slipped into the gown she'd fashioned for her own wedding, and her daughter would feel the cascade of love—the love she'd felt for Amadeu—wash over her. Mamà had loved my father with all that she was and all she had, and in that moment, nothing could have given me more peace apart from my own love for Tibèri and his for me.

"Gorgeous," Jenofa pronounced, clasping her hands with color rising in her full cheeks. Her snow-white hair wasn't in a braid down her back today but was swept up in an elegant chignon. "You look like an angel."

"She looks like her mamà."

"No greater compliment."

Wal knocked on the frame of my open bedroom door. Estèva flashed him a brilliant smile that made *my* breath rattle. "Let's leave these two alone for a moment. We need to head out in about fifteen minutes."

Estèva, looking resplendent herself in a pink dress that accentuated her lithe form and lifted the color in her cheeks, paused as she left the room to kiss Wal's cheek. There was an intimacy in their gaze that wasn't meant for me to see, but I felt delighted to see their relationship taking root. Jenofa followed after her.

"Estèva's a good friend to you, isn't she?" Wal asked, his eyes looking back at the doorway she'd just walked through.

"The very best. I've been fortunate to have both her and Jenofa."

"I'm happy for you, Tempèsta. Just don't forget your kid brother, okay? You promised you'd visit."

"We've been busy this summer since being accepted to the program. Running one of the most beautiful villages in France is a lot of work, you know. And I sent Estèva to see you, didn't I?"

He looked wistful at the memory of her visit. She'd gone alone, without Jenofa, Tibèri, and me to act as entourage, and I sensed they both preferred that it had been a solo visit. She'd come back with glowing tales of her tour of the city, and though she tried to keep her cool French façade, she gushed about Wal a fair amount as well. According to Estèva, Lucille had been gracious, which was a pleasant shock.

He cleared his throat, apparently forcing his mind back to the present moment. "I have a few things for you. I know the engagement party was the big to-do for giving family gifts, but I'm not much for public displays like that."

"Fair. Audeta was keen on being the center of attention anyway. She's probably glad you didn't steal her thunder."

"Probably right. Lucille sent these." Wal pulled a long ivory case from the breast pocket of his pristine navy suit jacket. The antique case creaked as I opened it to reveal a strand of beautiful uniform pearls.

"They were her mother's. I think your comment at the funeral hit home. She'll never say it, but in her heart of hearts, she knows she was blisteringly unfair to you."

"I think, in her weird way, she wanted to protect Dad. If I'd been a boy, it would have been even worse. Heir to the Luddington throne and all that."

"It still wasn't right."

"No, but at least I'm able to wrap my head around it in a way I wasn't able to when I was younger," I admitted.

"She considered coming, but she wasn't sure how welcome she'd be."

I wished I were the sort of person who could have truthfully said she was welcome with open arms. But I wasn't that person yet. I hoped to be in time.

"Maybe she can come visit with you sometime in the next few months. The warmth would do her good when the snows start to fall in New York and before the mistral winds set in here."

"She might go for that," he mused. "Especially since I plan on spending some more time here in the future."

I cocked a brow, waiting for him to explain.

"I bought the land where Mamà's house used to be. I contacted Tibèri's friend Matthieu and arranged the whole thing a couple of months ago. And Tibèri will help build the house. I swore him to secrecy until I had the chance to tell you."

I threw my arms around him. "We're going to be neighbors?" I shrieked. "Does that mean you and Estèva . . . ?"

"I hope so. I've never met a woman like her. I'm hoping we can split our time between the two places. Summer here, so she can keep the place running during peak season, and winter in New York, for the fundraising season. But I wanted you to know first. I hope you're okay with it."

"Of course I am. I couldn't be happier to have you close." *To have my brother back.*

He threw his arms around me this time, and my heart grew light. *This is exactly what Mamà would have wanted.*

"We'd better get you to church and married off, hadn't we?" Wal eyed my necklace. The omnipresent herbal charms that Lucille so hated. "Do you want me to help you put on the pearls?"

"Yes." I removed the pearls from their case and carefully wrapped them four times around my wrist and held it up for Wal to fix the clasp. It wasn't what Lucille—or he—expected, but I was growing more at ease with subverting those expectations.

"One more." He reached into his pocket and pulled out a tiny little velvet bag. Inside were the tattered remains of the embroidered hair ribbon Mamà had given me on my first day of kindergarten.

"Where did you get this? I searched for it for ages."

"I know. I found it in the trash. Grandmother finally found it and I knew if I gave it back to you, she'd find it again. I thought it was safer in my room. But I should have told you. It wasn't right to keep it, but I wanted a little of Mamà to keep close too. I suppose I was jealous."

"How so?" I asked. Mamà had lavished love on him just as much as she had me.

"I know you felt left out from the Luddington side, but I felt the same with you and Mom sometimes. I'd never share the same bond you two did, and I suppose this was my way of sharing that with you two."

"You should have given it back," I agreed. "But I'm glad you finally did."

"I hope you forgive me. For this and a million other slights. I wasn't a very good brother to you."

"I don't blame you for it, Wal. Not anymore."

I took the tattered remains of the ribbon and tied them to the pearls at my wrist. Not because I needed the boost of confidence any longer—indeed, I was more certain of this decision than of any other I'd made in my life—but to have another token of my mother's love with me as I married Tibèri. It was the best gift Wal could have given me.

Astre bounded into the room, now an adult cat in size but forever with the soul of the lost kitten I'd found in the leaves. He peered up at me with his big yellow-green eyes, meowed loudly, then curled up on the sunny-yellow quilt Mamà had made for Walt so many years before. I liked to think he was wishing me luck. He certainly had been my lucky charm since he'd come into my life.

Wal smiled, offered me his arm, and escorted me to my car, then proceeded to drive to the church, with Jenofa and Estèva in the back seat for support.

I walked down the aisle on Wal's arm, allowing him, as a representative of our family, to present me to my groom. And though I felt myself trembling as I walked, I had no fear about what my new life with Tibèri would be like. There could be nothing but the magic of sunshine and fresh basil in a life we spent together. After three decades spent wondering what I wanted out of life, I was still uncertain about many things, but never him.

And with my mother's dress, my grandmother's pearls, and a few tricks of my own, I walked toward that future with hope in my heart and a memory of lavender and sage in my soul.

Author's Note

Dear Reader,

If my historical works *A Bakery in Paris* and *Mademoiselle Eiffel* are my tributes to Paris (see if you can spot the subtle nod to *A Bakery in Paris* when Tempèsta and Tibèri are visiting the city!), then this is my love letter to Provence. I majored in French in college and went on to pursue my master's, so I've spent a fair amount of time in France, but it was to Provence I traveled as a naive eighteen-year-old kid who had never ventured farther from her Northern California home than Portland, Oregon. I was a student for two terms in Avignon, and it was one of the most transformative experiences of my life.

There are no monolingual native speakers of Occitan any longer, nor many villages where Provençal is quite as prevalent as depicted here. Indeed, Sainte-Colombe is a fictional town that time forgot (though not enough for Pau's liking) based loosely on a few real villages in Provence. Most notably, the remote but bustling Moustièrs-Sainte-Marie is what I envision as the healthy future for Sainte-Colombe.

In Tempèsta, I worried about creating an "outsider saves the day" narrative, but I also wanted to eschew the idea that all the big-city finance knowledge she gained while living with her father was useless. My hope was to depict a small village on the brink of ruin saving itself by using all the tools at its disposal, and Tempèsta was the catalyst to help Tibèri and Estèva get the village to see the dire situation they faced.

There are countless villages in France, and indeed all over Italy, Spain, Portugal, and elsewhere, where the youth flee for the jobs in the cities. Villages are left simply to age out, and the death knell of all of them is when the schools close.

And the truth is that Tempèsta is never really an outsider. It wasn't until she turned the clunky, iron antique key in the door of the Bastida that she ever belonged anywhere.

This was my first full-length work of contemporary fiction, and in the process of writing it, I gained even more respect for all my women's fiction colleagues who manage to make their pages compelling and fast-paced without the luxury of well-timed explosions and looming threats of invasion that I was able to depend on in many of my previous books. I doff my cap to those of you who make this look easy, because I assure you, it isn't!

But Tempèsta's story was a joy to tell. I loved spending sun-soaked days in Provence with her, even while I was actually braced against the Colorado snows in January. I hope you enjoyed this tale of love and found family as much as I enjoyed bringing it to you.

Warmly,
Aimie

Acknowledgments

As with all books, this began as a solitary endeavor and become the work of a vast village. I offer my profound thanks to:

Kimberly Carlton, my lovely and talented editor, for taking a chance on this new venture with me and for helping make Tempy's story shine. I appreciate the deep dives and the thoughtful notes.

Kevan Lyon, my wonderful agent, for always being a passionate advocate for me and my books. So glad to have you in my corner.

Julee Schwarzburg and her careful line edits, which have made this book better by an order of magnitude.

The entire staff at Harper Muse for being tireless in their efforts to make this book a success. And OMG, that cover art, am I right? You're a dream team.

Barbara Vance, professor of French at Indiana University, for her guidance in finding a French-Provençal dictionary suitable for the few phrases I used in this book. Any errors are my own.

J'nell Ciesielski, international treasure, for reading this book when it was barely fit for alpha reads, let alone outside eyes, and helping me get back on track when I was ready to throw the manuscript in the trash and get a job baking cookies.

My dear writer friends: Heather Webb, Kate Quinn, Andrea Catalano, Rachel McMillan, J'nell Ciesielski, Kimberly Brock, the Tall Poppy Writers, the Lyonesses, and many others, for being such sympathetic places to turn.

Amy E. Reichert for the titling brainstorm session. I love *The Memory of Lavender and Sage*, and it's thanks to you we settled on the perfect name for this book.

My dear friends Stephanie, Todd, Carol, Sam, and Danielle, for being the most amazing cheerleaders a girl could ask for.

My wonderful children, Aria and Ciaran, for their patience with me when I am lost in the story, and to the Vetter and Trumbly families, who always manage to find me and pull me back into the here and now for a little while.

My darling husband, Jeremy, for taking me all over Provence (and a huge swath of Western Europe) in a little red Peugeot that will have stories about the crazy Americans and the windy mountain roads in the Alps, Haute Provence, and the Pyrenees to share with all the other rental cars for the duration of her service. Here's to many more road trip adventures.

My sweet JijiCat, who was the inspiration for Astre, and the world's best writer's companion. I found him in a shelter when I most needed him, and he's been rescuing me ever since.

And to my readers, who make this whole thing possible: I am grateful beyond words.

Discussion Questions

1. Tempèsta's father's room causes her to have some strong emotions. Why do you think seeing the space after so long an absence is so powerful to her?

2. Tempèsta has a "dream job" that many people would aspire to—a food critic for a respected New York newspaper. Why do you think she finds the work ultimately unfulfilling?

3. Tempèsta's reaction to the condition of the Bastida is extreme but perhaps more than warranted. What do you feel are some reasons from her past that might be causing her to doubt her decision so strongly?

4. What do you think is the symbolism of Sarraut's shop and its larger meaning for the town? Why do you think Pau, Estèva, and Tempèsta react so differently to the shop?

5. In several interactions, Tibèri seems as though he's afraid to trust Tempèsta. How does that mirror her own situation with her brother and grandmother?

6. Jenofa serves as a sort of soothsayer and prophet throughout the book. Why do you think she withheld the truth about Tempèsta's parentage for so long?

7. Why do you think Nadaleta rarely used her gifts when she moved to the US, despite them being so hard to detect?
8. What is the significance of the pearls from Lucille? Do you think it was right for Tempèsta not to wear them in the way Lucille intended?
9. Which of the herbs from Tempèsta's greenhouse was your favorite, and what does it symbolize?
10. What recipe mentioned in the book would you most want to try?

Recipes

Here are a few of the more prominent recipes from the book for your enjoyment!

ESTÈVA'S FAVORITE

LEMON-VERBENA COOKIES

Warning: Addictive

Ingredients

$2^1/_2$ cups flour (I use a gluten-free blend with good success)

2 tablespoons dried lemon-verbena leaves (you can dry your own!)

2 teaspoons baking powder

$^1/_3$ teaspoon sea salt

1 cup high-quality butter, softened (European style is best. Don't skimp on this ingredient. It's where a lot of the flavor comes through.)

1 cup sugar

2 eggs

1 tablespoon lemon juice

2 teaspoons vanilla extract (try making your own!)

Directions

1. Combine the first four ingredients well and set aside.

2. In the bowl of a stand mixer, beat the butter until smooth (30 seconds to 1 minute). Slowly add the sugar, eggs, lemon juice, and vanilla and mix well at medium speed. Add the flour mixture slowly, in four batches, with stand mixer on low until well combined.

3. I recommend making drop cookies, about a tablespoon each, and chilling in the freezer for an hour (or several days if you want; just wrap them well).

4. Bake from frozen, spaced 2 inches apart on cookie sheet, for 8–10 minutes (until golden brown) in a 350-degree oven.

ENCHANTED PESTO

Not *guaranteed* to settle decades-old feuds, but I'm not saying it won't either. This delightful recipe is easy to make—the key is getting great ingredients and using a good food processor.

Ingredients

1/3 cup pine nuts (can be pricey; check bulk stores)

2 cups fresh basil leaves, preferably from your own patio, with stems removed

1/2 cup freshly grated Parmesan cheese

3 cloves garlic, minced

$^1/_2$ cup olive oil (good quality—very important!)

$^1/_4$ teaspoon salt

$^1/_8$ teaspoon freshly ground black pepper

Directions

1. Lightly toast the pine nuts in a dry skillet if desired.
2. In a food processor, blend the basil and pine nuts well, add in the cheese and garlic, then slowly add in the olive oil. Pulse several times, then season with salt and pepper to taste.
3. Serve on pasta or as a dip. A spoonful in soups, stews, or on potatoes is amazing too. Prepare and serve with love.

TEMPÈSTA'S MAGIC MINT MARGARITAS
(MAKES FOUR SERVINGS)

A perfect summer drink to share with a special someone.

Ingredients

6 ounces tequila or mezcal

4 ounces Grand Marnier or orange liqueur

3 ounces fresh-squeezed lime juice

Several sprigs fresh mint leaves

Simple syrup to taste (I prefer mine less sweet and just use a dash, or omit altogether)

Directions

Add all the ingredients to a cocktail shaker, muddle the mint, shake, strain, and stir!

TIAN PROVENÇAL

This is ratatouille's more fashionable sister. Though the ingredients are similar, tian is a roasted vegetable dish as opposed to vegetable stew. Artfully arranged layers are key here, making the tian lovely for important company or a romantic tryst. Best to source the ingredients fresh from a farmers market. You can substitute any similar vegetables that are fresh and in season.

Ingredients
  1 leek
  1 clove garlic (fresh!), minced
  1 zucchini
  1 summer squash
  2 Roma tomatoes
  1 small eggplant
  Olive oil
  1 tablespoon fresh oregano, chopped
  1 teaspoon fresh thyme, chopped
  Salt and pepper
  Grated Parmesan

Directions
  1. Preheat oven to 375 degrees.
  2. Remove the dark green leaves from the leek, cut it into quarters lengthwise, and rinse well. Chop into 1/4-inch chunks and cook in a few teaspoons of olive oil with the minced garlic until soft and fragrant (3–5 minutes). Spread on the bottom of an oven-safe baking dish, such as Tempèsta's green cocotte. This creates the base for the tian, so if you don't like leek,

consider alternatives such as yellow and green beans or sautéed onions.

3. Slice the *unpeeled* vegetables as thin (and even) as you can and arrange in alternating layers on top of the leek-and-garlic base. Take your time and arrange in pretty overlapping circles.

4. Gently coat the layers with 2 tablespoons of olive oil, or more as needed. Alternatively, you can add $1/4$ cup dry white wine and reduce the olive oil to 1 tablespoon.

5. Sprinkle the oregano, thyme, salt, and pepper on top and bake for 30 minutes. Drizzle on 2 more tablespoons of olive oil, then bake another 30 minutes or until vegetables are tender.

6. Serve hot with freshly grated Parmesan and some crusty French bread!

About the Author

Copyright © Aimie K. Runyon

Internationally bestselling author Aimie K. Runyan writes to celebrate unsung heroines. She has written eight historical novels (and counting!) and is delving into the exciting world of contemporary women's fiction. She has been a finalist for the Colorado Book Award, a nominee for the Rocky Mountain Fiction Writers' "Writer of the Year," and a Historical Novel Society's Editors' Choice selection. Aimie is active as a speaker and educator in the writing community in Colorado and beyond. She lives in the beautiful Rocky Mountains with her wonderful husband, two (usually) adorable children, two very sweet cats, and a pet dragon.

* * *

Visit her online at aimiekrunyan.com
Instagram: @bookishaimie
Facebook: @aimiekrunyan
Twitter: @aimiekrunyan
TikTok: @aimiekrunyan